Where The Heart Beats Strongest

The Strathavon Saga

Angela MacRae Shanks

Braeatha Books

Paperback ISBN: 978-1-9999624-5-6

e-book ISBN: 978-1-9999624-4-9

Cover Design by Rachael Horsburgh

ALSO BY ANGELA MACRAE SHANKS

Under A Gravid Sky (The Strathavon Saga)

The Blood And The Barley (The Strathavon Saga)

PROLOGUE

Strathavon, the
northeastern Highlands,
June 1769

M ORVEN M AC R AE TRAILED DOWN the slope of Tom Mòr after her
family. It was *An Fheill Sheathan*, Midsummer; it would barely get dark
tonight before the sky began to lighten. Yet as the light slowly died in the
west, it shone eerie and strange. She blinked and slowed her steps. In her
seven years, she had never seen a sky like it. 'Twas the kind of sky Rowena
would say foreshadowed something. Rowena was their neighbour. She said
the Creator sent signs to warn of things to come. Those signs could be read
if you knew how. Morven's innards tingled. Rowena was the wisest woman
she knew and the most beautiful. A pang of guilt niggled, and she hurried
after her mother, slipping her hand into Mam's warm palm.

The day had been long and exciting. They celebrated with a special
bonfire; she was allowed to carry a flaming torch three times around the
infield. Walking *deiseil*, the direction the sun moved across the sky, she
blessed the land and all that grew there, especially the barley. Her da would
distil most of their barley into whisky. Rowena kindled the needfire and
guided her in her first small part in the blessing. 'Twould not be her last.
Highland folk were superstitious; most still followed the old ways.

When the flames had died, they buried the blackened bones of the
bonfire around their home to protect it and walked to Balnedin for their
neighbour's wedding. Balnedin cot-house sat on a hillside looking down
on the river Avon and out over heathery hills. After crossing the river,
they travelled there in a rambling, roundabout way to fool the gaugers.
Excisemen were sly, always searching for illicit whisky. 'Twas unwise to
draw their attention.

After the service, led by Father Ranald Stewart, they celebrated with a
ceilidh, a feast with pipe and fiddle music and many breath-robbing jigs and
reels. The bride passed around the Loving Cup filled with whisky so many

1

times even hardened herdsmen were soon whooping and kicking up their heels in the heather. In the still moment when vows were softly repeated, a hush fell, the cries of moorland birds fading away. A sweet breeze blew, cooling the young couple's cheeks. It carried the fragrance of mountain flowers, and Morven hoped it would blow away their troubles.

The day had been magical, but 'twas late now, and there was still a deal of trudging to do before they reached home. As they approached the river-crossing, the air freshened, the Avon singing over her stony bed. The trees parted to reveal more of the extraordinary sky. The sun had slipped below Ben Avon, but beyond the range, a pool of luminous blue shone. Morven stretched her head back. Clouds ribboned the night sky, sea foam strewn across a vast ocean, caught by the dying sun and stained glorious red and gold. She stumbled on. The strange clouds grew fiery, the sky deepening to violet. What did it mean? Was it a warning, or did the spectacle promise something wondrous? Rowena said the heavens could foretell things. Entire futures could be read in the stars, but what was this sky trying to tell her?

Mam jerked her hand to regain her attention. They could hear a strange wailing, a woman weeping in the trees fringing the riverbank ahead. Her parents exchanged fearful looks. Da passed Rory to Mam to carry and slipped his *sgian dhu* from his hose. Gripping the knife, he jerked his head at Alec and made toward the river. Her brother followed, adopting the same crouching gait.

Mam's alarmed expression warned they must keep quiet and out of sight whilst their menfolk investigated. Morven sighed. Alec was allowed all kinds of adventures forbidden to her when she was just as fearless.

The wailing subsided to a muffled sobbing, and Da returned and beckoned to them. He led them to the riverbank where the boatman, Robbie Grant, was waiting to ferry them across. Robbie moved aside, revealing another family standing in the willow: a man and woman with a boy clutching the woman's skirts. Two horses were tethered in the trees, not shaggy highland garrons but tall, slender-necked animals with sleek coats and proud heads. These folk must be wealthy to own such horses.

'I kent ye'd be coming,' said Robbie. 'With ye haeing the wee one and the river so high, I judged it best to stay and ferry ye safe across.'

''Twas good o' ye.' Mam eased Rory from her shoulder. He stirred, and she rocked him back to sleep.

'We're indebted.' Her da peered at the strange folk.

The man was dark-haired and bearded, handsome, his eyes thickly lashed. His clothing looked as fine as his horses, his sark of soft linen, not rough homespun like her da's. He pulled off his bonnet and gripped her da's hand.

'Thomas Gunn, His Grace's principal tacksman in Badenoch,' he said in Gaelic. 'We wish no trouble.'

'Malcolm MacRae,' her da replied. 'Tenant at Delnabreck in Stratha'an. Ye'll get nae trouble from me.'

Her da also spoke in Gaelic, and the man half-smiled, conceding his point. 'We've dealings with the priests o' Scalan. We're to meet them on the far bank. Ye'll understand my caution?'

'I ken o' Scalan,' Da replied. 'Many here still follow the Roman faith and know o' the place, but we dinna speak openly o' it.'

'We must all be cautious,' Robbie warned. 'Dragoons are patrolling, as ever looking fer smugglers. I spied them moments ago through the trees at the far bend in the A'an. They'll be upon us directly.' He looked at her da. Da was a notorious smuggler, well-known to the redcoats.

'McBeath was wi' them?'

'I didna see him.' Robbie shrugged darkly.

'Try and keep the bairn quiet,' Da urged, and they melted into the undergrowth. The light was dwindling, the shadows deepening to conceal them. On this, the shortest night of the year, the sky would lighten again in a few hours, but for now, the sun's disappearance was welcome. They shrank into a hollow in the alder and willow. Mam beckoned to the Gunn family to follow, and they squeezed in, snapping twigs, crunching dead wood under their feet, and crouched awkwardly beside them. The stink of river mud filled their nostrils. Robbie led their horses away and hid them in a thicket.

Morven peeped sidelong at the boy. He was about Alec's age but more delicately made. Even with his head bowed, his face shone white in the gloom. Sensing her scrutiny, he looked at her. He wore a hunted expression, tears shimmering on his long eyelashes. She gave him what she hoped was a reassuring smile, wondering what ailed him. His mother was still weeping and had not loosened her grip on his hand. When Mister Gunn scolded her, the boy made a choked sound and lowered his head. He must have done something wrong, yet Morven sensed his fear was real.

Robbie returned and nodded to the family. 'The priests are waiting fer ye on the far bank. I signalled to them, warning them o' danger. They've hidden themselves, but ye must do naught to draw attention to them. Popery's forbidden. 'Twould be the worse fer the fathers should they be discovered, and fer you should the redcoats find some connection atween ye.'

'God help us,' Mister Gunn groaned.

The drum of hooves extinguished further talk. Robbie scrambled from the undergrowth for the soldiers to find him sitting guileless as a half-wit by his boat. Stretching her neck, Morven peered through a gap in the foliage. There were six of them, grumbling in their harsh English tongue, complaining of the miserable conditions in the glen, the poor lodgings and lack of sport since local smugglers had grown wily to their movements.

Much of what they said escaped her. Her grasp of English came from her da at the urging of Father Ranald, who spoke it fluently and encouraged others to. 'Twas wise to learn the occupier's tongue, he preached to his scattered congregation, if they wished less trouble from them. Yet in his disguised chapel, he used only Gaelic, the language of the Highlands. Her da agreed and had taught his family what he knew of the southerners' tongue, a language Morven at first considered gibberish. Da must speak English when he ventured into Lowland towns to negotiate the sale of his whisky.

The dragoons reined in their horses and leant down, questioning Robbie intently. The most hostile of them, a man with a snarling face and voice, drew his sword. Robbie gave a convincing performance, shrugging and feigning ignorance, or perhaps he truly knew little of their tongue. They quickly tired of questioning him, the sword-wielder resheathing his weapon. As they regrouped to leave, Robbie cursed them, making Morven catch her breath. Understanding his sentiment, if not his words, the soldiers spat on him and rode on.

As the thud of hooves faded, they emerged from their hiding place and climbed into the boat. Robbie hauled on ropes slung through iron rings on either side of the gunwale, heaving the boat across the river. The family clung to the hull, water slapping the sides, likely imagining the consequences should they be pitched into the surging blackness. Once on the far bank, Mister Gunn pressed payment on Robbie for safely delivering them and promised further payment for the return crossing. He drew the boy away from his mother and squatted to his level.

'Now, Nathaniel.' He lifted the boy's chin, forcing the lad to look at him. 'I'll have no more tears. You're a Gunn. Ye must remember it. Your family and kin need your help and trust you will do your duty. Be a diligent student and make your family and kinsmen proud.' He inhaled fiercely. 'Who knows, when the Popery Act is finally repealed, ye might even become a bishop. Naught would please me more.'

He patted the boy on the head and rose to his feet as two figures appeared from the trees. Morven recognised Father Ranald. The man with him was younger but also wore a long black cassock. The father had left the wedding before the *ceilidh* began. She remembered him trotting away on his pony after the bride and groom exchanged vows. He must have ridden to the Braes of Glenlivet.

Her parents greeted the father warmly and nodded to his companion, a man Father Ranald introduced as Mister John Thomson, master at Scalan. Scalan was the hidden college where boys were secretly trained to be Catholic priests.

'Well, young Morven.' Father Ranald smiled down at her. 'Did you enjoy your first wedding *ceilidh*?'

'Aye, Father.' She was about to tell him that she'd also enjoyed the Midsummer rite but stopped herself. Rowena said the father didna approve of heathen traditions. 'I sang and danced 'til my insides swooped,' she said, and he chuckled.

Nathaniel's father produced a fat package and handed it to Mister Thomson. 'As agreed, payment for my son's lodging and instruction. I understand you'll educate Nathaniel far better than anywhere I could send him, will nurture in him the foundations of the true faith.' He took the boy's hand and drew him forward, placing his small hand in the master's weathered one. The boy's lips trembled as he stared up at the tall black figure. Morven exchanged a look with Alec. He nodded, recognising the boy's distress.

'The duke and I share blood,' Mister Gunn said. 'His ancestors granted mine a sizeable tack of land in Badenoch. Land my family has held for generations. As such, I am one of the Duke of Gordon's principle tacksmen with many kin as sub-tenants.' He half smiled. 'A man of some importance held back by my faith or the authorities' judgement of it.'

The master nodded. Morven sensed Mister Gunn's words had pained him.

'I place my son into the Church's safekeeping in the hope of His Grace's continued protection, knowing his sympathies still lie with Rome, however tacitly. In these intolerant times, I pray my lands willna be taken from me.' A muscle in Mister Gunn's cheek flexed. ''Tis my hope the penal laws will soon be repealed, the Catholic faith no longer outlawed, then we may again practise our faith freely and without fear.'

'Amen,' Father Ranald muttered.

'I wish my son to be ready for that day, to rise swiftly within the Church as soon as 'tis again possible.' He looked at the top of his son's bowed head. 'Nathaniel knows what I expect.'

Nathaniel's mother began to sob, Father Ranald patting her hand to soothe her. Morven looked at her parents. They appeared gripped by the drama, Mam tightening her hold on Rory.

Aware of their disquiet, Father Ranald explained, 'Although young, Nathaniel has been accepted as a student at Scalan. A great honour for his family. You may know the seminary has been secretly rebuilt, rising anew from the ashes Cumberland's troops made of it after the disaster of Culloden.' Pride crept into his voice. 'Hidden away in the Braes o' Glenlivet, the lad will study history, figures, the grammar and syntax of language like any student, but also scripture, theology, the lives of the saints, Latin, Greek, and perhaps Hebrew if he has an ear for it, not forgetting Gaelic. He will devote himself to piety and prayer, finishing the many years of his education at one of the continental colleges. Once grown to manhood, if worthy, he'll be ordained and armed with the Lord's protection, will venture into the glens as I have long done, ministering to the faithful who've clung to the true faith through the darkest times.'

Da crossed himself. 'I did hear Scalan had been restored, Father. Lang may it endure.'

Morven stared at the boy. He was being given to the Church, something she could see neither he nor his mam wanted. A lot seemed expected of him, yet he looked so small and timid.

'Nay, Father,' Mister Gunn countered. 'Once ordained, Nathaniel must return to Badenoch to serve those of our land who still follow the auld faith. There are many of our name. 'Tis my hope my son will help secure our claim to the land.'

'Well, now,' the corners of Mister Thomson's mouth twitched in a patient smile. 'Perhaps we should let Nathaniel decide about that when the time comes.'

Not understanding, Morven looked at Alec, aware that Nathaniel's father was using him in some way, a way that served the man, not the boy. Alec frowned back, just as puzzled. She tried to imagine how she would feel in Nathaniel's place. She'd feel burdened by expectations, overwhelmed and desperately unwanted. She'd be afraid to go with the black-robed master, wanting more than anything to stay with her family.

Nathaniel swallowed and raised his chin. She could see the battle waging inside him as he fought not to cry or shame himself. It took an effort of will, but he firmed his jaw, facing his daunting new life with courage and dignity. Her throat tightened. He looked so trusting, his face so earnest; something tender stirred inside her. She had a sudden urge to seize him by the hand and run with him helter-skelter through the trees to safety. Her eyes nipped. She couldn't do that; only adults could save Nathaniel.

Nathaniel looked up at the master, and Mister Thomson nodded and led him away. His mother wailed, Father Ranald patting her hand again to soothe her. At the last moment, the boy looked back, seeking a final communion with his mother. They shared a look of kindred yearning, a look Morven understood must sustain them through the long years of separation. Before he turned away, his gaze found her, his expression softening as he recognised her sympathy and appeared grateful for it. She gave him a tentative smile, then he vanished into the trees.

'Come away,' Mam croaked. ''Tis time we were getting hame.'

Never had she held so tight to her mother's hand. 'Mam?' she ventured.

'Now, dinna fret. I could never gie up any o' my bairns.'

'Nay,' Da muttered, 'to keep a roof ower our heads, such a thing can prove necessary and right.'

'Och, Malcolm,' Mam scolded. 'Thon's the whisky talking.'

But her da only grunted, 'Ye ken as well as I, Grace, 'tis mountain and glen that matter. Best nae forget it.'

When Morven stared at him, Da ruffled her hair. 'Be a guid lass, eh, else ye could end up at Scalan wi' the Gunn lad.' When Mam gasped, he added, 'Being accepted fer Scalan is a great honour.'

'Fer an older boy, mebbe, but nae a wee lad like that.'

'But Da,' Alec piped, 'I thought only lads could become priests.'

Da ignored him, and they trudged away, leaving Robbie to help

Nathaniel's mother back into the boat beside her husband. Father Ranald trotted away on his pony.

As they climbed the banking, Morven's thoughts were troubled. Could Nathaniel have sinned or been idle to make his da so eager to be rid of him? So eager, he would send him to Scalan in the bleak Braes of Glenlivet to become a priest? The boy had seemed too timid and respectful to do anything sinful, and if he had sinned, surely the priests wouldna want him. Maybe he was just a disappointment. She shivered. Was *she*? She didn't always do what she was told, nae upon the first telling. Da said she was thrawn, and she supposed she could be. Fear tightened her chest—she must do better.

That night, Morven made a decision, one that would shape her life—she would prove her worth. She might be naught but a lass, but she would work as hard as Alec and give Da no excuse to be rid of her. She drew a quivering breath. She must be careful who she trusted. Land mattered, highland land, to some even more than a bairn, especially, she supposed, a female one. She shivered and glanced over her shoulder. A fat moon winked at her through the trees. It hung low in the sky, silvering the foliage, throwing up shadows. She stumbled on. The strange sky had been a warning.

CHAPTER ONE

Strathavon, March 1781

THE SUN WAS ON the brink of rising, a pearl-grey dawn lightening the sky. Morven stood at the window, watching lapwings display over Druimbeag's infield, their tumbling flight and wheezy cries calming her racing heart.

Feeling a little easier, she returned to Jamie and gazed at his sleeping face. Freed from its lace, his dark hair had curled in his sleep, something he disliked. She longed to run her fingers through it. Wasted on a man, she thought, gazing at his sensual lips, and she yearned for their touch. She thought of their nights together, of soft skin and whispers, tenderness, trust, now unquestionably given, the breathless coming together and the hitherto unimagined feelings, and her heart ached for this man she once so mistrusted and miscalled. She now trusted him with her life.

Jamie was now her husband, yet she sensed he was only truly hers in these rare moments, vulnerable in sleep for all his strength and stature. She must hoard them like treasure. There were never enough hours in the day for Jamie. If he was not working to build a life for them, a home, and a living from the land, he was helping others to.

Two days ago, they sowed Druimbeag's first crop in over twenty years. Rain held off long enough for Jamie to till soil warmed by gentle spring winds, and together, they scattered their precious seed grain on the ground. Since gaining the lease of Druimbeag, Jamie had worked like an ox, digging out saplings, stones, ragwort and thistle, turning soil that had not seen a plough since he was in swaddling. Even knowing his strength, his achievement was extraordinary. But then, love drove him.

Morven gripped the bed frame as dread again tightened her chest. A dream had woken her. She saw them standing at a fork in the road, a crossroads that would take Jamie from her. A shadow reared up between them, cleaving them apart in some cruel, inescapable way. She released a quivering breath, but her foreboding remained. Something threatened their happiness, something still unrevealed.

Since girlhood, she had been learning from Jamie's aunt Rowena, a healer and wise-woman, and her dear friend. Over the years, Rowena had passed on her skills, especially with herbs. She spoke with reverence of nature's magic, teaching that to heal, a student must first align with the earth's invisible energies. 'Twas through those energies, foresight and healing came. Morven was not yet the spaewife Rowena was, a living dowsing wand sensing all manner of wondrous and ruinous things, a cunning witch some unjustly called her, but already, she had seen much that mysteriously transpired.

Rowena held that the earth was a living being with a spirit and a soul. Her spirit was the force of nature. It wove a magical web over the land, an invisible tracery linking all beings, quickening the land and all that grew or walked upon it, much like nerves and vessels animated limbs, organs, and minds. Guided by the Creator's hand, nature's energies ebbed and flowed like people's; only hers were infinitely more complex. They connected everything—man and beast, every tree, stone, and flow of water, every forest, mountain, and sea. Even every thought. These energies had flowed since the dawn of time. Stilling the mind was the surest way to align with nature's energies. With practice, compassion, and long hours observing her ingenuity, a broader understanding came.

Feeling suddenly nauseous, Morven's mouth filled with water. She dashed outside and retched into the midden. Trembling, she rinsed her mouth at the rain trough and paused to catch her breath. When had her courses last come? She'd been too busy to pay heed. Her heart bounded, and she spun around, gasping and laughing. She reeled across the yard to the byre and startled the cattle awake. They lowed indignantly at her.

'A bairn,' she laughed. 'Jamie's and mine, made from this aching love we share.'

They backed away, snorting and blarting, eyeing her from beneath long fringes. Sobering, she sat on the quern stone and forced breath back into her lungs. But a new mouth to feed so soon after gaining Druimbeag with the holding nae yet able to support them. How would they manage? More importantly, would Jamie be pleased? She rubbed her brow. This must be her secret until she was sure, but whatever the hardships, a child was a precious gift to love and cherish, a dear soul to guide through life until it grew into its finished self.

Still giddy, she got to her feet. ''Twas only a dream,' she whispered. 'All will be well. Let him be pleased. Let him love the wee soul as much as I do already.'

She smoothed her fingers over her shift, picturing the infant forming inside her. 'Twas likely little bigger than a tadpole, but 'twas half Jamie. Already, she felt the same tenderness for the tadpole that she felt for him. Would he feel the same, though? He might think it a burden, something to make their hard lives even harder. She sighed. A child could make up for the family he'd lost. Rowena and his cousins were Jamie's last remaining kin. She frowned; she was getting ahead of herself. Childbirth was risky. She had attended enough births to know that.

Inside, Jamie was sitting on the edge of the bed, pulling on his sark, the pale linen ghostly in the dimness. She moved to the hearth and brushed away the night's peat ash. Beneath, the embers still glowed. She blew on them and added dry pine needles until they flared, sending out a welcome burst of warmth, then poked birch bark and twigs into the glow. When they caught, she fed the fire with dry peats.

Jamie got to his feet, searching for the rest of his clothing. 'Something affrighted the cattle. Ye should've woken me, my love. I've no business acting the sluggard. I promised Rowena I'd help wi' the sowing.'

She nodded, wishing he would tarry. 'I think 'twas me startled the beasts, though I didna mean to.'

He studied her, his brows drawing together. 'You look worn out. I work like a demon, but ye mustna think ye should do the same. Have I made ye feel that?' When she struggled to answer, his face fell. 'I have.' He drew her up into his arms. 'I hope ye can forgive me.'

'Nay, I'm fine,' she croaked.

He cradled her head against his chest, stroking her hair. 'Ye're frozen.'

His heart sounded reassuringly through his sark. She wound her arms around him, feeling the power harnessed in his warm body. Jamie only returned to Strathavon last year after the death of his parents and sisters. Growing up in exile in Inverness, he'd become aware of new farming practices—land drainage, crop rotation, green crops like clover to enrich the soil. He now wished to put them into practice at Druimbeag. They'd toiled for months, digging ditches, clearing heath and gorse, most of all, planning their future together as man and wife.

Jamie kissed the top of her head, then searched for her mouth, his kiss prompting a familiar flutter in her belly. She shivered, inhaling his scent. He smelled of pine resin, of earth, and hard toil. She drew his scent into her lungs, earthy, intoxicating, and reached up to touch his cheek.

'I should learn to temper my passion,' he murmured, 'and let ye sleep. You work as hard as me.'

She smiled; his passion had made their wee tadpole. 'Nay,' she whispered, 'I yearn fer our closeness as much as you.'

He smiled in relief but continued to gauge her intently as if to be sure. She held his gaze, letting him tuck wayward tendrils of chestnut hair behind her ears while he searched her face. She had always been forthright. Growing up with three brothers, her youngest, Donald, now seven, competing for her da's approval, especially with Alec, who was only ever her champion and defender, she had learned to be.

'How did I ever deserve ye?' Jamie kissed the tip of her nose, then let her go while he finished dressing. 'What will ye do whilst I'm gone?' He ran his fingers through his hair and laced it deftly at his nape.

'I'll visit Annie Shaw wi' Rowena. Annie lost a deal o' blood when her infant came. I've herbs to gather, a tea to brew. 'Twill help her regain her strength, and Rowena will bring a special tincture.'

'Then, ye must take the pony. I can walk.' He helped himself to a handful of bannocks from the table and crossed to the door, stuffing them into his pouch. 'I dinna like to take from Rowena's table.'

She nodded. Rowena's husband had been gone more than two years, murdered by the devil-exciseman Jamie helped bring to justice. Since losing Duncan, Rowena's life had been a constant struggle.

'Jamie.'

He looked back at her.

'I ken I once doubted ye.' She bit her lip, remembering how bitterly she once accused him, her anger blistering the air between them. 'I believed terrible ill of ye.' She hung her head, ashamed to look him in the eye. She had gone too far, calling him a gutless excuse for a kinsman. Her heart shrank at the memory.

He frowned, pain marring his handsome face. 'You were led to believe the worst o' me. 'Tis how it looked. Dinna punish yerself. In yer place, I'd have believed me a traitorous louse, too.'

She sighed. He was being kinder than she deserved. Jamie had been prepared to give his life for his kinswoman and cousins, fighting an illegal duel with the exciseman, exposing the gauger's deceit to the factor and the whole glen so Rowena might remain at Tomachcraggen. Rowena's home meant everything to her. Jamie felt the same; his parents were put from Druimbeag when he was still in swaddling clothes. Yet, although the exciseman tried to take his life, Morven knew Jamie would risk it again in a heartbeat.

She no longer doubted Jamie's courage. His principles and decency defined him. He would sacrifice himself for those he loved; she understood that now. Land meant everything to him, Strathavon land, this wild highland glen where they had both been born. His family's eviction was unjust. Now that he had regained Druimbeag, his resolve to hold onto it moved her deeply. Daily, he near worked himself into the ground. He would fight any injustice threatening what he held dear, but knowing that made her fearful.

'I wish ye to ken how much I regret my sore words.' She frowned, wishing to express her feelings for him in a way not graceless and clumsy. 'That I've ... althegither beached my heart on yer shore.' She blushed, knowing herself no poet. 'I love ye more than I have fine words to tell ye.'

He laughed. 'You said it well, but I love you more.'

'Nay,' she wrung her hands. 'What ye did, the risks, joining the gaugers, and the duel, all to protect Rowena and yer cousins. No man could've done more. I'm proud to call ye my husband.' She frowned, thinking of her fearful dream. 'I couldna bear it if aught came atween us.'

He sobered, puzzled. 'Naught will.'

'Ye swear?'

He flashed her a mystified smile, then frowned as he tried to gauge what had prompted her strange question. His right hand moved to his left hip where his sword hilt would have rested had King Geordie in faraway London not outlawed Highlanders carrying arms—one of the Crown's many attempts to crush their way of life. To the authorities, they were all still rebellious Jacobites.

'My heart is yours, Morven.' He smiled crookedly. 'I hope ye ken that. I swore afore God to love and protect ye. I didna make that vow lightly. Nae fer any man nor any reason will I break it. So, naught can come atween us. I give ye my word.'

She nodded, feeling foolish.

He inclined his head to her. With a twitch of his plaid, he was gone.

CHAPTER TWO

As arranged, Morven met Rowena on the outskirts of the village of Balintoul. She carried her herbs and simples in a basket strapped to her back, the tea of shepherd's purse, yarrow, and motherwort sloshing in a flask against her pony's flank. Four days ago, they delivered Annie Shaw's infant, a flailing baby girl with thin arms and legs and an even thinner cry. Annie named her Miriam, hoping she might watch over the brothers she would surely have, as Moses' sister had watched over the infant Moses among the bulrushes of the river Nile. Morven remembered Father Ranald telling the story in chapel and liked the name. She hoped the infant would thrive, but she would only do well if her mother made good the blood she had lost. If not, Annie would have barely enough milk to feed a sparrow, and little Miriam might die.

They rode east from Balintoul, following the rough track around the foot of Tom Trumper into a forest of birch and pine. A thin trail of smoke rose above the pines. Following it, they came upon Tomnalienan, half hidden in the trees. Morven spoke little during the ride, her thoughts elsewhere, Rowena respecting her silence. How to broach the matter of her possible pregnancy?

Sheltering in a clearing in the trees, Tomnalienan was humble, little more than a crumbling pile of field-gathered stones thatched with heather, a ramshackle byre, and a few meagre strips of weedy ground. Annie's husband and father were whisky smugglers, although on a lesser scale than her own da. Since Hugh McBeath's arrest, smuggling had become less hazardous. His replacement clamped down hard on any brazen smuggling, but he understood that whilst smuggling continued and he handed in a token tally of seized barrels, he might remain safely employed with the Scottish Excise Board. Stamping out all smuggling, even if possible, would mean the end of his career.

As they neared the cot-house, their garrons grew restive and wilful, snorting and tossing their heads. The reason for their nervousness became plain on entering the clearing. A great draught-horse stood tethered outside the byre. Bay in colour, the animal was well-muscled with an arched neck and broad shoulders, its hooves fringed with long hair. Bridled in polished leather and gleaming brass, it chomped from a bag of oats, pausing mid-chomp to eye them through gimlet black eyes.

Morven looked at Rowena. No Glenlivet cottar could afford to keep such an animal, never mind acquire one. Highland garrons were stocky with dense badger-like hair, keeping them warm and dry in all kinds of weather. They were the only ponies used in the glens.

'It canna be the factor,' Rowena muttered. 'McGillivray rides a sleek black hunter, nae a great workhorse like thon.'

'Who, then?'

She shook her head.

They tethered their garrons and were poised to rap on the door when a shrill cry from within made them jump. There came a series of piercing shrieks followed by the tremulous cry of a startled infant.

'If the foolish girl is unwilling,' a male voice boomed, 'then in God's name, hold her down. I didn't come all this way for a witless lass to question my authority. The impudence of her!'

They exchanged startled looks; the man had spoken in English. Rowena pounded on the door. The shrieking ceased. Annie's mother Janet cracked the door open. Her eyes widened when she saw them. 'A medical man's here,' she hissed. 'John Dalrymple, physician o' Edinburgh. The Kirk minister sent him, though how I'm to pay the man, the Lord only kens. Annie wasna fer being bled.'

'Bled?' Morven stared at her. 'Annie near bled to death when her infant came. Whatever's he thinking?'

Rowena gripped her arm. 'Have a care,' she warned. 'I've heard o' this Dalrymple. He's nae a man to cross.'

Morven had also heard rumours of a physician in the area but was unclear what that meant. He might be a barber-surgeon or an apothecary or even hold documents from a college of medicine. But what wisdom did such documents bestow? Rowena was the most accomplished healer she knew, having spent her entire life studying nature, the true source of all healing.

'He's likely an educated man,' said Rowena, 'come armed wi' scientific methods from the south, using Latin words to fool folk into trusting him.' She frowned. 'Yet his patients are usually wealthy landowners, nae humble folk. They say he talks a good cure, but can he work one? The factor rates his skill in shooting game, but that hardly makes him a healer. He prescribes fancy concoctions common folk havena the coin to afford.'

'A trickster, then?' Morven stared at Rowena. She had heard about men who claimed a piece of paper entitled them to charge outrageous fees, but never had she expected to find one here.

Rowena shrugged. 'Be wary. He may judge our methods witchery. 'Tis hard to imagine he'd recognise the value o' wisdom gathered ower the centuries and passed down to women like us.'

Morven nodded. 'Why's he here, though? Annie could never afford him. Look at his horse.'

'Aye, 'tis puzzling.'

Concerned, they pushed their way in.

The physician glared up at them from his bottles and vials. They had spoken in Gaelic; if Dalrymple was from Edinburgh, he would likely have no Gaelic. He was a big man with bushy red sideburns and florid cheeks. His shirt sleeves were rolled to his elbows, his hands bloody. He wiped them on a filthy rag, glowering at Morven's basket of herbs.

'Folk healers, are you? Henwives? Or is it witches? I heard these glens were plagued with cunning women practising the dark craft, but I hardly imagined you'd peddle your wares door to door.' He turned back to his vials. 'Your services are not required.'

Glancing at Morven, Rowena lowered herself into a respectful curtsy. 'Sir, I am Rowena Forbes,' she said in English. 'You may call me a folk healer if you wish. This is my student, Morven Innes, although Morven is well-nigh as skilled as me. We've come to ask after Annie and her child.'

'An honour, sir.' Morven attempted a similar curtsy.

He stared at them, perhaps astonished they had spoken in English, likely even more astounded that they possessed such a thing as good manners. He bowed stiffly. 'John Dalrymple, physician. As I say, your services are not required. I'm more than qualified. I've bled the girl and was about to purge her.' He lifted a flask holding an evil-looking liquid. 'This will settle her humours. Her sickness will soon remedy itself.'

Morven stared at him. 'Sickness? Annie has no sickness, sir. She bore a child four days ago. When the afterbirth came away, she bled more than was good for her, bright blood with clots like lumps of liver. If she's weak, 'tis from hard toil and from losing so much blood.'

Dalrymple recoiled. 'Good God, madame, you disgust me.'

Morven frowned. Dalrymple claimed to be a physician, yet he seemed to find childbirth and the workings of a woman's body distasteful. He perhaps left the work of bringing new souls into the world in the hands of women since he appeared to find the subject offensive. She made a scornful sound in her throat.

'You question my diagnosis, Mistress Innes?'

'I do, sir.'

'By what authority?'

'That gained through tending glen women and what ails them. By the authority of having eyes in my head and the wits to understand what they tell me.'

'The gall of the piece!' Dalrymple spluttered.

Baffled by their exchange, Janet rushed to placate him. 'Sir, Morven is a skilled *leighiche*,' she soothed. 'A *bean-ghlùine*. Rowena, too. 'Twas they helped oor wee Miriam into the world.'

He glowered uncomprehendingly at her. She had called them healers and midwives.

Nodding at Janet, Morven set her basket on the table. Her eyes had grown more used to the dimness. Annie was nursing little Miriam by the fire, her older sister Elspet standing rabbit-struck at her side. Elspet moved aside, revealing Annie's arm extended over an upturned barrel by her chair. A bowl placed under her arm was slowly filling with blood from a vein opened in the crook of her elbow. Dalrymple's blood-stained instruments and fleam lay by the bowl.

'Nay!' Morven lunged forward. 'Annie mustna lose more blood.' Grasping Annie's hand, she bent her elbow to pinch off the punctured vein. 'Quick, Rowena! Moss to press upon this wound.' She spun around, reaching for her basket, and clattered the physician's metal instruments to the floor.

'God's blood!' Dalrymple turned on Janet. 'If you'd rather these meddlesome witches tended your daughter, good luck to you. You didn't imagine I'd come here out of the goodness of my heart?'

Janet flinched, looking blankly at him.

'I only came to this godforsaken hovel upon the urging of Reverend Dundas, Kirk minister. An act of the noblest charity.'

Janet swallowed, searching for understanding. Her family were Catholic, though, like the other papists of the glen, they were careful to hide it.

Dalrymple rolled his eyes. 'I retract the commitment I gave to the reverend. You've made your choice. I hereby absolve myself of any obligation to your family. Do you understand me?'

Janet's blank expression failed to change.

'Dundas be damned!' Dalrymple glowered around the room, dismissing Janet's meagre home with a scornful curl of his lips. 'He can do his own investigating.' Glowering at Morven, he stooped to collect his instruments from the floor.

Rowena rushed to help, picking up his shiny brass clyster syringe. She held it out to him. 'Sir, no harm was intended.'

He snatched it from her and threw it in his bag along with his vials and flasks. Shrugging on his coat, he clapped his tricorne on his head and made for the door. Pausing there, he squared his shoulders and turned back, fixing Morven with a hostile glare.

'The factor will hear of this. I doubt it'll please him to learn witchery's grown so rife amongst His Grace's tenants, the cunning pieces free to interfere in the proper practice of medicine by a qualified physician. You've not heard the last of this. Most assuredly, you have not.'

'We've done naught wrong, sir,' Morven returned. 'Whilst you have just bled a lass who near bled to death four days ago. Should aught ill befall poor Annie, it will, *most assuredly*,' she echoed, 'be on your head.'

'Holy God!' he sputtered. 'The brazen piece dares to threaten me. A pox on your insolent tongue!'

'I threaten no one. I state the truth.'

Dalrymple whitened with rage. 'Innes, is it? William will have a full account of your actions, madame. He won't tolerate a witch on his rent roll.' He wrenched the door open and stalked out, leaving it swinging on its hinges.

CHAPTER THREE

Rowena squeezed Morven's shoulder. 'I fear ye've made a powerful enemy o' that man.'

Morven snorted. 'Was he ever likely to be a friend? Ye saw what he made o' our methods—judging, quick to misconstrue. Yet we both ken what nature's magic can do when used wisely.' She flattened a wad of peat moss over the puncture wound in the crook of Annie's arm. 'I didna mean to vex the man, but I couldna let him bleed poor Annie.'

Rowena nodded, looking troubled.

'Did he call ye a witch?' Annie whispered.

'Aye, a brazen one.' A sudden fierceness flushed Morven's cheeks. 'But if a witch is a woman who wields nature's magic to help others, then I stand guilty as charged.'

'Please.' Annie touched her hand. 'Be careful who ye say that to.'

She nodded.

'What did he shout at me?' Janet stroked little Miriam's hand. The infant fanned her tiny fingers, closing them around her thumb. 'Forgive me, Annie. I should niver have held ye doon whilst he cut ye.' Janet shuddered.

Morven took away the bowl of blood. Dalrymple had tried to shame Janet and her family. She had no wish to do the same, but she must tell them no lie.

'He said he only came here to please Reverend Dundas. A kindly act. He never meant to charge coin. The minister mebbe thought charity might lure ye to the Kirk from the wickedness o' Rome.' She rolled her eyes. 'But since ye'd rather have twa meddlesome witches tend Annie, he'll have no more truck wi' ye. He means to tell the factor witchery's grown rife amongst His Grace's tenants.'

'Oh, Lord.' Janet sat down hard. 'He means to cause trouble?'

'Maybe the factor will pay him little heed,' said Rowena.

'Is that likely?'

''Twill depend on how much importance McGillivray places on what the physician has to say. How close their acquaintance has grown.' Morven's chest tightened. 'Twas only six months since the factor granted Jamie the tenure of Druimbeag. Jamie chose the derelict holding as a tribute to his father, throwing himself into restoring the land and cottage. His way of righting old wrongs. But what if the factor now evicted them thanks to her runaway tongue? Would Jamie ever forgive her?

'He tricked us,' Elspet blurted. 'He said he held a license to practise from the Edinburgh College o' Physicians.' She pulled a face. 'Whatever that is.'

Rowena sighed. ''Tis likely a gentleman's school. A place where wealthy menfolk go to learn the new science o' medicine. Men from distinguished families. But knowledge isna wisdom; I've long learned that.' She tucked a lock of dark hair under her kertch. 'Nature's been teaching us since the world began. She needs no colleges or licenses. She offers her lessons freely, trusting we'll use her wisdom wi' careful judgment. Some have become so enamoured wi' themselves they've forgotten how to hear her voice.' She looked at the women around her. 'If we still our minds, we'll hear her. She speaks the language of the Creator, spreading harmony and healing.'

Janet nodded, crossing herself.

'Morven mightna be so tactful,' Rowena went on, 'but she was right in what she said. We must build up Annie's strength, nae tear her down. Wee Miriam needs her.' She rummaged in her basket. 'I have a tincture, and Morven has made a special tea. I'll work a charm ower them; they'll make powerful medicine.'

Janet touched her hand. 'Ye've aye been wise, Rowena, a green woman, straddling the cleft atween realms. Ye've walked that path all yer life. We're grateful.'

Morven shivered. She had long known Rowena was special. She drew her inner grace from the wild places and magical glades where she spent so much of her time. Rowena was sensitive to the *sìth*, the faeryfolk who shared their glen, a counter to their devilment.

'We're indebted,' Elspet muttered. The girl was tall and thin, her fair hair uncovered, indicating that she was unmarried. A cleft lip disfigured her face. 'Ye'll tak' a sup o' ale wi' us?'

'Please,' Annie whispered.

'Da would wish it,' Elspet urged. 'And Annie's Rob. They'd be offended if they thought we'd nae been hospitable.'

Rowena nodded, accepting their generosity. The family had little, but what they had, they shared. Chairs were fetched, and while Rowena worked a charm over the tonics they'd brought, Morven bandaged Annie's arm and examined little Miriam. The infant was well, although small and fragile. She tucked the child into her fleece-lined cradle, wondering if she would soon be doing the same with her own littlin.

Janet poured the ale, and they sat companionably around the fire. The brew had only a hint of alcohol, just enough to keep it sweet. Morven let a mouthful slide down her throat. The physician's wrath had unsettled her more than she cared to admit.

Elspet glanced sidelong at her. 'Is marrit life to yer liking, Morven?' She slipped a dry peat into the fire.

Three pairs of eyes turned on her.

'It is.'

'And Jamie?' Janet's mouth twitched. 'How fares he as a husband? The man whose courage and swordsmanship saved the glen smugglers from the Black Gauger's wiles.'

'Fine,' she answered, unsure what Janet was asking.

'Is he tender?' Elspet pressed. 'When ye lie thegither.'

'Elspet!' Annie gasped. 'What a thing to ask.'

'Ach,' Elspet muttered, 'ye wish to ken as much as me. He defended his kinswoman's honour wi' such gallantry.' She glanced at Rowena. 'I'm wondering if he's as gallant when ye're alone thegither?'

Morven's cheeks grew hot enough to toast bannocks. She puffed them out whilst she considered how to answer. That Jamie loved her was the greatest wonder of her life. Their union had been sanctioned by God, a bond she would guard with her life, yet she understood the curiosity he aroused. She was once as curious about him.

'He makes me laugh,' she said, 'wi' his manners and politeness. He thinks me made o' eggshells, likely to break if he doesna take the greatest care.'

'Oh, Lord,' Elspet swayed in her chair, a hand clutched dramatically to her chest. 'I've long dreamed o' such a man, but I doubted he existed.'

'He acted wi' great courage at the duel,' said Janet.

''Twas no act,' countered Rowena.

'I meant—'

'Aye, I ken what ye meant.' Rowena closed her eyes, and Morven knew the memories were crowding back. For her, too. She breathed the mossy air again, felt cold drips slither down her neck from the sodden trees fringing the duelling ground. Hidden in the undergrowth, she'd watched with her heart in her mouth, cringing at the deadly ring of steel on steel, unable to tear her gaze from the clashing figures for fear only the force of her will kept them from killing each other.

'And the cot-hoose our menfolk helped Jamie rebuild,' Annie ventured. 'How d'ye like bideing there?'

Morven let the harrowing memory go. Strathavon folk had near tripped over themselves in their eagerness to pitch in and show their gratitude. Passing stones from hand to hand, they rebuilt the walls one stone atop two, two stones atop one. They laid turfs over the roof ridge and tamped down the earthen floor with their feet. By the greying of the day, a home had arisen from the ruin. Donald Gordon of Craigduthel helped Jamie re-thatch the roof. As a younger man, he helped Jamie's father thatch Druimbeag, ready for the day he would carry his young bride Mhari over the threshold. That was over twenty years ago, and Craigduthel was now in his twilight years. He needed help onto the roof but was eager to do his share. Such kindness touched Morven's heart. Jamie belonged at last.

'I'm thinking 'tis the most beautiful holding in the glen,' she said. 'But every glen wife likely thinks that o' their own wee scrape o' land.'

Annie's delicate face was half hidden under her kertch. 'Rob hasna yet convinced the factor we can raise the quarterly coin fer a holding o' our own. 'Tis our hope fer the future, though. Subdividing holdings is forbidden, so fer now, we bide here. I help Mam wi' the beasts and the milking, and Rob helps wi' the ...' She blinked and reddened, but she didn't need to finish. She meant Rob helped with the whisky. Few in the glen could afford the duke's rents without the coin from whisky smuggling. Jamie would begin distilling as soon as they had reaped their barley. He was new to whisky-making, while Morven had distilled her first dram at the age of twelve. During her growing years, whilst her da and Alec secretly toiled through the hills leading convoys of keg-laden ponies, her da had trusted her to work his pot-still.

Rowena nodded at Annie in sympathy. 'Rents have risen across the Highlands. Young folk must think long and hard afore taking on a tenure from His Grace. The burden o' payment weighs heavy wi' the risk o' default too dire fer many to consider.'

''Tis what Rob says,' Annie whispered.

Rowena sighed. 'Folk once paid the chief of clan Gordon in kind. They gave him the first fruits o' the land in return fer his protection, swearing their allegiance wi' the sword. Those days are gone. His Grace now considers himself a landlord, his people no longer his children but his property to do wi' as he pleases.' She frowned. 'During the rising, he pledged his support to the Hanoverian king, perhaps unwillingly, yet his people remained loyal to the Stuart cause. The authorities havena forgotten.'

Since Culloden, the Crown's reprisals had been brutal. Much had changed in the Highlands, with lairds and clan chiefs now looking to the south, envious of the lavish lifestyles they witnessed there. Jamie said some lairds were even putting tacks of land up for auction, renting land not to their people but to the highest bidder, whoever they might be. The duke hadn't done that, but there had been a shift in attitude amongst those holding power over their lives. Highland people were considered less valuable now. Profit was king.

'In truth,' Morven admitted. 'I dinna ken how we are to afford our first payment. Jamie says we must keep faith and work all the hours God sends, but I confess I lose sleep ower it.' For Jamie, the burden of payment lay heavy and was deeply personal. His parents had been forced from the same tack of land they now held. How would he bear it if history repeated itself? 'Yet Druimbeag feels like home,' she said. 'The land's still half wild. It charms me more each day.'

Rowena sipped her ale with a faraway look in her eyes. 'I've ofttimes thought an enchantment was long-ago laid upon Druimbeag, holding all who venture there under its spell.'

Morven felt the same. There had been a tangible sadness about Druimbeag when they first took possession. The land lay fallow, untilled and overgrown, thick with bracken, deer grass, and heather. Nature had claimed the cottage as surely as she had retaken the land. 'Twas hard to imagine the ramshackle pile had ever been a loving home, yet Morven sensed the spirits of Jamie's kin still lingered in the old timbers and stones, their voices whispering around the firestone.

Jamie's parents had dreamed of working the land and building a herd of cattle, as their ancestors had done. But those dreams proved forlorn.

The victim of a wicked crime, Jamie's da left for Inverness with his wife and infant son before the factor could evict them. Morven shuddered. Being dispossessed shamed all Highlanders. Her da had instilled that understanding in her early on.

Janet laid her cup down. 'I should've said it afore, but 'twas shameful how folk treated Jamie when he first returned here.'

Elspet clicked her tongue. 'I think what he did on Carn Liath was heroic. 'Twas heartless to distrust him so.'

Morven stiffened. What happened on the hilltop had been her doing. Jamie rescued her from the Beltane flames, but in saving her, he defiled the ancient rite. Some believed his actions cursed the whole glen. But since his duel with McBeath, opinions had changed. The exciseman and his hirelings now languished in gaol awaiting trial, and Jamie was respected the length and breadth of the glen. When McBeath finally came up before the local magistrate, most expected McGillivray would make him pay dearly, his sentence lengthy, even final.

Rowena shifted in her chair. She had more reason to want the gauger gone than anyone. ''Tis only thanks to Jamie McBeath's now gone from our lives.' Her voice held a bitter edge. 'The lad holds the same principles his da held. He did what was right; he saved Morven's life. For that, I'll always be grateful.'

'And me,' Annie whispered.

'I dinna believe saving a life can ever be wrong, and the lad had only good in his heart. The magic conjured upon Carn Liath seeks harmony and peace, all earth magic does, and anyhow, 'tis simple enough to recognise goodness in a soul. The Creator sees into every soul. In my life, I've witnessed nature's wisdom. I've seen that kindness and decency are always rewarded. 'Tis only the how and when of it are mysterious.'

''Tis what Father Ranald says,' Janet murmured.

'What ye sow ye will always reap, mebbe many times ower. Jamie now enjoys the place in the glen he deserves.' Rowena picked up her cup, although she did not drink. 'But 'tis hardly right to speak o' the lad behind his back, however generously.'

Annie shot her mother and sister an accusing look. 'Ye must forgive us, Rowena.'

'Aye.' Janet lowered her head. 'The lad's lugs must be burning.'

Morven was relieved. Raking over the events of last year made her uncomfortable. She had mistrusted Jamie more than anyone, coming to all the wrong conclusions, hardly something she was proud of.

Elspet muttered, 'Ye'll have heard aboot the sickness in Glenlivet, Rowena?'

'Sickness?' Rowena looked sharply at her.

'The Ardregan bairns hae it. A fever wi' flaming cheeks and a burning throat. Folk are saying 'tis rush fever.'

'Father Ranald called it scarlet fever,' Janet said.

Rowena's eyes widened. 'I hadna heard, but if true, we must prepare. It could take many innocent young lives.' She got to her feet and began gathering her things.

'Ye think 'tis serious?'

Rowena met Elspet's alarmed expression. 'I've seen rush fever afore, though 'twas years ago. It swept through Stratha'an in a great tide, something Southerners call an epidemic. 'Twas the young it took, nae so much swaddlers but bairns two years and older, but striplings, too.'

'God help us,' Annie whimpered.

''Tis still early in the year; there's little to be found, but we must scour the hillsides and forest margins for nature's most potent medicine, treading little-used paths for the herbs that help counter it.'

Morven got to her feet, her thoughts in ferment. Which herbs best fought an infection that took the young and the innocent? She hooded her arisaid over her head, thinking of the wee soul quickening inside her.

At the doorway, Rowena turned back. 'Dinna go to Ardregan. Nae into the house. If ye wish to bring gifts o' food and such, leave them at the door. Ye must be mindful nae to bring the sickness hame.'

Janet nodded, glancing back inside. Annie now sat alone at the fire, anxiously rocking little Miriam.

CHAPTER FOUR

Morven was quiet on the ride home, her troubled expression reflecting her unease. Rush fever could blaze through a settlement, infecting every home. Could it infect an unborn child? She didn't know, but she must find out before she entered an afflicted home.

Rowena looked across at her. 'Have ye told Jamie?'

She blinked, her cheeks reddening. 'How did ye …?'

Rowena smiled. 'I see the subtle colours that shine from folk revealing their spirit. We've spoken o' it if ye mind. I ken yer colours, they're vibrant, full o' passion, but I'm seeing a new colour, a gentle hue. From yer child, I'm thinking.'

Morven gave a choked laugh.

'How late are ye?'

'I hardly ken, but I have the waking sickness.'

Rowena nodded in sympathy. ''Twill pass.'

'But how will we manage? And will Jamie be pleased?'

Rowena slowed her garron and reached over to grip Morven's hands. Her dark eyes softened. ''Tis only a year since the morbid throat took his kinfolk. He grieves fer them, as I do. He struggles to understand why the Lord took them and left him untouched. Jamie believes it his fault.' She smiled sadly. 'Family is what he yearns fer. 'Tis what ye're giving him. How could he nae be pleased?'

Relieved, Morven nodded. 'Only how will we manage?'

'Ye'll find a way. Love does that.'

'I hope so.'

'Something else troubles ye?'

She shook her head, loath to speak of her disturbing dream. 'Twas likely naught but foolishness.

'Then I'm heart-glad fer ye both.' Rowena chuckled. 'Yer mam will be beside herself, though 'tis best nae to spread the tidings just yet. Some pregnancies are but fleeting. I'm certain yours has quickened,' she added hastily. 'But there's nae sense in raising the lad's hopes 'til the first perilous weeks are behind ye.'

Morven nodded, appreciating the wisdom of that. Many infants were lost in the first weeks of pregnancy. She swallowed. 'Might rush fever smite a babe in the womb?'

Rowena retook the reins, clicking her tongue to her garron. It walked on with a swaying gait. 'I've niver seen that. It can make anyone sick, so it could smite you, though I've long held that working wi' herbs can shield a healer to a degree. But I've never seen a child miscarried or born malformed through its mother catching rush fever, though I've seen that wi' other afflictions.'

Morven exhaled in relief and urged her pony on.

'Try nae to worry.'

'Which herbs are best?'

Rowena stared ahead. 'Pine needle fer its oil. Burned in water, the oil cleans the air and helps prevent the spread o' contagion. Wild garlic. When added to broth, garlic helps the body fight virulence. Marsh mallow root fer its power to soothe and flush the kidneys.' She frowned. 'White oak bark. An infusion eases complications o' the throat. Wolfsbane if we can find it. I've seen it cure the disease outright in older bairns, though 'tis harder in littlins, and deadly nightshade.'

Morven stared at her. Wolfsbane and deadly nightshade were mortal poisons. Folk rightly feared the plants. 'Wolfsbane?' she croaked.

'In the wrong hands, both herbs can kill,' Rowena confirmed. 'Many can. Nature's medicine chest brims wi' powerful poisons. But when used wisely, these herbs cure stagnation o' the kidneys. That'll kill a bairn quicker than any fever.'

Morven acknowledged Rowena's point. When a child ceased to pass water, convulsions quickly followed. If not remedied, the end would be sudden and violent.

'Ye should stay away from Ardregan fer now,' Rowena advised. 'I ken what I said, but 'tis wise to be cautious. I'll go there alone. Ye might forage fer herbs. Pine needles will be easy to find, the others harder.'

Morven was already picturing the best places to search, the sheltered groves where winter's icy breath had failed to ravage everything it touched.

They skirted the fringe of Balintoul village and drew their garrons to a halt. A colourful notice had been hammered into the ground at the side of the track. Neither woman could read but its meaning was clear. Painted in deft strokes and lavish colours, it showed a likeness of the Duchess of Gordon in her finery entertaining local folk in the village square. Families were shown sitting on the grass with pipers and fiddlers playing in the background. They looked at each other. The duchess was known for her love of Scottish music and dancing, particularly the strathspey. This was an invitation to join her for a fair.

Excitement fluttered in Morven's belly. 'Twould be an opportunity for her and Jamie to enjoy themselves. He was an accomplished dancer, confident yet graceful, attentive to his partner. Every eye would be upon them, particularly the female ones, something she had once found insufferable. Now, the notion filled her with pride.

Rowena groaned. 'Folk must keep to themselves to curb the contagion, but the whole glen gathering thegither ...' she made a despairing sound.

Morven swallowed; she hadn't thought of that. 'What d'ye suppose 'tis fer?' she asked. 'I mean, what have we to celebrate? Folk survived the winter, but rents are due at Whitsun. Most will struggle to pay. 'Tisna like His Grace to be so generous wi'out cause.'

Rowena frowned. 'There's something behind this, something to profit His Grace and his wife. The duchess is said to enjoy a wager. Nae matter how it looks, I doubt this will benefit common folk, and wi' fever in the glen, 'tis hardly the time to be gathering.'

'A great crowd will come.'

'Aye, and they'll bring their bairns.'

CHAPTER FIVE

April 1781

Jamie inched himself from the bed he shared with Morven. He winced as the frame creaked and glanced at her. An air of peace radiated from her sleeping face. Gentling his movements, he got to his feet, a chill striking his bare skin and reached for his sark and plaid. He still wore tartan despite knowing the penalty for clothing himself in forbidden garb. Wearing Southerner's breeks felt like a betrayal of his ancestry, yet he was increasingly conscious that wearing the plaid marked him out. Tartan was only permitted to soldiers in the king's army. Wearing it could signify the wearer's willingness to serve in the king's ranks, something many Highlanders found abhorrent, himself included. But as he pulled on his sark, a thought struck. Many would wear tartan to the duchess's fair. He might honour his da's memory by wearing his da's old plaid.

His mind made, he knelt on the earthen floor and dragged out the kist he kept under the bed. Cracking the lid open, he felt in the half-dark, his fingers closing on the beloved garment. He brought it to his face, filling his lungs with the scent of lanolin and old peat smoke ingrained in the wool. His chest tightened, for his da's faint but discernible scent was still fixed in the weave. Tears pricked, but he blinked them away. This should be a joyous day, a respite from the back-breaking grind of bringing Druimbeag back into fruitful production. He intended to spend it with his wife, a rare indulgence after all their hard work.

The fair was the talk of the glen with rumours of dancing and merriment. The duchess wished to entertain her husband's tenants, a community he was now proud to be part of. Known as the Flower of Galloway and reputed to be strikingly beautiful, she would stir great excitement and flutter a few hearts. The whole of Strathavon and Glenlivet would come to admire her and down her husband's whisky, yet Jamie couldn't help fearing it might prove a pretence for the duchess's recruiting efforts on her husband's behalf. His Grace was eager to levy more men into his regiment, the Northern or Gordon Fencibles.

For months, there'd been rumours of competition between those lairds and clan chiefs granted warrants to raise regiments, rivals poaching recruits from neighbouring lands, vying to outdo each other in the king's eyes. The duchess had even claimed she could enlist more fighting men with her womanly wiles than any man with a beating order, but the land was being emptied of men when barely a lad could be spared. What Highlandman would wish to join the king's army? The occupying redcoats were viewed with contempt, as were England's wars. Many Highlanders would rather fight for France.

But this was not a day for discord, so Jamie let the thought go and carried his father's plaid to the table, where a feeble shaft of light from the window let him see what he was doing. He gathered the fabric, smoothing his fingers over the muted reds and greens, pride tingling through his innards. Wearing the *fèileadh-mòr* did that to a Highlandman; the great kilt stirred the age-old warrior spirit. Once pleated, he belted the plaid at his waist, letting the folds fall to his knees and mantled the length over one shoulder, securing it beneath his belt.

He moved to the window. A green haze blanketed the infield, strong young barley shoots poking through the soil. Once harvested, he would malt and distil most of their barley and smuggle it south with Morven's da, Malcolm. 'Twas the only way to make a living from Druimbeag. His da's experience had taught him that. He shivered, feeling his presence.

Growing up in Inverness, he'd become aware of some shame in his parents' past. They never spoke of it but 'twas always there—a quietness in his da. As he grew, he began to question why he had no kin like other boys. Were they dead? If not, where were they? Eventually, his mother explained they'd been forced to leave their home in Strathavon. His da felt responsible, his guilt beating him down. His mother wore her sadness with a lighter touch, likely to spare the husband she adored, but once Jamie knew the truth, they began to speak of the glen and the kin they had left behind in longing tones. Their yearning to return stirred a curiosity about the fabled Strathavon and a desire to reclaim all his family had lost. By the time he reached manhood, Jamie had formed two firm beliefs: kinship was precious and holding land in the glen of his birth even more so.

Although his parents dreamed of returning, sickness struck. God took his mother and sisters with merciful swiftness, but his father's suffering was lengthy and torturous. After their deaths, Jamie despaired. Rootless and adrift, desperate to find lost kin, he could think of no earthly reason why he should not return. He might have kin still living in Strathavon, such as his paternal aunt, Rowena, and her husband, Duncan. Also Grace—not blood kin but as good as. He longed to meet his grandsire Lachlan, a man he'd heard so much about he felt he already knew.

But on reaching the remote glen, Jamie found Rowena a widow, Duncan killed in suspicious circumstances. Of his granda Lachlan, he found only a grave. Rowena told him her father never recovered from losing his son, Jamie's da, and knowing he would never see his grandson grow to manhood broke his heart. Jamie wished he could have met the man. But Rowena was kind and welcomed him into her home despite her troubles. He found he had two cousins, William and Sarah, and threw himself into working Rowena's holding.

His hard work was bearing fruit when Rowena revealed the local exciseman was blackmailing her. Hugh McBeath, known as the Black Gauger, wanted her for his wife. He gave Rowena an ultimatum so offensive it made Jamie's blood boil. He resolved to snare the man. But his plan failed, leaving him little choice but to challenge the gauger to an illegal duel.

He shuddered, pushing away memories of that fateful day. The outcome could so easily have swung the other way. Yet he was content now. In loving Morven, light had come back into his world. With Morven at his side and his name on the lease of Druimbeag, he had begun to live again.

He breathed on the warped glass of the window, rubbing it with the side of his fist until it shone, and he could better see the land his father had once worked. 'Twas fine tillage. As the Avon flowed from her mountain source to join the Spey, she snaked through Strathavon, flooding and receding, carrying down rich silts and sediments and spreading them over the land. In few places had she better done that than at Druimbeag. Here, her minerals enriched land that once belonged to his da, at least in every way but a legal one. Now, it belonged to him. Jamie tightened his fist; he mustna lose it.

His da had been principled, impressing upon his son the need to always do what was right. He never wanted to smuggle. Once wed, he hoped to prove it possible to meet the rental with only a parcel of land and a few beasts, but his venture was a gamble from the start. It ended as badly as any gamble could. Later, working as a gravedigger in Inverness, his da sorely regretted not smuggling. 'Twas a folly Jamie had learned he must not repeat.

'Twas known the duke had established the new settlement at Balintoul to woo his tenants away from whisky smuggling and cattle reiving toward a legitimate occupation in the linen industry. But His Grace had little understanding of the rough hill grazing in these glens. The land and climate were suited to raising cattle and barley, not flax. Hence, cattle herding continued, as did smuggling, an activity Jamie was eager to turn to as soon as possible.

He shifted his gaze to the in-field with its run-rig strips. Morven had worked hard, planting potatoes, sowing cabbage and turnip. He smiled. When first they met, she had been guarded, a guise she wore like a tough outer shell to protect herself. Skilled in whisky-making, she became his teacher. He needed to make Rowena's holding pay. But as she came to trust him, her guise slipped. He discovered she was loyal and driven, but her loyalty made her vulnerable. She was in constant danger, both in her da's hidden whisky bothy and as a healer. He longed to protect her.

His guts twisted. But he'd failed her and mustna fail her again, yet he feared he would. The thought undid him. Sudden movement caught his eye. A pair of hares were standing on their hind legs, flailing at each other. He smiled at their antics. Something disturbed them, and they leapt and capered, then bounded away, eager to mate, he supposed. He glanced back at the bed, finding it empty.

Puzzled, he flicked his gaze around the room. Morven must have gone to the spring to fetch water, yet she'd made nary a sound. She could move with the fluid grace of a cat and had the same jewel-like green eyes. She had no notion how lovely she was. Making for the door, he almost collided with her.

'Jamie!'

She blushed as if he'd caught her at mischief. She was still ashamed of her lack of faith in him. He hadn't realised how much until recently, but he wished she would not be. Without her, his life was empty. He supposed losing his family had made him love more deeply, needing to fill the empty well inside him, yet love and loss walked hand in hand: the deeper the love, the more heartrending the loss. Every moment with her was a potentially fleeting gift.

He shook the thought away and took her in his arms. She shivered, still in her shift. He wrapped the loose end of his plaid around her to enclose them both, fighting the urge to carry her back to bed. That was likely the reason she looked so tired.

'I hope I didna waken ye,' he murmured.

'Nay, 'twas ... something else.'

'Ye look tired.'

'I'm fine.'

He frowned.

She stepped back, taking in his father's old plaid. 'Oh, Jamie, ye look that handsome.'

''Twas my father's.' He blushed, fingering the faded wool.

'Fine work.'

He nodded. She was likely tired from her hours spent searching burnsides and scouring along forest margins for the herbs to counter the sickness Rowena warned about. A contagion which thus far had failed to ravage the glen as Rowena predicted.

He smiled. 'If I'm to take yer arm at the fair, I must look my best. I'm keen to show ye off.' He took her hand and spun her around, catching her about the waist. 'Ye're the fairest lass in the glen, and I'm far and away the most fortunate lad.'

She laughed, looking at her crumpled shift. 'I'd better be dressing, then.'

'Och, I dinna ken.' He slid his hand down her back. 'I like the feel o' ye in yer shift.' But he left her to dress.

Once Jamie had done the work that could not be left undone, he returned to the cot-house and sat by the fire, warming his knees while he watched Morven plait her chestnut hair and fix her kertch in place. Only married women wore the long white, traditional piece of linen. Upon rising on the first morning as a married woman, Morven had tied hers in place, letting the long, finely worked point trail down her back. The delicate piece was a gift from her family, the MacRaes of Delnabreck. It heightened her beauty, adding a new dimension to her face. Wearing it signified she had bound herself to him, heart, body, and soul. Never would he weary of watching her tie it in place.

He looked at her gown. The wool was dyed a dark shade of mulberry, her arisaid spun in similar checked earthen hues. She draped her arisaid around her shoulders, pinning it with a brooch. It fell in folds from the crook of her elbows, revealing the tightly laced bodice of her gown and her slender waist. She looked beautiful, although he hoped one day to buy her something finer, perhaps spun in French silk. He shifted his gaze to the window and a hazy view of the hills where Druimbeag's summer grazing lay. First, he must freckle those hills with cattle.

Turning back, he leapt to his feet. Morven was slumped over the table. 'What is it? Are ye ill?' He helped her into a chair.

'Forgive me; my innards are queasy and rebellious.'

Perturbed, he knelt at her feet and felt her forehead. It was mercifully cool.

She leant into him, letting him caress her back. 'Forgive me. I dinna feel like making merry. I doubt I even could.'

He blinked at her in bewilderment. 'What is it? Are ye feverish?'

She shook her head. 'Nay, but I dinna wish to spoil yer day. Ye must go wi'out me. When will there be another like it?'

He sat back on his heels. 'Leave ye here sick and alone? I canna do that.'

She swallowed and closed her eyes. 'I'll be fine. And feeling like this, I'd rather nae have company.'

'But I canna just leave ye. 'Tis something only a scoundrel would do.'

''Tis a spell o' sickness. 'Twill pass, and I'll be right again when it does. Ye've worked hard, Jamie. Ye mustna miss the fair on my account.'

'But ye've worked as hard, and I dinna want to leave ye.'

She smiled wanly. 'I'll be fine.'

He continued to frown at her.

'Ye've many friends in the glen now. They'll be expecting ye. Ye mustna be letting them down.' She swallowed. Speaking appeared an effort.

She would know if there was anything to worry about, but leaving her didn't feel right. And the fair wouldna be the same without her.

'I wished to show ye off,' he pouted, realising how peevish that sounded. What *he* wanted hardly mattered. He swallowed. 'I'll go, then, but I'll nae stay long. I'll be back afore ye know it.'

She shook her head. 'Nay, ye must mak' the most o' the day, Jamie. Do it fer me.'

He looked at her in dismay, but she thrust him aside and bolted for the door. Seconds later, he heard the same sound that startled the hares.

CHAPTER SIX

Approaching Balintoul, Jamie caught the rousing sound of music and merriment carried on the breeze. His spirits rose. It had rained during the night, the earth dark and loamy, but a watery sun now warmed his back, mist rising wreath-like from the ground. The breeze brought the scent of spring flowers, and he drew it into his lungs. In his time loading boats on the east bank of the river Ness at Inverness, accustomed to the stink of rotting seaweed and the foul stench of tanned deer skins that daily left the Highlands for London, never had he imagined such a scent existed.

As he entered the settlement, another aroma wafted to him—a mouth-watering one. He pictured roasting hogget, fatty and succulent, sizzling on a spit. The sound of music drew him up the main street past heather-thatched homes to the grassy central square. Pipers were playing there even though the bagpipes had been outlawed for nearly thirty-five years. A drummer kept the beat on a *bodhran* while fiddlers canted their heads, elbows flexing. Jamie's feet began to tap. He saw many families; Rowena's warning to stay away had deterred few. Folk leapt and whirled, led by a vibrant vision he supposed must be the duchess dressed head to foot in tartan.

Morven's da Malcolm was in the midst of things, surrounded by fellow whisky smugglers. Jamie headed toward him, his mouth watering as the aroma of bannocks baking on a hot girdle assailed his senses. Entering the knot of menfolk around his father-in-law, his nostrils flared at the sharp sting of whisky.

'Jamie!' Alec pushed a dram into his hand and drew him further into the huddle.

There were more cries of welcome. He was jostled on all sides, his forearms clasped and shoulders playfully punched. Since McBeath's arrest, smuggling had become less risky. Folk never seemed to tire of showing him their gratitude. He was now a valued member of the community. The wonder of that had yet to lose its charm—he hoped it never would.

'Ye made it.' Hal McHardy clapped a hand on his shoulder. 'I thought yer young wife might hae ye fettered to her side, wanting to dance the hind legs off ye. Or ye'd be wanting to birl her aboot.' He grinned. 'As I would if I'd wed such a bonny quine. Ye can mak' merry, then. 'Tisna every day the whisky's free and legal.'

'Morven wasna able to come,' he muttered. But Hal was right; 'twas a rare day they could be openly at ease with a dram in hand.

'Glad to see ye, lad.' Malcolm grinned at him. 'Alec, find nourishment fer yer brother-in-law. He's a growing lad.' He laughed. 'Though God help him if he grows any taller. He'll nae fit under his ane door.'

Alec reeled off toward the nearest laden table, Jamie watching him fondly. He had much to thank Morven's family for, especially her da. He raised his drink to him. Malcolm had already downed a deal of whisky by the looks of it. His face had a ruddy sheen, although Delnabreck could hold his drink. That was one of the things he had learned about his father-in-law. Young Alec, he noted with an inward smile, was less able in that respect. Already, he was showing signs of wear.

Alec returned inanely pleased with himself, carrying a hunk of meat skewered on a stick, his pockets stuffed with bannocks. Jamie accepted the bounty and tore at the meat, letting the juices run down his chin to rousing cheers and laughter.

'The lad's half-starved, Delnabreck. Whit's yer daughter been feeding him?'

'He's mebbe nae had time to eat,' Hal said with a wink. 'What wi' him haeing his marital duties to perform every chance he gets.'

Malcolm glared at Hal while Jamie choked on a mouthful of bannock amid more ribald banter at his expense. 'Twas all good-natured, but for once, he was glad Morven wasn't there to hear it.

'Whit's it all fer, then?' Donald Gordon nodded at the duchess. She was resting from dancing, fanning herself, surrounded by liveried servants. 'All this indulgence. Why d'ye suppose oor laird suddenly feels the need to act so generous toward common folk?'

Malcolm frowned. 'I'm thinking 'tis aboot the duke's ambition as an army colonel, as is much he does these days.'

The men nodded gravely. They took heed when Malcolm spoke. Since Duncan's death, he was likely the best smuggler in the glen, certainly the most successful. The others looked to him for guidance. Jamie intended to do the same.

Angus Munro grunted, 'The American war doesna go their way. French privateers harry the northern coasts. The authorities fear an invasion. 'Tis what the defencible regiments are meant to guard against.'

'Many've deserted,' put in Peter Cameron. 'He'll be efter fresh blood to mak' up his levy quota.'

''Tis robbing the Highlands o' men,' Malcolm growled. 'There's scarce men left to farm the land, never heed defend our shores from the French.'

Craigduthel sucked on his pipe. 'His Grace thinks owermuch o' his family name and pride, as do other lairds and clan chiefs.'

'Puffed-up vanity in fading family power,' agreed Hal. 'His Grace and the other lords compete fer glory raising regiments from their ane people. Nae just that—they poach men from rival lands. Even here.'

'Aye,' Malcolm muttered. 'His Grace must ken it goes on. And wi' men slipping awa fer the sowing, he'll be wanting new recruits to swell his ranks.'

''Tis undignified fer landed lords to lose men to a rival,' said Hal.

Malcolm snorted. 'So, befuddle the sod-turners wi' whisky and pipe music, a display o' tartan to stir the blood. That'll have them champing to tak' the king's shilling and mak' up his losses.'

There was a smatter of bitter laughter.

Peter scowled at the duchess. ''Tis a hiring fair, then.'

'Likely,' muttered Malcolm. 'Though I doubt 'twill work. Common folk see things different. Men are needed here to grow grain fer filling bellies and paying rents. Wi' all that's been done in the glens in the Crown's name, I canna see any Highlandman wishing to join the king's army.' He shook his head. 'Abandon hame and hill to indulge the vanity o' a lord who doesna even ken ye exist?' He made a scornful sound in his throat.

'Weel said, Delnabreck.' Hal downed a mouthful of whisky. 'Ye'll nae catch me signing up.'

'Nor me,' came the muttered consensus.

Jamie savoured a mouthful of whisky, letting its fire warm his belly, its peaty vapour clear his head. Few Highlanders had the stomach to don a scarlet coat and fight for a distant king, particularly one whose father sent his redcoats against them after Culloden, ordering the killing of rebel and farmer alike. Highlanders no longer pledged their loyalty so freely. Struggling under crippling rent rises and the crushing of their highland way of life, folk now put their trust in each other. Any loyalty to their laird must now be bought, he imagined, or extorted. Looking around, he saw little appetite for a military life among his companions. These men lived their lives on the land, all aware of the harsh conditions and brutal discipline maintained in the British Army. For himself, living in the hills with his young bride, herding cattle, growing barley and perhaps bairns amongst a community of fellow Gaels suited him fine. If he made a success of Druimbeag for his da, all the better. His life might have some meaning, their deaths feel less pointless. God must have spared him for a reason. Maybe Druimbeag was it.

His cousin Sarah appeared and dragged Alec off to dance. They were betrothed and keen to wed, although Father Ranald was less enthusiastic. He judged Sarah too immature to enter the holy state of wedlock. They must wait another year or more until she reached eighteen. With Alec gone and his belly full, Jamie wandered away, leaving the men to their whisky and conjectures.

Rowena was sitting on the grass with Grace, Morven's mother, anxiously watching the merriment. He joined them. Grace touched his arm. 'Where's Morven, Jamie?'

'She's nae well. Naught serious,' he added. 'I wanted to stay wi' her, but she bade me come without her.'

Grace's face fell, although Rowena merely nodded. He sighed as he turned away, knowing his explanation sounded lame. Sarah drew his attention. She was trying to outdo the duchess, not in elegance but in sheer exuberance, drawing many amused looks as she charged toward poor Alec and ruthlessly birled him around. Thankfully for Alec, the duchess signalled to the musicians, and they slowed the tempo for a graceful Strathspey.

Sarah returned flushed and breathless, and tugged on his arm. 'Dance wi' me, Jamie. Alec's swilled ower-much whisky down his neck. He's naught but an embarrassment.'

He looked doubtfully at her. 'Alec would never humiliate ye, cousin.'

'Nae knowingly, but they've been too free wi' the whisky wi' Alec. Ye'd think Her Grace wished him to mak' a fool o' me.'

'Hardly, cousin.' But he allowed her to pull him to his feet. 'Alec thinks the world o' ye. He wears his devotion like a book—written all ower his face.'

'*Humph.*' She glowered at him and dragged him away.

'Twas unlike Alec to drink to excess. The lad was aware of his limits with strong spirit. Puzzled, Jamie bowed to Sarah and took her hand, then skipped and hopped to the music as gracefully as he could, threading his way through the line of dancers to come together with her again at the end. As they danced, he searched the crowd. He spied Alec at the far side of the square in bad company. Ale-swigging rogues leaned in on him on all sides. One threw an arm around Alec's shoulders while another filled his cup. A third linked arms with Alec, crooning and swaying as he led him down a side lane.

Frowning, Jamie turned back to his cousin. Sarah was a striking young woman, but she was still very much a child—a fact he'd learned to his cost. Lost without her father, she initially resented his regard for Morven and wanting to punish them both, let Morven believe he was in league with McBeath. He shuddered. That vile business was thankfully behind him. He hoped never to see the exciseman or his hirelings again.

The dance ended, Sarah curtsying coyly to him, followed by a break in the music for the dancers to catch their breath. Sarah stalked off, hopefully to rescue Alec. Servants began laying out more food for the revellers while the men joined their womenfolk on the grass. Two liveried footmen helped the duchess onto a velvet-covered box, then began setting up makeshift tables, laying out pots of ink, paper, and quills. The duchess signalled to her manservant, then clapped her hands for quiet.

'Young men of Strathavon and Glenlivet,' she cried in English. 'I salute you!' She waited for her manservant to translate her words. 'I know you are brave warriors, honourable to a fault. Patriotic hearts beat strong in your chests. Now is the time to prove it! Your Lord needs recruits for his fencible regiment. I urge you to do your duty and defend your native land from the French. The War Office will pay you for the privilege. Think of that. You need never leave your own country. His Grace has given his word: you will not cross Scotland's border unless England is attacked. I have documents to prove it.'

She brandished a sheaf of papers in the air. 'So, enlist, brave lads, and I will pass a shilling to you from my own lips.' She winked and pretended to blush, fanning her face while her words were translated and time was allowed for them to sink in.

A gasp rippled through the gathering, followed by a murmur of excitement. She nodded in encouragement. 'Yes, young lads. A dram, a kiss, an honourable career with the opportunity to be legally armed and kilted again. Your uniform will comprise tartan, sword, pistol, and dirk—the ancient dress you have long been so attached to. You may wear it again with pride. No longer will it be forbidden you.'

She pointed with her fan in mock chastisement at those in the crowd already clothed in outlawed tartan and wagged her finger, then blew them a kiss. 'Come forth, then, let your name be recorded. I will slip a shilling between your lips.' She paused for her servant to relay her words. 'Upon successful enlistment, you will receive a full guinea in bounty from His Grace. I give you my word.'

She turned to a group of burly men who had appeared behind her, their highland dress and cockade betraying their trade. 'These men have been issued with beating orders.' A drum ruffled and took up a slow beat. 'So, who among you will be first to take the king's shilling?' She produced a coin from a purse hanging on a silken cord at her waist and held it up. 'Which of you is brave enough to steal a kiss from a duchess?'

One or two young lads staggered to their feet, plainly the worse for drink. 'I will!' one shouted. 'I'll tak' a kiss!'

'Shhh, sit doon ye great muttonheid.' His da yanked him down.

'If the boy wishes to do his duty, no man may stand in his way.'

'He's still a bairn,' his mother cried. 'Fifteen. He's needed here.'

The duchess pulled a face. 'Fifteen is old enough, particularly if the lad has the manful figure required and generally found in these parts. No man or woman may stop him.'

'Is it to be an army o' bairns, then?' Craigduthel quipped.

'Certainly not. Any man up to an age rendering him unfit for service may enlist.'

Grace leaned across and touched Jamie's arm. 'Where's Alec? Sarah's looking fer him.'

Jamie stared across the square to the last place he'd seen Alec, but there was no sign of him. He flicked his gaze among the crowd. Malcolm was still with his band of whisky smugglers, a group Alec had earlier been part of—not now. Jamie got to his feet, feeling a vague sense of disquiet. He had foolishly allowed Sarah to distract him. He should have paid more attention to the unsavoury characters taking a shine to his kinsman.

Sarah lay sprawled on the grass beside Rowena, irritably plucking at daisy heads. Hal McHardy appeared and tugged on Jamie's sleeve. He nodded toward a burly character in highland dress headed their way. They exchanged wary looks.

'James Innes?' the man said on reaching them.

'Who says he is?' demanded Hal.

'His size. I'm told James Innes is the tallest man in the glen.' The man lowered his voice. 'I have word of your kinsman, Alec MacRae. He's been trepanned. If ye act swiftly, ye may yet save him.'

'Trepanned?'

The man jerked his head, indicating they should move out of their womenfolk's earshot. They shifted to the edge of the grass, where the man said, 'Many recruiting parties scour these hills, what with all the fighting men needed. Those who hold your kinsman have the authority to do so, their warrants signed by Lord Barrington, the Secretary at War, and the Duke of Gordon, as regimental colonel. Once a man's taken the king's shilling, he's judged to be lawfully enlisted. Your brother-in-law has done so.'

'Alec? He'd never do that. Nae willingly.'

'You could say he was prevailed upon.'

'Pressed.' Hal spat in disgust.

Jamie fixed the man with a hard stare. 'What trickery's this?'

The man took a step back. 'Raising men is necessary work. Profitable, I'll not deny it, but any lad fool enough to let himself be tricked is fair game in my book.'

'Profitable work?' Hal thrust his chin out. 'Ye should be ashamed o' yerself.'

The man stiffened. 'I act for His Grace the Duke; his business is my business.' He softened his stance. 'I can take you to your kinsman if you wish.' He shrugged. 'Your choice. As I say, you may yet save him.'

Hal shook his head. ''Tis a trick, Jamie.'

Jamie inhaled strongly through his nose. Young Alec was a trusting soul, likely more than was good for him, yet Alec's honesty and lack of guile were among the qualities he most admired about him. That and his likeness to his sister. Morven would never forgive him if he let them take Alec without lifting a finger. Lord, he'd nae forgive himself. He sighed. 'Ye'd better be taking me to him.'

The man nodded with a flicker of a smile, then jerked his head, indicating they should leave at once but discreetly. When Hal made to go with them, he ran an appraising eye over Hal's small but wiry frame. He nodded. The duchess was talking again. They slipped down a back lane, following the duke's man to a stand of pines where two garrons stood saddled and waiting.

The man nodded at Hal. 'You'll ride with me.'

Astride the other garron, Jamie could do naught but shrug when Hal looked back at him, tight-faced. They would learn their destination soon enough. Urging his garron into a canter, he made away after them.

CHAPTER SEVEN

THEY TRAVELLED ROUGHLY SOUTH through hilly country, following a series of deer tracks in the heather. A birch-covered incline rose on one side, the scent of gorse blossom filling Jamie's nostrils. Patches of snow still lay in the hollows of the land, the light uncommonly clear. He shaded his eyes, taking careful note of their route. Morven would know where they were heading; as a healer, she had trodden every hill and searched every forest and glade whilst he, still a relative newcomer, was quickly lost in this wild land filled with the cries of moorland birds. He gritted his teeth. Though 'twas glorious to feel the sun on his thighs, his jaw ached with tension.

'Nae far now,' the duke's man called back to him.

He had given up trying to glean anything of use from the man. All he would tell them was a little about the law regarding recruiting, which he said was vague, allowing recruiters to exploit their victim's ignorance and fear. The customary method was to soften up the target with whisky and bagpipe music, known to quicken the martial spirit. With some good-natured leg-pulling, this usually won the unsuspecting man's trust. Jamie recalled that was what he had earlier witnessed.

The intoxicated man was then tricked into taking the king's shilling, or, failing that, the coin was hidden about his person once he was too drunk to notice. Upon total inebriation, he was carried off and held in some secret place until the time allowed as a cooling-off period when he might change his mind had passed. That was four days, the man said, though at some point during that period, the recruit must appear before the nearest Justice of the Peace. Magistrates were anxious to promote enlisting, having been called upon to do so and tended toward deafness regarding claims of foul play. But once before the magistrate, the recruited man would have the opportunity to withdraw his enlistment provided he returned the king's shilling with another twenty shillings of charges known as smart money. This sum must be paid within twenty-four hours.

Jamie tightened his grip on the reins. Dear God, how would Alec find such a sum? Regardless, most recruiters took their quarry before the magistrate, having given the impression the withdrawal time had already expired. Jamie frowned. Why would the duke's man tell them this? He needed to get Alec before McGillivray as soon as possible. Their factor was also the local Justice of the Peace and was notoriously unsympathetic to the plight of his employer's tenants. How might such a hearing go? He recalled his da's account of his dealings with the factor and felt sick.

Finally, a stone hut came into sight, the only dwelling they had seen since leaving Balintoul. It looked abandoned. The duke's man faltered at the rickety door, then turned shamefaced to Jamie.

'I pray you'll forgive my part in this.'

Jamie stared at him, then followed him in. As his eyes grew accustomed to the gloom, he made out Alec crumpled on the floor, guarded by three ruffians. He looked in a bad way. Jamie hurried to his side, elbowing the men back.

'Alec?' He lifted his kinsman's head.

'What've they done to him?' Hal growled.

Alec reeked of whisky and appeared so drunk he had passed out, but a livid bruise on the side of his head, a half-shut eye and thick lip told a different story. The men guarding him eyed Hal with suspicion but showed no surprise at Jamie's arrival. They were the men he had seen at the fair, rough types, their faces craggy and scarred, showing signs of a life hard lived. One turned and shouted into a back room.

'Weel, weel, twa fer the price o' one! You pair have landed mair than ye bargained fer.'

To Jamie's horror, Dougal and Ghillie appeared, the Black Gauger's hirelings, both heavily armed. He peered past them, fearing McBeath would follow them in.

Dougal drew his pistol, a smirk creasing his whiskered face. 'Nay, Mister McBeath has been detained elsewhere.' He chortled at his own wit.

Following the Act of Proscription, the law governing their lives since Culloden, Jamie was unarmed. Hal too. He gaped. He had assumed these men were in gaol.

'Nae need to look so surprised,' Ghillie drawled. 'Since we were only following orders from an officer o' the Scottish Excise Board, we've been pardoned. We're free men.' He winked at Dougal, who smirked back. 'Now enjoying profitable careers as recruiters, though nae commonly in this glen. Here, oor faces are too well-kent.'

In Strathavon, these men were rightly scorned and despised. They had collected payment extorted by McBeath from local smugglers, raiding bothies, smashing stills, and confiscating whisky. They took pleasure in their work, persecuting anyone who failed to comply with the exciseman's demands. They'd been present at the duel as McBeath's seconds, there to finish Jamie off should the exciseman fail to do so. In Jamie's judgement, neither man possessed honour or decency.

'What d'ye want with my kinsman?' he rasped. He stared into their gloating faces. 'Ye surely didna return here just to enlist poor Alec?'

At the sound of raised voices, Alec groaned and probed his swollen face with trembling fingers. 'Jamie—what's befallen me?'

'Ye dinna remember?'

'Lord, have I been a fool?'

'Nay.' Jamie squeezed Alec's shoulder, struggling to hold back his anger. Since the duel, he had tried to purge his hatred for McBeath but had only half succeeded. Seeing the exciseman's hirelings again brought it all back. Father Ranald had even taken him aside before he took his wedding vows. ''Tis a sin,' he'd warned, 'to harbour hatred in yer heart. Let it go, Jamie.' But despite his best efforts, his hatred for McBeath lived on.

'Yer brother-in-law here,' Ghillie drawled, 'patriotic soul, has chosen to join His Majesty's army.'

Blinking, Alec rose to his knees. 'Nay, Jamie, I'd never do that, I swear. I'd nae leave Sarah or my kinfolk to fight fer those who only wish to trample us.'

'I ken that, Alec. Rest yer mind.' Jamie slipped an arm around Alec's waist and dragged him to his feet. Grunting, he staggered with him to an upright barrel and left him slumped over it, clutching his head. Hal moved close to guard Alec, prompting Dougal to chuckle. He and Ghillie were now lounging on ramshackle chairs.

Jamie fixed them with a hard stare. 'Ye've carried my kinsman here against his will, beaten and abused him. Let him go, and that'll be an end to it.'

Dougal snorted. 'Ye speak as if ye hae an army wi' ye. I see naught but scrawny McHardy, a farmer nae a soldier. Anyhow, we didna come fer the MacRae whelp, though 'twas a rare treat gieing him a seeing to. Lang owerdue,' he added. ''Tis you we came fer.'

'Aye,' Ghillie drawled. 'His Grace wishes ye levied into his fencible regiment. Since the duel, yer fame's spread far and wide.' He laughed. 'We hear tales o' yer bravery and swordsmanship wherever we go. Those tales grow taller by the day. Eh, Rab?' He looked at the duke's man, who frowned and nodded.

'Those tales have reached the ears of the duke,' Rab confirmed. 'And the duchess, who's anxious no other Lord snares you. I am to ensure that doesna happen.' He removed his bonnet. 'Robert Chisholm, but you may call me Rab, tacksman to His Grace the Duke of Gordon, at yer service.'

Jamie frowned at him. 'I've nae wish to join the king's army, be it the duke's regiment or any other. I fear ye've gone to great trouble, abducted my brother-in-law, all fer naught. I'm grateful to His Grace fer granting me a tenure o' land. Druimbeag means a great deal to me. But I'm nae so grateful I'd give it up to go fight fer him.'

Rab half smiled as if explaining to a child. 'Allow me to clear up any confusion. It hardly matters what *you* want. His Grace wishes it, and 'tis my duty to achieve whatever His Grace desires. My duty and that of his factor, Mister William McGillivray. We imagined you'd wish to save your kinsman.'

'I do.'

'How might you do that? By taking his place, of course.'

Jamie reared back.

'I understand you're an honourable man.' Rab looked him up and down as if to verify that were true. 'Hence, we assumed you'd wish to do your duty, both for your country and your kinsman here.' He nodded at Alec. 'I trust you don't intend to prove us wrong.'

'What are ye saying?'

'Only that we, Mister McGillivray and I, find ourselves loathe to believe you're a coward.'

Jamie stared at him.

'... a blackguard who deserves to lose his farm.'

'*What!*'

'Should you fail to enlist,' Rab went on, 'the factor will regretfully have you turned out of your holding. You and your wife. I understand you've recently acquired a bonny young bride.'

Anger flushed Jamie's face. 'Are ye threatening my wife?'

'Thon's aboot the size o' it,' Ghillie confirmed. 'If ye enlist, we'll release yer kinsman here, Alec MacRae, provided he returns the shilling the king lent him. Once he's done that, he may consider himself withdrawn from military service.'

'What shilling?' Alec lurched across the room. 'I took no shilling.'

'I think ye'll find ye stashed it in yer sporran,' one of the ruffians said. He sniggered.

Alec rummaged in his sporran, finding, to his horror, a shiny shilling. '*Aaaagh*!' He flung it into a corner as if it scalded him, where Dougal swooped on it, pocketing it with a smirk.

'More o' yer kin could find themselves homeless.' Ghillie rocked leisurely in his chair. 'Yer father-in-law, Delnabreck, and certainly yer aunt.' He smiled to himself. 'The bonny witch Rowena, along wi' her son and thon brazen daughter o' hers.'

Jamie gaped at him. 'That's blackmail!'

'Call it what ye will.'

Rab silenced Ghillie with a sharp look. 'I fear military service is the price you must pay to keep a roof over your family's heads.' He held up a hand to ward off Jamie's outraged protest. 'But thankfully, there is some sugar to coat the pill. Should you make the wise decision to enlist in the duke's regiment, the Northern or Gordon Fencibles, His Grace will make you a corporal. But be in no doubt, you *will* be enlisted—'tis just a matter of by whom. I think you'll find our methods gentler than our rivals.' He glanced at Alec's swollen face, then frowned at Dougal. 'Usually, anyway.'

'Gentler?' Hal gaped at him. 'Then, I'd nae like to sample the methods thon others use.'

Rab frowned. 'Any rough handling of your kinsman is regrettable, Innes. At least, 'tis regretted by me.' He drew a long breath. 'But the fact remains, I cannot let you be enlisted in a competing regiment. The humiliation would be beyond His Grace's endurance. Rivals march openly through his lands, stealing his tenants' sons, bartering men like cattle. You're a valuable asset, a symbol his lands are still well-stocked with loyal men willing to fight for their king.'

'Cottars and herdsmen,' Hal growled. 'Most still loyal Jacobites.'

'Warriors like yourself, Innes.' Rab ignored the interruption. 'An indication that His Grace still commands loyalty from his people and can raise dutiful men for his king. 'Tis why you're so important and why he employed these two,' he shot a look at Ghillie and Dougal, 'professional recruiters to find a way to convince you.'

'Ye expect me to take Alec's place?'

Dougal sniggered. 'Noo ye're catching the drift.'

'Nay, Jamie,' Alec cried. 'Ye mustna. Think of Morven. She needs you. Ye canna expect her to manage Druimbeag on her own.' He clutched his battered head. 'What's befallen me was down to my folly. My ower-trusting nature. Ye mustna pay the price fer my foolishness.'

Jamie nodded, anger and dismay darkening his face. Yet he couldn't let them take Alec. His family needed him. Sarah would never forgive him. Nor Morven. 'Twas his duty to save his kinsman. He thought of Rowena. After all he'd done to safeguard her place in the glen, he could hardly be the cause of her losing it. His guts tightened. And Delnabreck, a man he'd come to admire ... Lord, he cared about all Morven's family. He kneaded his brows. He'd only just regained Druimbeag. What would his da think if he let them take it from him? But his da was dead, and the thought of leaving Morven too hard to bear. He'd sworn to protect her; he could hardly abandon her. Yet he was unarmed, Hal too, while these men, six of them, carried pistol, sword, and dirk. He'd taken careful note of their weaponry on entering the hut. What hope had he of freeing Alec? Even supposing he somehow managed it, McGillivray would be incensed. He'd serve eviction notices on all his kin.

Jamie's stomach churned. He had resented the occupying troops all his life. Their swaggering superiority and contempt for highland people, their deliberate undermining of his language and culture sickened him. Most occupying soldiers weren't highland and knew little better, but to be part of it, to participate in the king's colonising endeavours, his search for ever more wealth and power. He squeezed his eyes shut. He'd never imagined doing such a thing, but what choice had he? He must become one o' them.

''Tisna like it'll be forever,' Ghillie soothed. 'Yer enlistment will only last 'til the end o' the American war, or five years, whichever comes first, though the fighting will be ower lang afore that. Then the regiment will be disbanded.'

'And ye can return to the bosom o' yer bride,' Dougal added. 'And dinna forget the enlistment money.' He toyed with his pistol, stroking it as he might a woman's thigh. 'They'll pay ye a full guinea once ye're attested, and there's the bounty coin, paid in cash, and regular wages to send hame. Coin yer bride can use to pay the rent whilst yer away.' He laughed. 'Soothing her pining heart. That is, should ye mak' the wise decision nae to let yerself be dispossessed.'

'And think, Jamie,' Rab coaxed. 'May I call you Jamie?' No answer appeared required, for Rab barely paused for breath. 'Once enlisted, you may bear arms and proudly wear tartan. Lawfully,' he added, eyeing his da's plaid with a derisory smile. 'As your ancestors did. You'll never leave Scotland. 'Tis a defencible regiment; you'll not be drafted. No overseas campaigns, no deadly swamp-fever jungles to capture. You'll not even cross the border into England.' He puffed his cheeks out, appearing mystified anyone in their right mind would not leap at such an opportunity. 'You'll only be garrisoned in Scotland, defending your country from invasion.'

Jamie stretched to his full height, towering over the manipulative tacksman. His country was only under threat of invasion, thanks to its ruler's greed. Yet that hardly seemed to trouble Rab. He advanced on him, bunching his fists.

Rab stumbled back. 'And you'll be safeguarding your family by giving the factor no cause to evict them.' Rab used the word cautiously, mindful that eviction was a dangerous word, sticking in the throats of landless tenant farmers, striking fear in their hearts.

Jamie stared at him. Folk to the north and west of Strathavon were being put from their homes as Rab spoke, cleared to make way for more profitable sheep—a tidy answer to a thorny problem, at least for indifferent lairds. But then, being the duke's man, would Rab care? He exhaled, rage building explosively inside him.

Rab swallowed. 'I hope you understand I'm only doing my duty. 'Tis naught personal. I like you, admire you even. I've no wish to harm you or your family, but I have a task to do.'

'A shameful one,' Hal growled.

Rab turned to him. 'Perhaps, but I wouldn't want to see my beloved country overrun by the French or that traitor, John Paul Jones.'

Ghillie chuckled. 'Ye'll be doing yer patriotic duty, Innes, same as Dougal and me. Only ye'll be on the sharper end o' things if ye tak' my meaning.'

Dougal sniggered.

Jamie stared at them. Patriotic duty? Neither man would recognise patriotism, supposing it slapped them in the face. He looked at Rab. 'Ye're saying I've no choice?'

'Nane,' Dougal cheerfully confirmed. 'Ye must go fer a soldier, though I doubt ye'll be the only one. Many will tak' the shilling, swayed by the duke's whisky and a kiss from his teasing wife.'

Jamie fought the urge to smash his fist into the weasel's smug face. He flicked his gaze to the three unsavoury cut-throats and finally to Rab, the duke's man, who at least had the decency to glance away.

'Lord, Jamie,' Alec choked. 'Can ye ever forgive me?'

He exhaled. 'What's to forgive? This,' Jamie flicked his hand at the rogues before him, gritting his teeth, 'this *snare* wasna your making.'

Alec's face tightened. ''Tis generous o' ye, but we both ken 'twas born o' my folly.'

'I dinna hold ye responsible.' Jamie moved to his kinsman's side and squeezed his shoulder. 'We need never speak o' this.'

'Oh, God. I dinna deserve yer kindness.'

''Tisna wise to dwell on it,' Hal advised Alec. He flashed Jamie a crooked smile. 'I canna be letting ye tak' all the glory. Ye'll need someone to keep ye out o' trouble.' He turned to Rab. 'It seems I'll be taking the king's shilling, too.'

Jamie stared at him. 'I canna let ye do that.'

''Tis done.'

Rab raised his brows in grudging admiration. 'Regrettably, 'tis not yet done, but I thank you for your gesture. You must take the king's shilling from the duchess, not me, and be seen to do so. Everything must appear above board.' He frowned. 'There can be no rumours of underhand recruiting. 'Tis His Grace's reputation at stake. His good name. It mustn't be sullied.'

'Of course,' Jamie said bitterly. 'We canna have that.'

'I'm glad you understand. I'll ride back to Balintoul with you and have you both enlisted.' Rab frowned. 'McGillivray will be there by now. Once you've taken the shilling from Her Grace, you must swear allegiance to the king and make your mark on official papers. That way, 'twill all be legal and binding.'

Jamie nodded grimly. 'What about Alec? I canna take him back looking like that. 'Twould shame the lad. And his family,' he added, thinking of Sarah. She might call off their betrothal. She hated the merest whiff of humiliation.

'Clean him up as best you can, then. Only be quick about it.' Rab indicated a pail of water by the door.

Jamie drenched Alec's face and wiped away all traces of blood. Unlacing Alec's hair, he let it fall forward, concealing most of his bruises. If he stayed out of sight at the fair, his battered appearance might go unnoticed. He prayed so for Alec's sake. Sarah was his world. He'd take it badly if she broke her promise to him.

Still lounging in their chairs, Dougal and Ghillie watched his efforts with great amusement, finishing off the whisky used to disable Alec. With Alec looking more respectable, Hal bolstered him under the arms, and they helped him to the door.

'Mind and gie them Frenchies a good seeing to,' Dougal sniggered.

Jamie grasped Dougal by the collar and hauled him to his feet, slamming his fist into the weasel's startled face. Ghillie leapt up, gaping as his companion reeled by and crashed headlong into a jumble of barrels in the far corner. Jamie jabbed again, catching Ghillie a glancing blow to the side of his head. Ghillie staggered but kept his feet long enough for Jamie's next blow to land squarely in the centre of his face. He joined his companion in a sprawling heap amongst the splintered barrels.

'By Christ,' Hal blurted. 'They had that coming.'

CHAPTER EIGHT

Morven's rebellious stomach had settled by the time Jamie returned. He had been gone the whole day. That pleased her. She hadn't ruined the fair for him, although she prayed the fever would not spread as Rowena warned. Three families in Glenlivet already had the sickness. No child had died, but Rowena warned there would likely be deaths. The afflicted families must keep to themselves, but the fair made that harder. Attendance was expected. Failure to appear would be noted, and the culprits deemed to have given offence, something no glen family would want. Even the sick might feel obliged to show their faces. Lord, what might that mean?

Watching Jamie negotiate the infield in the gloaming, her heart fluttered, anticipating the feel of his arms around her, but her joy dwindled as he crossed the yard. He trudged doggedly, staring at his feet, an air of despair about him. Remembering her dream, she shrank back from the window. He closed the door softly behind him but seemed to take an age to turn and look at her. When he turned, his face looked pinched and wretched. He crossed to the hearth and sat down heavily.

'Jamie,' she whispered.

'Ye're feeling better?'

'I am.'

'Come and sit wi' me. I've something I must tell ye.'

'Twas something terrible; she knew it before he said a word. She lowered herself onto the edge of a chair and laced her fingers together to stop them trembling.

Jamie leant forward to warm his hands. His knuckles were stained with blood. He had yet to look fully at her and drew a quivering breath, rubbing his face, deciding how to word what he must say. She waited, her heart thumping.

'It seems,' he rasped, lifting his gaze to her face, 'the fair wasna just a day o' revelry but a ruse. His Grace wished more men levied into his regiment, and he had one man, most particularly, in mind.'

'Lord,' she breathed, 'nae you?'

'Word of the duel has reached the duke and other lords. I'm considered a prize catch.' He exhaled angrily. 'His Grace wanted me recruited, fearing a rival would enlist me if he didna catch me first.'

'Mother Earth,' she whispered. 'Dinna tell me ye've joined the king's army.'

His face twisted, and he reached for her hand. 'Please believe me; never would I willingly don a red coat. I'd rather cut off my sword arm. Nor would I ever choose to leave ye.'

'I hope nae,' she whispered. 'Fer I've something I must tell ye, too.'

He didn't respond to that but stared into the fire. 'The thought of leaving ye here to struggle ...' he squeezed his eyes shut, stroking her hand. 'I love you. I hope ye ken that.'

'And I you.' *Mother Earth, what was he trying to tell her?*

'You've brought light back into my world. You *are* my world. But I was given little choice.' He let go of her hand and picked up the poker, stabbing at the peats on the fire. They shattered in a shower of sparks. 'I'm to be held hostage for the leases on our holdings.' He met her appalled gaze. ''Twas enlist or be evicted—nae just you and me but every soul at Delnabreck, Rowena and my cousins at Tomachcraggen, kin who last year I risked my neck to safeguard.' He sat back, bitterness twisting his face. 'Hardly a choice. I'd lose Druimbeag. I couldna let that happen.'

'Ye've taken the king's shilling?'

He nodded.

She stared at him.

'Please, dinna look at me like that.'

'How am I looking?' She had no notion how she looked nor cared.

'Like I've betrayed ye.'

'Nay, I dinna think that. I believed ill of ye afore. I'll never do that again.'

He retook her hand and squeezed it tenderly. 'When we wed, I swore to protect ye. I swore it afore God, Father Ranald, our kin, and most o' the glen. I meant every word.'

She nodded, a lump hard as granite lodged in her throat.

'Only now I find I must break my promise.'

'Please,' she whispered. 'Please dinna.'

He groaned and clutched his head. 'God forgive me, 'tis already done, my oath given, the papers signed. I can only beg yer forgiveness.' He swallowed, his throat convulsing. 'Ye must hate me. I dinna blame ye. I hate myself.'

'I dinna hate ye,' she choked. 'I … I dinna ken what I feel, but 'tisna that.'

He looked up, a flicker of hope in his eyes.

She stared into the fire, her mind reeling. She'd known for weeks something cruel would cleave them apart. The dream had shown her. Only why could she nae have been wrong? Around them, the room had darkened, filled with flickering shadows. Without Jamie, it would become her lonely prison. She thought of the child growing inside her and tears stung. She blinked them back. She must be strong.

She met Jamie's despairing gaze, tracing the strong angle of his jaw, the curve of his brows. They framed eyes sick with grief, and within her, a burst of love flared, flooding the aching chambers of her heart, the dark recesses where her doubts lingered like goblins. She shivered. Those who held power over their lives had forced Jamie to their will.

He watched her, his gaze moving over her face, following the flow of her emotions, perhaps misreading them. His throat spasmed. He longed to hold her, but the enormity of what he'd done held him back. The authorities had used him. Those who made the rules governing their lives had ruthlessly exploited Jamie for his principles, knowing he would never let his kin be dispossessed.

Her strength hardened like steel at her core. 'I once told ye I'd beached my heart on yer shore.'

He nodded.

'I meant it. This cruelty changes naught. What I feel fer ye is stronger than the conniving o' powerful men. 'Twill endure, I swear, fer yer sacrifice only makes me love ye more.'

Relief flooded his face. 'Oh, my love,' he choked.

She drew a quivering breath. 'All I ken o' ye, I've learned the hard way. Curse my doubting heart, fer it makes me quick to judge, yet I understand ye better now. Ye would give yer life fer those ye love.'

He pressed her fingers to his lips. 'I dinna deserve ye. I thought you'd turn your heart from me, harden it. That you'd be lost to me.'

She knelt at his feet. 'But ye are my heart.'

'And you mine.' He pulled her up beside him and dried her tears with his thumbs, his breath warm on her neck.

'When?' she choked. 'When must ye go?'

'The morrow. We have this night, then I must report wi' the others who took the king's shilling. Come full light, we march to Fort George.'

'So soon. To return when?'

'I pray His Grace gives me leave to bring in the harvest at summer's end, but I've signed for five years. Or until the end o' the American war.'

Five years. Mother Earth, a gaol sentence. But she slipped on as brave a face as she could muster. 'Da says the war goes against the British, that the fighting will soon be ower.'

''Tis my hope.'

'Then I've something I must tell ye. I wished to wait 'til the first weeks were past, but I see I must tell ye now.'

'First weeks?'

'I'm carrying yer bairn. Rowena thinks 'twill come at Samhain.'

'Oh, God,' was all he managed. He stared at her, the flames rippling on the hearth all that filled the silence between them but for the raggedness of his breathing as he digested this.

'Are ye pleased? I feared ye might think it a burden.'

He squeezed his eyes shut.

Disheartened, she looked at his hands as he held her, thinking of their nights together—the tautness of his muscles as she gripped him, the silk of his skin, the glow he ignited inside her, followed by the inner earthquake that shattered her to her core. Mother Earth, she'd nae done this on her own. 'Twas more than sensations he'd made grow in her belly.

'Say something,' she blurted. 'I need to ken what ye're thinking.'

'A child,' he breathed.

'Aye, does that please ye?'

He swallowed, trying to master his grief. 'If it werena that I must leave ye afore sunrise, I'd brim ower wi' joy. But to make a child with you and then ... then callously leave ye both. To abandon the child as if 'twere unwanted when no child could be more wanted!' He let out a wounded cry. 'Lord God, 'tis something only a scoundrel would do.'

'Yet it canna be helped.'

He swallowed, looking at her mid-section, still flat as a bannock spade, and tentatively pressed his hand there. 'Here lies the beginnings of our family.'

She nodded, covering his hand with hers. 'I'm glad 'tis wanted.'

'Ye doubted it?'

She hesitated a fraction, then shook her head.

'My love, this infant is more wanted than any child could be. The tragedy is I must abandon ye both to don the betrayer's red coat. That I must become a scoundrel.'

'Ye mustna say that. Ye're nae a scoundrel. I dinna think it, and you mustna either. As soon as the bairn's auld enough to understand, I'll tell the truth o' this. Never would ye willingly leave us.'

He swallowed. 'This is what made ye sick?'

'Did I nae say 'twould pass?'

He gave a strangled laugh. 'Who else knows?'

'Only Rowena.'

'She'll help ye when yer time comes.'

'I'd trust her wi' my life.'

He nodded, doubtless aware that childbirth was always something of a gamble.

''Tis you I fear fer,' she whispered. 'A Highlandman in the king's army when 'tis known what the authorities think o' highland folk.'

He stroked her back. 'The duke's regiment is made mainly o' men from his own lands. And I'm to be a corporal.' He grimaced. 'It hardly honours me, but I'll nae let the officers treat us wi' less than the respect we're due.'

She hoped he could do that but doubted it.

'And 'tis a fencible regiment. If I must fight, 'twill only be in Scotland, though I'll likely waste my time on guard duty and drills. But ye see, there's nae need to fear fer me.'

'Yet I do.'

'Aye, your heart's tender fer all yer fierceness. 'Tis how *you'll* manage that matters. Alec will help ye. He's beholden to me. Sarah, too. And there'll be bounty coin and wages to send home to help wi' the rent. Still ....'

He didn't need to finish. She would have to toil from dawn to dusk. 'Twould be backbreaking work on her own, becoming harder as the bairn grew in her belly. Should she fail, they'd lose their home and their living, and Jamie would lose something more precious—his link to the past. Druimbeag meant everything to him. She mustna be the one to lose it.

'I'll keep Druimbeag safe. I gie ye my word.'

He smiled sadly. ''Tisna wise to make promises ye mightna be able to keep.'

'But I will, supposing it kills me.'

He frowned. 'Bless you, but I'd rather lose my land than lose you.'

There was a look in his eye, a huskiness in his voice that she'd come to recognise. It meant he wished to lie with her. She wanted it, too. She said no more as he carried her to bed, but she made herself a promise. Supposing it near killed her, she would keep Druimbeag safe.

That night, their loving had a new raw edge, a desperate, despairing feel. Jamie was at first hesitant, fearing he would hurt the child, but when she assured him he would not, his restraint fell away. 'Twas as if he wished to lose himself, to push away the world and its injustices, to blot out what he must do come morning and escape into a world filled only with her. She clung to him, sharing his despair, letting him carry her to new heights of passion, only for her to crash back to earth with the hopeless knowledge that come morning, he would leave her.

They said their farewells on the ridge forming the boundary of Druimbeag land as the first glimmer of daylight split the darkness in the east. She shivered in her shift, her tears soaking Jamie's shoulder. He held her tight, as loathe to leave her as she was to let him go.

'Ye'll come back to me?' she pressed.

'Soon as I'm able.'

'Promise me.'

He lowered one knee and gripped her hand. 'I swear it.'

She exhaled with a shiver. 'Then dinna be looking back; 'twill bring ill luck. And should a hare cross yer path, turn yer face away, fer it might be the silent folk in one o' their guises.'

He nodded, tight-faced, and tore himself from her side, striding through the heather without a backward glance, his back unnaturally stiff.

She watched him until he vanished into the darkness, thinking of her chilling dream. They would both need all the luck they could find, yet she couldn't help fearing there was worse to come. 'Dinna let me lose Druimbeag,' she whispered. 'Oh, please, let me keep it safe.'

CHAPTER NINE

Scalan, the Braes of
Glenlivet, June 1781

Catching the low murmur of voices, Nathaniel Gunn opened his eyes, his hands still clasped in prayer, and shifted his focus from the suffering boy to the dormitory door. The latch clicked, the door opening to admit Father Ranald, who ushered the physician inside, a man Nathaniel had found disagreeable on every one of his previous visits. He rose from his knees and bowed to the two men, then crouched under the low rafters and retreated to the window recess in the south gable end. The window was set at floor level. Crossing his legs, he sat on the hard planks, waiting for the men to conclude their business so he might return to Andrew's side.

Young Andrew was desperately ill, his life in danger, which meant his immortal soul was in even greater peril. Nathaniel cared too much for Andrew to contemplate letting him die unprepared to enter the Kingdom of Heaven. Letting such a fate overtake his young friend was unthinkable and made him wish to weep, but with the master sick and Father Ranald running the college in his stead, Nathaniel knew that as Scalan's senior student, he might have to perform that task. He must be ready to do his duty.

Only the thought of Andrew dying, gentle, earnest-faced Andrew, who at ten had barely begun his life, filled Nathaniel with such grief his mind struggled to function. Instead of recalling the words of the Apostle's Creed, a vital part of the Last Rites, his mind hurtled back to the night his father prised him from his mother and handed him to the Church. Even now, having long since accepted the life chosen for him, the pain of that deed still cut deeply.

Night after night, he'd lain awake, conjuring his mother's face, longing for the refuge of her arms, the reassuring murmur of her voice, knowing he might never see her again. That emptiness he now recognised as the pain of loss and fear of its return consumed him.

Having devoted twelve years to scripture, study, and prayer, Nathaniel was on the brink of ordination. If worthy, he would receive holy orders at the bishop's next visit. As a priest, he would never marry or have children. Other than God, who was always with him, he would live out his life alone. Yet the other boys training to enter the priesthood were his dearest friends. He cherished every one.

Hunching his shoulders, he peered through the warped glass of the window at an upland scene: a view of the Ladder Hills in the near distance, the dark slash of the Crombie Burn and the desolate surrounding moors and pastures. He feared for Andrew if this Dalrymple was his best chance for a recovery.

'Why, I believe the boy looks a little better,' the physician declared, peering at Andrew's deathly face. 'My treatments have had the desired effect, as expected.'

Turning back into the room, Nathaniel saw the leap and warp of shadows on the far wall, Andrew's face bathed in golden light. He had foolishly left his candle on the floor, throwing a misleadingly warm glow over the boy's face.

'You imagine so?' Father Ranald's brows rose in disbelief. 'I hardly share your opinion—far from it. The lad has kept naught down in days, violently ejecting all sustenance, while your purging seems only to have made him weaker. Fever and chills wrack his body. Since the rash, his skin has peeled away, even from the poor lad's tongue. Last night, I found him delirious. Now, this.' He indicated Andrew's still form and deathlike appearance.

'Hmmm.' Dalrymple pressed a hand on Andrew's forehead, then furtively wiped it on his breeches. He prised one of Andrew's eyelids open, then his mouth, recoiling at the strawberry appearance of the boy's tongue. 'Has anyone else been treating him?' His voice was laced with suspicion.

'No one but you. The boys have prayed for him, and Nathaniel has seen unfailingly to his needs, attending to the purging and clysters ye prescribed. To little use, I fear. As you can see.'

'There've been no folk healers here? No hen-wives or cunning women?'

'Women are not permitted at Scalan, Mister Dalrymple, except for Janet, the housekeeper, and a girl who assists her. I assure you, there's naught in the least cunning about Janet or Annag. 'Twas one of the rules laid down by Bishop Gordon when the seminary was first founded. A rule followed faithfully to this day, as are all the bishop's rules.'

'You're sure?'

'Quite sure. With the master ill with the grippe, so you tell me, I took it upon myself to isolate the lad here, moving the other students' beds to the study to prevent the spread of this pestilence.' He rubbed his balding head. 'Scarlet fever, I believe 'tis called.'

Dalrymple snorted. 'You're a contagionist, then?'

'A what?'

'An adherent to the theory of contagion. Most serious and learned graduates of the College of Physicians know better. They understand that all illness results from a derangement of bodily fluids. Humoral balance is needed for health; any imbalance leads to disease. This is what we are witnessing, not a contagion.' Dalrymple nodded at Andrew, whose breathing had become noticeably shallower since the physician's arrival and now whistled in his throat.

'I speak only of what I've seen,' Father Ranald replied. 'In my years attending those who near the end of their lives whom I must try to absolve of sin, I've seen that disease ofttimes spreads from person to person within a family and from family to family, perhaps through the breath or upon clothing. I worry I might have brought the sickness here myself. In my pastoral duties, I visit throughout Glenlivet and Stratha'an.'

Dalrymple grunted. 'You've spent too long listening to the cunning women practising the dark craft in these glens.' He glanced at a statue of the Blessed Virgin balanced on a plinth above Andrew's bed and seemed unable to prevent his upper lip from curling. 'I suggest you put away your false idols and adhere to the true faith. Then, the boy may have some hope of recovery. In the meantime, I will bleed him again.' He rummaged in his bag. 'Bring me a bowl.'

Nathaniel rose from the floor and stood uncertainly at the end of Andrew's bed, instinctively aware that Andrew could not tolerate another bleeding. The physician had implied that their faith, the true one although forbidden, was preventing Andrew's recovery. Indignation reddened his face, a response hardly proper or pious. 'Andrew has passed no water in two days,' he ventured. 'I fear what that means.'

Dalrymple grimaced. 'It means a complication of the kidneys. As I said, all disease stems from an imbalance of bodily fluids. It means the boy nears his end, but I will attempt to bleed him again. A bowl, then.' He snapped his fingers.

Nathaniel turned in consternation to the father.

Father Ranald's face hardened. 'No more bleeding, Mister Dalrymple. If that is your only remedy, I hereby end your employment.'

'*What?*'

'You heard me. I'll not have the lad's death spoken of in his presence. I've long found that those most desperately ill, who appear beyond our reach, may still hear. Predicting the lad's death within his earshot can only make that tragedy more likely.'

'You're terminating my services?'

'I am. I'll have no more of Andrew's blood on my hands.'

Nathaniel stared at the ageing priest, his chest swelling with admiration. Could he have spoken out like that? Found the courage to blast this arrogant physician as Father Ranald just did? Likely not. Cloistered away, he still had much to learn about people and how to interact with them. They frightened him, this physician especially.

'You have no authority,' Dalrymple spluttered. 'The master engaged me to care for these boys. Only Mister Paterson—'

'I hold authority in his stead,' the father quipped. 'Until the master has recovered enough to take back the reins, I wield them in his place, though I fear John may never recover with a heathen like you treating him.'

'You'd have me forsake these boys and their master?'

'Not forsake. I would deliver them from you. I don't rate your skills, Mister Dalrymple. I don't even consider them skills, and as for your blasphemy, that I abhor.'

Dalrymple's ruddy complexion flushed to an even more livid shade. 'It seems you've forgotten that *yours* is the forbidden faith,' he flashed, 'sequestered here in defiance of the law. And that,' he jabbed a finger at the holy statue, 'is rank idolatry.'

The father smiled thinly. 'I've forgotten naught, Mister Dalrymple. Nathaniel will show ye out. I'll see that any outstanding fees are paid to you. So ends your engagement with Scalan Seminary. Ye'll excuse me.' He left the room.

Dalrymple looked Nathaniel up and down. 'So, that's the lie of the land, is it? I believe I'm capable of finding my own way out.' He sneered at the spartan dormitory. ''Tis but a wretched hatchery, spitting out popish priestlings, squatting in as godforsaken a wasteland as the devil could devise. Little wonder its inhabitants are racked with disease.'

Nathaniel gaped at him.

'I'll return for my fees,' Dalrymple snapped. 'Lest the father should forget what's due me.' He stomped down the stairs and banged the door so violently the windows rattled in their frames.

Shaken, Nathaniel found Father Ranald standing in the master's bed alcove, staring at Father Paterson's sleeping face. The master was so thin the bones showed through his skin. 'What'll we do?' he croaked. 'I fear for Andrew, and for the master, of course.'

Father Ranald turned wearily to him. 'I know of a healer in Stratha'an. Rowena Forbes. I believe her skills are God-given. I will ride for her. Forgive me; I must leave you in charge.' Seeing Nathaniel's alarmed expression, he added. 'I ask only that you pray for Andrew and ... and try to keep the lad from slipping away before I return. I ask much.'

Nathaniel swallowed. How might he do that? Prayer was all he knew.

'I'll speak with the students on my way out, keep them to their studies.' The father hurried away.

Nathaniel returned to Andrew's bedside. The boy's eyes were open, although unfocused. 'Andrew, can I get you anything?'

'Mam?'

'No, Nathaniel.'

'I'm cold.' Andrew's voice barely rose above a whisper, his mouth so dry his tongue clicked. ''Tis dark. How will I find my way home?'

'You're already home, Andrew, amongst friends, but I will fetch you a blanket.'

'Dinna leave me.' Andrew thrust out his hand.

'I won't. I'm here.'

Nathaniel didn't take Andrew's hand, although part of him wanted to. He was at a loss over what to do. Throughout his years at Scalan, he had received no demonstrations of affection, and learning by example had shown none. No one had held his hand or embraced him; hence, such behaviour now seemed alien. He could only express himself to God; then, his prayers might follow a prescribed formula. If he allowed his emotions free rein, they might engulf him. He'd kept his feelings private for so long, maintaining an aloofness was now instinctual. Yet, deep down, Nathaniel knew detachment was foreign to his nature.

Andrew's hand hung forlornly, calling him to take it. He stretched forward on his knees, his thumping heart urging him to show the boy he was not alone in what might be his final moments, but uncertainty held him back. Clasping his hands together, he prayed urgently for guidance.

Andrew's eyelids fluttered. Beneath the lids, his eyes dulled. His breathing slowed.

'Don't leave me, Andrew. Please.' But Nathaniel sensed the boy could no longer hear him. He made the sign of the cross over Andrew's face. 'I couldn't bear it.'

Andrew must die in a state of grace, forgiven of his sins, or he might never enter God's kingdom. But as he was, Andrew could not confess his sins or show remorse. Only by blessing him through Extreme Unction, anointing him with sacramental oil blessed by the bishop and praying fervently for his soul might he safeguard Andrew's journey to heaven. He stumbled away to find holy oil. Andrew was still a child; his sins could not be so grievous.

Returning with the oil, Nathaniel got down on his knees and began reciting the Latin words. '*Per istam sanctam Unctiónem et suam piisimam misericórdiam, indúlgeat tibi Dóminus quidquid per visum.* Through this holy Unction and His most tender mercy, may the Lord pardon you whatever sins you have committed by sight.' Dipping his fingers in the oil, he traced the sign of the cross over Andrew's closed eyelids, then repeated the prayer, anointing Andrew's ears, nose, mouth, hands and feet, parts of his body he may have used to sin. Unsure if he had done enough, he lapsed into the Lord's Prayer, 'Our Father who art in heaven,' repeating the prayer over and over, focussing every ounce of his will on his young friend's salvation.

He was still on his knees when Father Ranald returned, his hands cold as stone, all feeling gone from his legs.

'Nathaniel.' The press of a hand on his shoulder. 'Thank you, but ye must stop now.'

He opened his eyes to find a young woman with the father. She wore a white kertch, signifying that she was a married woman, yet this couldn't be the healer the father spoke of. She seemed too young. He had expected a henwife, as the physician described, and there was something about her that made him stare. He inhaled sharply. Hers was the face that visited his dreams, a face he had never forgotten. How many times had he relived that painful night of separation? Too many to count. Always, he remembered a young girl, her gaze searing his back as the master led him away. Because of her, he had known he must be brave, not just for his mother but for the girl—not to frighten her. It had been his first lesson: his life would no longer be his own. He must give it to God, serving Him, thinking of others, not himself. He remembered the girl's tentative smile; how grateful he'd been for it. Through the years, her face had stayed with him. Now grown to womanhood, she looked as he remembered—tender and lovely.

'Nathaniel, this is Morven.' Father Ranald was out of breath, having doubtless endured a wild dash over hill and moor to find this girl. 'Rowena's skills were needed elsewhere, but Morven has been her student for many years and is now as skilled in the healing arts as her teacher. Move aside now so she may examine young Andrew.'

He rose painfully, gripping the bed frame as the blood surged back into his legs and feet. The girl caught his arm, steadying him, and searched his face. He returned her gaze, afraid to look at Andrew for fear his prayers had been lacking and he'd failed him.

The young woman waited until he could stand unaided, then knelt in his place, taking Andrew's outstretched hand, something he had been too afraid to do. She turned Andrew's hand over, pressing her fingers to his wrist, frowning in concentration. She rose and bent over his chest, listening. She was so tender; a lump rose in Nathaniel's throat. His mother had acted that way, fretting over every cough and sniffle, pressing her cool fingers to his brow. He swallowed as the memories crowded back.

The girl sat back and closed Andrew's eyelids. 'I'm sorry, Father.' She stroked Andrew's cheek. 'We're too late. The poor lad has died, his ... his soul has slipped to the next realm.'

Father Ranald's face tightened. 'I feared as much.'

She looked at Nathaniel. 'He was yer friend?'

He nodded.

She rose and took his hands, rubbing them tenderly, her eyes full of pity. 'I'm sorry. He nae longer suffers, at least.'

He nodded, intensely aware of her touch, how much he'd missed that small comfort, but it was too much. He pulled his hands away, a surge of grief engulfing him. His face twisted, a grotesque wail breaking from his lips. Mortified, he turned away, trying to cover his unconscionable behaviour, but there was nowhere to go. He hid his face in his hands, choking on his sobs as they ripped from his throat with a vulgar shuddering sound. Nothing could excuse such a raw outpouring. He was embarrassing himself and the father ... and the girl, making an undignified spectacle of himself.

Another wail racked from his body. He bent double with the agony of it. He should have held Andrew's hand. Andrew was only a boy, a frightened lad who missed his mother. He had once been such a boy. Why hadn't he comforted him? This girl who knew nothing of their lives, had instinctively known to do that. Not him. He'd been too afraid hidden emotions might surface and shame him.

He fell to his knees, past caring, and wailed and wailed.

CHAPTER TEN

Morven turned to Father Ranald. She had seen grown men weep before, but not like this, not this harrowing grief racking Nathaniel's body, making him wail and sob. Her eyes nipped in sympathy.

'My dear.' The father took her arm and tried to steer her away. 'We should leave Nathaniel to his grief. If ye feel able, I would have ye look at the master. John's affliction is different. I'm told he suffers with the grippe.'

'But ...' she stared at the dead boy and the sobbing young man kneeling beside him, now gripping his hand. 'Should we nae try and give comfort?'

'Maybe later, although, in truth, I think it best to leave him. Women are not entirely welcome at Scalan. The master will make an exception for you with your healing skills, but 'twould not be proper. Perhaps ye can understand?'

She looked blankly at him. Feeling guilty, she was obliged to step around the weeping young man, a man who, despite the passing years, she recognised almost at once by his delicate features. She could still picture him as a boy, full of fear as his father handed him to the black-robed master at Scalan. She'd felt for him then and did so again. Over the years, she had often thought of Nathaniel Gunn. How did he fare in his new life? A life of isolation and discipline filled not with family but with study and prayer.

In the corridor, the father patted her hand. 'Nathaniel was always sensitive. In times of tragedy, sympathy can devastate any man. D'ye not agree?'

Confused, she murmured, 'I wished him to ken he needna suffer alone.'

'I understand, but Nathaniel stands upon the threshold of priesthood. He may be the best priest Scalan has ever produced. As such, he must seek his solace from God.'

'I see,' she croaked, although she did not. 'What about the other boys? They might have the rush fever, too.'

'I'd have you look at the master first.'

Feeling confused and unjustly chastised, she blinked her tears back and followed the father. A corridor led from the boys' dormitory to the master's chamber and the chapel beyond. She glanced up at the intricate joinery and dense thatch above her head. Although hidden in this desolate place, the college had plainly been built by craftsmen. The limestone walls were two feet thick, the interior clad in well-finished wattle and daub. On climbing the stairs, she had admired their smoothness. Yet the house felt cold and smelled stale. It needed a woman's touch, pinecones to burn on the hearth, fresh flowers and strewing herbs.

The master's chamber was a little warmer, although the temperature change made her shiver. A fire burned in an iron grate, the scent of burning peat filling her nostrils. A partition wall screened the master's bed from his desk and study, where many books were piled, forming a private alcove where Father Paterson lay asleep. He was younger than she expected and so tall his feet stuck out over the end of his bed. He looked thinner than was healthy for any man, his face pale as bone. She felt his hands and feet, finding them icy, while his forehead and chest burned. She probed his neck with her fingers, feeling a slight but definite swelling. He awoke at her touch and stared at her.

'John.' Father Ranald cleared his throat. 'This is Morven Innes, a healer studying with Rowena Forbes. I've mentioned Rowena if ye remember. I hope you'll forgive me, but I have dismissed Doctor Dalrymple. I believe he exaggerated his abilities. And outrageously overpriced them,' he added. His face tightened. 'Forgive me. I bring terrible news.'

'Andrew?' the master rasped.

'He died a short time ago. I suspect the physician only hastened his death. I've taken the liberty of bringing Morven in his stead. I believe she'll help you and will ensure the other boys don't succumb as Andrew did.'

The master's gaze shifted to rest on her face. 'Thank you, child.'

Although he said no more as a fit of chest-deep coughing overtook him, the master had managed to convey a weight of sincerity in those three simple words. Once he had recovered and was slumped back on his pillows, Morven wiped some bloody sputum from his chin and glanced at Father Ranald. He had not been entirely truthful in implying Rowena had been too busy to come. There was more to it. She'd been with Rowena at Tomachcraggen when the father arrived in something of a lather.

'Perhaps, Father,' Rowena ventured, 'ye might take Morven in my stead? She's long been my student and kens how to treat a child wi' rush fever. She'll easily fill Dalrymple's shoes.' Rowena frowned. 'I've William and Sarah to help me, but Morven ...' she glanced at her, seeking forgiveness for revealing what was not hers to reveal. 'Wi' Jamie gone, Morven's alone and carrying his child.'

Father Ranald's brows shot up. 'Oh, my dear.' He patted Morven's hand, trying not to glance at her midsection. 'How wonderful. Please accept my congratulations. When can we expect the young Innes to arrive?'

'Thank ye, Father. Around Samhain.' She exchanged a look with Rowena; Rowena was wise and generous, and her pregnancy would be common knowledge soon enough anyway. 'Jamie had nae choice but go fer a soldier. His Grace threatened to evict us and every one o' our kin if he didna.'

The father reared back, anger flaring in his eyes. 'Lord help us. I can scarce believe the powers that rule us have dealt Jamie another cruel injustice. Has the lad nae suffered enough? I heard he'd taken the king's shilling and was surprised, knowing his loyalties lie here. As mine do.'

She nodded. Father Ranald was a loyal Jacobite. Rowena called him a warrior priest. He'd been one of the few chaplains active at Culloden, barely escaping with his life. He held no love for the redcoats.

'But to hear the lad was blackmailed!'

Morven could see how much that angered him. A lump tightened her throat. Folk were whispering about Jamie. They said he'd taken the king's shilling from the duchess's lips, although Rowena assured her all those recruited at the Balintoul fair took the shilling that way—all but Ned Munro with his rotten teeth and poisonous breath. The duchess had refused to kiss him. She must pay no heed to talk that Jamie's kiss had been a deep, lingering thing.

'Leave this to me, my dear,' the father said. 'If you can demonstrate your skills at Scalan by keeping the boys in sound health, I believe you'll win even the bishop's approval.' He sighed. 'Though I fear ye mightna be able to save young Andrew. Nevertheless, I wish ye to try.'

She nodded and gathered her herbs and simples, packing them into her creel. There was little time to waste. Strapping the basket to her back, she climbed onto the father's garron, and they made away.

Now, acknowledging the father's encouraging smile, she knew this was her chance to prove herself. Caring for the Scalan community was a great honour and could prove a valuable string to her bow. If she could keep the community in sound health, the mission might even reward her with coin. She drew a quivering breath, feeling the feverish heat radiating from the man before her.

'Forgive me,' she murmured. 'I would listen to yer chest.'

He allowed it with a feeble movement of his hand.

She loosened his sark and pressed her ear to his bony chest. She straightened, perturbed. The whistle was impossible to miss. 'Twas the frothing of air with blood, revealing damage to the master's passageways and lungs. 'I'm wondering,' she ventured, 'if ye suffer from sweats in the night, and if yer fevers seem to ebb and flow, each leaving ye weaker than the last?'

His eyes widened, and he nodded.

'And if ye've suffered from these bouts afore, mebbe years ago? If they reappear when yer spirits are low, after some exertion, or after being caught in foul weather?'

'Why, yes. How did you know?'

'Ye dinna have the grippe, Father. I believe ye have the wasting sickness. Folk call it consumption, fer it appears to eat its victim.'

He lay back, considering. 'Over the years, I've feared as much. Can anything be done?'

'Much can be done, but I'll nae lie. 'Tis hard to make a permanent cure.'

'Then, please do what you can, Mistress Innes. I've much I still wish to achieve at Scalan.'

She nodded, grateful for his trust. 'My healing is wrought through knowledge o' herbs and nature's wisdom. 'Twas taught me and to my teacher and her teacher afore her down through the ages. I believe the auld wisdom will help ye, sir.'

'Old wisdom?'

She swallowed at his scepticism, knowing she must convince him her abilities were God-given. Only how? At Scalan, everything rested upon the scriptures. She cleared her throat. 'Everywhere in nature, we see the Creator's hand. When we marvel at nature's beauty and perfection, 'tis truly God's splendour we praise. As a healer, I've learned to appreciate that splendour.'

He quirked his brows at her.

'I've learned that fer every affliction to strike man, nature provides a remedy, be it from leaf or flower, root, stem, seed, or even a lowly mushroom. The Lord made the healing herbs fer us to use. Why else would they grow all around us?'

'God is bountiful,' he murmured.

'The key is knowing how to use them wisely, fer they hold the power to kill as well as cure. I ken the best herbs fer yer affliction, sir. 'Tis only a matter o' finding them and distilling their magic.'

'What are they?'

'Bullock's lungwort is king amongst herbs fer the wasting sickness.'

'Lungwort,' he wheezed. 'Sounds fitting.'

'All the lungworts are helpful, and the figworts where there's swelling in the neck.'

His hand jerked involuntarily to the base of his jaw. 'Where might this bullock type be found?'

'It grows amongst dry grass on hillsides, sending up tall yellow flower spikes to guide folk where to look. 'Twill be flowering now, so shouldna be so hard to find. Other herbs will be needed, though I'm mindful only to gather what I need. Coltsfoot flower, syrup o' white poppy fer preventing the spitting o' blood, juniper, bog myrtle, hart's tongue, and sage fer easing yer night sweats.'

He blinked at her.

'Afore I gather aught, I seek permission and give thanks. 'Tis important to be respectful.'

'You offer a prayer?'

''Tis a form o' prayer, fer it must be deeply felt. My remedies are a communion wi' nature, never thoughtless plunder. I've many herbs laid down: dried, preserved in whisky, made into rubs, tinctures, and balms fer their special properties.' She hesitated, hoping she had persuaded him to trust her. 'I canna promise to cure ye. 'Tis the Lord will decide that. But I'll conjure the most powerful magic in my power.'

Seeing his strange expression, she fell silent.

'You make it sound like witchcraft.'

'Folk have wrongly judged it so, but 'tis just healing from the earth.' She looked down at her hands, hoping she had not shocked or offended him.

'From the earth,' he echoed. 'And did not God make the earth and all that grows from and walks upon it? *"All things were made by Him, and without Him was made nothing that was made,"* John, chapter one, verse three. So, in truth, all healing stems from God.'

She nodded, pleased that he understood.

He gave a winded sigh. 'How to begin, then?'

'I must first bring down yer fever. A high fever fights sickness, but a constant, simmering fever does naught. If it helped, ye'd have seen some benefit by now. 'Tis wearing ye down, sir.'

'Please, call me John. Or Father John if John feels too familiar. I imagine you'll need to become familiar with me if you are to help me regain my health.'

She smiled, liking this humble man with his gentle face and voice. 'Then ye should call me Morven and less o' the Mistress Innes. Ye make me sound older than my mam, and I'm scarce nineteen.' She blushed at her boldness.

'Morven, then.' He laughed. 'Why, already you've lightened my spirits, and you're little more than a child.'

'I'm a marrit woman.'

'Already?'

She nodded. And soon to be a mother. If women weren't encouraged here, a pregnant one would likely be even less welcome.

'Despite her youth, John,' Father Ranald said, 'Morven has wed a fine man. I married her and Jamie last year on the feast of St. Martin. I was familiar with Jamie's father, a sore loss to the glen when he was forced to leave us, but Morven could not have wed a more principled young man.'

'Glad to hear it.'

'I have herbs wi' me, Father John: woodruff and bog myrtle. I'll infuse them in a tea. They'll help lower yer fever. I would speak wi' yer cook if 'tis allowed. Ye'll need nourishing food to resist these bouts o' fever: milk and clabber, broth, fruit, berries especially. I can forage fer those. Only ale or whey to drink, nae meat or strong drink, and never take snuff.'

He nodded, trying to keep a mental note.

'When the weather's fine, ye must fill yer lungs wi' fresh air and let the sun warm yer limbs. 'Tis healing and will lift yer spirits. And the students,' she added, 'if ye tak' them oot yonder fer their lessons.' She nodded at what lay beyond his window. 'But ye must avoid cold, damp weather.'

'I believe I'm in good hands,' he said before another coughing fit overtook him.

She helped him up so he could expel the mucus pooling in his airways. Now that she understood his affliction, she was anxious to work on his recovery.

'Before you focus on me,' he wheezed, 'I wish you to look at the boys. I fear Andrew's sickness may have spread. Is that possible?'

'I'd say 'tis likely.'

'Then time may be of the essence.'

'I'll have her do that, John.' Father Ranald took her arm. 'I'll have poor Andrew moved to the chapel whilst I attend to his funeral. His parents must be told. A difficult letter, I fear.'

'Thank you, Ranald. I'd be grateful if you'd order timber for his coffin and make the arrangements. We'll have the wright assemble it here.' The master looked sorry for imposing such a task on the old priest. 'But I must be the one to write to his parents.' He sighed. 'I'll spend time with Andrew first and pray for his soul. Please ensure the boys pray for him, and any boy who wishes to see Andrew may do so.' He lay back and closed his eyes. 'I'm indebted to you both.'

Father Ranald led Morven back down the stairs into the main classroom and study. An oak table extended the length of the room. Six boys of varying ages were sitting around it with their heads bent over their books. Nathaniel sat at the head and rose to his feet. He had recovered his composure, although his eyes looked puffy and red. She could see the boy she remembered in his expression, his gravity and deference, which seemed even more apparent now.

'Ah, Nathaniel.' Father Ranald made no mention of what they had earlier witnessed. 'I must leave Morven in your care. The master wishes her to examine the boys. 'Tis possible they've caught the fever from poor Andrew, and she will be treating the master. Please help her as much as you can. Sadly, duty calls me elsewhere.'

Nathaniel bowed to the father and glanced awkwardly at her.

'There'll be no more lessons today.' The father looked around the table at the white faces staring back at him. 'You will pass the time remembering Andrew and may see him if ye wish. This is Morven.' He pulled her forward. 'You must do as she tells you. What happened to Andrew was a tragedy neither I nor the master wish repeated. She will replace Doctor Dalrymple, whose methods I found objectionable, not to mention useless. Her task is to prevent the fever taking more of ye.'

He frowned as young eyes fixed fearfully on him, perhaps unaware that he had been none too tactful. Sensitivity was needed when dealing with youngsters. Morven was surprised the father didn't know that.

'We will pray for Andrew at evening prayers. If I've not returned by then and the master is unable, Nathaniel will lead you.' The father hesitated, appearing to think better of saying more. 'I'll leave you with Morven, then.'

CHAPTER ELEVEN

Once the father had gone, the boys turned to stare at Morven in wary silence. All were sober-faced; many were tearful. It must have been a shock to lose one of their own. She imagined the news had yet to fully sink in, and their pillows would bear witness to their grief later that night. Wishing to be gentle, she lowered herself onto an empty chair, likely Andrew's, and attempted as reassuring a smile as she could muster.

'As the father said, my name is Morven. I'm from Stratha'an, where I learned my healing skills. Andrew caught a sickness called scarlet fever. It spreads quickly.' She frowned and cleared her throat. She mustna frighten them. 'Yer hearts must beat sore, grieving fer yer friend. I dinna wish to add to yer troubles, but so I may tell who amongst ye most needs my help, I must look fer signs o' sickness upon ye.'

Eyes widened and darkened with fear.

'I'll only do that wi' yer permission, though.' She glanced at Nathaniel, wondering if Dalrymple, with his crude methods, had instilled this fear in the boys or if, having witnessed Andrew's suffering, they dreaded to learn who might share it.

'I'll only need to look at yer chest and throat and feel yer forehead, and only if ye agree.'

The boys looked at each other in puzzled silence and it dawned upon her they had not expected to be asked to give permission. They assumed they'd simply be told what they must do. That wasna her way. She always explained and sought permission; 'twas how to nurture trust.

'There's nae need to be afraid. Even if ye've caught the sickness, there are herbs to treat it, but they work best if I catch the sickness early. Might ye let me look at ye?'

There was an audible release of tension, and the boys became more animated, breathing easier, shifting in their chairs and blinking at each other. They nodded.

She breathed a sigh of relief. 'Thank ye. 'Tis my hope we can become friends. My remedies come from nature, hence from the Lord and can be found in what grows all around us. Perhaps ye've walked through a forest and seen nature's rich colours and patterns, especially in summer when she's most bountiful?'

They smiled and nodded.

'Then ye've seen how skilled an artist is our Lord.'

There were more smiles now. She could see the boys enjoyed exploring the surrounding forests and hills. Book learning looked like tedious work.

'The skill is knowing the right plants to use and how to draw out their medicine. Ower the years, that knowledge has been passed down to those deemed most able to use it wisely. I was fortunate to be chosen, but anyone may learn from nature. Trees and plants are our oldest teachers, yet most folk pay them little heed. All my potions come from nature.'

'We're grateful,' Nathaniel murmured.

She glanced at him, and they shared a moment that made her think he remembered her from that long-ago night.

'So, then,' she rose to her feet, looking at the lad she imagined was the oldest, hoping he might lead by example. 'Who wishes to be first?'

'I will,' he said. 'I'm James Cattanach.'

'James. A good name.'

'It comes from the bible,' he informed her. 'Saint James was one of the twelve apostles.'

She picked up her chair and carried it around the table so she could sit beside James. Before she examined him, she wished to learn a little about him. He told her he was fourteen and the son of Catholic gentry, his family among the dwindling population of highland chiefs and tacksmen left in the glens. He had been born in Strathglass and hoped to return there after finishing his training at the Scot's College in Rome. A confident boy, he let her peer in his mouth and feel his neck for signs of swelling. When asked if his head or throat hurt, he said he felt well, and she found no telltale rash.

She examined the other students in the same way, learning that there were two MacDonald boys, Roderick and Struan, and a MacRae, Christopher. He was not her kin but from Cromarty in Easter Ross. There was another James, James Sharp, and a Cameron boy named Thomas.

Nathaniel hovered at her shoulder throughout, anxious to make himself useful, urging the boys to trust her. She was grateful, especially since he had no more knowledge of her than did the boys. They paid great heed to everything Nathaniel said, treating him like an older brother.

The youngest boy drew Morven's attention from the start, but not wishing to single him out, she left him until last. Struan could barely hold his head up. His eyes were heavy-lidded, his cheeks shiny and flushed. A faint shiver ran through his body. When she opened his sark, sure enough, an angry rash covered his chest. He stared at it in horror.

'Struan,' she said, 'this rash means ye've caught scarlet fever, but ye mustna be alarmed.'

His eyes widened. 'Am I going to die?'

She held his fearful gaze with her steady one. 'I mean to do everything in my power to prevent that, and I have a great deal in my power.'

He nodded, but Nathaniel fell to his knees.

'Holy Father,' Nathaniel pleaded, 'show us what we must do. Make Struan well again so he may serve You in piety and grace. You are the bringer of all healing through thine own son, Jesus Christ our Lord. Amen.'

''Tis all right,' Morven soothed. 'I ken what to do.'

'Then, you are surely the Lord's emissary,' he gasped, 'sent to guide us.'

'I dinna ken aboot that, but I must separate Struan from the other boys to stop the sickness spreading, then burn pine needle oil in water to clean the air o' contagion.'

'The sickness travels in the air?'

'I believe from the breath o' those afflicted.'

Nathaniel raised his brows but nodded to show he accepted her word. 'Please, I wish to help. Tell me what I must do.'

She asked him to take the boys outside or elsewhere in the house so she could isolate Struan in the study and then fetch her a pot of water. Nathaniel attended to these tasks at once, shepherding the boys outside. She saw them from the window, kneeling in a circle on the green at the front of the house with their heads bowed in prayer. He returned carrying an iron pot filled with water and hung it over the fire.

Morven stoked a blaze and waited for the water to simmer, then dripped pine oil on its surface, where it spread its iridescent sheen, giving off a pungent, woodsy scent.

Nathaniel drew the vapours into his lungs. ''Tis like being in a forest.'

She nodded and sent him to the boy's dormitory to repeat the process there. 'Andrew's bedding must be burned.' He promised he would see it done.

Alone with Struan, Morven dragged the table to one side, upended the chairs on top, and made the lad comfortable on a chaff-stuffed mattress by the fire. More mattresses were piled in a corner; the boys had plainly spent the last few nights here. Whoever had thought to move them here, likely Father Ranald, appeared to know more about preventing the spread of rush fever than the educated Doctor Dalrymple.

Leaving Struan to rest, she went in search of the college kitchen and the housekeeper. She had potions to brew; 'twould be easier if she could use the kitchen. Scalan was not only a school where boys lived year-round but also a farm. During her wild gallop up the lonely track, clinging to Father Ranald's back, she'd seen cattle grazing, an ox, and a small flock of sheep. A draught-horse stood tethered in a barn, and a kailyard had been laid out to supply the community with produce. As they entered the walled courtyard, a flurry of hens had run out to meet them.

She discovered the kitchen in a separate building attached to the north wing of the house. Unsure if she should enter, she did so cautiously, seeing a woman dressed in aprons standing on a stool in what appeared to be a larder, counting off items under her breath. The woman looked plump and ruddy-cheeked, in her middle years with braided hair, her head uncovered, indicating that she was a spinster. She gaped at Morven over the rim of her spectacles.

'Merciful heaven! Who might you be?'

'Beggin' yer pardon. I'm Morven. I didna mean to affright ye.'

'Morven?'

'A healer. Father Ranald rode fer me after ... I believe 'twas after he dismissed Doctor Dalrymple.'

The woman lifted a box of candles down from the top shelf. They were of beeswax, likely for burning in the chapel, not the tallow kind that smelled of cow. 'A healer?' She stepped down, blatantly sizing Morven up. 'I've only heard o' one healer hereabouts, and 'tisna you, so best be telling the truth. Who are ye?'

Eager to gain the woman's trust, Morven's explanation came in a garbled rush, a breathless description of her years of training at Rowena's side.

'Aye, I ken who ye are now.' The woman smiled. 'I heard Rowena was bringing on an apprentice—only I didna think on ye being such a young thing.'

'I'm old enough.' Morven was pleased the woman knew Rowena; that made things easier. She needed an ally here.

The woman's lips twitched. 'Women are nae permitted in the hoose; even the boys' mothers are forbidden. 'Tis feared they would disturb the students' study and the nurturing o' their piety. 'Tis why I was so chary o' ye.'

Morven understood, although it seemed cruel to deny the boys their mothers. 'I'm here wi' the master's permission,' she said. 'Struan has scarlet fever.'

'Lord, Struan, too.'

'I've potions to prepare. Might I use the kitchen?'

The woman laid the candles down. 'Ye must treat the kitchen as yer own. Whatever it takes to save those boys. I'm Janet, the housekeeper.'

Morven smiled in relief. Janet's rosy cheeks revealed a warm heart, not just long hours toiling over hot cauldrons and pots. 'I must prepare an infusion to keep Struan passing water. The sickness begets poisons in the body. He must pass them out, or they'll overwhelm him. I fear 'twas what killed poor Andrew.'

Janet snorted. ''Twas thon leech Dalrymple killed him, wi' his bloodletting and purges. He even bled the poor lad under his tongue, and Nathaniel let slip he burned the boy's skin 'til it blistered.' She clicked her tongue. 'God rot the man. Efter all that, he let the boy die.'

Morven shared the woman's anger. 'I dinna hold wi' burning or bleeding. I use herbs and charms to heal. I mean to do everything in my power to heal Struan. And the master. Father John suffers wi' consumption.'

'Aye, I feared that was what plagued the poor man. Then, ye're doubly welcome. The master's worsened these last weeks.'

'I must lower his fever; 'tis doing him only harm, but Struan must come first. I've brought white oak bark.' Morven unwrapped what looked like curls of wood. 'A linctus of this will ease Struan's painful throat, but should his condition worsen, I must use more powerful medicine. 'Tis necessary I have it prepared should I need to use it.'

Janet peered into Morven's creel, staring at the roots of wolfsbane and deadly nightshade that doubtless looked innocent enough, just clumps of roots entwined limb-like at the base of her basket. 'If Rowena taught ye, 'tis good enough fer me. I'll show ye where ye can work.'

Janet led the way into a large kitchen dominated by a great hearth. Morven had heard of such hearths but had never seen one. Built into the wall, the fire was contained within an iron grate raised from the floor by an enormous hearthstone. Drystone walling to either side had been finished with layers of smooth clay, making shelving for pots and platters, while a hooded canopy drew smoke from the room through a stone chimney. A square worktable polished to a deep shine took up much of the room, surrounded by rush chairs. Light from the window picked out the glint of copper cooking pots, silverware, and pottery displayed on a dresser. A box-bed filled one corner hung with linen for privacy. Another bed near the fire was piled with blankets. A spindle lay on the pillow. The scent of broth and baking bannocks filled the air, making Morven's mouth water.

'Annag's bed.' Janet indicated the smaller bed by the fire. 'She assists me and bides here most o' the year. The boys are nae allowed to come to the kitchen, except fer Nathaniel. He's nae longer a boy and may go where he pleases. He often comes here.'

'I've met Nathaniel.'

Janet smiled wistfully. 'Aye, 'twill be a sore loss when he leaves us. Nathaniel's been here longer than me. When he tak's the cloth, he'll be a true heather priest, all his training gained hidden away in these lonely hills.'

What did that do to a boy? Little wonder Nathaniel seemed so unworldly. But Morven put the thought away and began infusing mallow leaves in hot water to make a hydrating tea. She left the oak bark steeping in whisky and returned to Struan.

He was asleep, Nathaniel sitting cross-legged at his side. He rose when she entered. 'Struan was nauseous,' he said. 'He brought up some bile.'

She set the tea down, noting that Nathaniel had cleaned the boy, removing whatever he had brought up. She tried to imagine her da dealing with such a task, or most glensmen, and failed miserably. Feeling Struan's forehead, she found him hot but not yet worryingly so. Still, she must prepare the tinctures of wolfsbane and deadly nightshade and have them ready. If his condition worsened, time would not be his friend.

'Forgive me. Would ye sit wi' Struan a little longer while I prepare further medicine? I'll be as quick as I can.' She glanced out the window. The clouds gathering over the hills were tinged with red. 'Twas later than she'd realised.

'I'll sit with Struan for as long as he needs me. I can give him that if you'd like.' Nathaniel nodded at the cup she'd brought. 'Once I've led the boys in their evening prayers, I'll return here for the night.' His face tightened. 'I don't intend to fail Struan.'

She looked curiously at him. 'There's nae need. I'll sit wi' Struan through the night.'

He looked at her in surprise. 'You mean to stay here all night?'

'If 'tis allowed.'

'But won't your husband expect you home? I mean, whatever will he think if you don't return? Surely, he'll imagine something ill has befallen you?'

A pang of loss caught her. No one waited for her at home. No soul but a few hens, and they would manage well enough without her for a day or two.

She frowned. 'My husband is ... away.'

'I see.' He blinked at her.

She could feel his confusion and knew he did not see. Her face grew hot, the silence thickening between them, crammed with questions Nathaniel was too polite to ask. She felt them gathering against her. Jamie's leaving still confused her, especially with the rumours spreading about him, but she'd not justify his actions, especially to Nathaniel, who had spent most of his life cloistered away, well-educated but likely ignorant of the hardships of the outside world.

After a moment, Nathaniel said, 'Well, I hope he returns to you soon. Do you live with your kinfolk, or have you a farm to run?'

'We have a holding, though 'tisna quite a farm. Druimbeag. The land's still half wild, but I hope to bring in our first harvest at summer's end.'

'Sounds like arduous work for a woman on her own.'

'Aye, but I've kinfolk to help.' With a sinking sensation, it dawned on her Nathaniel might think that Jamie was in gaol. She cursed herself. She should have explained he'd been pressed.

'I'm glad of it.'

She nodded, thinking of her cattle grazing on summer pastures with Rowena's beasts, watched over by Sarah. Jamie had said Alec was beholden to him, Sarah too, although he had not explained why. But it seemed so, for Sarah had not complained about the extra work.

''Tis necessary I sit wi' Struan through the night,' she said, 'lest his condition worsens. I must be ready to give him more powerful medicine if needed. Ye're welcome to sit wi' me if ye like.'

'Thank you, I will if you don't mind or think it improper.' He smiled awkwardly, little dimples indenting the smooth lines of his cheeks. She hadn't noticed them before, but then, she hadn't seen him smile.

'You're different from Doctor Dalrymple,' he observed.

'I hope so.'

He blushed. 'I don't mean in how you look. You're a delicate young woman, while he …' he frowned, appearing reluctant to put his impression of the physician into words. He hardly needed to. Dalrymple's manners were as crude and lacking in tenderness as his treatments. 'I meant different in your care of the boys. Doctor Dalrymple never stayed here overnight or longer than needed to conduct his treatments and never lingered to observe the results. He appeared to have little patience, always assuming his treatments would help his patients, although I did not observe that. You're different. You put your patients' needs before your own.'

Morven thought a moment. 'I'm well and strong and nae as delicate as ye imagine, whilst my patients are at their weakest when I see them. They trust me to help them. I mustna abuse their trust.'

He stared at her, and they again shared a moment that made her think he remembered her from that long-ago night.

'You must forgive me,' he stammered. 'I'm little used to female company. I fear my manners are not as gracious as they might be, especially regarding Mister Dalrymple.'

She laughed. 'Yer manners are fine.' Nathaniel's honesty put her at ease.

He frowned down at his hands. They were slender and pale, as he was, and not at all like Jamie's. Nathaniel's hands were made to hold a quill or be clasped in prayer, not wield a sword or grasp a plough shaft.

'Thank you,' he murmured. 'I remember you from that night by the river when I was a boy—the night my father gave me to the church.' He gave her a shy smile. 'You're kind. With your earth medicine and my prayers, I'm certain God will make Struan well again.'

She blushed into her lap, but before she could respond, Struan moaned, and they turned their attention to him.

CHAPTER TWELVE

Despite Nathaniel's words, the night proved long and difficult. Come the darkest hour, it was plain Struan was gravely ill. The lad was too exhausted to sip the mallow tea. He wanted only to sleep, yet his sleep was fitful, broken by frequent bouts of vomiting. His rash spread over his body but for the skin around his nose and mouth, which appeared yellow in contrast. His skin felt hot and dry—an ominous sign. Sweating was one of the ways the body cast out poisons. This dry heat meant Struan was retaining them. Likewise, he passed little water, and what he passed was dark in colour with a pungent smell. He complained his head hurt, and Morven felt the rapid beating of his heart and knew more potent medicine was needed.

Nathaniel despaired, gripping the boy's hand. He prayed endlessly. His prayers were like naught Morven had heard, impassioned, rich with scriptural phrase and description. They sent her mind back to the night his da handed him to the Church. She remembered his da telling the earlier master he expected his son to rise swiftly within the Church. Already, Nathaniel prayed as she imagined a bishop might. His sermons would be a joy to sit through. She often struggled to keep her eyes open through Father Ranald's functional liturgies, but Nathaniel spoke so lyrically, his voice rising and falling with the soft inflexion of the Gael, that not once during the night did she tire of listening to him. Hearing the tremble in his voice, she prayed she had allowed enough time for her tinctures to develop full potency. Even so, dilution was their key; these herbs were potent poisons. Five drops each tincture of wolfsbane and deadly nightshade in a cup of water. Struan must take a teaspoon of this every hour.

He vomited up the first dose, and Morven fretted whether any part of the herbs' healing powers had made it into his body. Knowing their deadly reputation, she was too afraid to repeat the dose and could only wait out the hour, praying he would keep the next dose down. Alongside Nathaniel's impassioned prayers, Morven offered her silent ones, too clumsy with words to pray aloud in front of Nathaniel. He could elegantly express himself, where she had gained her schooling roaming the hills and forests of Stratha'an in Rowena's footsteps and in her da's secret bothy, learning to distil whisky. Her prayers invoked Mother Earth's deepest magic, but Nathaniel might think it heathen witchery and judge her unfit to treat an innocent like Struan.

The night wore on, but at some point, she looked up to find the master swaying in the doorway in his nightshirt, staring at Struan's flaming face.

'Father.' Nathaniel rose to his feet. 'You mustn't distress yourself. Struan is in capable hands. We must put our faith in the Lord and in Morven, His able servant.'

The master's face tightened. He made the sign of the cross and let Nathaniel lead him back to his chamber.

Morven pressed a cool cloth to Struan's forehead, hearing the rattle of his breathing. She must do more to have any hope of saving him. 'We must mak' the lad sweat,' she told Nathaniel when he returned. 'This dryness o' skin is an ill sign.'

'How might we do that?'

'I need vinegar and a sheet and blankets.'

He hurried away to fetch them.

When he returned, she sponged the boy's body with a solution of vinegar in cool water and doused the sheet, wrapping Struan from neck to foot in the wet linen. Against his hot skin, the sodden sheet must have felt frigid. He gasped and shivered. She quickly swaddled him in dry blankets, tucking them around him to seal in the damp heat from his body.

Nathaniel looked anxiously at her. 'How long must we leave him like this?'

She felt the back of Struan's neck, then his forehead and her heart beat a little easier. He had begun to sweat. 'An hour, mebbe more. If his skin grows hot and dry again, we must repeat this.'

She lifted Struan's head and held the second dose to his lips, the boy blinking to show he was ready. Mercifully, he kept it down. 'D'ye wish to drink now?' When he nodded, she lifted the cup of mallow tea to his lips. He gulped it down and looked for more. She poured him a second cup and met Nathaniel's gaze. They shared a faltering smile of relief. Whose lips trembled most, she couldn't tell.

Twice more, she wrapped the lad to induce sweating, each time producing the desired effect. Come the first glimmer of daylight, the lad's fever had subsided, and he had passed the first danger point. She sat back and closed her eyes, letting the tension flow from her body.

'Before you sleep, Morven, and I want you to sleep, for no one more richly deserves rest, but before you do, I want you to know how indebted I am.'

She opened her eyes. Nathaniel was watching her, his face tight with emotion.

'You saved Struan's life, although I hardly know how, but you and your earth medicine saved him as surely as the Lord. I wish to repay you, only I've little notion how. I hope the master will find a way.' He blinked, and a tear tracked down his cheek. 'Perhaps you will speak of your methods when you're rested. I wish to learn of your ways. But for now, I give you my heartfelt thanks for Struan's life and for the sympathy you showed me all those years ago, on that night that changed my life.'

She smiled crookedly. 'I mind that night well. I confess, ower the years, I've dreamed o' it more oft than I care to remember. 'Twas the look on yer face that struck me most. I've never forgotten it. Fer long ye haunted my dreams.'

His face fell. 'Forgive me. I never imagined I had caused you such distress.'

'Fer such a young lad, ye looked so earnest and brave, even though yer heart was breaking. I felt that sorry fer ye; I thought to flee wi' ye to safety.' She smiled sadly. 'But I was still a bairn and saw life through a bairn's eyes.'

A flicker of pain crossed Nathaniel's face before he checked it. 'Ah,' he croaked, 'to see life as a child does—that is a rare thing.'

She nodded and half closed her eyes, studying Nathaniel from beneath lowered lids. He was handsome and likeable but not in Jamie's rugged, masculine way. His attraction was more subtle. He was still that vulnerable boy; perhaps he always would be, where Jamie was most assuredly a man.

'Anyhow,' she looked down at Struan. He was sleeping soundly. 'I fear the lad isna yet safe, though his sickness now follows a more welcome course. As his fever wanes and his rash clears, he must keep passing water. His skin will scale and flake off. 'Tis important he doesna swell wi' the dropsy as that happens. Fer now, though, he's as safe as I could hope fer.'

'I thank the Lord for it, but I also thank you.'

'Ye can thank me when he's back at his lessons.'

'I will.' Nathaniel grimaced as he stretched his spine against the wall. 'Do you wish to sleep now, or are you hungry?'

She had eaten naught in hours although she felt no hunger, but she should eat for the sake of her child. 'I wish to sleep, but I should likely eat something first.'

'Janet will still be asleep.' He got to his feet. 'I'll see what I can find.'

She brushed his arm as he turned to go, and he flinched. 'Dinna touch the pale liquid in the bowl by the hob. 'Tis Struan's medicine. Should ye drink it, 'twill kill ye. I've warned Janet.'

He smiled as if she jested, although she did not. He returned with ale, cheese, and wedges of cold bannock. The bannocks were a day old and had hardened but were still good.

'Janet's a fine cook,' he said, gnawing on his bannock. 'And Annag is learning. Janet mothers her.'

'I ken ye were close to yer own mam. Ye saw her again, Nathaniel, aye?'

His face tightened, and he swallowed and put his bannock down.

'Forgive me—'

'I saw her only once again, when she was in her coffin.' He frowned. 'I was thirteen when a letter came from my father saying my mother was ill. Father Paterson allowed me to return to see her, but she was already dead, lying cold and waxen-faced in a wooden box.'

'Oh, Nathaniel, I'm sorry.'

He frowned into his lap. 'I was overcome with grief and behaved badly. My father already believed me weak. I only confirmed it with my sobbing.'

She exhaled at the absurdity of that. 'I dinna believe 'tis weak to weep when ye lose someone ye love. 'Tis what folk do, whether they wish to or nae. Tears show ye care. Surely to feel naught is the true weakness.'

He reddened, and she recalled the startling display of grief she had earlier witnessed from him.

'You are wise. That is almost exactly what the master said.'

'Then I think ye should heed the master and never mind yer da.'

He laughed, then sobered, his face twisting. 'I never said goodbye to her. I didn't tell her I loved her, that I didn't hold her responsible for sending me away.' He swallowed. 'That was another's doing.'

She supposed he meant his da. 'Yer mam kent ye loved her. Even I could see ye cared fer each other, and I was only a bairn.'

'I hope so.'

'Do ye doubt it?'

'I wrote her many letters, but she never replied. Perhaps she didn't receive them.'

'Maybe she couldna read. I canna. Or write. I'm stupid o' letters.' She blushed even though she supposed Nathaniel would know that.

'You're not stupid, only unread. I imagine that is because you have had no opportunity to learn.'

She nodded, fingering the letter knotted in a fold of her arisaid. 'Twas from Jamie and came by runner two days ago. She had no notion what it said, but the knowledge that he had sat down with ink and feather and thoughts of her in his heart filled her with such a yearning for him she struggled not to weep. Only finding someone who could read his message was her difficulty. She had hoped Father Ranald might, but he was taken up with other things. Perhaps Nathaniel, but first, she must make him understand Jamie's plight. Nathaniel's world was far removed from theirs. Would he understand their troubles?

Nathaniel smiled brightly, dismissing his torment. 'I am a younger son and was always the weaker sibling.' He glanced down at his slender frame. 'I am the runt of the litter. My brother Samuel is my father's heir; hence, he is the one my father taught to manage the land. He always considered me less important. I understood. I would not inherit, so he wished me for the church, although, as you saw, knowing it did nothing to lessen my dread at having to leave my mother.'

'I'd have been afraid, too. 'Tis why I felt so bad fer ye.'

He flashed her a smile, again trying to make light of his pain. 'My only value is in what use I can be to my father and our people. If I cannot fulfil my father's expectations, I will have no value.'

Frowning, Morven set her flagon down. 'I canna believe that, fer every man has value. 'Tis measured in the things he cares about, in how he treats others and in how he rises to help folk in times o' trouble.' She thought of Jamie and all he had been willing to sacrifice for his kin. He'd have given his life for Rowena and his cousins. 'I believe a man's worth is measured in the respect he inspires in others and in the love he leaves behind when he passes from this world.' She cleared a thickness from her throat. 'Anyhow, what is it yer da expects?'

'That I will return to Badenoch as soon as I'm ordained and minister to those who still follow our faith, particularly his kinsmen who bear our name.' He frowned. 'I expect I'll return soon. If I'm judged worthy, I'll be ordained when Bishop Hay next visits. My father hopes I'll become a bishop one day.'

She frowned. 'He expects much.'

'He knows I've always been anxious to please him.'

'But what do *you* want? Do ye wish to be a bishop or even a priest?'

Nathaniel smiled patiently. 'It does not matter what I want.'

'But ye must hae dreams o' yer own.'

'Perhaps once, but they no longer matter.'

Morven exhaled in exasperation. 'A man's life is a precious gift, Nathaniel. It should be lived to the full. Ye shouldna live yer life to please yer da. Can ye nae see 'tis what ye're doing?'

He gave no answer but smiled patiently, looking at his clasped hands. She wondered if he prayed.

At a loss, she sat back. But then, had she nae done the same? Desperate to win her da's approval, hadn't she been trying to prove her worth since that same fateful night? She looked at Nathaniel's bowed head. The morning light found the copper in his hair as it curled at his collar. He was earnest and sincere; he could hardly be more malleable in the hands of others.

He looked up, aware that she was studying him. 'I know my failings, Morven. As a child, I had them repeatedly pointed out to me, first by my father and then by my brother. They are why becoming a priest is best for me.'

'Failings? I think ye're honest and loyal.'

'You are kind, but I was always weak, not just physically but my character. I tend toward shyness and lack courage and brawn. I was always more interested in books and learning than manly things.'

She supposed that might be true, but Nathaniel had been brave the night his da handed him to the black-robed Scalan master. 'Have ye been happy here?'

He laughed bitterly. 'Not always. I was miserable at first. Mister Thomson, the master back then, was stern. I felt desperately alone and unwanted. I missed my mother and everything I had ever known. I felt rejected by my father. Even my mother, I unfairly concluded, did not care enough to fight for me. I supposed something must be wrong with me that my father was so eager to be rid of me. I felt imprisoned by the hills that conceal our defiant existence here, imagining this lonely place with its strict rules would crush my spirit.' He sighed. 'Yet, in time, I learned to embrace the hardships and discipline and accept the dangers of training for an outlawed faith. I formed friendships with the other boys and a deep respect for the new master, Father John. I've not always been happy, but I've found peace here.'

'I'm glad o' it.'

'And I've learned so much. The more I learn, the more I crave to know.' He looked away as he thought, and she sensed his mind soaring. 'The written word especially enchants me. Marks made on a page, how they make me feel, the images they evoke and the message they convey enthral me. That is especially true of the scriptures, for they are the most sacred writing. And unlike at other schools, corporal punishment has no place at Scalan. Despite the strict rules, the students are treated with respect, something I realise I never received from my father, although I hope my ordination will please him.'

'I'm sure it will.'

'Father John's teachings especially inspire me. I began to see that my life had not ended as I once imagined but had just begun.' He smiled softly. 'My life will be the most wondrous adventure any man can have, for I will live it with God. I've learned that kinship, though valuable, is not everything—there is something greater.'

She nodded. 'I see the Creator's hand everywhere in nature.'

'That is because you are wise, Morven. You did not need books to tell you what you instinctively knew. Although, if you wish to learn the rudiments of reading, with the master's permission, I would be honoured to teach you. It would perhaps be a way to repay you.'

She stared at him. 'I have a letter.' She delved within the folds of her arisaid, unknotting the precious bundle with trembling fingers. ''Tis from my husband. I long to know what he writes.'

'Why did you not tell me?' He took the package from her and carefully unfolded it, spreading the pale brown paper on his knee.

'Twas a mite crumpled; she had unfolded and refolded it many times, fingering the thick paper, admiring Jamie's artistry with quill and ink, most of all, wondering what it said. She'd slept with it pressed against her growing belly.

'This is his address.' Nathaniel pointed with his finger. *'Fort George, Nairnshire.'* He frowned. 'Your husband is in the army?'

Her cheeks grew hot. 'Jamie took the king's shilling twa months ago, though nae willingly. He had to, or we'd be put from our holding.'

'You were threatened with eviction?'

'Wi' all his kinfolk and mine.'

'What? But why?'

'His Grace wished Jamie enlisted in his fencible regiment. He thought him a prize catch and feared others might press him if he didna catch him first.'

'A prize catch?'

'Jamie fought a duel last year. He challenged the Black Gauger, the exciseman who was blackmailing his kinswoman and ruining folks' lives.' She swallowed. How to explain Jamie's actions to a man with no knowledge of gaugers, never mind folks' need to smuggle whisky to afford their rents? 'McBeath was corrupt,' she finished.

'But duelling's illegal.'

'Aye, but 'twas the only course left to him. McGillivray witnessed the duel and stopped it. Ye'll ken he's the duke's factor and a magistrate. He spoke up fer Jamie against the gauger, though he later whispered tales o' Jamie's bravery in His Grace's ear, adding to the fables spreading about him.'

'Then, your husband is a courageous man?'

'Loyal and principled.'

Nathaniel raised his brows and turned back to the letter. 'Your husband writes in Gaelic:

My love, though I be miles away, my heart is always with ye, nae matter where I must go. I think o' ye day and night and pray that ye're well, that my absence and the hardships my leaving must have brought havena undone ye. I imagine our littlin must grow strong inside ye, and I wonder if the lamb yet moves and if ye can feel him. Thoughts of our child fill my heart, yet I despair o' the world he'll be born into. It grieves me, for as Highland folk are reviled in the glens, mistrusted, believed ignorant and superstitious, lacking in any virtue, so highland recruits and our Gaelic culture are just as despised here.'

Nathaniel lowered the letter and stared at her. 'You are with child?'

She nodded, cradling her belly to protect the innocent inside from the hostile world Jamie described.

Thrown by this, Nathaniel blinked at her. 'Had I known, I would never have let you sit up all night nursing Struan.'

'I told ye, I'm nae as delicate as ye imagine. I havena the luxury.'

Nathaniel drew a flustered breath and read on:

'From the start, I determined to keep my head down and follow orders, acting the model soldier, eager to please my officers and colonel, and secretly even more eager for the end o' the American war. But my restraint is sorely tested. The duke is nowhere to be seen, our officers all anglicised, speaking no Gaelic, and worse, despising the highland tongue and those who speak it. Daily, my men and I suffer our officers' contempt. I strive to bite my tongue and not rise to the offence but 'tis hard to stomach. Only thoughts of you and our child keep me strong. I dream of the day I can return to you at Druimbeag. I see you standing on the ridge to welcome me, our babe in yer arms, ripe barley rippling around ye. Those dreams keep me strong through the brutal treatment and shameful scorning I and my men suffer at the hands o' our supposed betters.'

Nathaniel looked up at her. 'Your husband speaks of his men. Is he an officer?'

'He was given the rank o' corporal. The duke's way o' making his enlistment easier to swallow.'

Nathaniel frowned back at the letter.

'We are kept together, all those who enlisted wi' me, ten glensmen from Stratha'an and Glenlivet embodied into Captain Cumming's company and garrisoned for now at Fort George. I am made corporal, as promised, in command of our unit of raw and mostly reluctant recruits. Most of these men were seduced by the duchess with her talk o' bounty coin and romantic notions of once more being armed and kilted. One lad deserted on the road here. You'll know him—young Archie Munro of Ardriachan, a lad o' sixteen. Recruiters stupefied him wi' drink. When he sobered, they told him he was enlisted. He remembers naught. He lay down beside me as we made camp by the roadside on our march here. Come morning, he was gone. Had I known his intentions, I'd have stopped him. I'd have tied him to a tree if need be. He was caught trudging the long road home and brought here five days ago, a bound prisoner. He's been sentenced to four hundred lashes by beat o' drum, poor lad. Gordon Fencibles will form the square, though the whole garrison

must witness his agony and the shame and brutality of his sentence. That is the order.'

Nathaniel lowered the sheet of paper, his face white. 'Forgive me. I had no idea your husband's letter would hold such disturbing news. Should I go on?'

She nodded. 'Jamie tells the truth. I would hear it and nae be coddled or kept in the dark. And to hear his words is still a comfort, even be it the things he speaks o' chill me.'

Nathaniel looked tenderly at her. 'If you're sure.' He cleared his throat and continued.

'Our pay is in arrears, a pittance even when paid, for we must buy our own bread and ale and are expected to pay for the upkeep of our arms and clothing: shoe polish, tallow for oiling the lock and barrel of our muskets, flour for powdering our hair, candles, ink, paper, even peat for the fire in a cruel deduction they call poundage. It leaves us meagre rations to live on. No man among us has received the enlistment guinea due us, and we've seen naught o' the promised bounty. I'm told most o' this coin must anyhow be handed back to pay for our hated uniforms. We are deceived, my love. I hoped to send coin home for the rental due at Lammas. It shames me that I cannot. I hope you'll find it in yer heart to forgive me, but I canna help but feel I've betrayed ye.'

Nathaniel cleared a gruffness from his throat. 'This must be hard to hear.'

'Yet I must hear it.'

'I fear so.' He read:

'Even our uniforms are nae what was promised. The plaid is government tartan, the hated military pattern pushed upon the Black Watch, they who the authorities betrayed. I pray we will not be similarly betrayed. Our tunics are cut from brick-red cloth. I am a redcoat now in every sense and feel the rankle o' it bitterly. The promise that we would wear our ancient dress was a thin one, for this is a grotesque parody. No Highlandman ever dressed like this. Our blue bonnets are made ludicrous pillboxes diced in scarlet and white, cocked with plumed yellow wool made to look like feathers. Our coats are braided and edged in lace, our shirts frilled and flounced to humiliate our national dress—monstrosities we must pay for and so dearly nae a coin remains to send home to family and kin.

'I'm bitter, my love; pray excuse me, yet I am sorely galled. The candle gutters and I must finish this letter. I have many to write. No man among us

can write, yet all wish their kinfolk to know they are safe. I will keep Father Ranald busy reading my scratchings to wives, mothers, and sweethearts. Lord knows what I am to tell Archie's folk. I pray the Lord grants him the strength to endure his sentence.

'It grows dark. I see silver pinpricks through the dreary panes of my window and know they are the same stars that shine for you in Stratha'an. I despair that I have no coin to send you and fret how ye'll manage, but ye mustna worry for me. I'll get by and will help the others to as best I can. Until we are together again, know that ye are my heart and my life. I remain always yer loving husband, James.'

Nathaniel swallowed and folded the letter. 'Your husband writes well. Where did he learn?'

'From a priest in Inverness when he was a lad.'

'It pleases me to hear that. Forgive me; do you wish me to read his words again?'

'If it isna too much trouble. 'Tis as if I hear Jamie's voice when ye speak his words.'

Nathaniel smiled tenderly. 'He cares a great deal for you.'

'And I even mair fer him.'

'Yes,' he said softly. 'I can tell.'

CHAPTER THIRTEEN

Fort George, near
Inverness

JAMIE FIDGETED BESIDE HAL, uncomfortable in his ill-fitting uniform. The cartridge pouches the men must wear when in full uniform were bulky and cumbersome. A wooden box covered in lacquered leather and deep enough to hold thirty paper rounds of powder and ball, the pouch needed an extra wide shoulder belt to carry it. The men complained that the belt and box chafed viciously. They were impracticable under a flowing plaid. If they were to be kilted like their ancestors, why could they nae carry powder-horns and shot-bags?

Jamie suffered like the rest, his belt and pouch digging in cruelly. Shifting in the line of Gordon Fencibles, he frowned down at his ludicrous goat-skin sporran hung with tassels and bells. He detested it even more fervently. What was wrong with their ancestors' plain deerskin pouch, a basic but essential part of highland dress? This desire to have them tasselled and frilled like choir boys was a mocking insult, not to say a deception since the cost of the anglicised abominations would be deducted from their promised bounty. The ridiculing of their national dress was but another way to subjugate the men who must wear it.

'D'ye think they'll go ahead wi' this?' Hal muttered in the line beside him.

'Lord, I hope nae. Archie's only a lad. But why else are we here?'

They were assembled in a square formation on the main parade ground, facing inward, waiting to witness the flogging of their fellow glensman. Captain Cumming's company of Gordon Fencibles formed the inner square, the deserter from their ranks, but every man garrisoned at the fort and not on guard duty had been ordered out. They stood in the drizzle, a murmur of disquiet rising above the constant pitter of rain as they waited for young Archie to be brought to the halberds. Every soldier must witness the lad's punishment, the spectacle doubtless intended to daunt the men into obedience.

To Jamie's front, a scaffold of sergeants' halberds had been erected as a flogging post. The murderous tripod of three-headed pikes reinforced by the pole of a fourth as the crossbar was the frame they would tie young Archie to.

'Stay in formation,' barked their sergeant. Prowling the lines, he halted in front of Jamie and jabbed him in the ribs with the blunt end of his halberd. 'Well, well, Corporal Innes, got yourself a ringside seat for the entertainment? Still, I doubt ye'll relish the spectacle as much as me. I like to see a stripling's pride flayed away along with his flesh.' He laughed. 'Especially a heiland muck-the-byre. Better yet, a witless heather-lowper from God-forsaken Strathavon.'

Jamie lunged at him, but Hal held him back. ''Tis what he wants,' Hal hissed. 'He'd hae ye trade places wi' Archie in a heartbeat. Dinna go playing into his hands.'

'Lord,' Jamie groaned through clenched teeth. 'Give me the strength to endure the devil's gibes.'

The sergeant winked at him, his left eyelid twitching, and stalked on, wielding his halberd to straighten the Gordon line.

'Did ye tell Morven who oor sergeant is?' Hal whispered. 'In yer letter, did ye tell her he's nane other than Hugh McBeath, the Black Gauger?'

'How could I?'

'Aye,' Hal conceded. 'I suppose nae.'

'She'd only fret all the more. She's carrying my bairn.' Jamie said no more, unable to bear the thought of what could befall his pregnant wife. Already, she must be overworked and half-starved through his neglect. He could hardly add to her troubles. This dire turn of events, an inexplicable blow he was still reeling from, he must keep to himself.

A low murmur rose from the ranks. Captain Cumming came into view, leading Archie surrounded by burly drummers, the regimental surgeon bringing up the rear. Archie looked white-faced and bewildered. His eyes roved, searching the ranks for a friendly face. As he drew level with Jamie, they made eye contact. Powerless to help him, Jamie could only grit his teeth as Archie stumbled on.

The group halted in front of the flogging post, where Captain Cumming ordered two sergeants to tie Archie to the halberds. Sergeant Shaw bound the lad's hands at the wrist and tied them to the crossed blades above his head. McBeath kicked Archie's legs apart and belted them at ankle and thigh to the staffs of the pikes, his chest resting on the crossbar. The surgeon then took a moment to inspect the bonds, ensuring that regulations had been followed. The bindings were not so tight they restricted blood flow. Satisfied, he nodded to Sergeant Shaw, who stripped Archie to the waist, taking care to fold the lad's uniform and place it a safe distance from the flogging post. Archie shivered, drizzle pattering on his bare skin. His back shone white and unblemished as a babe's, every rib visible through his stretched skin.

At Captain Cumming's order, the relay of drummers moved up, the first man holding the cat o' nine tails, drawing the tough knotted cords of the whip through his fist to straighten them. Jamie grew sweaty despite the chill creeping up his legs from standing in a puddle. His breathing shallowed, his heart thumping. Four hundred lashes. Lord God, 'twas inhuman. Two hundred and fifty was the maximum any man was thought capable of enduring in one day. The remainder must be laid on the next day and the next if the sentence demanded it, opening the bleeding scabs forming over the previous day's cuts. Poor Archie's ordeal would stretch over two days.

Captain Cumming stamped his buckled shoes, making the ostrich plume in his hat quiver. A hush fell. Satisfied he had gained the rank and file's attention, he read the Articles of War aloud, stressing the section on desertion, the crime Archie had been found guilty of committing. He addressed the men in clipped English, calling no officer forward to translate his address into Gaelic. Perhaps there were no Highland officers, no Highlandman trusted enough to bear rank. Or if such officers existed, they were landed noblemen, their commissions bought, men educated in the south and now so anglicised they had forgotten the tongue of their forebears or considered it so primitive not one amongst them wished to admit knowledge of it.

Jamie exhaled in anger. He was the only man of his unit who could understand the Englishman's tongue, especially when delivered with a brusque clip. Even McBeath's Lowland Scots must be translated for most Gaelic speakers. Jamie carefully reworded all their orders into Gaelic for his men. That way, there could be no misunderstanding about what was expected of them. Poor Archie must understand not a word of Captain

Cumming's address.

The captain lowered the sheaf of papers. 'Go ahead, drum major. On beat of drum. The sentence is four hundred lashes.'

A drum rolled. The first man swung the whip around his head, the flail whirring as it gathered speed. On the tenth rap, he brought it down with a sharp crack between Archie's shoulder blades. The lad jolted and arched against the holding straps but uttered no sound. The strike had broken his skin, drawing blood. A livid weal now marred the white perfection of his back.

'One,' called the drum major.

The drum rolled again. The second strike landed just below the first but curled cruelly around Archie's ribs. The lad shuddered at the electrifying shock of it.

'Two,' came the count.

The drum rolled again. Jamie's palms were damp, his jaw rigid. He glanced sidelong at Hal. Hal's grim expression reflected his fury and despair. 'Bastards,' he growled.

The third stroke landed lower. Archie let out an agonised shriek, his flesh quivering with the sting of it. Each strike seemed to take an age to come, the rhythmic roll and tap of the drum drawing out the agony, yet every blow must come too soon for Archie. By the time the first drummer had dealt twenty-five strokes, Jamie's clenched fists shone white at the knuckles. The drum major called a halt. The man stepped back, handing the whip to the next drummer. This was a younger man. He showed signs of reluctance, having likely never flogged before other than in practice on a sack of sawdust tied to a post. He drew the flails of the whip repeatedly through his fist to remove the build-up of blood that would otherwise splatter his face and clothing, although Jamie imagined the clotted blood might have cushioned the sting a fraction for poor Archie. Wiping his hand on a rag, he surveyed Archie's rutted back.

Again, it took what felt like a lifetime for the next twenty-five strokes to be inflicted, the rhythmic rat-tat of the drum beating a throbbing tattoo in Jamie's head. Shining scarlet in the drizzle, Archie's back was now lacerated and raw. Blood trickled down, soaking his bunched plaid.

When the young drummer's quota was finally complete, he handed the cat with some relief to a fresh drummer. This man was stouter with muscular arms and showed no hesitancy. Swinging the cat expertly around his head, he brought it down with clinical precision, lacing a bloody pattern into Archie's flesh, giving the lad some terrible cuts about his ribs.

Jamie's jaw ached; he clenched it so hard. There was an odd coldness at his core, from anger or grief, he couldn't tell. His mouth felt dry, yet the wetness of tears chilled his cheeks. He glanced around. Many along the Gordon line were also weeping, their cheeks wet and faces taut with anger. He shared their fury. 'Twas intolerable to stand by and watch one of their own be brutally beaten, and a boy more than a man. The savagery sickened him. As he stood there in frustration, a strange sound permeated his consciousness. It came from further back among the lines of men, a massed sniffing as men collectively inhaled their tears rather than let them fall. The sound came as one with the crack of the whip, a shared inhalation from fifteen hundred nostrils and throats, a sound like naught he'd heard before.

Archie sagged against the belts, his body quivering. He had cried out only once during his ordeal and must have near bitten his tongue in half to keep so quiet. He might be a lad of sixteen, but Archie was a proud Highlander from Strathavon. He would keep the shreds of his dignity no matter the cost.

Jamie's heart began to pound, his taut muscles itching to spring into action. Injustice had always incensed him, especially when 'twas inflicted upon those he cared about. Perhaps rage was a sin, yet standing in the rain, hamstrung by the allegiance he'd been blackmailed into swearing, an impotent witness to this barbarism with no outlet for his fury, Jamie's rage boiled relentlessly to the surface.

'Forgive me, Lord,' he growled through clenched teeth, 'but I can stand this no longer.' Stepping forward, he shouted, '*Mercy!* Fer the love o' God, show the lad some mercy!'

'Shut your muzzle.' McBeath butted him in the chest. Winded, he staggered back, but the essence of his cry had taken hold amongst the men.

'Pity,' cried another. 'Show the lad some pity. He's still a halfling.'

'Cry a halt to this,' another shouted.

'Cut him loose!' came the men's shared cry.

Jamie stamped his shoes on the cobbles. Within seconds, the parade ground echoed to the tramp of fifteen hundred military shoes.

Hal leapt forward, drawing his broadsword. 'Heartless brutes!' he bellowed. 'Cut the lad doon.' Sergeant McBeath butted him in the stomach.

He staggered back, McBeath wrenching the sword from his hand.

Captain Cumming's voice rose above the clamour. 'I'll brook no dissent from the men.' He called his officers to him. 'Once this matter's been dealt with, I'll have the ringleaders disciplined. I will not tolerate defiance.'

The officers glanced nervously along the lines of men. There was further discussion, none of which Jamie could hear, although he drew a sense that it boded ill. Their behaviour would be deemed rebellious. McBeath would undoubtedly identify him as the ringleader. They had history, he and the exciseman-turned-soldier.

The burly drummer delivered his last blow with a degree less swagger, doubtless aware of the mood of the men.

'Seventy-five,' came the count.

'Halt now,' Captain Cumming ordered. 'Take the private down. Munro is a young soldier. Let this disgrace be a lesson to him. I want it known Private Munro was extended every mercy. Desertion is a capital offence. I could've had him shot.'

Jamie turned to Hal in astonishment.

'Nay,' Hal muttered, 'dinna fool yerself they stopped this cruelty through compassion. They fear a mutiny. Highland men canna be trusted.' He laughed without humour. 'While Highlanders trust the British Crown and its War Office far less. Why d'ye suppose Highlandmen are aye first to be sent into battle or to foreign service in some swamp-fever colony to put doon the natives whose land King Geordie wishes to steal? 'Tis because oor loss is no great sorrow. Less o' us highland rogues to cause trouble. Punishment fer past uprisings, fer failing to show loyalty to a king and government that only wish to crush us.'

Jamie looked at Hal with respect. Hal spoke as he saw, and he saw things clearer than most. He nodded slowly. 'I suppose control can be gained through mercy as much as through punishment. 'Tis a careful calculation balancing the illusion o' leniency against glaring cruelty.'

''Tis the truth o' it.'

They fell silent as Sergeant McBeath stalked toward them, smirking at their wary expressions.

'Captain Cumming says he willnae tolerate defiance,' McBeath drawled. 'Yet it seems Corporal Innes must learn that the hard way. 'Twill be the worst for you both,' he prophesied. 'I intend to make sure o' it.' He laughed until he wheezed, then turned on his heel and stalked back to the flogging post where they were untying poor Archie. He left a reek of sour whisky in his wake.

'The weasel's drunk,' Hal muttered.

Archie groaned as they brought his arms down, a fresh flow of blood running from the lattice of cuts on his back. When they untied his legs, he staggered and would have fallen had the surgeon not caught him. Gordon men rushed forward, but they were ordered back. Four privates from Lord Seaforth's regiment were chosen. They bolstered the lad under the arms and dragged him to the waiting cart. Laying him face down in the straw, they pulled his blood-soaked plaid up to cover his back. The cartwheels rumbled into motion, and the cart clattered and jolted over the cobbles toward the infirmary.

Wincing, Jamie crossed himself. 'God grant the lad a swift recovery,' he muttered. But Archie's ruined back was only the visible damage inflicted on the lad. His wounds must go deeper, damaging his spirit, maybe damaging all their spirits.

With the spectacle over, Captain Cumming ordered the men back to their duties. They wheeled about in their companies to the ruffle of grenadier drums. As Jamie about turned, a hand clamped on his shoulder.

'No' you, Innes. You and Private McHardy are for the Black Hole. Captain Cumming agreed wi' me; four weeks in the cold and dark on bread and water will soon temper your rebellious streak.'

Jamie looked at Hal, but they both knew there was naught to be gained in arguing. Orders must be obeyed. They had seen what happened when a recruit dared to defy the British Crown. Stripping them of their weapons, McBeath marched them away.

CHAPTER FOURTEEN

Scalan Seminary

MORVEN WOKE TO BRIGHT sunlight. Blinking, she stretched her stiff limbs, then sat up with a jolt as the night's events came back to her. Struan was awake and turned his head toward her. Relieved, she rose from a mattress she had no memory of lying upon and knelt to feel his forehead. It was cool, and the livid hue had faded from his cheeks.

'How d'ye feel?' She stroked Struan's hair, noting that he lay under dry blankets that no longer smelled of vinegar.

'Better. Have you been here all night?'

'Aye, but doesna matter.' She caught movement and glanced up. Nathaniel was sitting in the shadows at the far side of Struan's bed. He drew his chair into the light. He had not slept, judging by his face; his eyes were bleary and heavy-lidded, the delicate bones of his face visible through his pale skin. A twinge of guilt pricked. He had kept a vigil at Struan's bedside while she slept.

'Struan was thirsty,' Nathaniel said. 'I let him finish the mallow tea you made. I hope I did right. He appears much better.'

'Thank ye. 'Twill keep his kidneys flushed. Has he been passing water?' She blushed at having to ask such a question.

'Enough to water the whole college garden,' Struan boasted, and Nathaniel nodded.

'Then I'll make a fresh brew. Struan must keep passing water as his rash clears.' She got to her feet, searching for her kertch. She had worn it every day of her marriage. It felt disloyal to go without it, as if she had forsaken Jamie. Her heart clenched. His absence hit her afresh every morning, a dull ache in her chest. Today was no different, worse since she'd woken somewhere not Druimbeag. For the thousandth time, she wondered what hardships Jamie faced, and as a Highlander in the king's army, what prejudices he struggled against.

She cleared her throat. 'Might ye manage some broth, Struan?'

'Maybe a little.'

'Janet will have some,' Nathaniel said. 'She makes a fresh pot every day.'

Feeling guilty, she said, 'I shouldna have slept. Please forgive me. I dinna ken what came ower me.'

He frowned at his hands, appearing to find his fingernails inordinately interesting. 'Your condition, I imagine. It made you more tired than me. You must rest for the sake of your child.'

Struan's eyes widened. He propped himself on one elbow, staring at her middle.

Morven's cheeks reddened, and she struggled for something to say. Nathaniel handed her the missing kertch, likely to distract the boy and ward off any questions he might be thinking of asking. It still retained the shape of her head with the pins in place. She had no memory of taking it off. She always took out the pins and folded the linen before lying down to sleep.

Nathaniel nodded at the wool-stuffed mattress she had risen from. 'I found a fresh bed for you. I hope you were comfortable.'

'Aye, thank ye.' Had he been obliged to help her onto it as exhaustion overtook her? When first she learned she was expecting a child, she had assumed she would carry on as before, at least until her time drew close, but already the strains of pregnancy were showing. She cleared her throat. ''Twas unfair to leave ye to care fer Struan alone.'

'Oh, I wasn't alone. God was with me, and I'd have woken you if I needed to.'

'Still ...'

'Please, there is nothing to forgive.'

She nodded, recognising Nathaniel's sincerity. He would make a compassionate priest; the needs of others were important to him. If not for the vow of celibacy he must take, he would make a devoted husband. 'I wish to look upon the boys,' she said, 'if 'tis allowed.'

'You may go where you please.'

'Even though I'm a woman?'

'The bishop's rules don't apply to healers. The master has said so, and I know Father Ranald agrees. And you saved Struan.' He smiled at the boy until he slumped back in his blankets. 'Father John has yet to learn of

Struan's recovery. He'll be overjoyed. I expect he will wish to thank you.'

'Struan's nae yet fully recovered,' she reminded him. 'We must keep him strong whilst he purges poisons from his body so the sickness canna reclaim him.'

Nathaniel blanched at the notion. 'You'll do whatever is necessary, I'm sure. And I'll help you as much as I can.' He looked earnestly at her. 'Perhaps some of your skills might even rub off on me, knowledge that could help the scholars and my parishioners once I have some. I enjoy learning.'

'I'd be grateful fer yer help,' she replied guardedly. 'But it takes years to learn all the herbs and simples. Rowena began teaching me when I was a bairn.'

'I imagine it takes as long as it does to train for the priesthood.'

'Years ranging the hills,' she admitted. 'Foraging in the depths o' the forest where nature keeps her most precious gifts. Many plants look alike, but ye must learn the difference. Some harm, others heal only when diluted enough. There's skill in extracting their properties, in turning roots and leaves into medicine. I ken only a trace of all there is to know. Mother Earth is generous. She has many gifts to share.'

Nathaniel looked intently at her. 'What you speak of fascinates me. I cannot hope to become skilled in my brief time with you, but anything I learn I would count a blessing.'

She twisted her hair back and fixed her kertch in place. Not all her abilities had been taught to her; many were inborn, so Rowena said. But since meeting Nathaniel, seeing him weep at Andrew's bedside, she had longed to take him into the hills and forests so nature could put colour to his cheeks, breathe vigour into his slender frame.

'Then, ye might help me gather the herbs I need. 'Twould likely be good fer ye to escape here fer a time.' She moved to the door. 'Pine oil's a powerful guard against rush fever, but the other boys may still have sickened.'

'They seemed well when I woke them, but I refer to your greater knowledge. Father Ranald has returned. He's dining with them in the kitchen since they cannot come here. The master is feverish again. Father Ranald will stand in for him, leading the boys in their studies. Oh, and he has brought your garron. You're no longer stranded here.'

She blinked at Nathaniel. 'I was never stranded here. I hope ye didna think that.'

'Forgive me; I meant only—'

'I came at Father Ranald's urging and stayed when I saw I was needed. There's little waiting fer me at hame anyway, naught but an infield full o' weeds. They'll still be there the morrow. 'Tis hard to keep atop o' the ragweed and thistles.'

Nathaniel swallowed. 'If only I could help you more.'

'I can manage,' she replied. 'All folk must if they wish to keep their holdings. 'Tis Druimbeag that matters, that I keep it safe fer Jamie.'

CHAPTER FIFTEEN

July 1781

IT WAS SO LONG since Nathaniel had walked through a forest he had forgotten what a treat it was to the senses. He struggled to remember the last time he'd done so, recalling long-ago games in the woods with his brother Samuel, sword-wielding games with sticks instead of swords that Samuel had always won. Samuel was older and stronger but never as clever. Their father had been quick to point that out whenever he sensed Samuel growing too lordly or overweening. He especially stressed the point in the days leading up to them leaving for Scalan, an event that had loomed over Nathaniel's life from the moment he learned his father wished to give him to the church.

Lying awake at night, he tried to imagine living with silent, black-robed priests instead of with his family. When his mother came to kiss him good night, he clung to her, breathing her scent into his memory with a shadowy likeness of her face. When he looked into her eyes, bright with love, the thought of leaving her brought such unbearable grief his throat tightened and swelled. He could not speak, not even to tell her how much he loved her. When she finally managed to prise herself free, his hiccuping sobs must have chased her down the passageway.

But his father's mind was made. 'Twould be good for him, giving him a backbone. What was there for a second son but subservience to the first? He was doing Nathaniel a service, cutting the apron strings binding him to his doting mother, dragging him out from behind her skirts, something Nathaniel would one day thank him for. Besides, where at best Samuel would only ever be a tacksman and a farmer, Nathaniel might become a bishop if he worked hard enough.

Nathaniel remembered what Samuel had thought of that. He'd called him a milksop and a weakling, fit for naught but wearing a preacher's frock.

No sooner was their father's back turned, and Samuel had beaten him with his stick, careful to leave no bruises on his face.

Yet, despite the painful memories, there was a simple joy in walking in a highland forest at the height of summer. The only woman to ever accompany him on such walks had been his mother; hence, walking with Morven felt unfamiliar, although not in the least awkward. Despite their dubious start, when he must have embarrassed her with his unconscionable weeping, he felt at ease in her company.

They left their garrons at the forest's edge, noisily cropping turf with their yellow teeth, and picked their way through a scattered woodland of pine, birch, and rowan. Beneath their feet, the going was springy, a rich patchwork of heather, pine saplings, and great hummocks of spongy moss. The air was cool and still but never silent: leaves whispered, birds called, the occasional pinecone dropped to earth with a soft thud. An earthy fragrance saturated the air. The colours were a delight. He fingered the parchment notebook he kept in his pocket, hoping for a chance to capture what he saw in inky images.

They were looking for juniper and woodruff, hart's tongue, although Morven said they would be lucky to find that. She knew where to look, and he followed her without question, silently thanking the Lord for sending her to Scalan. She had known what to do for Struan. If only she'd come in time for Andrew. His eyes nipped. He thrust the regret away, fearing he would weep again. Morven cared where Doctor Dalrymple had not. That was the greatest difference, although her whole healing philosophy differed vastly from the physician's.

A vista opened before them, a sunlit grove amongst the leaning, lichen-crusted trunks, clover green and lush. He gaped at the beauty of it. How could such a place exist so close to Scalan, yet he had no knowledge of it?

'There!' Morven sprinted ahead. 'Hart's tongue.' She squatted by a clump of glossy green ferns sprouting from the base of a tree.

'This bracken stuff?'

''Tisna bracken. See how the leaves point up as they unfurl, thick like writhing snakes?'

'Why, yes.' She was far more observant than him. On closer inspection, the leaves looked like a nest of angry green vipers, although he assumed also a bit like deer tongues.

Morven laid her basket down. 'Infused in hot water, these leaves mak' the best linctus fer slackening a consumptive cough.'

Intrigued, he stretched his hand out to pick some, but she tightened her fingers around his wrist. 'First, we must seek permission and give thanks to the power that placed this medicine in our path. Ye must never take wi'out first giving thanks.'

Chastised, he murmured, 'I won't, I promise.'

She released his wrist and closed her eyes, whispering her thanks. She spoke reverently, a strange ardency lighting her face. She looked so earnest, and the act appeared so holy, Nathaniel's chest filled with admiration. Following her lead, he also whispered his thanks, although he was careful to direct his appreciation toward the Lord and not Mother Earth.

'A linctus of this will help the master?'

'I believe so.' She began harvesting some leaves. 'I only take what I need. Ye must do the same. 'Tis important nae to weaken the plant; that way, ye can return here.'

'Couldn't we just dig up the clump and plant it at Scalan?'

She looked at him as if he were a foolish child. 'But then 'twould lose its magic. Hart's tongue thrives here, amongst the trees that shelter and protect it. Even if it survived, its healing properties would diminish. Special herbs grow in special places, or they lose their specialness. This is such a place. And here, the herb is free to all who need it.'

He nodded, seeing the wisdom of that.

'A forest is a living being, Nathaniel. The trees protect all the other life, even the silent folk who keep themselves hidden.' She gave him a faltering smile. 'Though ye can plant common herbs at Scalan like nettles, comfrey, and that. They grow all ower the place.'

He blinked at the depth of her superstition. The master had warned him that most rural folk believed as Morven did, taking as gospel that all manner of supernatural beings lived in almost every hillock and knoll. He fished his notebook from his pocket with a pot of ink and a quill and began sketching a likeness of the herb so he might recognise it again.

She peered over his shoulder, watching his deft strokes capture the plant and its surroundings. 'How clever! Where did ye learn to do that?'

He shrugged. 'I'm not sure I did. 'Twas born in me, I think.'

'As I was born wi' the healing in me.'

He nodded, his thoughts turning grave. 'Can you cure him, Morven?

The master is very dear to me; he is the father I never had. All at Scalan depend on him. Our mission there hangs on a thread. Father Paterson is that thread.'

She looked into his face, her expression softening so he feared what she saw, likely his many weaknesses, although she was too gracious to comment on them. Regard for her fluttered in his chest. He had long known he was different. That was likely the reason why his father rejected him.

'I canna promise to cure him. The master's been eaten wi' consumption fer years, damaging his lungs and Lord knows what else, but I'll bring all my healing power to work. Combined wi' yer prayers,' she gave him a crooked smile, 'we may work a miracle. Dinna gie up hope.'

'I won't.'

He continued to sketch, filling another page, this time with a drawing of a willowy young woman with a tender face and wary, cat-like eyes. Puzzled, Morven drew back, slanting her head, not recognising herself.

'So,' she ventured, 'efter yer da left ye wi' the master, did he never come back to see ye?'

He stilled his hand and looked up at her. 'He wrote to the master to check on my progress but not to me, other than to tell me that my mother was ill. I've not seen my father since the day my mother was buried.'

Morven's brows came together, making two sad little clefts. 'I'm sorry fer that.'

He put the finishing touches to his sketch and helped her to her feet. 'Such hardships are sent to try us,' he said, quoting the master. 'They help shape us into the guardians of the faith we must become.' Those had been the master's measured words when he'd asked about his father's lack of interest in him. 'I have tried to be worthy of the vows I will take by forgiving him.'

Morven looked curiously at him. 'And have ye?'

He frowned. 'I confess, I am still resentful. I understand what my father did was for the greater good of our clan and kinsmen, but I also know he gave little thought to my feelings or wishes. With God's guidance, I hope to fully forgive him.'

She snorted. 'Then, ye must hae a better heart than me. I doubt I could forgive such a thing. I'd still be bitter and hurting. I might try and hide it, especially from the master, but all the while, my wounds would fester.' She sighed, her sudden fierceness leaving her. 'But I'm quick to doubt and judge. That's long been my trouble. I once doubted Jamie. I near lost him through my doubting heart. I'm thinking 'tis as well ye're to be the priest and nae me.'

He blinked at her. No one had ever spoken to him in quite such a blunt and candid fashion. It was inspiring to know humble folk had the courage to do so and even more heartening that a young woman would. He had not known women could be so direct. But then, what woman had he known? Only Janet and she wished to mother him.

'You speak plainly,' he said. 'I like that.'

'What other way is there?'

'No, no. You're right to do so.' He stared at her, his admiration growing. Nothing daunted her, whilst almost everything frightened him, everything beyond the protective walls of Scalan. He imagined life outside the church would bring many opportunities for further rejection. That was why being a priest was best for him. Priests must give up all hope of a common life—a life that frightened him anyway. They lived a step removed from the flock they shepherded. In taking his vows, he could distance himself from the outside world, avoiding threatening situations and people, especially his father and brother. He would never have a wife, someone who might spurn him. Nor children. Youngsters were particularly perceptive at noticing flaws and weaknesses. Any child would quickly discover his defects and scorn him. At Scalan, he lived amongst those who shared his unwavering faith in the Lord, the only source of love for him. He could indulge his love of books and learning whilst fulfilling his father's wishes, and once ordained, his father might finally ascribe him some value. Over the years, Nathaniel had come to understand that taking the cloth was the safest, indeed, the only solution for him.

He blew on his drawing and closed his notebook, slipping it into his pocket. As a child, he had not thought that way. He considered Scalan a gaol, surrounded by the bleak hills that concealed its presence from the authorities. Only with time had he come to see Scalan as a refuge, the wild surrounding hills his armour, shielding him from the hurts of the outside world. He swallowed and gave Morven a brighter smile than he felt. 'So, what now?'

'We look fer coltsfoot fer the master's cough, juniper and woodruff to counter his fever. Then we climb the Bochel in search o' bullock's lung-wort.'

CHAPTER SIXTEEN

The Bochel was a rounded, dome-like hill, long thought to be a faery hill, although its name from the Gaelic *buachaille* meant shepherd. It guarded the entrance to the Braes of Glenlivet, watching over a wild landscape of hills and moors and concealing the northern approach to the college, rendering Scalan invisible to any but an informed traveller.

'Twas a steep climb, first on grassy, flower-strewn slopes, then through stubbly heather. When they reached the summit with its rocky cairn, they were both breathing hard, the toil more strenuous than Morven remembered. She kept forgetting about the bairn in her belly. 'Twas worth the effort, though; from here, the glen stretched away, revealing a wondrous landscape. A bewitching patchwork of rough grazing, heather moors and woodland snaked through with gushing burns and ringed by hills all far taller than this faery hill.

She spun around, laughing at Nathaniel as he wheezed, bent double, his hands on his knees. She pulled off her kertch, letting the wind rip her hair free. It billowed about her shoulders. She shouted over the wind. 'It quickens the heart, aye? All this.' She threw her arms wide.

Nathaniel pressed a hand to his heaving chest as he stared at the wild expanse. 'What grandeur the Almighty has made.' He turned apologetically to her. 'Though, of course, the company I enjoyed during the climb also had a hand in lifting my spirits.'

She dropped him a mock curtsy, pleased at the healthy flush on his cheeks, although conscious that she had half killed him putting it there. Nathaniel was hardly used to climbing hills.

'So,' he wheezed, 'where might we find this bullock's lungwort?'

'Nae up here. 'Tis too delicate a herb.' She pointed to the lower reaches of the hill.

'What? Then why ever did we climb up here?'

'Just fer the joy o' it.'

He stared at her, the wind bringing tears to his eyes, and then slowly smiled back, a rare sight but one that pleased her. Finally, he began to laugh. He spread his arms wide, staggering as the wind pummelled him, his sleeves and the legs of his breeches flattening around his limbs. Still laughing, he cried, 'The Lord breathes his glory upon us!' He dropped to his knees and clasped his hands together.

She turned away so he might commune with God in private.

On their stumble back down the hill, they were both lighter in spirit, their legs running away with them, making them laugh even more. When had Nathaniel last laughed? 'Twas hard to tell, but she thought it had been a while.

During their climb, Morven spied what looked like lungwort growing amongst the rich tapestry of flowers blooming on the hillside. She took note of the herb's position and now went straight to it, kneeling in the grass to give thanks and pinch off a harvest of downy leaves. A decoction, strained to remove irritating hairs, would make potent medicine for the master.

Nathaniel gaped at how quickly she made the find.

'Ower the years, I've grown keen forager's eyes,' she told him.

'I thank the Lord for it.' He drew out his notebook and began sketching.

By the time they were reseated on their garrons and trotting back to Scalan, Morven was satisfied with the contents of her creel. Juniper grew on the lower slopes of the Bochel, while woodruff, a plant of damp woods, grew deeper in the forest. Coltsfoot and knotgrass were easy to find, but bullock's lungwort was her crowning discovery. With these herbs, she had the makings of powerful medicine to counter the master's sickness.

When they reached Scalan, two men were working outside, hammering and sawing, constructing Andrew's coffin. They stopped and removed their bonnets, bowing their heads respectfully. Nathaniel crossed himself. The sight of the pitiful little coffin sank Morven's spirits. Somewhere, a mother was grieving. Andrew's family would be inconsolable.

A flutter in her belly made her catch her breath. She pressed a hand to her middle. The sensation came again, a rippling feeling, this time stronger, the wee soul making its presence known. She shivered with excitement. Yet her joy was tempered with guilt. What right had she to feel blessed when others suffered unimaginable sorrow? At times, 'twas hard to understand how the Creator worked.

A draught-horse was tethered to a tree inside the walled courtyard. Recognising the animal, Morven's heart sank. She glanced at Nathaniel, but he paid it no heed.

The physician was in the lobby with Father Ranald when they entered, stuffing a package inside his tailcoat. He fixed Morven with a cold stare, then narrowed his eyes at her basket of herbs. Florid blotches appeared above his sideburns.

Father Ranald took her arm and drew her forward. 'Your replacement, Mister Dalrymple. Morven has proven herself a skilled healer, invaluable to us here at Scalan what with scarlet fever running rampant through the glen. She knows how to cure it.'

'Good God,' the physician choked. 'You mean, you've given the care of your students over to this henwife?'

'She's hardly that,' the father retorted. 'The lass is a skilled herbalist.'

'And cares about her patients,' Nathaniel added.

'Meaning I do not?'

'I meant no ... no slur,' Nathaniel stammered.

'I think we all know Andrew died through your neglect,' the father flashed. He nodded at the bulge spoiling the hang of the physician's coat. 'You've been well paid for the harm ye've done. I've no wish to see you here again.'

'Nor I to come here.'

'We're agreed, then.'

Scowling, Dalrymple drew in his considerable girth, bowed to the father, and made a meal of squeezing past Nathaniel as he made for the door. He paused in the doorway and looked back, allowing himself a half-smile. 'You should know I've given the factor a detailed account of your actions, Mistress Innes. Mister McGillivray is now aware that a tenant he considered valuable has wed a practising witch who plies her craft openly in these glens despite the law forbidding witchcraft.' His lips curled in distaste. 'Concocting potions from poisonous weeds gathered on His Grace's own land.'

'Harmless herbs,' she countered, 'free to anyone who cares to gather them, unlike the sugar o' lead and vitriol o' iron ye use yerself. Such concoctions likely kill folk quicker than the afflictions they're meant to cure.'

Dalrymple's face reddened. 'The impudence of the piece! Hark at the tongue on her. Her neck must be harder than brass. She couldn't hope to understand real medicine, yet she turns the poor from established procedures practised by a trained physician. McGillivray will have something to say about this. He's an acquaintance, not least a magistrate.'

'Ye're threatening me?' Morven's chest tightened. How many times had Rowena warned her to bite her tongue?

'I am, madam.'

'Come, now,' Father Ranald soothed. 'The lass has done naught to challenge your position here. You did that yourself. I asked her to come; indeed, I fetched her. My doing, not hers.' He turned to Nathaniel.

''Tis the truth,' Nathaniel rushed to confirm. 'Morven has only done what was asked of her. And what she has achieved is little short of miraculous.'

Dalrymple scoffed. 'She's taken you in, then? A gangling, idol-kissing misfit, fooled by a pretty face.'

Father Ranald's nostrils flared. 'You'll leave Nathaniel out of this. And the poor you speak of haven't the coin to afford your fees, although that is only one reason they turn to women like Morven. She understands what ails the folk of these glens, their hardships. Generations of gathered wisdom lie behind her cures.'

Dalrymple dismissed the father's assertions with a derisory grunt, re-aiming his wrath at Morven. 'Well, I hope you've counted out every coin owed on your holding for the Lammas quarter day. 'Tis less than a week away. There'll be no clemency should the factor find you short.' He smiled thinly. 'I hear your husband's a brave man, though reckless. He took the king's shilling and serves in the duke's regiment. His Grace thinks highly of him.' He chuckled. 'And the duchess even more. Let's hope he's behaving like a model soldier. If not, if he so much as puts a foot wrong, I'll wager he'll find himself without a holding to return to.'

Morven reddened, but Nathaniel pulled her into the study before she could reply.

'Don't listen to him,' he urged. 'Only His Grace and his factor can make that decision. You said it yourself: the duke values your husband. He will want to keep him as a tenant. This man is trying to frighten you.'

She exhaled with a quiver. 'Dalrymple kens how to rile me. I suppose 'twas his intention.'

'I don't doubt he meant to alarm you.'

'But I canna lose Druimbeag. Jamie was born there; 'tis land his father once held. Druimbeag matters most to Jamie in the world.'

Confusion flickered in Nathaniel's eyes. He frowned. 'From your husband's letter, I gained the impression you matter most to him. I don't want you put from your home, but you mustn't let this man bully you, especially into giving up your healing craft or abandoning your patients.' He looked down at Struan.

The lad's brows shot up. 'Who's here?' he whispered. 'Is it the doctor who treated Andrew? I don't want him to cut me.'

Morven knelt and took the boy's hand; the skin had begun to peel away. 'I'll nae let him do that, I promise.'

Struan slumped back, his eyes full of trust. A precious thing, trust, something Dalrymple seemed not to value. She stroked the lad's forehead until his eyes grew heavy. She would abandon no one.

The front door slammed, followed moments later by a shrill whinnying. Morven peered through the window, watching horse and rider tear down the lonely track, the physician flogging the animal mercilessly, clods of mud flying from its hooves.

'How will you manage?' asked Nathaniel. 'Have you money set aside to pay your rent? Or is that a foolish question?'

She looked wretchedly at him.

'Perhaps I could write to the factor to plead your case. Or to His Grace. The factor is no friend to us here at Scalan. He despises papists and has repeatedly attempted to cancel our tenure and allot our acres elsewhere. Over the years, it has always been His Grace who saved our mission here, perhaps reluctantly, but he tolerates our presence, affording us his protection. I'm told his ancestors were devout Catholics, that he even follows the Roman faith himself, although not openly.'

She stared at him. 'Ye'd do that fer me?'

He looked puzzled. ''Tis no burden to write a letter, although I have never written one to a duke, and daring to go above the factor's head might anger Mister McGillivray. There is that to consider.'

'Or His Grace. Mightna yer letter anger His Grace?'

Nathaniel reflected. 'It's possible I could worsen your situation, yes.'

She groaned. Any letter would likely enrage both the duke and his factor. Pleading for leniency directly to His Grace was unimaginably bold. She knew of no one who had ever done such a thing or would know how. Yet, with no wages from Jamie and their first crop still in the ground, she'd be sunk should the factor demand payment. 'Twas customary to allow new tenants time to bring in their harvest and fatten their beasts for selling before demanding coin. McGillivray would hopefully extend her that grace. He had not asked for coin at Whitsun, pleased Jamie had brought the land back into production. 'Twas land few wanted. Many thought it cursed, believing that turning soil once worked by folk evicted from it would bring the same ill luck, especially when those put from the land had been treated as cruelly as Jamie's kin.

'Are you all right, Morven?'

She nodded. Her head ached with it all.

CHAPTER SEVENTEEN

Fort George

THE CELL'S MASSIVE IRON door creaked open, a shaft of light flooding in. Jamie winced and shielded his eyes. Groaning, Hal rolled to his feet from the stinking pallet they shared. Neither man could make out who stood in the doorway, their eyes smarting after days of solid darkness, but since their visitor had extended no greeting other than a grunt of amusement, they knew who he was.

'Dinner is served.' McBeath lobbed a loaf of bread into their cell, Fort George's infamous Black Hole. The brittle thud spoke of its staleness. 'Bon appetite.' He slid a jug of water across the cobbled floor.

Hal lurched forward to catch it before it toppled over, managing to right it in the nick of time.

'Dinnae go gorging yourselves, now.'

'What day is it?' Jamie croaked.

McBeath advanced into the cell, whacking the stone wall with his drill cane. Jamie jumped. 'Friday, and you will call me Sergeant.' He glanced back through the open door where two guards flanked the entrance.

'I meant, how long have we been here, Sergeant? I've lost all sense o' time or even if 'tis day or night.'

'Your defiance hasnae yet been forgotten if that's what you're asking, though I hear you're to be released.' McBeath laughed. 'Doubtless to fatten up for your march to Edinburgh. You look like scrawny beggars. It stinks in here.' He moved deeper into the shadows, turning so the light fell on him and Jamie could better see his face. He recognised the man's twitching smirk. Despite his vow to bite his tongue and not rise to any offence, the sight boiled his blood.

'Wonder how you'd fare pitted against me now?' McBeath mused. 'No' so well, I'll wager. You're naught but a bag o' bones.'

'Even half starved,' Hal growled, 'Jamie could outmatch ye wi' a sword any time he chooses. He could smash yer face wi' the swing o' one fist.'

'Is that so?' McBeath advanced on Hal, pinning him against the wall with his cane. 'And I could flatten you under the heel of my shoe and no' even notice I'd trodden on slime.'

'Lying drunkard,' Hal muttered.

'We are to go to Edinburgh?' Jamie's chest tightened. He would be even further from Morven and their half-made child. With every day that passed, Strathavon called more urgently to him.

'You heard.'

'When?'

'In ten days.'

'But why?'

'Some military matter that doesnae concern you.' McBeath pushed himself away from the wall, whipping his cane through the air with a flourish.

'What aboot the hervest?' Hal protested. 'I dinna ken what the weather's been doing in Stratha'an, if it's been fine or foul, yet I'm supposing my barley's been ripening. Who's to bring it in if I'm to march awa' sooth? My Eilidh's eight bairns to keep and a babe on the breast. Ye're surely nae expecting her to do all the reaping and gathering?'

McBeath rolled his eyes. 'I care no' a jot about your wife, McHardy. She and your brats can rot. Do you imagine I give a tinker's curse what betides any Strathavon muck-the-byre?'

'Suppose nae,' Hal muttered.

'And what made you think you'd be allowed furlough to bring in your grain?' McBeath scowled at Hal. 'Ye'll only turn it into whisky.'

'I just thocht—'

'Well, don't. Thinking doesnae suit you.'

Jamie rose to his feet. 'Harvesting's sore work,' he muttered. 'It must be done when the weather's fine. Left owerlong, crops rot in the ground. A ruined crop means hunger and suffering, even eviction. I dinna expect ye to care about that, but 'twill be hard toil fer the women we've left behind.'

McBeath wheezed with laughter. 'Ye're right. I mind no' a jot.'

Jamie drew an irritated breath. 'But the men imagined they'd be given leave to return for the harvest, that His Grace would want that. Rents depend on a decent harvest. His Grace must ken that.'

'Must he? I wouldnae know. I'm well rid o' the place.' McBeath whacked his cane. 'And you will call me Sergeant!'

Jamie tensed, watching the man swagger like a cock pheasant, arrogantly whipping his cane through the air until it whistled. Garrisoned here, his men had no way of knowing how their kinfolk fared in the glens. They must waste their days suffering the pointless drill parades called every morning and afternoon, or worse, like Hal and him, rotting in a dank cell. Having to address this heartless devil as Sergeant stuck in his throat.

'How did ye escape gaol?' he ground out through clenched teeth. 'I've been wondering about that since I got here. Since I learned that *you* were our sergeant. I supposed McGillivray would hang ye or at least have ye thrown in gaol for a lengthy stretch, that if he couldna stretch your neck, he'd stretch your sentence to make up for nae seeing ye swing. Yet here ye are, and a sergeant, no less.'

'Aye, wouldn't you like to know?'

'I would.' Jamie sank back onto his pallet, the only comfort in the miserable cell save for a brimming pail stinking in the far corner. 'I'd like to ken how ye accomplished such a thing.'

As he suspected, McBeath couldn't resist the urge to crow.

'You'll have heard o' the Recruiting Act?'

'The law that lets magistrates press criminals into the army?'

'And smugglers.'

Jamie shot McBeath a look—his jibe had needled. Most glen folk had little choice but smuggle if they wished to keep a roof over their heads.

McBeath chuckled. 'Who'd have thought the law would come to my aid?'

'How did it?' Jamie choked. Seeing the former exciseman strut in government-issue scarlet was disturbing enough, but seeing him kilted in a mocking travesty of highland dress offended him to the core. McBeath had never hidden the fact that he hated Highlanders. He believed them a lesser breed, populating the lowest rung in society. Jamie turned away, the reek of sour whisky in his nostrils. McBeath's cheeks were pitted and reddened through drink. He fingered his own chin, now bearded. He had lost count of how long he'd been here, half-starved and frozen despite the garrison beyond their cell's thick walls enjoying the gentle warmth of a highland summer.

'Since the jury decided I wasnae so corrupt I needed hanging,' McBeath went on, 'McGillivray turned to the Recruiting Act. He wanted rid of me and had me enlisted in the Northern Fencibles, no doubt collecting the levy coin for his trouble. After all, I'm a fine example of Scottish manhood with years of experience defending the duke's lands from smugglers and ruffians.' He puffed his chest out and strutted to the door, furtively checking the guards were still in place. 'In return, I gained my freedom ... of sorts. You'll understand I had no choice in the matter, but since I'd little desire to spend the rest of my days in gaol—'

'But if McGillivray wanted rid o' ye, why nae just leave ye to rot?'

McBeath shrugged. 'I was an embarrassment, a reminder of his humiliation, something he's no' forgiven me for. With me enlisted, he perhaps thought his humiliation might be removed along with me. We were once valuable allies.'

'But ye soured all that by playing him for a fool.'

McBeath laughed. 'Yet made a tidy profit. I'm told McGillivray never wants to see me again. Suits me. I've no wish to see him or godforsaken Strathavon again. The glen's infested with papists and Jacobites. Rife with witchery,' he added.

Jamie prickled at the insinuation he knew was aimed at his aunt, yet he was relieved to hear McBeath had no wish to return—if it were true. The man was still a danger to Rowena.

'I doubt McGillivray expected the army to promote me.' McBeath laughed. 'My methods of discipline saw to that.'

'Yer ruthlessness,' Hal muttered.

'Call it what you want, but once I let Captain Cumming know I was familiar with Strathavon, where the duke's latest recruits were levied, he put me in charge of the Strathavon unit. Hence, you.'

Jamie stared at him. 'Are ye saying ye planned this?'

A smirk spread across McBeath's face. 'Did I expect you to enlist? Oh, aye, I knew you would. No' only have I been expecting you here, I paid Ghillie and Dougal good coin to make sure o' it.'

'*What?*'

'I had them spread rumours of your prowess in the neighbouring glens, knowing rivals would prick up their ears. Any suggestion a rival lord might poach one of his tenants would enrage His Grace, particularly if that tenant had already proven himself able with the sword.' McBeath sniggered. 'The duke wouldnae stand for that.'

'Scheming bastard,' Hal growled.

McBeath stiffened. 'My parents were legally wed. I doubt the same could be said of yours.' He lifted Hal's chin with the point of his cane and stared coldly at him. 'My faither's a Kirk minister, and you'll no' speak ill of my mither.'

'Twisted divil,' Hal choked.

McBeath whipped his cane away. 'I'll admit, McHardy, I didnae expect you. You were a wee surprise.'

'You mean,' Jamie stammered. 'The business with Alec?'

'Worked as intended.'

Jamie stared at him. 'But ... to what purpose?'

McBeath looked pityingly at him. 'Repayment for past wrongs, for deceiving me, for whipping up feelings in Strathavon so that the blasted muck-the-byres were baying for my blood.'

'Ye did that yerself,' Hal flashed.

McBeath's breath rasped murderously. 'An eye for an eye, Innes. I've dreamt of little else since the day o' the duel.'

'But how does this settle scores? You're trapped in the army, same as me.'

'You'll see. I've barely gotten started. If you thought the last few weeks were hard,' McBeath chuckled. 'They were only a taster.'

'Christ,' Hal groaned.

'Months I mouldered in Elgin's tollbooth awaiting trial.' McBeath bared his teeth at Jamie. 'That was *your* doing. Now that I'm free, I will have my pound of flesh.'

'Yer what?'

McBeath gave Jamie another pityingly look. 'You were doubtless spawned in some smoking dunghill, so I'll concede 'tis unlikely you were favoured with the education I received. I'll make it plain. I passed the time imagining how I'd make you suffer, how it might be done. I saw it in my head, and when 'twas safe to sleep, even better in my dreams. Took my mind off the rats and filth, the constant danger of having my throat slit by a fellow prisoner, one I'd likely put there myself. Time dragged slow as torture, but I used it well, honing my hatred to a razor's edge. A weapon to hurt ye with.' He stalked to the door and turned back. 'And dinnae imagine I've forgotten about your aunt. I thought about her, too, though most o' that at night on the flat o' my back.' He laughed. 'I swear, I will have her yet.'

'Nae whilst I draw breath,' Jamie growled.

'What can you hope to do about it?'

Turning, McBeath strode through the open door, kicking his leg out at the last moment. The water jug spun into a corner, spraying its contents. A dark stain seeped into the cracks between the cobbles. The door slammed shut, plunging them back into darkness.

'Jamie,' Hal said after a moment.

'Aye?'

'I've found the bread.'

'Good.'

'I dinna ken if thon's how I'd put it.'

'Meaning?'

'Have ye a chisel on ye?'

'Christ!'

They huddled together for warmth, gnawing on the bread, trying to soften it with their tongues.

'My gums hurt,' Hal muttered.

'And mine. 'Tis like eating rock.'

'I've never eaten rock, but I'm thinking it mun taste better than this. What d'ye suppose the divil plans to do to us?'

'Lord knows. I pray he doesna hurt Morven. I should never have left her.'

CHAPTER EIGHTEEN

THEY WERE RELEASED AT dawn and stumbled out onto the parade
ground, dragging in lungfuls of air rich with the tang of the sea. Jamie
blinked as a growing light in the east transformed his world from darkest
black to soft grey. Above, stars were fading into the morning sky, gulls
skirling and wheeling. He turned to Hal, able to make out his face for the
first time in weeks. He looked ghastly. Hal's face was grey, his eyes ringed
with dark circles.

Drums sounded the reveille, a long roll on the snare drum, signifying
the start of the military day. Jamie again took in the bewildering scale of
the place. Fort George was colossal, a fortress of earthworks and sloping
stone ramparts built on a promontory jutting into the Moray Firth. The
fort bristled with canons and heavy guns. No expense had been spared to
ensure the Highlands could never again rise in rebellion. But there was
little time to dwell on the impossibility of escaping such a place; they
were quick-marched back to their barracks, struck with the blunt end of
a halberd whenever their trembling legs stumbled beneath them.

'Morning parade in ten minutes,' McBeath barked. 'You will assemble
for inspection.'

Their barrack room was home to all ten raw recruits from Strathavon,
cramped quarters stuffed with crude wooden berths and the meagre belongings of Jamie's fellow glensmen. Knapsacks and clothing hung from
wooden pegs by each shared berth, a hearth in the far wall giving some
warmth. An appetising aroma wafted from there. Although spartan, the
room felt like heaven after their wretched cell. Here, the men slept, cooked,
shared what food and news they had and kept their weapons and uniforms
clean.

Jamie swayed in the doorway, gripping the wooden frame as the room darkened.

'Steady, now.' Hal braced him under the arms until his legs ceased trembling, and the room came back into focus.

'Forgive me.' He glanced at the first berth. Archie lay face down there, his naked back crusted with half-healed scabs. Sickened, he knelt and touched the lad's forearm. 'Have the others been looking after ye whilst I mouldered in the Black Hole?'

'Jamie!' Archie gaped at him. 'Thank the Lord.' He gripped his hand. 'I'm told Captain Cumming only reduced my sentence because o' you. I canna tell ye how grateful I am.' He swallowed, his throat convulsing. 'And how sorry fer the trouble I've caused.'

'Och, I put voice to my rage, certainly, I couldna help myself, but I did naught to help ye. Such is my shame. I stood powerless in the face o' British justice.'

'Still, I couldna have taken more. My will was spent.' Archie hung his head. 'I'm shamed to say, by then, I wished only to die.'

Jamie felt for the lad. 'But ye didna die,' he said softly. 'Ye held onto yer dignity. Were I in yer place, I dinna ken if I could've done the same. I'd mebbe have squalled like a babby. Naeone kens how they'd endure such a thing.'

Archie's eyes filled. 'Bless ye,' he whispered.

'They publicly flayed yer flesh to break the men's spirits,' Hal growled.

Jamie agreed. 'Likely supposing 'twould deter others thinking o' deserting, but I doubt 'twill work. Brutality only ever breeds resentment.'

He looked up as his fellow glensmen came crowding around, still scrambling into their uniforms. It took a moment for some to recognise him. Once the first shock at his appearance passed, the men's faces lighted in recognition, a response that heartened him. But expressions darkened again when they took in his haggard appearance, his and Hal's wasted bodies.

Allan Ross cleared his throat. ''Tis good to see ye, Jamie. And you, Hal.'

There was a ripple of agreement.

Jamie rose to his feet with some difficulty. 'And you, Allan. 'Tis good to see anything again.'

'We've rotted in the dark these past weeks,' Hal said. 'Shivering like rats in a burrow.'

Jamie frowned. 'I hope you understand it wasna my choice to abandon ye.'

'Now, dinna fash, lad, we ken that.' Willie Thom pressed a hand on his shoulder. 'I'm only glad ye had each other, and no man was left to rot alone. That could drive ye mad.'

Hal forced a laugh. 'We've grown closer than man and wife, though dinna go telling my Eilidh.'

Jamie drew a weary breath. 'I can still hardly believe McBeath's now our sergeant. He means to have his revenge fer the duel we fought. I pray 'tis only me he makes suffer, and he's more lenient with the rest o' ye.'

Robbie Fraser snorted. 'Leniency isna in McBeath's nature. We've all felt his ire and suffered his temper.'

'I feared as much.'

'But he'll nae better us,' Willie Thom said. 'We're men o' Stratha'an and Glenlivet. Strong in heart and blood. He might scorn us, but that only makes us stronger.'

Jamie nodded. 'If we can come together as a well-disciplined unit, he'll likely find it harder to hurt us.'

'Aye, army discipline could shield us from the scheming divil's mischief,' Robbie Fraser muttered.

The idea was already growing in Jamie's mind. Playing McBeath at his own game was likely the best way to thwart him. 'The devil has the army's full authority behind him,' he mused, 'sanctioning his every action, nae matter how brutal or offensive. But if we work as a well-oiled military unit, drilled and practised, fighting men to make any colonel proud, we could frustrate the devil.' He hesitated. McBeath had already made it plain he gave no thought to who he hurt in his eagerness for revenge. He couldn't care less if their families starved. In suggesting they work together to thwart his plans, was he putting his men at risk?

Willie Thom gave a low whistle. 'Well said, Jamie. What hope has the divil against smuggling men who've long worked thegither to thwart the gaugers?'

'Aye,' said Allan Ross, 'we're neighbours and kinsmen. We share the same love o' our hills. I say we use that allegiance against the divil.'

Jamie nodded, looking at Archie. 'One man is easy prey for him, but ten men of kindred heart will be harder to break.'

They cheered and lifted him onto Willie Thom's shoulders, and he let himself be carried around the room. For long, these men had contrived to thwart the gaugers. They were used to colluding against the authorities, only now they would be doing so under the guise of performing their patriotic duty for the king—a hard thing for McBeath to fault or punish, especially if they became the best at what they did. He gripped the hands lifted up to him. Not so long ago, these men had distrusted him; now, he shared such an allegiance with them it stirred his blood. As their corporal, they were his responsibility. He must do everything he could to keep them safe and ultimately return them to their families.

John Gordon helped him down. 'Ye're half starved, Jamie. I can feel yer ribs.'

'Hal, too.' Allan Ross shook his head. 'He's slender as a stripling.'

'Who're ye calling a stripling?'

'Are ye hungry?' Angus Grant lifted the cooking pot lid and peered inside.

'Hungry doesna near cover it,' Hal muttered. 'But thirsty more. My tongue's dry as an auld quern stone.'

Angus emptied the water pail into two cups. 'Go easy,' he warned. They lifted their cups with trembling hands and drained the water in one long draught.

'Niver tasted sweeter.' Hal looked longingly at the empty pail.

'I'll run to the well fer more.' Young Atholl Birnie grabbed the pail and headed for the door.

'Quick, then,' warned Allan. ''Tis almost roll call. Ye ken what he'll do if ye're late or havena right laced yer hair.'

'Has he been hard on ye?' Jamie searched the men's faces.

Robbie Fraser shifted uncomfortably. 'He might be a drill sergeant now, but at heart, he's still the Black Gauger. He calls us muck-the-byres, especially when officers are within earshot. Or heather-lowpers.' His face darkened. 'When he explained what he meant by that, the officers fell aboot laughing.' He shook his head. 'He scorns all Highland folk but Stratha'an folk most o' all.'

'And Glenlivet folk,' Willie said.

'Aye, and Glenlivet folk.'

Jamie nodded uneasily. Their officers would side with McBeath, especially against highland men, although in assuming that, he perhaps did some a disservice.

'Why must our officers speak wi' such foul mouths?' Donald MacKay scowled. 'I dinna understand their need to debase us at every turn. Ensign Stubbs called me a dim-witted turd when I asked him to repeat his order in Gaelic. He says oor language is heathen and primitive.' He shook his head. 'The ancient tongue o' the Gael.'

Hal sank onto his berth. 'He says it to crush yer pride.'

'I ken he does. It mak's me want to knock his teeth out.'

Willie Thom flexed his fingers. 'And me, but 'tis best nae to heed his insults.'

'Willie's right,' said Jamie. 'Try nae to rise to the offence. It only gives them more excuse to punish us.'

'I dinna want to fight them,' said Donald. 'We're meant to be on the same side.'

Jamie sighed. 'I like to think they canna all be bad.'

'Some are fair,' Archie said from his bed. 'The junior officers mostly.'

Allan Ross tactfully changed the subject. 'We kept yer weapons in good order, taking turns to oil yer swords and sharpen yer musket flints. Now we must ready ourselves fer inspection.'

Hal fingered his beard with grimy fingers. 'We've been told to appear fer inspection.'

Allan stared at him. 'What? Looking like that? Ye'd better clean yerselves up, then.'

Hal dragged himself to his feet, searching for a lace to club back his lank hair. Atholl hurried in with the water, and they drank again before using the rest to wash. They were struggling into clean shirts when the drums and fifes began beating the Troop, calling them to assemble for inspection.

'Hurry,' said Allan. 'Help me get them into their tunics.'

The men gathered to fasten buttons, strapping their belts across their shoulders. Allan passed them their muskets and swords whilst Angus Grant gave their scuffed shoes a quick buff and clapped their bonnets on their heads. Jamie glanced at Hal—he looked far from respectable. Marshalling what remained of their strength, they followed the others out to the main parade ground. Captain Cumming had a reputation for being a hard man to please; the men knew it to their cost. McBeath must also know it. That worried him. It was still half-light, but he could see McBeath waiting alongside Captain Cumming, an anticipatory smirk stretching his lips as he watched the men gather in their companies.

Roll call went without incident, with the men answering when their names were called. The drums then struck a quick march, and the ranks wheeled about, parading before their captains and flanking lieutenants. Jamie glanced at Hal. His face was grey and greased with sweat. After weeks of inactivity and little food, the sudden exertion made Jamie's head swim. He also broke out in a sweat. Weak like this, neither of them could keep this up for long. As they marched past Captain Cumming, McBeath extended the blunt end of his halberd and prodded Jamie in the back.

'Stand tall, man!'

He stumbled, keeping his head down, then halted abruptly, Captain Cumming's silver-tipped cane preventing him from marching on.

'Good God!' the captain exclaimed. 'This rascal's bearded.'

Hal slammed into his back, and the captain exclaimed again. 'God alive, and this one!'

'Highlanders are often loathe to wash and shave, sir,' McBeath observed. 'These two wretches in particular.'

'Wretches indeed. They're both nasty ill-dressed, and dirty beyond sufferance.'

'But sir,' Hal blurted. 'There wasna time—'

'Keep quiet,' McBeath barked. 'You will speak when you're spoken to.'

'I'll have the rascally fellows' names,' Captain Cumming snapped. 'They're not fit to be seen. Look at them; they're half fagged. The drunken sods have been in their cups.'

McBeath eagerly supplied their names. 'Corporal James Innes, sir, and Private Haldan McHardy.'

Cumming frowned. 'Innes? I've heard some good of him, although I recall his conduct was insubordinate at the recent flogging of a deserter, bordering on outright mutinous.' He tutted in displeasure. 'Now he's disgraced himself and his whole company.' He beckoned them out of the ranks. 'In punishment for dishonouring your fellow men,' he snapped, 'Corporal Innes will endure ten days of hard drill in marching order.' He turned to Hal. 'You, Private, will suffer five. Now get out of my sight. And get yourselves clean-shaven.'

'Aye, sir,' they stammered.

The captain moved on, encircled by junior officers, all pulling faces and acting as if he and Hal had given off an offensive smell, which Jamie reflected they likely had.

McBeath smirked back at them.

CHAPTER NINETEEN

Strathavon

THE SUN HAD NEWLY risen as Morven picked her way through a forest of pine and rowan, avoiding the many moss-covered stones strewn between the trees. The final stretch to Druimbeag's shieling was a punishing climb up windswept pastures but 'twas a glorious day for it. The land shone burnished emerald, mist lingering in the hollows, a sweet, hay-rich scent carried on the breeze. Despite the child growing heavy in her belly, long hours toiling on the land had kept her strong, that and her treks to Scalan. Thankfully, the master had responded to her treatments, although he was still weak. He ofttimes wished to do more than she thought advisable, and the risk of a relapse was great, but already, he was more robust. His breath whistled less, and he could speak without exhausting himself.

The stone hut and dairy were empty when she reached them, save for a few staved wooden coggs and churns and a cheese press. She shaded her eyes in the doorway, seeing Sarah in the distance, herding the cattle with a switch of hazel. She raised her hand to her. Sarah returned the gesture and waited for her to catch up.

As she neared, the beasts crowded forward. Morven greeted them affectionately, scratching behind their ears and murmuring to them. The calves were less sure of her and kept to their mother's sides, one woolly youngster giving her a snorting sniff. They were in fine condition. Lush summer grazing had put a sheen on their coats. Most of the cattle were Rowena's; only three cows and their calves belonged to her and Jamie. It had been Rowena's suggestion to keep the folds together over the summer months and make them Sarah's responsibility. Then, Morven could devote her time to tending Druimbeag's fields and the Scalan community, work that would hopefully yield a return she could put toward her rental.

She smiled at Sarah over the backs of the beasts, grateful for her help.

Herding and dairying were considered women's work. She should be helping, but without Jamie, there weren't enough hours in the day to do everything that needed doing. She hoped Sarah understood and didn't feel forgotten up here with naught but a few cows for company.

Their curiosity sated, the cattle wandered away, flicking flies from their haunches with their tails. Shaggy heads were soon bent to the turf, tongues and jaws busy.

'Ye're doing a grand job, Sarah,' she said. 'I hardly ken how to thank ye. I'm beholden fer all the butter and curds I've found at my door, a welcome sight after long nights tending those still sick at Scalan.'

Sarah's expression didn't change, but a muscle tightened in her jaw. She dropped her gaze to Morven's belly. 'Ye're a size now,' she said in greeting. 'Does it hurt?'

'Nay,' Morven laughed. 'But I'm slower, and 'tis harder to bend down.'

Sarah grimaced. 'Ye'll be regretting yer tender nights wi' Jamie now then since he was planning on leaving ye.'

Morven blinked. 'Jamie never planned to leave me. He had nae choice.'

'Didna look that way where I was standing.' A layer of scorn coated Sarah's words. 'He looked right keen to tak' the king's shilling. Took it from Her Grace, plundering her mouth wi' his tongue to find it.' She snorted. 'He made the deed look that scandalous, folk cheered him on. Lads lined up fer a chance to do the same. 'Tis why so many enlisted.'

Morven's heart clenched at the image. 'Ye're wrong,' she choked. 'That's nae what happened.'

'I was there. 'Tis still the talk o' the glen.'

That much was true; folk were whispering about Jamie. Morven had heard some of the talk and couldn't help feeling bitter. After everything he'd done for the folk o' Stratha'an, risking his life with her granda's old sword, did folk still nae understand the kind o' man he was? But then, he hadna put the gossips straight. Jamie told no one of the duke's threats but her. Her heart thumped. She was doing it again: doubting him. How could she? Jamie was given no time or opportunity. He was an honourable man; he would put others before himself and carefully consider his actions. She must never forget that.

'I'm sorry if ye think that,' she countered, 'and of yer own cousin. I thought ye kent Jamie better.'

'I thought so, too, but folk are calling him a turncoat, quick to join the king's forces. They say he must've forgot all the ill the redcoats have done here ower the years, burning and plundering, killing innocent ferming folk as well as rebels. They killed my da's folk.' Sarah swiped at the grass with her switch. 'How could he forget that and march off to join them?'

Morven's chest tightened. She'd seen the looks folk gave her in chapel, their reluctance to meet her gaze, but she'd imagined it sympathy for the plight she found herself in, pity for the way Jamie had been used. *Mother Earth, did they pity her her choice o' husband?*

'Might I walk wi' ye?' she asked, frowning. The cattle had almost vanished over the brow of a hill.

Sarah shrugged without enthusiasm and trudged after them.

'Who's saying this, Sarah?'

'Near everyone.'

Only months ago, folk had rushed to help Jamie restore Druimbeag. How could they change their opinions so quickly? Morven swallowed. 'D'ye ken why Jamie joined the duke's regiment, Sarah? Wi' all the idle talk there's been, the spiteful blither blather, have folk whispered about that?'

Sarah gave no answer only tramped on, scything her switch back and forth, lopping off seed heads in the grass. Eventually, she muttered, 'I suppose folk think a man like Jamie must want more from life than just toiling fer a crust.'

'They imagine the army will give him a better life?'

'Mebbe. Most suppose he was seduced by the glamour and thrill, wearing the plaid, carrying arms. Many lads were. When they saw Jamie tak' the shilling, they wished to do the same. Folk look up to him. He's a passionate man. I'm sure ye ken that better than most. He can read and write. He could rise through the ranks and lead an easier life in the army than ever he could here.' Sarah glowered at the surrounding hills. 'Here there's naught fer him but struggle and toil, working land that'll never be his.'

'Ye think Jamie yearns fer a soft life?'

'Why nae? He's naught to his name but an agreement binding him to work land the law says belongs to another. A wife he must provide fer through the sweat o' his brow.'

'I can provide fer myself,' Morven flashed. 'I've healing skills folk will pay fer, even if 'tis only in kind.'

'So has Mam, but she still struggles. Even when Da was alive, she spent much o' her day bent to the grind.'

Morven sighed. 'We all must if we wish to survive.'

'Aye, but now there's a bairn coming, Jamie must graft even harder. Mebbe, he thought to escape that by joining the army.'

Morven stared at Sarah, but the girl only tramped on; she was forced to hurry after her. How could Sarah judge Jamie so cruelly? He lived by his principles, yet Sarah had casually cast him as a scoundrel. 'Ye're wrong,' she returned. 'Jamie enlisted because His Grace left him nae choice.'

'Aye, so ye said.'

Again, the inexplicable scorn. Did Sarah truly believe her cousin would abandon his family to join the redcoats? It went against everything he held dear. Mother o' God, was that what folk were saying? She peered sidelong at Sarah. Did she resent being left alone with the beasts, fancying some indignity in that? Or feel overlooked by her mother? There had been some jealousy before. Yet they'd put that behind them. She pictured Jamie striding away in the half-dark the morning he left her, ordered to join his regiment. 'Twas the last she'd seen of him. Could folk truly have turned against him? Another thought struck. Perhaps Sarah still coveted her cousin. Oh, please, let it be that.

'D'ye still feel something fer him, Sarah?' she ventured. 'I ken ye once had feelings fer yer cousin. Are ye nae happy wi' Alec?'

Sarah scowled at her. 'Leave Alec out o' this. He'd never do such a shameful thing. Ye might be lawfully wed wi' a bairn in yer belly, but my Alec would never leave me like that, nae matter what choice he was given.'

'I didna mean to suggest he would. I love my brother. But did the tattle-tongues tell ye the whole tale?'

Sarah looked warily at her.

'Jamie enlisted to save his family. The duke threatened to evict us all if Jamie didna join his regiment. You, William, yer mam at Tomachcraggen, all those at Delnabreck and Druimbeag. Jamie couldna let that happen.'

Sarah appeared unsurprised by this. She stalked on, scowling at the ground.

'D'ye still think 'twas shameful? Should Jamie have let that happen?'

Sarah's pale eyes flashed. 'Weel, mebbe what he did wasna shameful, only the way he did it.'

'What? How did he do it?'

'He turned up near the end o' the fair, likely as full o' drink as the rest and went storming up to Her Grace, bowing and scraping. I swear, he stooped as low as any treacherous southron bootlicker. That pleased Her Grace. She laughed and clapped her hands, fooled by his manners and handsome face. She made a great show o' choosing a shiny shilling, holding it up fer the crowd to see, then slipped it atween her lips. Folk gasped to think Jamie would tak' it from her. I imagine they thought better o' him.'

Morven's heart clenched.

'Yet up he stepped, bold as ye like and took her in his arms. He pressed himself that brazenly upon her, she staggered back whilst he ravaged her mouth wi' his tongue.' Sarah snorted. 'He made such a meal o' it, folk cheered him on, whistling and calling out what else he might do wi' his tongue. All so he could join the red-backed divils,' she finished in disgust.

Sarah's description left Morven speechless. Her eyes nipped with grief. After a moment, she rasped, 'Nae matter how it looked, he didna do it willingly. It tore him apart, especially when he learned he must leave me carrying his bairn.' She exhaled, trying to calm herself. 'Ye see that, aye?'

'I suppose.'

'I'm glad. I wouldna like to quarrel ower this. 'Tis done, nae matter how, though I'd give all I have fer it nae be so. I dinna ken when I'll see him again.' She quelled the quiver in her voice. 'When he'll see his bairn, but I mustna think on that. I've the harvest to bring in, the rental to find. I swore I'd keep Druimbeag safe.'

They walked on in silence. She could feel Sarah's thoughts fermenting but hadn't the heart to chide her further. The lass had been a great help. She was young; Jamie's actions had plainly scandalised her.

Sarah sniffed. 'They'll be starting the hervest at Tomachcraggen if the weather stays fine. Alec and yer da will reap.'

Morven's throat tightened. If he were here, Jamie would scythe Rowena's fields. He thought the world of his kinswoman.

'I canna believe folk think so ill o' him,' she choked.

Sarah shrugged. ''Twas how it looked. 'Tis just talk, though.'

'Well, if you hear any more, I hope ye'll set folk straight.'

Sarah nodded and tramped on, Morven stumbling after her. Her heart thumped woodenly; Lord, her world was falling apart.

As they trudged on, it became plain the cattle were no longer grazing but heading toward a gully where a fast-flowing burn cascaded, a sheltered place rich with birch and alder. The wind had picked up, and the gully offered protection from blustering winds. The weather could change quickly in the hills, something they were both aware of. The cattle even more.

Sarah glowered at the darkening sky. 'Ye'd best be turning back afore ye end up as droukit as I'm aboot to be. Ye've the bairn to think o'.'

Sarah was right. To the south, Ben Avon and the Cairngorm peaks had disappeared in louring cloud. The wind had a damp feel. Morven looked into the distance. Under the storm clouds, a golden light still shone, all that remained of what had promised to be a fine day. Grey wisps streaked its brilliance, revealing the rain that sheeted down in the mountains and was headed their way.

'What about you?'

'I'll shelter at the bothy on the next hillside, the Gaulrigs shieling wi' the McGrigor women. Ye've likely more important things to do. Lads to nurse at Scalan.' Sarah's mouth twitched. 'I hear there's a handsome young priest there wi' the face o' an angel.'

'Ye mean Nathaniel?'

'Aye, that'll be him.'

Morven frowned. Nathaniel was earnest and sincere, but he didn't make her heart leap like Jamie did. He was a sensitive young man, perhaps a damaged one, his face more that of a child than a man. She frowned. 'I dinna like to leave ye like this.'

'I'm used to it.'

A gusting crosswind caught them. Morven staggered, shielding her belly. 'I'll go, then, but I'm sorry we had sore words.'

Sarah nodded, and Morven reluctantly headed back down the hill. Pushing a hand into the folds of her arisaid, she found the package knotted there. 'Twas from Jamie; she knew his spidery handwriting and could tell he had penned his words in haste. It came that morning by runner, the lad slogging through the night to bring it. She longed to know what it said. Nathaniel would tell her, but she was needed at Tomachcraggen for the harvest. Everyone must lend a hand, though what use she'd be with her belly growing larger by the day 'twas hard to see.

The storm nipped at her heels all the way home, catching her on the final stretch as she broke from the trees. Rain battered against her back. She gasped, pulling her arisaid up to cover her head, blinking water from her eyes. Two mounted figures were waiting in her yard. The smaller got off his horse and held the other's reins while he also dismounted. The larger then strode about the yard with his hands clasped behind his back, peering into the byre and barn, then made his way to the rigs to examine her ripening crop. She knew the factor's swaggering gait. Lord, what did he want?

They were sheltering in the cottage doorway when she reached them. Highland hospitality, not to mention common decency, decreed she must invite them in. 'Sirs,' she said in English. 'Will you come in out of the rain?'

The factor raised his brows, perhaps surprised that she had spoken in English. He grimaced at her rustic home, likely thinking it a hovel, but when a sudden squall pummelled and soaked him, he muttered, 'I believe we'll do that,' and pushed his way in. His manservant followed.

The fire was still lit despite the rain hissing on the hot peats. Morven shook off her wet arisaid and indicated the chairs by the fire. She had left her latest gathering of herbs on one and quickly removed it. 'You'll have a seat?'

The factor pointedly ignored the chairs, forcing his manservant to do the same. He loitered by the window, blocking out most of the light. Sitting in such a primitive place, dark and reeking of peat smoke, was perhaps beneath a man like McGillivray. He frowned up at the cross beams from where more herbs hung.

'I'll come to the point.' He frowned, appearing to only now notice her condition. 'Please,' he indicated one of the chairs, 'perhaps you should ....'

She shook her head. She would hear whatever he had to say whilst standing at his level.

'Very well. Certain allegations have been levelled against you. Accusations of an unsavoury and disturbing nature.'

She looked blankly at him.

He grew irritated, frowning at his manservant.

'He says,' the man began in Gaelic.

'I understand him.'

'Madame,' the factor went on, 'it has been suggested that you are a practising witch. Or, at least, a folk healer who presumes to know more about medicine than a trained physician legally licensed to practise.'

So that was it; Dalrymple had carried out his threat. 'I help sick folk, sir,' she replied. 'I'll not deny it, but I'm no witch. That is Dalrymple's word.'

McGillivray held up his hand, appearing already tired of her. 'As I told Doctor Dalrymple, his accusations bear investigating, but my main concern must always be for His Grace and his property, that those given the care of it are doing so to the letter of their lease agreement. And that any money due is paid.'

'Of course,' she stammered.

He cleared his throat, appearing ill at ease. 'I understand your husband has joined the duke's regiment. I commend him for that, but he has left you in a vulnerable position.' He indicated her swollen belly with an embarrassed flick of his hand. 'Since you are without your husband, I feel I should extend you some clemency.'

She blinked in astonishment. 'Thank you, sir.'

'Having examined your holding, land cleared and put to the plough, the difference wrought here, ripe grain almost ready for harvest, I can see that thus far you and your husband have honoured the articles of your lease agreement. You've worked hard, Mistress Innes. That pleases me. What I've seen here, at least outside your home, pleases me.'

Astonished, she opened her mouth to reply, but he was talking again, eager to leave her distasteful home and presence.

'I initially offered the lease of Druimbeag to your husband after observing his extraordinary bravery, his grasp of the principles of honour and fairness. I feel justified in my decision even though no feu duty has yet been received. I expect that to change. Any dispute Doctor Dalrymple has with you shall therefore remain a matter for him. I'll not be drawn into it. But,' he stressed, 'I expect you to pay the full amount owed at Martinmas. Is that clear?'

Mother Earth, less than three months to find a year's rental coin.

'Mistress Innes?'

'Yes, sir,' she croaked.

He nodded at his manservant, who was standing expressionless. 'Donnell.'

The man crossed the floor and wrenched the door open, scurrying out to fetch the factor's horse. McGillivray turned back to her. 'I should bring in your grain before the weather worsens. That is my advice to you.' He bowed stiffly. Ducking under the door lintel, he lurched out into the rain.

CHAPTER TWENTY

Fort George

JAMIE'S HEAD SWAM, WEARINESS washing over him in waves. Beside him, Hal stumbled, made clumsy by the relentless musket drills and endless marching exercises they must practise. Sergeant McBeath reacted instantly, lashing out at Hal with his fist. He sent him reeling into the long grass, where he landed on his belly, his kilt fanning up his back, exposing downy white buttocks.

'Blundering plank o' wood!' McBeath aimed at Hal's buttocks with his shoe. 'Get up, ye useless muck-the-byre.'

'Let him be,' Jamie growled. 'Fer pity's sake, he's long past had enough.' Lowering his musket, he trudged into the grass to help Hal up.

McBeath smirked as he swung his leg back and took perverse pleasure in slamming his iron-tipped shoe into Hal's vulnerable flesh. He kicked Hal to his feet to the sniggering laughter of the watching soldiers.

Jamie gritted his teeth. The impotence of their situation incensed him. Naught in life had prepared him for a situation where he must take a blow he could not return, an insult he could not hurl back at his tormentor, not without dire repercussions. He couldn't even defend the friend he most trusted from a beating he hardly deserved. He squeezed Hal's shoulder. 'Never heed him. Try nae to rise to his bate.'

Hal nodded, by now too exhausted to put up any but the most token resistance. Re-shouldering his musket, he looked dazed and beaten and glanced darkly at the watching soldiers. There would be no rescue from that quarter. They were there as witnesses should either of them think to retaliate and as protection for McBeath should they be so foolhardy. Their presence exposed McBeath's spineless nature, but Jamie knew all about that. At last year's duel, McBeath had hidden arms about his person, thinking to finish Jamie off should the contest turn against him.

Jamie exhaled bitterly. Should any counterblow have only a cost to him, he'd gladly take the chance to settle scores, but any furious response would bring his court martial. McBeath would see to that. What would that mean for Morven and the kin he'd left behind? He shuddered to think. 'Twould enrage His Grace.

He fell in beside Hal, praying the afternoon's exercise would soon be over. Every day after morning parade, McBeath dragged them out of the ranks with his halberd and marched them through the fort's main gate to a strip of coastal grassland. Bringing a drummer and a carefully selected squad of privates, he made them march in mock parade for another two hours. After full-dress parade called at eleven, if they were not on guard duty or delegated other tasks, McBeath again marched them away from prying eyes. Beyond the fort's walls, he drilled them for up to another four hours until their legs trembled, their shoulders and feet ached, and all they could think about was when it would end. Yet neither man would plead for clemency; they'd not give the devil the satisfaction.

Away from his superiors' scrutiny, McBeath could discipline his men as he pleased. Punishment of almost any kind was encouraged in the British Army, especially when doled out to Highlandmen considered the dregs of humanity. Regarded as natural criminals, they were assumed to need it most. Under the pretence of carrying out Captain Cumming's orders, McBeath could extend his discipline beyond even the British Army's bounds of accepted brutality.

'You will go through the standing drill again,' he barked. 'Rest, order, and club, secure, shoulder and present. Damn you, you will do it until you can do it in your sleep.'

Jamie suspected he already could.

'You will meet regimental standards, supposing it kills you.'

Daily, Jamie suffered a more detailed inspection of his person, uniform, and equipment than the rest of his unit, singled out for McBeath's withering scrutiny and caned for the slightest imagined lapse. Yet, thanks to McBeath's vindictive and gruelling training, Jamie's strength was slowly returning as he gained new skills. Without knowing it, McBeath was assisting with his plan.

Thwarting McBeath was now the Strathavon men's primary goal, their method of choice: unfaltering obedience. Despite needing their orders translated into Gaelic, once the men understood what was expected of them, they worked together like clansmen of old, helping each other master the complex manoeuvres of British Army drill. Gone was their ancestors' fierce highland charge. That howling onslaught, a horde of sword-wielding clansmen charging down half-naked upon their enemies, had served their ancestors well until Culloden. Even now, most glensmen scoffed to think these exercises could hope to replace it. But by cooperating as Highland-men had always done, they were quickly mastering the rigidly controlled series of movements demanded of them: three for resting their firelock, four for grounding it, twenty-one for priming and loading, nineteen for firing, as dictated by the British Army's Manual of Arms, a publication McBeath liked to high-handedly quote from.

Likewise, come evening, in the flickering firelight of the barrack room, instead of resting weary limbs or conjuring memories of home by retelling the sagas of Gaeldom around the fire, they again went through their musket drill. With Jamie barking out orders in imitation of McBeath, braying like an ass Hal called it, they swiftly learned what each guttural sound meant they must do. They rehearsed the correct placement of arms and feet, the precise angle at which the musket should be held, taking pains to encourage any man less able until they could all perform the movements to the same high standard. They practised fixing and unfixing their bayonets, presenting arms, levelling the barrel of their flintlock at an imaginary target, for soon they would practise live firing with powder and ball. On the parade ground, they learned to march upon the centre, wheel to the right, and left about turn. They quickly learned to discern each ruffle of the snare drum and obey its subtle shifts without hesitation, marching as a unit by rank, file, company, and in battalion order. They were becoming, as Jamie had hoped, and to the astonishment of the rest of the garrison, a well-drilled military unit, fighting men McBeath was now finding it harder to fault, although that hardly stopped him from trying.

As their competence grew, McBeath took to strutting along the fort's ramparts with a gloating swank. Full of self-importance, he puffed his chest out, glorying in the undeserved praise conferred on him by his superiors for the professionalism of his unit. Yet the Strathavon men knew better. 'Twas not for his elevation they practised so hard, but for his downfall.

Jamie caught Hal's eye. Hal nodded back with a wry half-smile. Nay, the smile said, try though the devil might, he'll nae beat us.

The next day, Sergeant McBeath singled only Jamie out of the ranks and marched him through the fort's main gate. Hal's punishment was now complete, Jamie supposed. His stomach knotted. He would now be the sole focus of McBeath's hatred, but with that thought came a perverse sense of anticipation. Damn him. The devil wouldna break him.

The day was hot and airless, the marching ceaseless. After two hours of wheeling and turning, marching, and presenting arms, sweat trickled down Jamie's back. His head thumped, and he longed for water.

'I would drink,' he said at last, lowering his musket. 'I've a powerful thirst.'

'You'll drink when I say so and no' before.' McBeath stretched back on a grassy hummock, his chosen place of repose for the morning's exercise. 'I've a powerful urge to bed your kinswoman, but since I must do without that pleasure for now, you must do without water until I decide otherwise.'

Jamie's jaw tightened; a nerve ticked in his cheek.

'You'll be missing your new wife.' McBeath chuckled. 'I hear you wed last Martinmas, your bride none other than the witch's apprentice. I forget her name ... Delnabreck's getling. A comely piece, though too wilful for my liking.'

'What if I did?'

'You must be pining for the nightly pleasures of her ripe young body.'

Jamie gritted his teeth. *Come again wi' yer coarseness, and ye'll feel the force o' my fist.*

'Of course, who knows when you'll see her again. Especially now.'

'What d'ye mean?'

'If ever,' McBeath mused on, 'if the rumours are true. And you will call me Sergeant.'

'What d'ye mean, *Sergeant*?' he ground out.

'We march to Edinburgh in five days. The duke intends to address all the Northern Fencible companies before you embark.'

'Embark?'

'Go on board ship.'

Jamie's heart missed a beat. 'On board ship? To where?'

'You'll learn that when you reach Edinburgh and join the rest of your regiment. The men will be told all they need to know when their betters decide to tell them. That's how things work in the British Army. I thought you'd have worked that out by now.' McBeath jerked his head. 'Get back to your exercises.'

On board ship? But they werena to leave Scotland. 'Twas the promise they'd been given. What treachery was this? The blood began to pound in Jamie's head. 'Ye'll tell me o' these rumours.' His voice was edged with steel.

'I'd also like to know of them, Sergeant, if you'll forgive my boldness.' During their exchange, the young drummer chosen to beat time for the day's exercise had rested in the shade of a tree. He now straightened to attention. He was an English infantryman, quiet and mild-mannered from what Jamie had seen. More a musician than a soldier.

McBeath fixed him with a cold stare.

'Is there trouble back home, Sergeant? We were told the Fencibles would only leave Scotland if England was threatened, that they were to defend her shores from the French. I've family in Kent, Sergeant. Folkestone, a small town on the coast. Have I reason to fear for their safety?'

McBeath rolled his eyes. 'How would I know? I care no' a jot for Kent, wherever that is. I listen to what concerns me. I sharpen my ears when I see officers huddled together discussing orders. I know naught of Kent, ye fool. Get back to yer drumming.'

The lad flushed. 'Sorry, Sergeant.'

'The rumours, McBeath.' Jamie glanced at the watching soldiers. 'What rumours?'

McBeath laughed. 'Military logistics hardly concern you. You'll go where you're ordered and no' question it.'

The breath whistled in Jamie's nostrils. 'My men will go nowhere that breaches the terms of their enlistment.' He nodded at the drummer. 'That lad spoke the truth. We were given assurances, told we'd nae leave these shores unless England was invaded. Has England been attacked?'

McBeath chuckled, irritation sharpening his sly expression. 'I'll no' be interrogated by the likes o' you. You'll learn what's to become of you when the other men do.'

'Ye said we were to board ships.'

'Did I? I might've heard that.' McBeath sniggered. 'Or maybe no'. You'll march to Edinburgh with Captain Cumming's company and join the rest of the regiment mustering at the castle. That I know. Preparations are being made.'

Jamie stared at him, trying to gauge from the devil's twitching expression how much of that was true. 'Ye ken more than that,' he growled.

'Do I? Then, 'tis for me to know and you to wonder about.'

God rot the man. Maybe the devil knew naught but wished him to think he knew something, hoping to rile him into an action he'd regret, something Captain Cumming would punish him for. Blast the man. He was playing with his head.

'Get back to your exercises.' McBeath stretched out in the grass, flicking a fly from his chest. He adjusted his bonnet to shade his eyes. 'Where was I? Oh, aye, congratulating you on your nuptials. How is the bonny bride? Enjoying married life?' he sniggered. 'No' so much lately, I think.'

Jamie re-shouldered his musket and tried to ignore him.

'I'd have broken her in for you if you hadnae stopped me. Last year at Delnabreck's bothy if ye mind.' McBeath cast a wary glance at the watching soldiers. They stood in uneasy formation. 'She's a headstrong piece, though you doubtless know that. Maybe that's how you like your women. I was poised on the brink, ye could say, ready to teach her a lesson.'

'Shut yer foul mouth.'

'Dinnae like to hear the truth?'

Jamie flushed. He had tried to put that sickening day behind him, but it manifested afresh in every shocking detail. The attack had been his fault. He'd dithered too long, at a loss over what to do, foolishly leaving Morven alone and defenceless with the twisted devil. When he came to his senses, he managed to prevent her rape, but not her beating. McBeath had already lifted his fist to her. Intervening dressed as a gauger, Morven understandably assumed the worst. Betrayer, that was her word. It still lanced his soul. She knew the truth now, but that hardly freed him of blame. He failed her that day in every conceivable way and despised himself for it.

'My blood was up,' McBeath bragged on. 'I'd have blazed a trail for ye, spearheading the way, ye could say, so there'd be no difficulty on your wedding night.' He chuckled. 'After a good time with me, she'd have known what to expect. Only ye spoiled my sport.'

'Shut yer mouth,' Jamie hissed. 'Or I'll shut it fer ye.'

McBeath chuckled at the threat. 'She's a spirited piece; I'll give ye that. I'm sure I would've enjoyed her.'

Jamie's face darkened. 'Ye foul braggart.' His hands tightened into fists. 'Ye'll nae speak like that o' my wife.'

'I'll speak any way I please and of anyone I choose, and you will call me Sergeant. Show respect for my rank, or the cat-o-nine-tails will lick yer back.'

Blood thrummed in Jamie's head, skewing his judgement. Knowing he mustn't rise to McBeath's taunts hardly meant he could stop himself. He reached for his dirk, but one of the privates had taken it from him. He threw his musket down. Two strides and he was upon McBeath. He grasped him by the collar and yanked him to his feet, slamming his fist into the devil's startled face. His fist connected with a pleasing crump.

McBeath staggered back. 'Guards!' he shrieked. Blood spurted from his nose. 'Seize him! What are ye waiting for?'

Soldiers piled onto Jamie, bringing him down, his arms pinioned behind his back. He twisted as he fell and kicked out, feeling the gratifying sensation of iron-tipped shoe thump into soft flesh. McBeath dropped to his knees with an agonised squeal.

Jamie crashed to the ground beside him, pinned down by what felt like a mountain of bodies. He tasted blood, but satisfaction was sweet. The foul-tongued devil would enjoy naught for some time. A bony knee pressed into his back. He groaned, writhing to dislodge his assailant, his face pushed into the grass. More soldiers straddled him. Spitting soil, he twisted his head and drew in a desperate drag of air. His lungs burned, but he could see out of one eye. McBeath lay moaning in the grass. He ceased struggling to savour the sight. The weight lifted from him, and he felt his hands being tied behind his back.

'I mean ye no harm,' he choked. 'I only wished to silence that midden mouth.'

There was a deal of muttering. Jamie sensed some sympathy for him, although not for his actions. He had shown outrageous defiance. He doubted these men had ever witnessed such an unthinkable display. The only question now was what form his punishment would take.

They left him trussed and panting in the grass. His chest ached, his knuckles too, though they in a satisfying way. His thirst was fiercer than ever. McBeath was still crippled. He rolled onto his back. His face was purple, his nose likely broken. Jamie had registered the dull crunch of gristle.

Two soldiers dragged Jamie to his feet and made him sit with his back against a tree while they waited for McBeath to recover. It took some time, but the devil's colouring slowly returned to a more normal hue, then he fell to cursing instead of moaning. Any trooper would have blushed at his language.

'Would water help, Sergeant?' The drummer hovered at McBeath's side with his canteen.

'Leave me,' McBeath snapped. Then, 'Aye, give me water. I'll have that heather-lowper hamstrung. Bring me his musket.' Wincing, McBeath levered himself into a sitting position. He spat foulness into the bushes and blew out a long breath, a hand pressed to his midsection. Jamie wondered if he would vomit. Finally, he let the drummer help him up. 'Yer name?' he growled.

'Drummer Edward Aitken.'

Grunting, he drank from the lad's canteen, then snorted and hawked a glutinous red glob at Jamie's feet. 'Someone cut me a bough. A long, straight one.' He took a few faltering steps, then halted, breathing hard.

Jamie's chest gripped. It looked like his punishment would be immediate; the devil was going to beat him with a stick or have the men do it. But as he waited, the purpose of the bough became clear.

Still looking like he might swoon, McBeath steadied himself on a tree. 'Give me yer belts,' he snarled at the men. 'Drag the upstart into the sun and bind his ankles. Tie his hands beneath his knees.'

The men did as instructed, hauling Jamie to the centre of the makeshift marching ground. They made him sit with his knees drawn up, his hands bound at the wrist beneath them. A private hacked a bough from a nearby tree. At McBeath's instruction, they pushed Jamie's musket under his thighs and used the bough to force his chin down onto his knees, pressing the length of the pole down on the back of his neck. He gritted his teeth as hard timber ground down on the small bones of his neck.

'Give me yer belts,' McBeath growled.

The soldiers looked at each other.

'Now, blast ye.'

They jumped to it, unbuckling the belts holding their ammunition pouches and handed them over. Grunting, McBeath knelt and looped the first belt around the musket butt and the bough. He tied another around the musket's barrel and the bough. More belts secured the device. Tightening the belt buckles, he drew what had become instruments of torture as close together as he could force them.

Jamie thought his back must break. Trussed in a folded-over position, he struggled to breathe. His neck and back screamed at him, but there was no way to relieve the agony. McBeath swiped Jamie's bonnet from his head and beat him about the head with it, then hurled it into the bushes. 'Now we leave him.'

'Sergeant?' Jamie could hear the uncertainty in Aitken's voice. 'For how long, Sergeant?'

'Until the sun slowly bakes him. 'Til thirst cracks his lips and tongue. I've seen it done. Given enough time, his back will pull itself apart.'

Jamie stifled a groan. Bent over, he could see naught but the sandy grass beneath his knees. He waited for a blow or a kick, but none came. They were simply going to leave him. Sure enough, there came the rustle of knapsacks and belongings being gathered, then the tramp of military shoes fading away, the owner of one pair decidedly slower than the rest. He drew in a painful breath, and then there was naught but the suck and slap of the sea on the shingle shore below, and the cry of a lone gull.

CHAPTER TWENTY-ONE

Strathavon, August 1781

THE SONG FLOWED THROUGH Morven's body, its ancient rhythms rising and falling with her movements. Around her, her kinfolk's voices flowed to the same rhythm, binding them in their toil. *Arc and swing, bend and straighten.* The rhythms were timeless, held together by abiding threads woven through the melody. *Stoop and rise, sweep and bind.* Her forebears' voices seemed to come to her through the ages, echoing the rhythms of centuries-old toil. How long had folk been singing these old reaping songs? Likely as long as folk had been reaping. The patterns were ageless, flowing to an ancient current that seemed to rise from the soil, the harmony as tireless as the tides, as enduring as the rising and setting of the sun.

Her da scythed the swath to her right, her younger brothers Rory and Donald gathering what he cut into sheaves. Rowena's son William banded the sheaves and stacked them. Morven worked behind Alec and his swinging scythe, banding the sheaves Rowena gathered. She did less bending that way.

Regardless, her back ached, and she glanced at the dark sky, praying they would get through the harvest before more rain came. Once they had reaped Rowena's infield at Tomachcraggen, God willing, they would move to her da's holding at Delnabreck and then to Druimbeag, cutting the first crop there in over twenty years. She dreamed of Jamie's face when he learned she had brought in their first harvest. His eyes would light with pride as he took her in his arms. All her backbreaking toil weeding and spreading cartloads of dung had borne fruit. But that would only hold true if the Lord willed it. Much could still go wrong; the failed harvests and famines of past years spoke poignantly of that. And hanging over her was the knowledge that come Martinmas, she must find a year's rental coin.

Choosing the best time to harvest was always a gamble. Left too long, a crop could blacken and shrivel overnight should frost blight it. Blizzards struck early in the high glens. Snow could blanket the land as soon as October and lie well into spring, while rain could devastate a crop, rotting grain, encouraging mould to grow. Mouldy grain was dangerous, even for beasts, though folk ofttimes took the chance, preferring sickness to an empty belly. 'Twas useless as a seed crop and would fail to germinate.

Rowena's harvest looked decent. Seeing the bent stalks fat with grains lifted Morven's spirits. What folk paid Rowena for her skills—a clutch of eggs, a guddled trout, a turnip, or boiling of tatties—hardly paid her rent. Coin was needed, but finding it was the hardest thing. Folk might sell a beast or two to reivers, but they rarely sold their grain. Only His Grace profited that way with no need for meal to feed himself or his family. He dined on finer fare and controlled the mills and the prices.

'Are ye managing?' Rowena looked back at her.

Morven cast her dark thoughts away. 'I'm keeping up fine.'

'Ye'll say if ye grow weary or sore?'

She nodded.

Alec lent on his scythe. 'Ye mustna push yerself.' He looked at her belly. 'I couldna bear it if aught befell you or yer bairn. I promised Jamie.' A muscle tightened in his jaw. 'I swore I'd look efter ye.'

When had Alec promised that? Such a promise was news to her. What else had Jamie kept from her? But Morven pushed the thought away. 'I can manage fine.'

'A rider!' Rory whooped. 'Ower yonder.' He pointed to the east. A lone rider was galloping through the heather. Morven squinted, trying to make out the slight figure flattened over the horse's back. Dark clouds were gathering on the horizon again.

'I've seen that lad,' Rowena said. 'He's a student at Scalan, has been many years.'

Morven's chest tightened; something must be wrong.

As he neared, Nathaniel wrestled with his snorting mount. It reared, shaking its head in a jingle of bridle fittings and almost threw him. He was no horseman. Shut away in a pious world of prayer books and study, he had little need to be. Breathless, he slid to the ground, fighting to calm his skittish animal. It threatened to trample the barley they had still to cut, prompting her da to come running over, cursing and gesturing wildly.

Alec took the reins and calmed the animal with practised hands.

'My apologies.' Nathaniel bowed to Alec and even lower to Rowena, clutching his bonnet. His gaze seared Morven's face before he turned to her da. Her da glowered at him, the urge to give this reckless stranger a good tongue-lashing plain in his louring expression. Only Nathaniel's manners and well-cut clothing deterred him. He knew better than to rebuke a stranger, at least until he had established the intruder's identity.

'I pray you'll forgive my intrusion,' Nathaniel blurted. 'My name is Nathaniel Gunn.'

'Is it noo.'

'I'm a student at Scalan Seminary.' Still addressing her da, he indicated the work they were engaged in. 'I would not normally presume to trouble you at this time; only Father John, the Scalan master, has fallen gravely ill.' White-faced, he turned to Morven.

'Is it the wasting sickness again? Consumption can work that way. It may seem to go, only to come raging back.'

'I fear so, but I've never seen him so poorly. He travelled north to the coast in search of meal, against your advice, but our meal kists were almost empty. Managing to secure a boll, he barely made the return, a storm chasing him all the way. It caught him at Tombae, soaking him to the bone. Then the mists swirled down, soundless, impenetrable. Lost in their depths, he strayed into a peat bog, where he and his horse floundered for hours. One of the servants found him and carried him home. Yet despite his ordeal, he would not rest.' Nathaniel wrung his hands. 'He's too good a soul and tries to carry on. His work is endless. He allows himself no rest from the boys' lessons, ordering provisions, writing letters to the Mission in Rome, missives he must draft in code for fear of interception. He celebrates Mass in our little chapel with those poor souls who have no other way of receiving it. He was giving the Eucharist when he fell to his knees, a terrible constriction in his chest. The boys helped me carry him to his chamber, but even as I left to search for you, I could hear his brassy cough from the foot of the stairs.'

'He spits up blood?'

Nathaniel glanced at Rowena. 'Forgive me; he expels much thick bloody phlegm and suffers terrible pain in his chest. He will not eat but shivers and sweats racked with fever. He seems so weak, yet he cannot sleep. He says,' Nathaniel faltered, 'he says his soul has half slipped to the next realm.' His face twisted. 'What can I do? We cannot lose him. He is the father I never had, a man of childlike sincerity.'

Morven stretched her aching back. 'I will come. Whatever can be done, I will do.' She glanced at her da.

'Aye,' he muttered. The heat had gone out of his anger. 'Ye must go. I've heard much good o' the Scalan master.'

Tears shimmered in Nathaniel's eyes. He nodded, not trusting his voice.

'Ye must find bullock's lungwort,' advised Rowena. ''Tis the best remedy fer the wasting sickness.'

'I have it prepared,' Morven answered. 'A leaf extract seeped in whisky. I managed to rally the master wi'out it afore, thinking to save the most powerful medicine fer when he might need it most.'

'Ye did well.' Rowena held Nathaniel's tearful gaze. 'I could do nae more. My student is now as skilled as her teacher.'

'Oh, yes,' Nathaniel blurted. 'I have the greatest faith in Morven and her methods. Her remedies come from nature, hence from our Heavenly Father. They are His gifts to us wrought through her.' He swallowed. 'You are Rowena?' When she nodded, he said, 'We have you to thank for Morven's healing talent, I think.'

Rowena half smiled. 'Morven was born wi' her talent. I only helped draw it out.'

'I thank you for that. All at Scalan have been blessed to know Morven.' Nathaniel's gaze strayed to Morven's abdomen. Her pregnancy was now impossible to hide. His face fell. 'But in your delicate condition ....'

'I'm nae as delicate as ye imagine.' Morven indicated the work she had spent much of the day engaged in.

'Then, if you're sure.' He smiled in relief.

She climbed onto his horse, and he leapt up behind her. Taking the reins from Alec, she urged the animal away with a squeeze of her calves. As they crossed the stubble, her kinfolks' voices came to her again, slipping back into the rhythm of their toil.

CHAPTER TWENTY-TWO

Scalan

Nathaniel could hear the master's laboured breathing from the foot of the stairs. Exchanging a distraught look with Morven, he mounted the staircase with trembling legs. Father John's condition had worsened. Undaunted, Morven hurried to the master's side. Perching on the edge of his bed, she pressed a hand to his forehead. His fever was unmistakable; his cheeks were livid, his poor lips cracked and raw, a burning heat radiating from him.

At her touch, the master opened his eyes. 'Morven. Good of you.'

''Tis a pleasure to see ye again, Father, though I hoped to find ye in better health. Nathaniel was worried about ye, but ye mustna fear. There's much I can do, and ye must do yer part by letting yerself sleep. Sleep is the best balm, better than any potion.' She stroked his hot forehead until his eyes closed.

Watching from the end of the bed, his heart in his throat, Nathaniel had never felt more powerless. He had done all he could in fetching Morven. Now, it was down to her. She looked too young for such responsibility. Pressing his trembling hands together, he silently prayed. *Almighty Father, have mercy on your servant, John. Heal him, Lord, so he may continue your work. I'd do anything, give anything…* He sighed. The master would not thank him for presuming to barter with God. Wringing his hands, he withdrew to the window, afraid to crowd Morven or hinder her vital work. He had been fooling himself, imagining he might glean some healing knowledge from her, but where Morven knew what to do, he knew nothing.

Morven looked up at him with the soft expression she reserved for the sick and those who loved them, understanding they suffered as much. It was a look his mother had worn. A memory of her weeping in the riverside undergrowth came back to him. He turned away, tears burning the back of his eyes.

'Ye might fetch warm water and a compress,' she suggested.

He hurried off, glad of something to do. When he returned, Morven was listening at the master's chest. She probed his neck with her fingers and studied his throat and tongue. The master coughed suddenly. She wiped blood away and looked up gravely as he waited with the bowl of water. The master's lungs were even more damaged. She didn't need to tell him. Every breath was a painful wheeze. When he coughed, he sprayed a fine red mist over poor Morven.

'Forgive me.' Father John slumped back on his pillow. 'I've long had an eye on the next world. It calls to me, whilst the evils and sorrows of the valley here below only repulse me more. I don't fear death, but I still have much I wish to do.'

'Try nae to distress yerself,' she answered. 'Ye must rest.'

Dear God, the master believed his life was almost over—maybe he wished it. Nathaniel wrung his hands. How would he carry on with the shining light in his life extinguished? It was too much to bear. He clenched his jaw, trying not to weep. Morven must wield her earth magic to keep the master here, where he was loved and needed and could complete his mission. *Help her, Lord,* he prayed. *I'd do anything, give anything.* But even as Nathaniel prayed, he knew his motives were selfish.

'I hear ye were caught in foul weather.' Morven pressed the compress to Father John's neck, clicking her tongue as if to a child.

'Guilty as charged.'

''Twill make healing harder.'

The master licked his cracked lips. 'Is it even possible at this late stage?'

'Everything is possible if ye hae enough faith. I thought ye'd be kenning that. I forge my cures from the essence that binds all things thegither. I call it earth magic, but churchly folk likely call it God's grace.'

The master's face relaxed a fraction. 'God's grace extends everywhere. It touches every one of us, every one of God's creatures.' He wheezed into his kerchief, leaving it stained with blood. '"By the grace of God, I am what I am,"' he rasped. 'Those were Saint Paul's words to the Christians of Corinth.'

'God's grace flows through the earth, too, Father. It quickens every tree and plant that push their roots into the soil. 'Tis how I'm able to tap it.'

She looked at Nathaniel. 'Will ye stay with the master whilst I go to the kitchen? I've medicine to prepare.'

'Of course.' He knelt at the foot of the bed. What would Father Ranald do if he were here in his place? If only he knew. All he had was prayer.

He was still on his knees when Morven returned and rose to find the master twitching in his sleep, his cheeks crimson. His breathing sounded even more alarming, a wheezy gurgle threatening to stall in his throat. Nathaniel wrung his hands in despair.

Morven had brought a bowl filled with a pungent-smelling paste and a flask holding a pale yellow liquid. She set these by the bed. He expected she would encourage the master to drink the liquid, but instead, she moved aside the folds of her arisaid, revealing a leather pouch hanging from her belt. She untied it and tipped its contents on the bed. There was an assortment of dried herbs, some strange roots and bones, a large dusky brown crystal, and five stones, each with a hole worn through the middle.

'What are these?' Nathaniel touched one of the stones.

'Healing charms, each a rare find. I fished the hagstones from the river A'an.' She held one up. 'The eye was formed by the flow o' water ower many years. They've long been used in healing, fer a wealth o' earth energy is bound in them. That energy may be channelled to heal.' She smiled, seeing that he was drawn to her crystal. 'My cairngorm.' She took it from him, turning it to catch the light. ''Twas formed ower countless centuries deep in the heart o' the mountains in the faery realm. Look into its depths, and ye may catch a glimpse o' that kingdom, a world of shifting shape and shadow, a realm as real as our own, only hidden from the eyes o' men.'

He swallowed, unsure what to say. It looked like the trappings of witchcraft, but it couldn't be. Hadn't the Lord created everything in heaven and on earth?

'How will you use them?'

She put down the crystal and chose a hagstone. Closing her eyes, she recited some words over it. Nathaniel had studied many languages—Gaelic, French, Latin, Greek, but had never heard anything as unfathomable as this. Still whispering, she moved around the bed, placing the charms in a circle with the master at its centre.

'As the charms release their energy, 'twill flow into him, bringing harmony and healing. The force will strengthen.' She whirled her hands together, forming a graceful eddy, quickening to a swirling vortex. 'Empowering the medicine. 'Tis potent. He must tak' only a little at a time.' Pouring a spoonful from the flask, she touched the spoon to the master's lips. 'This will help ye, Father.'

He opened his mouth like a hatchling and sucked it in.

Nathaniel blinked. 'Lungwort,' he croaked, ''tis well-named, then?'

'When the Creator made the forests at the dawn o' the world, some plants were marked wi' features o' the disease or organ they help, showing their curative powers. Lungwort is marked fer the lungs.'

He nodded, prepared to believe anything if it helped the master.

'He must take a spoonful every half hour. I've made a rub fer his chest—quince seed, juniper, balsam, and water trefoil. Sage to help ease his sweats.' She untied the master's sark, exposing his bony chest, and worked the paste into his papery skin.

Nathaniel took the chair from the master's desk and drew it to the bedside, watching in fascination as she massaged the master's rib cage in gentle, circular movements. Her hands flowed and blurred, soothing him as much as they appeared to soothe the master. His eyelids grew heavy, the pungent aroma lulling him. A faint golden light seemed to emanate from the bed, enfolding the master in a sphere Nathaniel sensed was holy. He felt it draw him in, too.

Only a few moments seemed to pass before Morven was offering the master another spoonful of liquid. Again, he sucked it in. When next Nathaniel became aware of his surroundings, Morven was on her feet, mantling her arisaid over her head.

'You're leaving?' Alarm jerked him fully awake.

'If ye'll let me, I'll tak' the master's horse and ride fer silvered water. I must employ all the earth magic I know.'

He looked blankly at her, feeling foolish; he had never heard of silvered water. Glancing at the bed, he again saw the master haloed in swirling golden light. 'Of course. If it will help. Might I fetch it for you?'

She shook her head and was gone.

It was dark when she returned. The sun had set, pale moonlight bathing the room, yet it felt like no time had passed. The master appeared held in a powerful thrall, a magical shield spun around him so no harm might come to him whilst Morven travelled on her mission. Nathaniel sensed the magic had also worked on him.

Morven stoked the fire until it flared and spat, then lit a candle. Whispering in her strange tongue, she sprinkled the mysterious silvered water over the master. That done, she let him suck in another spoonful of elixir. His breathing sounded less noisy. He didn't shudder at the cold water. Pleased, she smiled and took Nathaniel's hand. His chest tightened in confusion. Still smiling, she uncurled his stiff fingers and held them to the master's brow.

Disconcerted, his instinct was to snatch his hand away and offer an apology, to mumble an excuse for the blatant impropriety. It took all his will not to. His fingers tingled under hers. His breath caught in his throat, then slowed and deepened. Inexplicably, he began to feel safe, his heart no longer leaping as if the devil himself pursued him. More disconcerting, a longing for further impropriety kindled. He wished Morven would hold him. Knowing she was with child soothed rather than unnerved him. Mothers were set apart. They carried new life, although he did not care to dwell upon the crude act needed to quicken that life. A yearning to be comforted had endured since childhood, no matter how hard he'd fought it. How many nights had he lain awake pining for his mother's arms? Not once had God's love given him that visceral feeling. *God forgive me.* He whimpered, trying to smother his childish longings. Priests did not take pregnant women in their arms. Releasing a quivering breath, he allowed his fingers to explore the master's forehead, finding it cool and dry.

'He's better!'

'His fever has broken, aye.'

'So quickly?'

'He'll sleep now.' Morven looked at him. 'The master strives fer holiness in everything he does. At heart, he's a humble man of the earth.'

'Oh, yes,' he sobbed. 'Father John is wholly sincere.'

'He spends his days praying and thinking deeply. There's nae anger in him, nae hatred. He's filled wi' spirit and light. I see it shining from him. You may call it what ye will, piety or something churchly, but his heart is pure. There's naught to resist the energy I've channelled. It can flood through him, bringing harmony and healing.'

'The golden light?'

'Ye saw that?'

'I saw something. It ... it held me in its thrall.'

Morven drew back, the cat-like flecks in her eyes reflecting what he hoped might be admiration.

'Mebbe the blood o' the *draoidh* flows in yer veins as it does in mine.'

He cradled the hand she'd touched. '*Draoidh?* Is that what you are? A druid.'

'Some say so, though others cry me a witch.'

He recoiled, rejecting that. 'How can they? You're an angel. You worked a miracle; I saw it. You saved him. He'll live, won't he?' Tears burned; he prayed she would say yes.

'I believe so, but wi' the wasting sickness, 'tis always hard to be sure. In the end, the Creator decides who lives and dies.'

He pushed that thought away, fighting back tears. He wanted to bless her for the momentous thing she'd done, to repay her, but the only way he could reward her in a way that mattered would be to ease her grindingly hard life. Only how? He had mere words. 'It sounds so puny, but thank you.'

'Och.' She smiled with the directness he had come to love about her.

'I wish to repay you. If ... if there is anything.'

'There is something.'

'Oh, God, anything.'

Frowning, she hunted among the folds of her arisaid, and he wondered if there was anything that traditional garment could not hide. Finally, she drew out a folded piece of paper.

CHAPTER TWENTY-THREE

JAMIE'S LETTER WAS A mite dog-eared; Morven had fingered it so much. Hurrying home in the rain, she was unable to keep it fully dry. The crinkled surface with its spidery lettering told her nothing yet evoked an uneasy feeling.

Nathaniel took the letter to the master's desk and gingerly unfolded it, flattening it on the polished wood. ''Tis from your husband; I recognise his writing, although his address has changed. It reads, *Castlehill, Aberdeen.*'

'Aberdeen?'

'You didn't know he'd been deployed there?'

She shook her head. 'He must go where he's ordered.'

'True.' Nathaniel squinted at Jamie's faded longhand. 'He writes in Gaelic as follows:

My love, I pray ye'll forgive me fer nae writing sooner. Fate has contrived against me at every turn. Please dinna imagine I've nae been thinking and dreaming o' you, fer in that I canna help myself. I think o' ye day and night—you and our child. I pray that ye still think kindly o' me, though ye must sometimes curse me. As the weeks pass, I pray ye dinna lose heart or worse, imagine I've abandoned ye. I could never do that. Ye are my life. When all my kin were lost to me but Rowena, whom I couldna remember, 'twas you lifted me from despair. 'Tis only because o' you my life is worth living.'

Nathaniel glanced at her, then read on.

'*We marched fer Edinburgh five days ago and are to quarter here in Aberdeen only as long as it takes to re-provision. We travelled by the post road, hugging the shoreline fer much of the way, sleeping by the side of the road in tents we carried upon our backs. Our backs suffer fer it. Mine especially. It rained most of the way, the track little more than a sucking mire, a cold, miserable slog, our thoughts on what may lie ahead of us. Our officers avoided the military road through the hills, the quickest route, fearing the men would desert, that the lure of the hills would prove too strong fer many.*

"Tis true some might've slipped away to their glens for the harvest. I longed to and might've found a way if I didna ken the penalty for desertion would mean a shameful flogging in front of the officers and men and even more dire consequences for you should His Grace learn of my actions. There's bad feeling on that score amongst the men. They assumed they'd be given leave to return for the harvest and chafe at the order that keeps them from their fields, fearing for their families. What misguided commander would draft an order leaving auld bodachs, bairns, and pregnant women to reap the precious grain? Yet that is what the duke's uncle Lord Adam Gordon has ordered. The men fret ower the hunger and suffering next winter if their crops are left to rot in the ground. I worry ower that, too.

'We are to join the rest of the Northern Fencible regiment at Edinburgh Castle. We've been told naught beyond that, but rumours are rife. All officers on leave have been recalled, all outposts summoned in; hence, we fear something is astir. In truth, 'tis plain something brews. 'Tis rumoured we are to board ships at Leith, Edinburgh's port; only the source of those rumours canna be trusted, though others do say the same. To where we know not. We were given promises, assured we'd nae leave Scotland unless England was attacked. Here in Aberdeen, there is no word of an attack; hence, I fear the War Office and its treachery.'

Morven's heart lurched. 'They are to board ships,' she breathed. 'To where?'

'Forgive me, I know not. Perhaps to England.'

'Mother Earth,' she whimpered. 'When will I see Jamie again?'

'I wish I knew, then I might ease your mind. Your husband writes further:

'If the rumours are true, I give ye my word; I will protect my men. They're a loyal band, the envy of every commander at Fort George for their discipline and conduct, their swift command of military drill despite the barrier of their Highland tongue. They have practised 'til they can barely stand, tireless in their wish to please and conform. I feel such affinity wi' them, Morven, I can scarce explain it. Every man is strong in heart. I'll nae let the authorities breach our terms of enlistment. We were given assurances. I will hold the scoundrels to their word. Yet I fear we're betrayed. Here, Highlandmen are counted of little value, chattel to be sold or thrown to the wind, wasted on our

enemies' guns. Forgive me, I'm bitter. Events have made me so.

'*Our drill sergeant goaded and prodded us all the road here, abusing the men as sorely with his tongue as he did with his cane. He's a cruel, vulgar wretch; many of our officers are little better. But this foul-mouthed ...*' Nathaniel frowned at the page. '*Forgive me, I believe he writes devil, yes, this foul-mouthed devil bears a particular grudge.*' Glancing at her, he read on. '*I'll not trouble ye with the details; they hardly matter. He willna win.*

'*My love, you know how I despise injustice, but in defending these men I care about, I can't help but feel my life may finally have some meaning. My guilt at surviving the sickness that took my family may finally be appeased, for it ever weighs on my mind. Why was I spared? I've asked myself that so many times. Perhaps I may only make sense of that dark time by doing something worthwhile with my life, proving I deserved to live. I hope ye can understand; if I do naught but while my life away, letting the authorities betray us, I will cheapen my kinfolks' lives. My father most of all, who taught me always to do what is right.*

'*In truth, the Stratha'an men inspire me. Hal McHardy, Willie Thom, Allan Ross and the others, every man is unshakeably loyal. The bond we share, Morven, I could scarce feel closer to them, supposing they were blood kin. After the mistrust and bad feeling my actions wrought last Beltane, they've welcomed me into their lives and, best of all, into the community I was born to. I belong now. I'm valued. Almost as much as you, these men have made me feel part of something ancient and proud. I canna let them be misused.*

'*'Tis possible I delude myself, but I harbour a notion God must've spared me for a reason. I know not His purpose, but what if 'twas to bring me to this place so I might make a difference? Yet in standing up for these cottars and smugglers, now made soldiers, I fear I might hurt ye again. I confess that thought undoes me.*'

A sob caught in Morven's throat.

Nathaniel faltered. 'Forgive me. This makes grim reading.'

'I would hear Jamie's words.'

He nodded, his voice rasping as he read on.

'*Still, we await our bounty coin, and our pay is far in arrears. That I have no coin to send you grieves me sorely, though ye mustna worry for me. As the weeks pass, I pray carrying our child hasna caused ye great trouble. The infant must grow heavy. He'll be here soon. More than anything, I wish I could be there to greet him. I dream o' his dear face, and yours, my heart. Yours is the face I see every night afore sleep claims me. I worry about the birth, knowing I can do naught to help ye trapped in the king's army. That you will have Rowena eases my mind. My kinswoman has seen many infants safe into the world. I pray she will see another.*

'Forgive me, the drums beat tap-too. I must snuff my light. I will write again as I can. Until we are together again, know that ye are my heart and my life. I remain always your loving husband, James.'

Nathaniel looked up. His face was white; his hands shook almost as much as hers. 'Your husband has hurt you?'

''Twas a foolish misunderstanding.'

'You're sure?'

'He hoped to save his aunt Rowena, the woman ye met at the reaping when ye rode to fetch me. He gave a false name to the Excise Board so he might join them and uncover proof against the gauger blackmailing her. Only I didna ken that. I thought he'd betrayed me. I thought the words o' love he spoke to me were part o' his deception.' She frowned at her hands, remembering the bitter accusations she'd hurled at him. Jamie had risked his life to save the last of his kin; she only blasted him with her temper. 'He couldna tell me the truth fer fear o' revealing his deception.'

'The hurt was unintentional?'

She nodded. 'I'm ower quick to judge, ye see. 'Tis one o' my failings. I'm a faithless creature. I've long owned a doubting heart.'

Nathaniel stared at her. 'Oh, no. You are the most faithful of women, fiercely loyal. And your husband, if I may say so, is exceptionally fortunate to have you.'

She smiled crookedly. ''Tis kind o' ye, but I ken the truth.' Coupled with her doubting heart, she owned a barbed tongue, a wounding one. She'd long been quick to use it, hoping to safeguard her precious pride. With Jamie, 'twas her heart she'd struggled to guard. Thinking he had played her for a fool, she held naught back, scorching him with her tongue. Scorn was her weapon. She wielded it with venom, hoping to hide how much he'd hurt her. Only later did she discover how wrong she was.

'Then, your husband is principled and courageous?'

'A hero, aye.'

'Knowing that must make you worry for him all the more.'

She swallowed. 'It does. If he thought his men had been betrayed, I fear he'd think naught of risking his life again.'

'Even knowing you and his unborn child wait here in dire straits for his return?'

Her throat tightened, and she struggled to answer.

'Forgive me. I should be trying to allay your fears.' Nathaniel folded the letter and got to his feet. His face looked pale. 'Twas his learned speech made him seem worldly, his earnest nature. Inside, he was still a shy and awkward boy. He held the letter out uncertainly. 'Perhaps you would like me to read it again?'

She took it and shook her head. 'I understood Jamie well enough. 'Tis hard nae to be alarmed by the betrayal he foresees and what he might do about it.'

'Your husband believes God may have spared him for a higher purpose. A powerful belief that could make him bolder than is good for him. As you say, such a notion might prompt him to take risks he should not. Then again, perhaps he is right. God's will is always at work. None of us know His plan for us, not this side of heaven.'

Nathaniel meant well, but she didn't care to hear that. Jamie had strong principles, while she was a more straightforward creature. He would let his principles guide him. Only to where? Riled, he was a powder keg. She looked down at her belly, swollen with his bairn who needed him as much as she did. That she loved Jamie was beyond her heart's command or control. Without him, she would wish to die.

She cleared her throat. 'I'm nae so sure I wish to ken God's plan fer me. Common folk have few paths to choose from in life. We must live the simple life given us, honour the family we were born to, the customs of the glen where we belong.'

'Forgive me, I spoke clumsily. I think we both know you are far from common or simple. I confess I have known few women, but among those I have met, you are by far the most extraordinary.'

That made her laugh; she regarded Nathaniel. He looked back steadily, his eyes shining with sincerity. There was not a false bone in him, and she was glad of it. 'Ye're kind, but if I am to do my best healing work, I must put away my fears.' She looked at Father John. He had not stirred during their exchange. 'I hope to make the master well again.'

'I pray for that.'

'He must tak' the lungwort elixir every half hour 'til this bout passes, and I'll burn the coltsfoot flowers we gathered. The vapours will ease the tightness in his chest.'

'You mean to sit with him through the night?'

'If 'tis allowed.' She looked at the master's carved wooden chair. 'Twas a thing of beauty and would give as much comfort as her lonely bed.

'Of course. After all, the master is in no position to object. I'll fetch a blanket if you're sure.'

'Will ye stay, Nathaniel?'

'No, no. 'Twould not be proper.' He blushed. 'I'll join the boys in the dormitory. The master is peaceful now. I'll look in on him later if I may.' He swallowed, his jaw tightening. 'I fear what might've happened if not for you.'

She nodded and tried to smile back, but her face was too stiff.

Nathaniel left her and returned with a pillow and blankets, laying them on the arm of the chair. He carried a bundle of dried yellow flowers. 'Coltsfoot, if I remember correctly?'

'Thank ye.' She fingered the brittle little blooms. 'As they burn, I'll fan the smoke ower the master, so he breathes it in.'

Nathaniel stared at the desiccated little heads, then nodded and took his leave.

She set to work as soon as he'd gone. As the tiny blooms smouldered in a bowl, they gave off a honey scent, soothing the turmoil inside her. Her hands ceased their trembling. She whispered the ancient words, conscious of the powerful vibrational energy bathing the sick man. Like Nathaniel, she discerned the healing field as swirling golden light. It brought harmony and a sense of lightness in mind and body. In her fragile state, she welcomed its effects. Drawn into the eddy, the smoke curled around the sleeping man. He sucked it in, much like he had the elixir.

The child stirred in Morven's belly, and her heart clenched. When would the wee soul see its father? She had never asked anything of Jamie. That he loved her was enough. Why could it nae be enough fer him? But he itched to right wrongs, believing he must justify why he still lived. Over the years, she had nursed many sick folk, yet rarely had she sickened herself. 'Twas a puzzle but not a new one. Perhaps it spoke of God's will or plan, as Nathaniel said.

She made an exasperated sound and rose to her feet. Most Stratha'an smugglers would say Jamie had already proven he deserved to live. *What more must he do?* Was it selfish to want him all to herself? A cottar, a smuggler, naught more. Nae a hero. Heroes didna live long, at least, nae in any fireside tale she had ever heard. Their lives were brutal and short. Jamie's passion for justice stirred her devotion, but it also confused her. Did he nae love her that he would sacrifice himself fer his principles?

She crossed to the window and stared out at a sky full of stars. As the child grew in her belly, so had her fears. Now, with this letter, they consumed her. She exclaimed, rubbing her brow. Why must she aye doubt him? 'Ye o' little faith,' she muttered. Yet, despite her confusion, she did know something: she must keep Druimbeag safe. That wild scrape of land mattered to Jamie. Holding on to it would prove her faith in him, her loyalty, then he would come back to her.

Throughout the night, she plied the master with lungwort elixir, reciting the ancient incantation over and over. Rhythmic chanting could take her to a place beyond the mind. 'Twas a welcoming place offering peace from the nagging voice in her head. Caught in the thrall of swirling energy, lulled by its effects, she travelled gladly to that blessed place, spending the darkest hours there. If Nathaniel looked in on her, she was not aware of it.

Dawn finally crept through the master's window, and she stared out at hills purple with heather. The dark clouds had gone and the day promised fair. The master stirred from what must have been the deepest sleep of his life.

'Morven.' He blinked at her. 'I hope you've not been here all night.'

''Tis no matter.'

'So, you have.' He rose on one elbow, staring at the healing charms placed around his bed. 'I feel lighter. I no longer sense the remorseless pull of the next realm, my spirit fading from this. How did you ...?'

'Nature worked the magic, Father. I only helped.'

He took a breath that did not wheeze and released it slowly. 'I can breathe without difficulty. If I didn't know better, I might think it witch-craft. Bless you.' He reached for her hand.

His touch made her fingers tingle. She smiled and stretched her stiff body. Her traitorous mind had finally stilled.

When Nathaniel entered a few moments later with Father Ranald, she had put away her healing charms and was feeding Father John some of Janet's savour broth. Nathaniel stared open-mouthed. Even Father Ranald seemed lost for words. He waited for her to put the bowl down.

'Lass.' His lips trembled. 'I hardly know what to say.' He stared at the master. 'John seems quite himself again. Praise the Lord! All at Scalan are in your debt.'

'I feel renewed, Ranald,' Father John said.

Morven smiled. The master's recovery was a fragile thing, but she would not dampen the joy in the room by saying so.

'Bless you.' Father Ranald clasped her hands. 'You've answered our prayers. When I think of what little use thon charlatan Dalrymple was.' He swallowed. 'You must rest now. Nathaniel will show you where you can sleep, and you must for the sake of yer child. I promise no one will disturb you.'

Nathaniel nodded, tears shimmering on his long eyelashes.

'I should stay wi' Father John.'

'Nathaniel will stay with him whilst I take the boys for their lessons.' The father caught Nathaniel's eye. 'Today's lesson is essential for any young priest hoping to provide pastoral care to the faithful of a highland parish.' He looked out the window at the growing radiance in the sky. ''Tis a perfect day for reaping, and Nathaniel tells me Druimbeag still awaits the scythe. We'll spend the day harvesting your infield.'

Morven's mouth fell open.

'As you know, I've long worked a holding. I'll wield the scythe, and the boys can gather what I cut. The fresh air and exercise will do them good.' He nodded to confirm it. 'Both their health and their wider education.'

Speechless, Morven looked at Nathaniel.

He nodded, tears brimming.

'Now, I'll brook no argument. 'Tis settled.'

CHAPTER TWENTY-FOUR

Edinburgh, September
1781

IT WAS LATE AFTERNOON, and the sun shone low in Jamie's eyes. He had travelled far from the mountains of home and stared at the wide firth opening before him. Unlike the Moray Firth, with its limited trade, this silver expanse seethed with industry. White-sailed frigates, schooners, and brigs cut across the froth-topped waves, carrying their wares to Edinburgh and Leith, a shoal of coastal smacks running into the many fishing villages along the shore. He caught the briny scent of salt and seaweed on the breeze and couldn't help staring at the stone dykes enclosing broad fields with strange new crops or patterned with corn stooks, at the breek-clad strangers working the land. They looked like a foreign race. He could see few trees, not a clump of heather, and reflected that in this fertile land with its civilised society, he and his fellow Highlanders were the foreign race.

He marched on, his back aching from neck to tail. He had still to fully recover from the hamstringing McBeath inflicted on him and longed to throw off the heavy knapsack, bundles of tent poles and canvas he trudged under. He glanced sidelong at Hal. Hal nodded back. If not for Hal, he might now be crippled.

Hal had been on guard duty on Fort George's ramparts on the last day of Jamie's punishment. From the east wall, he watched Sergeant McBeath return with his hand-picked squad of soldiers, noting with alarm that Jamie was no longer with them. Risking another stretch in the Black Hole, he abandoned his post to gather as many men of his unit as he could find. Between them, they scraped together enough pipe tobacco to bribe the sentry in the guardroom, and the man looked the other way as they stole out.

Hal knew where to search, but Jamie was never gladder to hear his gruff voice or the pounding of his fellow glensmen's feet as they spotted him.

Shocked at his treatment, they unbuckled the belts torturing him and carried him back to barracks, treading the stony ground gingerly not to jar or jolt him. Even so, every step was agony. Now, four weeks later, the torn muscles and sinews of his back had still to fully heal, while the extra loads McBeath spitefully piled on him only hindered his recovery.

As they neared the capital, a great crowd spilt from the city, eager to watch the spectacle Captain Cumming's company of almost one hundred Highlanders made as they marched to Castle Rock. Pipes inflated and wheezed into life, the snare drums rapping. A breeze rippled the pleats of their kilts as they marched in line, well-muscled calves bulging and flexing. The sound stirred Jamie's blood as much as it tugged at his heart. His ancestors had charged into battle to the skirl of the pipes. The sound awakened a memory of clan bonds and affinities, pride in all there still was and all that had been taken from them. He sensed the men around him felt the same. Putting the gruelling exhaustion of their march behind them, they straightened their backs and touched the hilts of their swords, lengthening their strides with the merest hint of a swagger.

To Jamie's surprise, the townsfolk cheered them. Young women called out what fine lads they were. They mustnae let themselves be sold to the Indies like their comrades before them. Most Highlanders understood little but Gaelic, but Jamie clenched his jaw at the mention of betrayal. He had heard about the brutal deception the Black Watch suffered at the hands of the king's father almost forty years before, but now there were rumours of more recent regiments—Lord Seaforth's Highlanders, the Argyle Fencibles. 'Twas said they had also been betrayed.

A young woman called out to him. 'Hey, bonnie lad, will ye steal a kiss?' She blew him a kiss and tossed a yellow flower to him. He knew better than to catch it and marched on, letting the bloom fall at his feet.

McBeath swooped on him, jabbing him in the lower back with the blunt end of his halberd. 'Eyes front! March in close order.'

He stumbled, exhaling through clenched teeth as pain flared up his spine. For the thousandth time, he cursed the man.

They marched on past yet more gentle farmland, finally entering the capital through the West Port, a gate in the city walls. As they tramped toward the castle, they passed a growing jumble of dark buildings tottering drunkenly together. Jamie had seen naught like it. Separated by narrow closes and wynds, the towering tenements of the auld toun leaned in all directions. Jamie stared up at the ramshackle storeys, seeing pinched faces peer out of the dark, whole families crowded in squalor and filth. He wrinkled his nose. An offensive stench hung in the smoke-filled air. Shouting a warning, a woman tipped the contents of a chamber pot onto the cobbles below. McBeath leapt aside, narrowly missing being foully doused. He cursed her, brandishing his sword. Dogs scavenged amongst rubbish and filth, hens and livestock free to wander the maze of narrow alleyways alongside traders with creels on their backs or guiding rumbling carts loaded with all manner of unfamiliar goods. Overshadowing this hubbub towered the castle, high on its crag, its turrets and walls guarding all it surveyed.

On command, the column wheeled to the left and marched up Castle Hill, entering the castle through the portcullis gate. Their approach had been observed for some distance. Captain Cumming was waiting to greet them, strutting in his scarlet and braid. He swiftly dismissed them to their barracks. The captain had not thought to humble himself by marching with his men. He journeyed to the capital by sea on the *Glenmore* with much of the baggage and those men too injured or sick to make the long march, young Archie amongst them. That their captain had chosen to do so told Jamie much about the man His Grace had appointed as their commanding officer.

On reaching the barrack building, the men discovered their quarters were even more cramped than those of Fort George, the northern fort being far newer. Even so, they were relieved to throw off their heavy packs and equipment and lie on a real bed, even if they must share that berth with another soldier. The walls of their barrack room soon echoed with grunts and groans as men stretched stiff limbs and rubbed tender shoulders and blistered feet.

Young Archie was waiting to greet them, standing by the hearth where a pot of something savoury bubbled on the hook. He smiled shyly as they crowded in.

'Archie! It is! Archie Munro.' Jamie grasped the lad by the forearm and gingerly embraced him. ''Tis good to see ye on yer feet.' He grimaced as he straightened his spine. 'How are things?' He nodded at the lad's back.

'Better, thank ye.' Archie tugged his sark free and pulled it up to reveal the ruined expansive of his back. The livid weals were no longer weeping but still sickened Jamie.

'Glad to hear it,' he muttered.

'I've been judged fit to rejoin my company. On the morrow, I'm to parade wi' the rest o' ye.'

'That's grand news, lad.' Hal ruffled Archie's hair before stretching out on his chosen berth, his hands clasped behind his head. 'We've missed ye. What news, then? What passed whilst we made the lang march from the Highlands to the civilised south?'

The men gathered to listen, their mouths watering at the aroma wafting from Archie's pot.

'We'll eat first, aye?' But Archie hardly needed to ask. The men had been on tight rations for much of the march, enduring a constant, gnawing hunger. Handed steaming bowls of mutton stew, they set to with their spoons.

Archie spoke between mouthfuls. 'Ours is the last company to muster here. The others hadna so far to come. The duke's brother Lord William is here, our lieutenant colonel. A private from another company pointed him out, and we watched him go into the governor's house. Other commanding officers are also here, even Lord Barrington, the Secretary at War. There's a full dress parade the day efter next, a formal affair to entertain the fashionable folk o' Edinburgh. Lord William will address the regiment efter the parade, though what aboot, I dinna ken. 'Tis a mystery, though there be rumours.'

'Rumours?' Allan Ross lowered his spoon.

'Some say we're to go to England.' Archie frowned. 'Others say farther, America or ... or even the Indies.'

'The Indies!'

''Tis what I've heard.'

'They canna do that!' Willie Thom exploded. 'We havena to leave Scotland.'

'Aye,' John Gordon growled. 'Her Grace promised. We all heard her, and 'twas writ on thon papers we put oor marks on.' He looked at Jamie, the only man amongst them who could read.

'Aye,' Jamie confirmed, 'we're nae to be drafted. The Northern Fencibles were raised to defend Scotland. We've nae to go for foreign service, even to England. Foreign service is naught but transportation to the king's colonies clad in a scarlet coat. A cruel punishment.' He exhaled, calming himself. There was no sense in alarming the men. 'Those were the terms on the letters o' service we signed. They read something like: I agree to serve His Majesty King George the Third as a soldier in the regiment of fencible men commanded by His Grace the Duke o' Gordon upon the condition I'm nae to be marched out of Scotland except in the case of an invasion o' England. I'm nae to be drafted into any other corps. There was a bit about having the Articles of War read aloud to us. 'Tis what we signed. I read the paper to the end, every word. I dinna see how His Grace can break his promise.'

There was a rumble of agreement, although Jamie knew doubts had been sown in the men's minds. That they rooted with ease was a consequence of their distrust in the authorities that ruled them. The men fell silent, looking uneasy. He understood their unease; he had harboured a sense of impending betrayal ever since McBeath's alleged slip of the tongue at Fort George. The devil had taken every opportunity to needle him further on the long march here, feeding him half-truths and rumours until Jamie no longer knew what to believe. He had tried to dismiss McBeath's tales, but his unease remained.

McBeath had likely hoped he would share his suspicions with the men, stirring their fears, but he had chosen not to. Instead, selfishly, he unburdened himself to Morven. He frowned. Had she nae enough to worry about? He must've frightened her. Yet deep down, he knew why he'd done it. If there was substance to McBeath's claims and trouble brewed, he would not have it come out of the blue for her. And should he, God forbid, do something unthinkable, he wished her to understand why.

He put his bowl down. Unbidden, her face came to him, delicate, intelligent, the proud set of her jaw, her sensual mouth. He groaned. Did she still think of him, miss him like he missed her, as if his heart had been wrenched from his ribcage? Or was she angry with him for leaving? He could hardly blame her for that. He left her with a child in her belly, something only a scoundrel would do. After all his fine words, he'd donned a red coat and marched away to join an army he despised. She must feel bitter, yet in the dreams he escaped to every night, she still loved him with all her heart.

He lay down beside Hal and stretched his aching back. Hal's even breaths told him his friend was already asleep. They should be seeing to their weapons and uniforms in readiness for this formal parade, but exhaustion dragged at his bones. Had he truly been given no choice but enlist? As time passed, he grew less sure. *Eviction.* The word struck fear in the hearts of all Highlanders, but 'twas poor land they worked when compared with the rich soil of these low-lying counties. They could grow crops in the Lothians highland folk could only dream about. The march south had shown him that. But the pull of mountain and glen was fierce. 'Twas the call of clanship and blood, of belonging. Eviction would make him a vagrant, he and his kin. How could he inflict that shame on them? The loss would be too great, the sadness too much to bear. He sighed, knowing what that sadness had done to his father. Like his da, Jamie longed to be in Strathavon, where his heart beat strongest, at Druimbeag with Morven at his side. Recalling her face, his breathing deepened.

'I dinnae remember granting ye permission to sleep, Corporal,' Sergeant McBeath growled from the door. 'You will stand guard on the Argyle Battery.'

Jamie sat up, blinking. 'But I've marched all day.'

'And now you'll do guard duty all night. Or would ye prefer to drill?' McBeath sniggered. 'I can arrange that.'

Groaning, Jamie swung his legs over the edge of the bed. At the sound of raised voices, the others had begun to stir. ''Tis all right,' he muttered. 'Go back to sleep.' He shrugged on his coat, fixed his sword belt over his shoulder, and picked up his musket.

McBeath waited in the doorway, a smirk playing on his lips, then stalked away, expecting Jamie to follow. He trudged after him.

'Here.' McBeath thrust a rolled-up newspaper at him. 'Something to relieve your boredom. I know fine ye can read.'

It was a copy of the *Edinburgh Evening Courant*. Jamie glanced at the headline: *Gordon Fencibles to sail from Leith*. His heart lurched. He unrolled the paper and scanned the front page. McBeath whacked him with his cane.

'Leave it for later when you've naught else to do. If you look north from the Argyle Battery, you'll see the waters of the Firth of Forth and lying out to sea, off the port of Leith, the transports waiting to carry you muck-the-byres to the south of England. Or so they say.' He sniggered. 'Once they have you below decks, the War Office can ship you wherever they please. Even sell ye.'

'Sell us?'

'Best I say no more.' The devil flattened his lips as if he had said too much.

'They wouldna dare. We were given assurances.'

'Assurances!' McBeath snorted. 'What use are they when the East India Company pay handsomely for heiland men?' He smirked. 'You might be naught but heather-lowping muck-the-byres, but being a barbarous race, Heilanders are thought hardy and dauntless, accustomed to fighting in wild country. The Company understand most are still treacherous Jacobites resistant to British rule—hardly a loss to the Crown.'

Anger tightened Jamie's throat. 'If what ye say is true, I suppose they'll be shipping you away too since ye pledged to serve in the duke's regiment same as I did, same as the glensmen o' Stratha'an.'

McBeath stared at him as if he'd lost his mind. 'Of course, no', ye fool.' He let out a gust of laughter. 'I'm far too valuable. I trained the best unit in the duke's regiment. My skill in drilling raw recruits is the envy of every captain at Fort George. I'm far too useful to waste on the East India Company.'

'The men learned despite ye,' Jamie growled, 'nae because o' ye.'

But the devil only smirked back. 'Once you're safely aboard the transports, I'll be sent back north to train the next enlistment of raw recruits.' He chuckled. 'Or maybe they'll keep me here.'

'God help the poor wretches.'

They had reached the walls of the Argyle Battery, where six carriage-mounted heavy guns were aimed over the capital, guarding the northern approach to the castle. Jamie stared out over the smoke-wreathed city, his thoughts in turmoil. Could any of this be true? There must be some truth to it; why else would the *Courant* print that they were to sail from Leith on the front page of their newspaper? He swallowed, feeling sick. Had they marched here only to be shipped away Lord knows where? But then, how could the Edinburgh press know about it before they did? Most of Edinburgh must know of it by now, yet the men had been told naught. Anger flushed his face. 'Twas treachery, sanctioned by the duke and War Office. Only what could he do about it?

He glanced sidelong at McBeath, noting the devil's smug expression, his twitching eye. Had he somehow played a hand in this? But how? McBeath was only a drill sergeant, and he'd hardly been that for long. Even he couldn't contrive this.

'There they are.' McBeath pointed with his cane.

Beneath the ramparts, a long loch glistened, the last rays of the sun silvering its waters. On higher ground lay sweeping avenues of grand new houses, many still clad in scaffolding. A whole new town was being laid out in elegant lines and symmetry, stately homes for the professional and merchant classes of the capital. Jamie stared. Naught in the glens had prepared him for such an expression of wealth and privilege. He lifted his gaze to the grey expanse of the Firth of Forth beyond. Outlined against the sky stood the dark hulks of six troop transports, their escort still under sail and standing out to sea.

His guts tightened. Was this to be their fate, the promises made to them broken, the whole regiment shipped away, sold even before they could grasp what was happening? *God rot the scoundrels.* Nae whilst he still breathed.

McBeath rapped the newspaper with his cane. 'Should you tire of the view, ye've always some reading to keep you entertained.' His breath reeked of whisky. 'I think you'll find this interesting. I certainly did.'

Laughing, he strode off across the ramparts.

CHAPTER TWENTY-FIVE

THE SUN SHONE STRONGER in these southern lands, the wind less raw. After two hours of relentless musket drill, Jamie longed for a biting breeze. Its cold fingers might steal under the tight collar of his scarlet coat, the thick wool of his plaid, taking the hot edge off his rage. All ten companies of Northern Fencible Highlanders were drawn up on the castle mound. They had spent the morning parading in their companies in tight columns and files, put repeatedly through their marching exercises.

In close formation, they about turned, shouldered their muskets, rested them, then went through the motions of priming, charging, and firing without discharging their flintlocks. Again, they marched and about turned, wheeling to left and right, a scarlet wave in perfect step, instinctively reacting to each rap and ruffle of the company drums. Standing to attention, they presented arms, sunlight shimmering off a wall of bayonets.

The display was to entertain polite Edinburgh society and the watching crowds, most of whom had generously shown their approval, yet marching with his fellow glensmen swelled Jamie's pride more than he could say. He was surrounded by the flower of Gaeldom, Gaelic-speaking Highlandmen who shared his customs and values, who had doubtless suffered the same hardships and been blackmailed in the same way. They were hardy, honourable men, finely muscled, handsome in their dark plaids and bonnets, most of all, committed to one another. In their company, he felt uplifted and emboldened. Flanked by the glensmen of Strathavon, men he now loved like brothers, the suggestion the British Crown would order their betrayal incensed him.

A piper began a mournful air, the plaintive strains tugging at his heart, sharpening his need to protect his fellow Highlanders. As he stood to attention, a lone word echoed in his head, a word he could not repeat aloud since the deed it described was judged treason and carried the death sentence. Yet he could no longer deny it. That word was *mutiny*. He exhaled, his nerve steadying, confirming the stand he had already taken in his mind, for sure as the sun would rise on the morrow, right was on their side. Buoyed by regard for his fellow men, he felt primed for battle. If they were ever to return to their glens, a battle there must be, for they must defy the might of the British Crown.

Before them stood their lieutenant colonel, Lord William Gordon, carrying their regimental colours and flanked by senior commanding officers. Save for Captain Cumming, Jamie knew none of these men. Most were older and portly with fleshy faces, wigged, feathered and braided to within an inch of their lives. Lord William was younger, his face impassive as he silently judged the ranks before him on their appearance, the condition of their weapons and uniforms, the steadiness of their lines, their response to the ruffle of the company drums. Said to be newly married, he was tall and handsome and wore an air of bored indifference. Perhaps he was too self-absorbed to see the unease in his men's faces, to recognise their sullen mood, still less to understand it. Yet Jamie fancied he saw a tightness in the young lord's jaw, a mild discomfort at what he must be about to announce.

He tightened his fingers around his musket barrel, his injured back throbbing. He had not been idle during his night on guard duty. Having read the piece in the *Edinburgh Evening Courant* more times than was good for him, going over every phrase, weighing its meaning, both apparent and hinted at until the blood pounded in his head, Jamie knew he must spread word of their betrayal to the rest of his regiment.

The *Courant* reported the Gordon Fencibles were to be shipped to the south of England in anticipation of a French invasion, an assault that had yet to happen and perhaps never would, that the transports to carry them already awaited them in the firth. They would be armed with four thousand loaded cartridges, enough ammunition to repel the enemy and protect the innocent citizens of England. The Edinburgh bailies and burgesses were rightfully enraged. The regiment sent to protect their citizens and coastal fleet would instead be deployed to England, leaving Edinburgh defenceless, her port easy prey to French and American privateers. The Crown must judge even the most rural villages of England more important than Scotland's capital.

The piece talked about resulting unrest in the city using language plainly intended to embarrass the authorities. Among civic leaders, there were rumours the War Office intended to betray the Gordon Fencibles as they had deceived other Highland regiments. The worst rumours centred around the allegation that the War Office intended to sell the regiment to the East India Company or had already done so. Jamie's guts tightened. Could McBeath's tales be true? The devil couldna be trusted, yet perhaps he had spoken the truth. The *Courant* encouraged Edinburgh's citizens to support the Fencibles. These men were highly regarded in the city for their mannerly conduct and handsome appearance. They should be garrisoned at the castle defending Edinburgh, not shipped away to England or anywhere else. The last line read: *'Good citizens of Edinburgh, by the grace of God, do not let the authorities waste the lives of these brave lads!'*

Lowering the broadsheet, Jamie stared out to sea in despair. As he stood there, agonising over what to do, another soldier guarding the battery wall called out to him in Gaelic, wanting to know what the ships were out on the firth.

'Who might ye be?' he returned. 'Name yerself.'

'Private Thomas Thain.' The soldier made his way along the battery wall. 'From Huntly. Recruited into the Duke o' Gordon's fencible regiment last Candlemas. Lord Haddo's company. We've spent the last months in Ayrshire, guarding against thon raiding pirate John Paul Jones. We marched here ten days ago.'

Jamie introduced himself and showed the lad the newspaper.

Thomas shrugged. 'I ken naught o' letters.'

He explained that according to the Edinburgh broadsheet, the troop ships out on the firth were waiting to carry them to England.

'England? But why? Has thon land nae soldiers o' its own?'

'Many, I imagine.'

Thomas frowned. 'But we havena to leave Scotland.' He swore under his breath. 'I might've kent nae to trust the laird. Oor pay's months owerdue, and we've seen naught o' oor bounty.'

'It seems the duke has betrayed us.'

The lad blanched and stared at Jamie. 'The blaggard.' He glowered out at the waiting transports as the sun sank in the west.

''Twould appear so if what this paper says is true.'

Thomas swallowed. 'Since they made us march here from Ayr, and you from Inverness where I ken there be few roads better than drove roads, why would they ship us to England? We're foot soldiers. If we must go to England, why can we nae march there?' He stared out at the dark shapes riding high in the water, their copper-sheathed hulls glinting in the last rays of the sun. Fear crept into his voice. 'I'm a cattleman. I've nae love o' the sea. I couldna abide being herded alow deck like cattle aboard one o' thon great beasts.'

Jamie felt the same. That they were to be transported by sea seemed suspicious. The thought of hundreds of men crowded in dank holds stirred a sick feeling in his stomach. 'I fear once they have us crammed alow deck, they can ship us wherever they please. The south of England lies a long way from the Highlands. Stranded wi'out friends so far from home, how would we return to our glens? And once there, as the paper says, they can ship us wherever they please. Even to the Indies.'

Thomas looked at him in alarm. 'How far's that? Be it farther than France?'

'Much farther.' Jamie knew that Highlanders measured distance from home, not in miles, but in the degree of longing for their glen the distance from it aroused. ''Tisna a land ye can return from.'

'Christ! What can we do?'

'Warn the others o' Lord Haddo's. Can ye do that?'

'Aye, but what then?'

'I believe we should ...' Jamie swallowed at what he was about to suggest. 'Refuse to board the transports.'

'Defy orders?' The lad's eyes widened. 'They'll punish us. I hear they send a letter to the man's parish wi' notice o' his crime fer the kirk minister to nail to the kirk door. 'Twould shame me.' He hung his head. 'My kinfolk are proud o' me. I dinna want to be shaming them.'

Jamie pressed a hand on the lad's shoulder. Such a letter would be the least of their worries. ''Tis why they do it,' he said softly. 'Shaming men deters others, yet better to be shamed than sold to India. The East India Company will only use ye to fight their petty wars. Canon fodder to defend their profits.'

'Christ!'

'Ye'll spread word, then?'

'Soon as I get off guard duty.'

Jamie gripped the lad's hand as they parted and wished him well. Once the young private had returned to his post, Jamie briefly abandoned his position to search for others to warn. He spoke to every fencible soldier he came upon, bringing the bitter news of their betrayal, urging them to spread word to their comrades. When he had done all he could, he returned to his post, staring out into the darkness at the transports he knew still lurked there, waiting to carry them away. His breath quivered, rage boiling inside him. He tugged at the facings of his hated red coat, tearing it open to drag in lungfuls of warm, southern air. It lacked the sweetness of highland air, redolent with the scent of heather and mountain herbs and did nothing to calm him.

Throughout the night, men came to speak to him at his post, treating him like their leader, asking what they should do. He showed them the broadsheet and read what it reported. He asked them to spread word. As the news sank in, he saw fear in the men's faces, although no man showed great shock. An undercurrent of suspicion already ran deep amongst the fencible men. Consternation swiftly turned to fury. Like touchpaper, a spark would ignite it.

Come morning, the bitter truth had spread throughout the regiment. Despite feeling sick with worry and exhaustion, instead of returning to his berth to sleep, Jamie spent much of the morning talking to men from his own and other companies. There had been rumours before the *Courant* published its piece, but now every story was believed, no matter how hard to swallow. As the day wore on, the men grew defiant, banding together, muttering in Gaelic.

McBeath watched them with a sly smirk but did nothing. That worried Jamie. He urged restraint on the most hot-headed amongst them. They should obey all orders but those to board the transports. Only that order should be disobeyed; it breached their terms of enlistment. They were reasonable men, known for their good conduct, but they mustn't let the duke get away with breaking his promise.

The plaintive drone of the pipes faded away, replaced by a murmur of disquiet that rippled through the ranks. Jamie glanced at the grim faces around him, the fencible men blinking in the bright sunlight. By now, every man who cared to look had seen the transports anchored in the firth and knew why they were there.

Lord William cleared his throat.

The assembled ranks fell silent, straining to hear the voice of this privileged young lord. Jamie supposed the duke had bought his brother's commission, making Lord William a lieutenant colonel at the stroke of a pen. The thought did little to warm the man to him. As he stood in line, his stomach churning, the desire to return every pressed man to his family burned in Jamie's breast. Such a feat would make his dead father proud, would be the greatest privilege of his life.

'My friends,' Lord William boomed, his voice deep and resonant. 'Fellow non-commissioned officers and men of the Northern or Gordon Fencibles. I have brought you here in consequence of a call from His Majesty to go to the south of England, where the king requests the regiment's aid, believing it will be of great service.'

He nodded to the adjutant standing at his side, a small, bespectacled young man who stepped forward and haltingly translated the lord's words into Gaelic. A murmur of alarm rose from the ranks.

'I can assure you,' Lord William went on, 'this call proceeds from His Majesty's good opinion of you as a regiment, his confidence in the good name you have deservedly acquired since your establishment. When I was last in England, it pleased me greatly to hear every person speak of you in the most flattering terms of endorsement.'

Once translated, the men received this praise in stony silence, the adjutant struggling to interpret some of Lord William's more complex sentence structures into Gaelic. *Every person in England had heard of them? How could they?*

'His Majesty,' Lord William boomed on, 'in taking into consideration the length of the march by land and the loss of time such a march would entail, has ordered transports and an escort to receive you. I am informed these have arrived and are being made ready for your comfort. Be assured other Scottish fencible regiments have likewise been called to England to answer His Majesty's call.'

Anticipating some favourable response, Lord William smiled, perhaps expecting applause, a burst of three cheers, bonnets waved in the air, even a shout of God save the King. When naught came but sullen silence, he frowned and went on.

'His Majesty expects at least eight hundred men from the regiment to go, rank and file, including corporals, with a proper number of sergeants, officers, and staff to accompany you. Of course, only the cream are wanted, men chosen for their abilities and good looks, youth, vigour, and strength of constitution. Most of all, men known for their loyalty. The king wishes this to be a voluntary act on your part, and I have assured him it will be.' He smiled with a patronising air. 'So, my friends, step forward; let every brave man and lover of his country come forth and vie to be among the first chosen to meet so noble a cause!'

He paused and looked along the ranks, expecting men to rush forward. Not a man moved. *Their country*? But England was not their country. They werena to leave *their* country unless England was attacked.

'Be assured,' Lord William went on, his voice more of a croak now, 'no one has your welfare more at heart than I do. You will find excellent quarters in England. A soldier can live much better there than ever he can here. However well you look at present, I expect every one of you will look ten times better before you've been a month in England. The voyage is nothing with good transports and a naval convoy.' He lifted their regimental standard aloft. 'So, I ask you to prepare with as much spirit and alacrity as possible.'

Finally remembering to let the young adjutant translate his message, he frowned at Lord Barrington while the young officer attempted to do so. The Secretary at War frowned back, irritably drumming his fingers against his breeched leg.

The fencibles reacted with anger.

'Has England been invaded?' one private shouted in English.

Lord William ignored the outburst. 'I trust I shall have it in my power to declare your readiness to answer His Majesty's call without delay. The king looks upon going by sea as the least fatiguing, least expensive, and most expeditious method of travel, which it most certainly is. So, then, let the first brave volunteer step forth that he may encourage his less certain fellows to their duty.'

Once translated, this appeal was greeted with angry shouts of defiance.

'Niver will we go to England!' came the shout, and the Edinburgh crowds cheered.

'We're sold to the Indies!' Hal bellowed, and he stamped his buckled shoes.

''Tis a trick,' others cried.

'We're deceived!'

'Remember the Black Watch!'

The men took up that cry to the thunderous approval of the watching crowds.

'We've niver seen a penny o' oor promised bounty!' one man threw to the wind.

Jamie shouted over the uproar. 'Fellow countrymen,' he bellowed. 'We're highland-born, and Highlanders honour their promises. Amongst Highlandmen, the shame of a broken pledge isna to be borne. Fer lang, we've given our laird our obedience, believing that as his tenants and kinsmen, he's honour-bound to protect us. Our fathers drew their swords for him and spilt their blood. Yet in allowing this shameful deception,' he gestured angrily with his musket in the direction of the waiting transports, then at the cluster of gentrified officers before him. 'His Grace has broken his promise. Shipping us to England breaches the terms o' our enlistment, and well he kens it. They all do!' He exhaled, struggling to keep his anger in check. 'There's been no invasion. 'Tis weasel words to lure us from our country. I say we stand firm. No man board their ships!'

A great roar went up.

He waited for the cheering to die down before repeating his charge in English for the benefit of his language-challenged commanders.

The men shouted their approval amidst a thunderous stamping of hob-nailed shoes. 'This was niver in oor papers. Damned if we'll board their stinking ships!'

'Who in God's name is that rabble-rouser?' Lord Barrington demanded. 'The man dares to incite the men in English, doubtless to inflame this seditious crowd. I want his name.'

Unable to prevent a gleeful smirk from twisting his face, Sergeant McBeath sidled up to Captain Cumming, eager to provide that information. He pointed at Jamie with his cane. The captain turned his head to listen to his best drill sergeant. His countenance darkened. Spluttering with rage, he approached the knot of senior officers.

Jamie was not privy to Captain Cumming's exchange with the British Army's top commanders, but the fact that they were all now glaring at him told him enough. They knew his name and that he had spent time in the black hole at Fort George for an earlier act of defiance. They accepted every malicious falsehood McBeath concocted to blacken his name. Already, they had him identified as the ringleader, which he supposed he was.

The shouting continued, men breaking from the ranks, milling over the castle mound in chaos and disorder. 'Where's His Grace hiding?' one man bellowed.

'Aye, where's oor colonel?' shouted another. 'The trickster hasna the guts to face us!'

The young adjutant stared in horror. He leant forward to translate the men's cries, but Lord William waved him away. The young lord appeared stunned by the men's anger. Cheeks flaming, he turned on his heel and strode from the field of exercise to jeers from the watching crowd, the sight of his stiff back retreating over the drawbridge only further inflaming them. He was followed by Lord Barrington, Lord Adam Gordon, the duke's uncle and an army commander and Member of Parliament, then by senior officers and staff, also to jeers and taunts from the crowd.

Captain Cumming glared at the crowds of mocking townspeople. 'Blast these pernicious reforming societies. They're responsible for this outrage, spouting their drivel about civil liberties and the rights of the lower orders. Good God, they even espouse the rights of barrowmen and fleshers. Washerwomen, for God's sake!' He narrowed his eyes at the raucous crowd. 'I see their wicked contagion in this, fuelling disaffection amongst the lower set, giving them aspirations above themselves.' He exhaled through flared nostrils. 'Look at them! They're a rabble, here to poison the men's minds and stir up trouble.'

'Very likely, sir,' Lieutenant Grant replied.

The captain glared at him. 'I'll have the men dismissed in their companies, Lieutenant. March them back to their duties in good order.'

The lieutenant stared open-mouthed at the chaos around him, likely wondering how he was to accomplish that.

'For the love of God, man, get them out of here!'

CHAPTER TWENTY-SIX

Scalan, October 1781

MORVEN INHALED SHARPLY AS she got to her feet, prompting Nathaniel to glance at her.

'Are you all right? I can do that. If you show me where each plant should go, I shall plant it. Won't you tell her, Father?' Nathaniel looked at the master.

Father John was resting in a wicker chair Struan had carried out to the courtyard for him. Having taken the students for their history and theology lessons, he now looked weary and pale. Father Ranald had gone with the boys to a small pool in the Crombie Burn where they liked to swim and play; their last opportunity before winter's chill dampened their enthusiasm. The master believed fresh air and exercise were conducive to a healthy body and a pious mind and encouraged outdoor activities whenever possible. His eyes were now closed against the watery sun leeching through the clouds, and he appeared asleep.

''Twas only a twinge,' Morven assured Nathaniel. 'Rowena thinks I've still a week or twa until my littlin comes. Nae need to look so worried.'

Although he nodded, Nathaniel did worry. How would she manage with an infant to care for? Her husband was unlikely to return from Edinburgh or wherever he was now garrisoned before the end of the American war—if then. Morven's grain was safely harvested, but there were only two weeks left to find her quarterly rent. He hoped Bishop Hay would authorise payment to her when he came to chair the annual administrator's meeting. They expected His Excellency any day. There was no question Morven had saved the master's life. If the bishop would go further and engage her as the seminary's permanent physician, she would have a regular wage, only mission funds were tight. He had known that since almost his first day here, and she was a woman. Women distracted from the business of learning and piety. Boys could not be their true selves in their presence; hence, they must be shunned as much as possible. He had once accepted that ruling. All women frightened him except Janet, but the rule now baffled him. Since the Lord was all-loving, He must love men and women equally and would not want women's lives restricted.

'The comfrey will do best there.' Morven pointed. 'Against the wall where the sun's warmth lingers.' She lifted a clump of roots and earth from her creel.

'Please, let me.' He took the clump from her. Since Morven had shown him the healing power of herbs growing in nature, he had read widely on the subject, even ordering the *Generall Historie of Plantes* by herbalist John Gerard to add to the college library. The volume had been enlightening. Scholarly men like Gerard had repeatedly proven the healing properties of the plants Morven spoke of. He had since learned about the medicinal garden Pope Nicholas the Fifth set out at the Vatican and about the physic garden at Edinburgh and the more famous one at Kew near London. With Morven's guidance, he hoped to plant a similar albeit far more modest one at Scalan.

He glanced at her. She was the source of his fascination with these miraculous gifts from the Lord that others seemed to carelessly overlook. Listening to her speak of nature's power and then witnessing that power in action had been truly inspiring. The more he learned, the more he realised his ignorance and wished to rectify it. The Lord had sent Morven to Scalan; there could be no doubt. Working alongside her and learning of her troubles, he had come to care about her welfare. Perhaps it was wrong, although he couldn't see how, but a friendship had grown between them. It was not the same bond between a man and wife; it could never be that, but it meant the world to him. He could speak freely with her, and she listened and made no judgements. In her company, his father's expectations faded in importance, something remarkable; they had ruled his life since he first learned of them. Even his fear of rejection was beginning to feel unfounded.

'I'll gladly let ye dig,' Morven said. 'Though I doubt a bit o' digging will hurt me.'

'But in your condition, I couldn't possibly allow it. Mightn't any exertion ...?' He fluttered his fingers in the direction of her swollen abdomen, unsure how to say what worried him. Not for the first time, he wondered how an almost full-term infant could fit in such a slender body and how it would get out. The situation was so far from his field of competency it left him flustered and lost. He hadn't even the right language.

'My bairn will come when 'tis time. I doubt aught I do will change that. I've already dug up all these.' She pointed to her basket piled with freshly uprooted herbs: comfrey, yarrow, wild garlic, bog myrtle, even nettles and dandelions, herbs she hoped would thrive in the relative shelter of Scalan's walled, west-facing courtyard. In such a harsh landscape, Nathaniel was not sure they would, but he prayed so.

'When I conceived the idea of an apothecary garden,' he replied, 'I did not mean for you to do all this. Especially in your ...' he swallowed, growing agitated. 'I only sought your advice.' And she had been sceptical, believing that healing plants thrive in particular places. 'I fully intended to do all the work myself.'

'A wee bit work niver killed a body, and I see now Scalan is special. Those who study and worship here mak' it so. You, the master, the pious young scholars, yer spirit and devotion raise this place.' Morven whirled her hands together, forming an invisible eddy as she'd done around the master the night she healed him. 'It pulses and thrums, singing a song that quickens my heart. I'm thinking these herbs will thrive.'

He smiled in relief. 'Then, if you show me where to dig, I shall do the planting.'

She nodded, rubbing the base of her spine. 'Though I dinna ken if 'tis what a future bishop should be doing.'

He laughed and began digging in the damp soil. An earthy scent rose to greet him. He breathed it in, savouring its glorious richness. 'I no longer know if I want to be a bishop.' He frowned, one foot poised on his spade. 'If I ever did.'

'Oh?' She studied him. 'Ye've nae lost yer calling, Nathaniel? But 'twas niver yours, was it? The priesthood was chosen fer ye.'

'I still wish to be a priest,' he said hastily. 'It's the only choice for me. I'll be ordained when the bishop comes if he judges me worthy. But a bishop? I wish to minister to the poor and would rather serve here, in Glenlivet or even Strathavon.' He smiled wistfully. 'Perhaps I could take over Father Ranald's parish when he can no longer manage. I have a friend in Strathavon.' His cheeks burned, knowing she must realise he meant her, but hopefully, in time, her neighbours and kin, even Jamie. Badenoch had faded so far from his memory he could no longer picture himself there.

'That'd be fine, Nathaniel. Father Ranald's a rare man; Rowena calls him a warrior priest. He was at Culloden on that fatal day, nae just as chaplain—he wielded a sword. But I've lang fretted ower what'll happen when he grows too old to carry on. Wi' all the priests seized after the rising, so few remain. 'Tis why Scalan is needed, and Stratha'an would be a better place fer having ye.'

'Thank you.' He lowered his head to hide the sudden rush of blood colouring his face.

'What aboot yer da, though?' She froze, a startled look on her face, and clutched at her skirts.

'What is it?'

She stared at her feet. A rush of liquid spread from beneath the hem of her gown, soaking the pile of earth by the hole he'd dug.

'Whatever's that?' He stared at it. 'From where did all that liquid come?'

She clutched her belly. 'From inside me.'

'Dear God. What does it mean?'

'That my bairn will come sooner than I thought.'

'*What? When?*'

'Now, or leastways soon.'

'Lord, but it can't!' He stared at the muddy puddle at her feet. 'Forgive me.' He averted his gaze. 'What should I do?' Never had he imagined finding himself in such a predicament.

'Ye might ride fer Rowena. Or send Janet to fetch her. I dinna suppose I should be riding fer her myself.'

'Lord, no.' He stared at her, his mind in turmoil. He knew how to pray and prepare a soul to meet its maker, how to deliver Holy Mass and a moving service, but of the mysteries of childbirth, he knew nothing. How a woman might bring forth a child paralysed him with embarrassment and fear.

Father John rose from his chair. 'Fetch Janet, Nathaniel. She'll know what to do.' He took Morven's arm and helped her into his chair.

Why didn't I think of that? He fled inside, silently thanking the Lord that Father John had only been resting his eyes. He returned moments later with Janet, her hands covered in flour.

'Ah, Janet.' The master smiled awkwardly. 'Do you know a woman named Rowena? I believe she's a midwife. Might you know where to find her? It seems our young friend here has need of her skills.'

'Oh, my!' Janet flicked her gaze to Morven, then back to the master. 'I ken Rowena Forbes, aye. D'ye mean the lass is—?'

'I fear so.'

'And ye wish the bairn born at Scalan?' She gaped at him. 'Ye mean to allow that?'

Father John smiled pragmatically. 'It seems that decision has been taken from my hands.'

Morven gave a little whimper, and Nathaniel's heart squeezed in sympathy. He should be helping her, not standing by like a halfwit. Only how? He had no idea, and it was hardly a priest's place. Or any man, he supposed.

The master patted Morven's hand. 'Try not to worry. Childbirth is natural. I'm sure all will go smoothly.' He turned to Janet. 'Can you ride, Janet?'

'I can manage a garron if 'tisna too skittish.'

'I want you to take my horse. Rufus is swift and surefooted. Please ride for this midwife with all haste.'

Janet blinked. 'Aye, Father, I'll do that.'

'Right away, Janet.'

She snapped her mouth shut and hurried to the barn, untying her apron as she ran. She used it to brush her hands, tossed it aside, and vanished into the building.

The master turned to Nathaniel. 'Is Annag here? I forget which is her rest day.'

He shook his head. He no longer knew what day it was. 'I'm not sure, Father.'

'Please fetch her and have her help Morven to the kitchen. I believe that would be the most suitable place. A midwife may boil water there. I understand hot water is needed. Since the kitchen is forbidden to the students, they need never know of this unusual breach of the rules.' He nodded to reassure himself. 'After everything Morven has done for us, it's only right we help her in her time of need.' He smiled at her. 'I wish your infant born with the smallest degree of trouble and distress. 'Tis the least I can do for you.'

'Thank ye,' she croaked. 'I wish for that, too.'

'You agree, Nathaniel? I know you two have developed a friendship.'

Nathaniel blushed, unsure if such a friendship was allowed. 'Yes, Father, wholeheartedly.' He looked at Morven.

'*Bless ye,*' she mouthed.

He fled back into the house, returning in time to observe a cloud of dust travel at pace down the college track—Janet and Rufus making away at a gallop. He had searched the house to no avail. It was Wednesday. He now remembered that was Annag's day off.

'I'm sorry, Father,' he stammered. 'Annag's not here. I believe 'tis her rest day.'

'Ah. A pity. I see I should not have sent Janet away.'

Morven rose cautiously from the master's chair. 'I can manage, Father. I've seen plenty bairns into the world. I'll take myself to the kitchen and put water on to boil whilst I wait fer Rowena.'

Unhappy with that, the master frowned at Nathaniel. 'Go with her.'

Nathaniel attempted a smile as he took her arm but achieved little more than a taut grimace.

'Ye needna come wi' me,' she whispered. 'I ken where the kitchen is.'

'I've little notion how to help,' he confessed, 'but I won't just leave you to go through this alone.'

She smiled softly. Nathaniel might be ignorant of childbirth. How could he nae be? But he would stay with her regardless. Bless him. No woman should toil in labour alone.

'I'm grateful, though I doubt I'll need help,' she said with more confidence than she felt. 'As the master said, childbirth is natural.' She stopped as a spasm gripped and waited with clenched teeth for it to pass. ''Twould be a dry birth and hence more painful. She had watered the soil with the birthing fluid, leaving naught to soften the strength of each contraction. Hardly the best start.

'How long until ...?' Nathaniel swallowed, trying not to look at her belly.

'Every birth is different, but I hope 'twill be ower soon.'

Puzzled, he opened the kitchen door for her. 'But wouldn't you rather wait until Mistress Forbes arrives to help you?'

She stifled a smile. 'Bairns wait fer naeone. They come when they come, nae matter what we'd rather. And I dinna ken where Rowena is likely to be.'

His eyes widened. 'You mean she might not arrive in time?'

''Tis possible, though ye needna fear. I ken what to do.'

His hand trembled as he held the door open, his attempt at a reassuring smile a dismal failure. 'But I do not.'

'Ye needna do anything, Nathaniel. The toil will be mine.' When first she learned she was carrying a child, she imagined Jamie would be there at the birth. Not in the same room, Rowena would never allow that, but waiting on nettle stalks on the far side of the door. That he was so far away made her wish to weep. Childbirth was bruising and could take hours. How would Nathaniel cope?

He looked uncertainly at her.

'Ye might talk to me. Let me grip yer hand. Allow me to moan and wail and ... and shut yer ears should I tak' the Lord's name in vain. When the pains grip fierce, a woman can do that, though if I do, I wish ye to ken I'm sorry fer it.'

His eyes widened in horror, but he nodded and led her to a chair by the fire. Whilst she rested, he filled the big boiling pot with water from the barrel kept there and lifted it onto the hook. He poked fresh peats into the fire, stirring the embers until they flared and sparked, and the peats began to burn, then knelt at her feet.

'I can do that,' he said. 'I understand you must suffer in childbirth; the bible tells us so. Only I know not how. In Genesis, God said unto Eve: *"In sorrow shalt thou bring forth children."* By sorrow, I understand was meant pain.'

She nodded, grimacing as another spasm gripped. This one was fiercer and made her whimper. During her years learning from Rowena, she had seen women writhe in pain as they toiled to bring their infants forth. 'Twas always harrowing to watch. She had also seen women die, but she pushed that thought away. Rowena would soon come, and all would be well. She need only endure until then.

'I would walk if ye'll help me. It eases things and might take my mind from the pain.'

'Of course.' He rose and helped her to her feet, offering her his arm. 'Lean on me as much as you need.'

She turned to look at him. 'I ken this isna where ye'd wish to be, Nathaniel. I'm grateful. I doubt the Church would approve o' ye attending a woman in her labours.'

He frowned. 'The Church might judge it vulgar, but if we are to serve our flock, we must understand something of their suffering. Women bring new life into the world. I believe that should be celebrated, not treated as shameful.' He regarded her earnestly. 'I have not always thought that way, but since you came into my life, you have opened my eyes in many ways.'

His kindness touched her. 'I'm thinking ye'll make a rare priest,' Morven replied. And an even rarer husband, but that she did not say.

They circled the room for the next two hours, Nathaniel stopping when she did, making soothing sounds as he waited for her pain to pass. He put his arm around her waist and let her lean on him. As they walked, she tried to explain what was happening inside her body, and he listened and marvelled at the wonder of it.

As time passed, their circuits slowed and became more broken, her pains coming stronger and closer together until she thought her back must break. Once each spasm had released its grip, all was well, and she could breathe freely, but no sooner had one pain passed than another swiftly clamped its teeth. Nature offered many herbs to deaden the pain, but foolishly, she had not thought to keep them here. The pain finally centred in her groin. She whimpered with the torment of it, wishing to rub aching flesh and bone but conscious of embarrassing Nathaniel.

'What can I do?' he begged. 'I cannot bear to see you suffer.'

'Pray Rowena comes soon,' she muttered through clenched teeth.

He dropped to his knees. 'Almighty Father, take pity on your servant, Morven. Deliver her from this torment, I beg you. Hasten the midwife to us, for I am of little use. I'd do anything, give—'

'Hush.' She raised him to his feet. 'Dinna be saying that. We'll get through, even if we must do it wi'out Rowena.'

He nodded, tight-faced, and slipped his arm around her waist. They began to walk again. She laid her head on his shoulder, breathing in the fragrance of incense, the musty aroma of old books, knowing she would always link these ethereal scents with the torment of labour and with Nathaniel's kindness. Yet how would she free her infant if the cord caught around its neck, turn the child if it lay wrong in the womb? What if the afterbirth didna all come away? She would need help.

''Twill be all right,' she whispered. 'Oh, Mother o' God.' She bent double as another fierce spasm gripped her.

Nathaniel's face twisted. 'Holy Father,' he pleaded, 'show me what to do. I cannot bear this.'

'Nathaniel,' she whimpered. 'I feel the need to bear down. Help me onto Annag's bed.'

He looked around wildly, perhaps unaware that Annag slept here, then helped her onto the heather-stuffed mattress by the fire. She cried out, the pains no longer coming in spasms but in a relentless torrent.

'A sheet to protect Annag's bed,' she gasped. 'Quickly, Nathaniel.'

He snatched the linen cloth from the table and thrust it at her. She bundled it under her skirts. She could feel the hard burn of the infant's head pressing on tender flesh and bone. The urge to bear down was overwhelming. She gave in to it, clamping her teeth to stifle her cries, but there was no quieting her. Her cries seemed too raw and primal for this quiet house of prayer. She panted, her head swimming, trying to catch her breath. Sweat soaked the bodice of her gown. Within moments, she was bearing down again, her vision blurring, squeezing the life out of Nathaniel's hand.

'Forgive me,' she gasped and clawed at her skirts.

He turned his head away.

The pain was different now, a deep tearing kind. She pushed through it, groaning like a rutting stag. 'I'm sorry,' she whimpered, but there was no helping it.

''Tis naught,' he assured her. 'Take a moment to regain your strength.'

She nodded, panting to prevent herself from bearing down again and groped with her free hand, feeling the slippery hardness of the infant's head crowning. The pain was excruciating. It filled every part of her.

The next push brought the worst pain of her life. She clamped her teeth, Jamie's face swimming before her. His eyes were dark and intense, softening as he gazed into hers.

'One more push.'

Her eyes flew wide to find Rowena smiling down at her, her eyes the same dark as her nephew's.

'Rowena! Thank God.'

The widow smiled, and with a little twist, the infant slipped into her hands. 'A lass,' she gasped. 'A dear wee soul wi' Jamie's dark hair. He'll be that proud. And to think, ye did it all yerself. Ye didna need me.'

'I couldna have done it wi'out Nathaniel.' Morven searched the room. 'Where is he?'

'I sent him away. I'll let him back later if ye want, after I've delivered the afterbirth and made you and the bairn look decent. He was wanted. The bishop is here.'

CHAPTER TWENTY-SEVEN

Edinburgh Castle

'I'D KEEP YER MOUTH shut this time,' McBeath warned. He came strutting down the company line, ruthlessly straightening any imagined aberrations with his halberd. 'They have your traitorous nature well marked, Innes. If you want to escape a court martial, you'd better no' whip up any more nonsense, though 'tis a sight I'd pay a fortune to see. James Innes, brave and principled, honourable to a fault, charged with leading a mutiny against the king.' He chuckled. 'What would His Grace say? Or his factor.'

'I've led no mutiny,' Jamie growled, but the devil had moved out of earshot.

Since the shambolic parade, the Northern Fencibles had followed all orders, behaving with civil if distrustful obedience, but no man had volunteered to board the king's ships. Fear of betrayal still darkened the men's minds.

The day after the parade, Captain Cumming separated his men into detachments and marched them into the castle's tiny chapel, an ancient shrine dedicated to Saint Margaret. Crowding them cheek by jowl in the stone nave, he mounted the pulpit, his face stiff with rage, and berated them like a Calvinist Kirk minister. Staring them down, his chest heaving, he called them shameful cowards and knaves for not honouring the king's call, cravens unfit to serve their country. 'Yet even now,' he growled, 'you may prove me wrong. Any man with an inch of backbone, step up to the pulpit and prove it!'

No man moved.

Choking with rage, Cumming stalked from the chapel, the men's obstinacy fuelling his anger, loading the flintlock of his wrath to fire at the next detachment of men. Their tongue-lashing would be even more vicious. White-faced, the men stumbled away. The captain's insults had only stiffened their resolve. Jamie urged restraint upon any man considering violence to show his resistance. They must remain obedient but stand firm. Right was on their side.

Sergeant McBeath watched the whole affair from a distance, loitering by the battery wall, his face twitching. Most days, he smuggled a copy of the *Edinburgh Evening Courant* to the men or the *Caledonian Mercury*, another Edinburgh broadsheet, smirking as he handed the papers to Jamie. The men's stubbornness to volunteer greatly amused him.

Both broadsheets warned if the fencibles refused to embark, the authorities would bring an armed platoon of dragoons against them. Those forces were already mustering outside the city walls, billeted in the homes of farming folk. Jamie's guts tightened, yet he said naught, keeping the alarming news to himself in the hope it might prove untrue. He warned the men they should give the authorities no excuse to bring force against them. If 'twas truly volunteers the king wanted, they must refuse to offer themselves. Yet he knew it would not be that simple. Highlanders were considered a lesser race, primitive and heathen, treacherous to a man. They must be bent to the king's will with an iron fist.

His Grace the Duke had now arrived in the capital, summoned by his uncle Lord Adam to shame and chastise his defiant regiment to their duty. That regiment now waited in the drizzle to hear what he had to say. A cold droplet slithered down Jamie's neck from his useless pillbox bonnet. He gritted his teeth, his stomach churning. His Grace had protected the Catholic seminary at Scalan, at least to a degree, and although he had repeatedly raised his tenants' rents and forbidden the sub-division of tacks, so had every other landowner and clan chief in the Highlands. The duke might be a better laird than many, but had he conspired with the authorities to break the promise given to enlist these men? They would learn the answer to that in the next few minutes.

The fencibles had spent the last hour parading on the castle mound before their colonel, wheeling and turning, put relentlessly through their exercises, content to demonstrate their competence in performing the British Army's complicated marching and musket drill on the understanding that on no account would they be boarding any ships. Now drawn to a halt, they stood to attention in their companies, the Grenadiers to His Grace's right, the Light Infantry to His left. Standing in the middle ranks beside Hal, Jamie was conscious of his height, more than a head taller than Hal.

He had no wish to draw the duke's attention.

Wigged and powdered, the Cock o' the North stood stiffly before them, appraising the men with prideful disdain. His uniform dripped with gold braid; an eagle's feather jutted from his hat. He was flanked by his brother Lord William, carrying their regimental colours, and Adjutant Abercrombie, again brought as interpreter. Behind these three, reinforcing the duke's authority, stood a wall of senior officers and staff, all wearing the same unyielding expression. Captain Cumming's face was set harshest of all.

Beyond them, a crowd of townspeople had gathered. These folk had likely read of the Highlanders' treatment and wished to see how their defiance would end. 'Twas only natural to be curious, especially about soldiers sent to protect them, but the townsfolk appeared genuinely concerned about the regiment and its fate. They whistled and cheered, calling them brave lads, urging them to stand firm.

His Grace frowned his disapproval. Alexander, fourth Duke of Gordon, was still a relatively young man, in his thirties, Jamie judged, his sour expression revealing his ill humour at having endured a jolting three-day coach ride south from the comfort of Gordon Castle to address his disobedient tenants. Tall and hook-nosed, steely-eyed, magnificently dressed, he made an impressive sight, his basket-hilted broadsword glinting in the sunshine between showers, a pair of chased silver pistols tucked into his belt. He made the men wait for long minutes in the drizzle while he satisfied himself of their nervous attention.

'My friends,' he finally boomed, 'brave men of the Northern Fencibles, many of whom I know bear my name. I come here with the expectation of bringing you to your senses. I stand before you as your colonel and laird, here to encourage you as my kinsmen as much as to admonish you as my tenants for your obstinacy. I cannot lie; your ignorance much wounds me.' Scowling, he scanned the ranks. 'Yet I console myself in the knowledge that you were aided in your stubborn bullheadedness by an evil undercurrent of sedition that runs like a sewer through the back wynds and closes of Edinburgh.'

This last comment prompted jeers and boos from the crowd. A muscle in his cheek twitched. He waited with barely concealed irritation for Abercrombie to translate his words into Gaelic, a task the young adjutant understandably struggled with.

'I'm told,' he went on, 'that troublemakers from the Society of Friends of the People have spread dangerous rumours in the city, stirring suspicion and hostility in your minds. Something I hope you are now ashamed of.'

At the duke's accusation, Jamie glanced at Hal, seeing him bristle. Should their colonel nae be ashamed o' breaking his sworn promise?

'Nonetheless,' the duke went on, 'I'll wager most of you are honest men who blush at the conduct of the minority, loyal soldiers who will stand by their colonel and king to the last. To you honourable men, I repeat, the king has called you to the defence of your country. All who remain true to their country and king, I urge you now—*step forward to the colours!*'

He turned to Lord William, who raised a pike in the air, displaying the silken yellow colours of the regiment. The flag hung forlornly, dampened by the drizzle. Even fully raised, it fluttered only limply. One canton showed the Union Flag with Saint Andrew pictured in the centre, surmounted by the crown of Scotland encircled by a strangling union wreath of roses and thistles. The regimental motto was emblazoned in Gaelic at the foot: *Cliù le Cruadail*—Renown in Hardihood.

A murmur of unease rippled through the ranks. There were no protests or demonstrations, but no man stepped forward. His Grace blinked in disbelief, his face draining of colour. Jamie's guts tightened. The duke would deem this a personal affront to his dignity and position. As a senior member of Scottish nobility and the ruling class, the Duke of Gordon was accustomed to being obeyed at all times.

The moment stretched on, straining the men's nerves as the duke's face whitened with rage. 'If any man is such a disloyal dastard he would refuse his king,' he spluttered, 'I disown him now. He may consider his lease in jeopardy, if not his freedom. Although you were raised for Scotland's defence, England is now in danger, and none but cravens would refuse her call!'

Jamie looked around in despair. *How could their freedom be in jeopardy?* They were all held men, only here because they had been blackmailed into taking the king's shilling, held hostage for their families' security of tenure. The loyalty of these men was not in question, but their loyalty lay not with His Grace and the British Crown but in the hills and glens to the north where their kinfolk scraped a living. Their allegiance was rooted in the peaty soil of the Highlands and at that moment, as fellow glensmen, in a fierce commitment to each other.

'I will urge you one last time,' His Grace growled. 'Rethink your folly, and by the grace of God, pray I can forgive your contemptible behaviour.'

The men reacted angrily, shaking their muskets at him, shouting that they would never embark. They had been betrayed.

'Ye promised we'd only march sooth to England if that land was invaded,' one man shouted in Gaelic. ''Tis what ye pledged, you and yer false-tongued wife. Cramming us alow deck on thon rotting hulks in the firth was niver part o' the bargain. Once alow deck, we'll be the king's prisoners!'

'Aye,' shouted another. 'Ye might be a noble lord, but yer word's neither noble nor honourable. 'Tis swiftly broken. Shame on ye! Oor pay's months owerdue, and what o' oor promised bounty? When will we see a farthing o' that?'

'As fer these abominations,' another man cried, 'ye can hae them back!' He threw his ammunition box and goat-haired sporran on the ground, then, rethinking the wisdom of discarding his supply of musket cartridges, hastily retrieved the box. Others followed his lead, tearing off their hated goatskin sporrans with their tassels and bells. They flung them into the crowd to cheers from the townsfolk who fought over them as keepsakes. The pouch was a mocking insult of their Highland dress. Known as a *sporran moloch* or hairy sporran, 'twas an anglicised purse they had been overcharged for from their promised bounty—coin which had still to materialise.

Jamie cringed. To disobey a chief was unthinkable, yet when that chief was bought and dishonest, a man must reserve his loyalty for his kinsmen and comrades. That was what the duke was now witnessing. These men, most tenants and kinsmen of the duke, had grudgingly put on a uniform that mocked their ancient dress in the misguided belief their laird would reward them with his protection. For that laird to then sell them, casting them to the wind on rotting troop ships, seemed the most shameful betrayal.

'We're sold!' Hal bellowed, stamping his musket butt on the ground. 'The duke has sold us to the Indies. The Edinburgh papers say so. He's shipping us awa' so he can clear oor kinfolk fer sheep!' He spat in disgust. 'We're sold to the East India Company, all to swell his fat coffers.'

'To better keep his mistress!' Willie Thom shouted.

Jamie winced, hoping Abercrombie would pause before attempting to translate that. Many men had drawn their swords. One, a man he recognised as Corporal Finlay MacKay of MacIntosh's company, was gesturing wildly.

'To me!' MacKay shrieked. 'Dinna be falling fer British tricks. We'll bring justice to the foul-tongued brutes who call themselves officers. They think themselves better than us. To me!' he roared. 'Northern Fencibles to me!'

All hell broke loose, men swarming around MacKay brandishing their swords, the crowd cheering them on. 'Twas suicidal madness. Jamie shouted for calm.

'Sheath yer arms, I beg ye! We're highland men. Nae matter what His Grace or these officers say, no man here is a coward. Our grievances are many, and this request, put to us like an order, feels like a shameful insult. I feel it as sorely as you. But I beg ye, dinna be drawing arms. That can only end badly. We're reasonable men. I'll wager His Grace can be as reasonable. We can settle this peaceably.'

Having given the men cause to hesitate, most grudgingly did so, lowering their swords. Jamie prayed they would pause long enough to see sense, for their rebellious spirits would be their undoing. A longing to protect every man gathered on the castle mound burned at his core, even if it must be from themselves.

With the wind knocked from their sails, most men blinked in contrition, many resheathing their swords. If dragoons were indeed mustering outside the city walls, any sign of a mutiny would be their signal to attack. The urge to rise against their deceitful leaders fermented as furiously in Jamie's guts as it did within the men, his blood pumping hot in his veins. He released his breath slowly through clenched teeth, struggling to master his rage. His muscles had tightened, the urge to draw arms almost impossible to resist. Clenching his fists, he forced breath deep into his lungs. Resist it, he must.

'His Grace wishes us to board ships bound fer the south o' England,' he shouted. 'Aye, England. Or at least, that's where he tells us the ships are bound. But that would breach our terms o' enlistment, terms His Grace devised in cahoots wi' the War Office. Those terms made clear we were to serve in Scotland, only crossing her border if England was attacked. Every man here kens the terms. They were read aloud to him, and he made his mark to show he understood. Ever we keep them in our minds.'

He thought of Druimbeag and the woman he'd left there carrying his child, of all he would give to return to her. 'If England were truly threatened,' he growled, 'do ye nae think the Edinburgh papers would be full o' it? But instead, they speak o' the Crown's treachery, that the duke means to trick us. Damned if a man here should be letting him!'

They cheered him for long minutes, reinforced by whistles from the crowd until he held a hand up that he might speak further. Bitterness drove him on. 'After the atrocities committed in the Highlands in the name o' the Crown, how can the king expect Highlandmen to trust his word? Are we to forget the barbarous crimes committed against our people, nae matter their loyalty? The killings and rapes, crops burned, land and cattle stolen. Does His Majesty imagine we can put those crimes behind us and leap eagerly to his aid?'

A keening sound rose from the men as they remembered the aftermath of Culloden and its terrors, the ill-treatment meted out to folk simply for being highland-born. To Jamie's surprise, that grief also echoed amongst the watching crowd. Shoving his way out of the disordered ranks, he strode toward the duke.

Captain Cumming leapt forward, levelling his pistol at him, but the duke raised his hand to stay him. Jamie bowed stiffly to his colonel, bonnet in hand. 'Your Grace, as you know, some of those atrocities were committed on your own lands. Not one has been forgotten or forgiven, for Highlanders' memories long endure. 'Tis arrogance to assume otherwise. Yet, despite our grievances, we wish no trouble. The men are prepared to serve as our terms dictate, but as to leaving our country, no man will board the king's ships.'

The duke stepped back in bewildered disbelief, and for a brief moment, Jamie gloried in the satisfaction of seeing the Cock o' the North less than cock-sure of himself.

'Nor do we forget the Black Watch,' Hal shouted. 'Their shameful betrayal at the hands o' the king's father or other highland regiments cruelly deceived. Damned if we'll let *this* King Geordie treat us the same way!'

The betrayal of the Black Watch regiment had grown legendary among highland soldiers for the enormity of the injustice wrought upon them. There was silence as the men grieved the treatment meted out to the Black Watch, likely wondering if the king would deal with them in the same way.

'If ye wish us to board yer ships,' another soldier shouted, 'ye'll need to dragoon us!'

Jamie winced at the man's choice of words, too close to the bone for his liking. Turning to face the men, he again raised his voice, hoping to temper their growing defiance to avoid bloodshed.

'I say we stand firm and refuse to embark,' he shouted, 'and dinna let ourselves be duped. But I urge ye nae to be drawing yer swords. 'Twill only give them cause to punish us. We're civil men. We can oppose this wrong peaceably!'

When the men answered his cry with a thunderous cheer, he carefully repeated his plea in English so the duke would be in no doubt of their stance and their desire to uphold it without violence. They wished no trouble but would not let him break his promise.

More men were now sheathing their swords. Jamie exhaled in relief. As the men slowly retook their positions, his heart slowed its wild thumping. The authorities would view the men's behaviour as unwelcome, even un-pardonable, but he prayed they might understand what lay behind it. In contrast, a violent revolt was another beast entirely. The Secretary at War would consider any violent resistance a mutiny, even treason. He turned to Hal and gave him a quivering smile, praying he had managed to calm the situation enough to protect the men he cared about. Whether he had presented their grievances and the position they'd taken without causing His Grace undue offence was another matter. 'Twas a slippery path to tread.

'Jamie!' Hal warned.

He caught the blur of movement too late—a beefy figure glimpsed from the corner of his eye. There was no time to react. McBeath raised his halberd to his shoulder and struck Jamie hard on the side of the head. He staggered, tasting blood. Pain exploded over his temples, the world tilting and pitching. He lurched toward the duke, then reeled away. Rendered useless, his legs folded under him. His teeth rattled as he hit the ground, a roaring sound in his ears.

CHAPTER TWENTY-EIGHT

JAMIE CAME TO SPRAWLED on a stone floor in near total darkness. He groaned and rose to his knees. His stomach lurched; the place smelled unimaginably foul. A tight band of pain crushed his skull. Exploring his temple with his fingers, he found a tender lump the size of a hen's egg and cursed, remembering the man who'd put it there. Taking his weight on one leg, he cautiously risked the other. Finally upright, he swayed, the room spinning, and steadied himself on a slimy wall. He lurched to the tiny window and peered down to the dark cobbles of the Argyle Battery far below.

'The Black Hole,' came a disembodied voice from the darkness. ''Tis a wretched chamber above the Portcullis Gate. Ye're here fer inciting a mutiny. And me. When will I learn to keep my muckle mooth shut?'

Jamie peered into the darkness. 'Who's there?'

'Corporal Finlay MacKay o' Captain MacIntosh's company. Ye can cry me Fin.'

Picturing the man, Jamie pressed his fingers along his brow line, trying to relieve the fierce ache. Corporal MacKay had foolishly drawn his sword and tried to rally the men to his side, an action that could well be considered an incitement to mutiny. But what had *he* done to deserve this treatment?

'I was trying to *prevent* a mutiny,' he croaked, his mouth dry as gunpowder. 'Could His Grace nae see I wanted to avoid bloodshed, to explain our refusal whilst keeping the men's behaviour within the bounds o' civility? I thought it the best way to protect them.'

'Ye spoke oot o' turn and to His Grace. I doubt he'll be forgetting that.'

'Aye,' Jamie conceded. 'I heard no assurances we werena sold. Nor a promise to pay the coin due us.'

Fin snorted. 'Ye're nae likely to.'

'How long do they mean to keep us here?' He moved away from the window, following the feeble band of light it admitted and tripped over a pair of outstretched legs. He pitched forward, but brawny arms caught him before he hit the wall. Lord God, this cell was even more cramped than the one he endured at Fort George.

'Here, sit yersel' doon.' Fin helped him to the floor, and he sat with his arms wrapped around his knees, cold seeping through his kilt and chilling his buttocks.

'Ye're Jamie Innes, then?'

'Of Captain Cumming's company.'

'Thought so. I dinna ken how long they mean to hold us. 'Til they decide how many lashes to flay oor backs wi'. Yer head must hurt. Thon McBeath's a wicked piece; naeone in MacIntosh's company trusts the divil.'

'Wise,' Jamie muttered.

'I swear I heard him afore.' Fin jerked his head toward what Jamie took to be the door. Hidden in shadow, it looked solid and heavy, darker traces revealing the iron studs that reinforced it. 'Oot by, laughing and jesting wi' the guards. Roaring drunk by the sounds o' it.'

'McBeath likes his whisky,' Jamie muttered. 'Especially when distilled by some poor tenant farmer who only wishes to pay his rent. He used to be an exciseman. He acted the tyrant, rotten to the core.'

'I'd say he's nae changed.'

Jamie gave a laugh. 'I'd say ye're right.'

'Did the divil ever go by anither name?'

'Stratha'an folk dubbed him the Black Gauger.'

'By Christ! Thon divil. He was feared all ower Strathdon, though I heard he met his match in Stratha'an. A young glensman bettered him at a duel, a lad wi' the courage to stand up to the rogue, and efter, a magistrate gaoled him.'

'Aye, but he later released McBeath on the condition he took the king's shilling.'

'Ye ken o' it?'

Jamie sighed. 'I was the young glensmen.'

'You? Ye're the man who bettered the Black Gauger wi' the sword?'

'I challenged McBeath to a duel to protect my kinswoman.'

'Christ, Jamie!' Fin let out a hoot. ''Tis an honour to share a cell wi' ye.'

He chuckled. 'The divil had his reasons fer clouting ye. 'Twas a spiteful blow fer outclassing him wi' the sword. Fer being the better man.'

Jamie grunted. 'Captain Cumming likely ordered him to seize me. McBeath's been poisoning the officers against me since my first day at Fort George. There's ill blood between us. He tried to blackmail my aunt, and I tricked him, secretly joining the excise to try and catch him out. He wasna ower pleased when he discovered who I was.'

'Christ, and now he's yer sergeant. What're the chances o' that?'

'I doubt 'twas down to chance.'

There was silence as Fin digested that.

Jamie rubbed his brow, wishing to change the subject. His eyes had grown more used to the darkness. 'What hour d'ye make it?'

'I've nae heard the drums beat Retreat, but it must be near nightfall.'

Jamie frowned, unwilling to mention the dragoons who might be poised to strike from outside the city bounds. 'Have ye heard any sound o' trouble?'

''Tis hard to hear aught in here. What was it happened to the Black Watch, Jamie? I've niver right heard their story.'

'The last King George betrayed them.'

'Aye, but how?'

Jamie sighed. 'The Black Watch regiment was raised in Perthshire to keep down clan fighting and raiding, to *watch* the Highlands. They were an independent company loyal to the king's father, later made part o' the British Army. Like the fencibles, they werena to serve beyond Scotland, but they were ordered to London, an order they considered contrary to their terms.'

'Same as us, then?'

'Aye, that's the point.'

'They agreed to it?'

'Their officers told them the king had never before beheld a highland regiment and wished to inspect them and satisfy his curiosity. Accepting this against their better judgement, they marched for London. When they reached the capital, crowds lined the streets, taunting and jeering them, calling them heathen savages. This bewildered the men since they were only there at the king's invitation. They were told the king had sailed for Hanover and ships were waiting to carry them to Flanders to fight the French in another o' the king's wars.'

'The lying scoundrel!'

'Aye, that shocked were they at their treatment, over a hundred o' them took it upon themselves to march home. They were surrounded days later by an English cavalry regiment. The officers listened to their grievances and told them they'd be pardoned if they surrendered. Thinking these officers honourable men, the Watch laid doon their arms and let themselves be taken back to London as prisoners.'

'To be betrayed again?'

'The authorities accepted the men had been deceived but judged such an outrageous breach o' discipline couldna be ignored. They were court-martialled and found guilty o' treason, every man sentenced to death.'

'*What!*'

'Their appeal failed, but thinking it wouldna look good to shoot ower a hundred Highlanders at once, 'twould make it harder to recruit in the Highlands where the War Office likes to fill its levies, the authorities decided to execute only those deemed the ring leaders. Two corporals, brothers from Laggan and a private from Rothiemurkus on Speyside, were shot at the Tower o' London. The others were transported to the West Indies, a swamp-fever posting as good as a death sentence. They never saw home again.'

Fin swore with startling savagery, venting a stream of oaths so vulgar Jamie imagined any Kirk minister would denounce him from the pulpit. He frowned. 'Ye see why we mustna be trusting their word?'

'I dinna trust a man o' them. How did ye learn o' the Black Watch's treatment, Jamie?'

'From the priest who taught me to read, though their story is well-known amongst highland regiments, their fate a warning to us all.'

'Christ, aye.' Fin drew an admiring breath. 'Ye can read, then?'

Jamie grunted. 'Little use it's been to me.' Yet he had been able to read the terms they had signed their names to and the Edinburgh newspapers' assessment of their situation. They would be ignorant of their true situation if he'd not been able to read. 'I long fer the end o' the American war,' he muttered, 'that the men might return to their families.'

'And me.'

Jamie peered at Fin through the gloom. 'Have ye a family, Fin? A wife, bairns?'

'A wife back in Corgarff and five bairns, anither on the way. You?'

'I'm newly wed. My wife is also carrying my child.' Jamie drew a despairing breath. 'God help them both. The child may be born fer all I know. I long to return to them. My wife is ....' He swallowed. How to describe her? His voice cracked. 'Morven is my life.' Anger drove a vein of steel into his voice. 'All I want is to work the land my da once worked, even if 'twill never be mine. I care nae a jot fer the king's plans.'

'Nor me.' Fin squeezed Jamie's shoulder. 'We should get some sleep. I doubt they plan to feed us.'

Jamie sighed, his stomach growling. They laid their heads down as best they could, trying not to think of the filth they were lying in. Jamie's head had ceased spinning, but a piercing cold seeped into his bones from the stone floor. Fin shivered beside him, and Jamie drew him close. They wrapped the loose ends of their plaids around each other. Sleep took its time coming.

Jamie had no notion what woke him.

Beside him, Fin stiffened and raised his head.

'What is it?'

'Dinna ken. Thought I heard sumhin.'

Jamie held his breath, straining his ears.

'There was laughter and brawling afore,' Fin whispered. 'Commotion I ken to be the sound o' men in drink. I'll swear McBeath was one o' them. It went quiet, and I supposed them asleep.'

Jamie stifled his breath, his heart beating in his throat. He could hear what sounded like the scuffle of many hobnailed shoes outside the door, then the heart-stopping rasp of metal on metal as levers were turned and bolts drawn back. He struggled to his feet. *Why would they come for them in the dead o' night?*

The door swung open.

He shielded his eyes against the sudden flood of light as men swarmed in and reached for his sword—his scabbard was gone.

'Jamie! Thank God!' Swinging lamplight revealed Hal's taut face, then Willie Thom, Allan Ross, young Archie, and the other men of his unit. More soldiers crowded behind: Fin's men. They hung back, keeping watch while the Strathavon men embraced.

Hal gripped Jamie fiercely, then thrust him away. 'Hurry, lad. We've work to do.'

'What—?'

'Later.' Hal thrust a sword and musket at him. 'Take these. Here, Corporal MacKay, arm yerself. The guards willna miss them, nae in their state. There's little time to waste.'

Bewildered, they did as instructed and followed Hal and the others, holding their breath as they crept past their unconscious guards—three men slumped over a table. Hal extinguished his lamp, and like silent wraiths, they crept down the stone staircase to the Argyle Battery, keeping within the shadow of the Mills Mount Battery with its gun platform high above. The air was cold and sharp, reviving Jamie. They skirted the perimeter of the main parade ground, passing Saint Margaret's Chapel, and made for their barracks.

Jamie's heart thumped as he looked up at the Argyle battlements. Guards were posted at regular intervals, black shapes standing motionless against a paler, moonlit sky. A man turned and peered down. He braced for the alarm, but the man only raised his hand and beckoned them on.

By the time he reached the relative safety of his barrack room, Jamie was breathless, the room spinning around him. He sank onto his berth and stared at Hal. 'What've ye done?'

Hal swallowed, avoiding his gaze. 'They mean to bring dragoons against us, to drive us onto the transports at sabre-point. I sent young Robbie oot to buy bread. The baker's lad telt him.'

'The baker's lad?' Jamie stared at Hal. 'After what happened this forenoon, the near mutiny I tried my best to put down, you ...' he exhaled, struggling to find the words. 'You overpowered our guards and released us on the say o' a baker's lad?' His voice squawked incredulously.

'Nay, Jamie. 'Twas reported in thon paper, the *Caledonian Mercury*.' Hal reached into his knapsack. 'See fer yerself. Ye ken I canna read.'

Jamie took the crumpled newspaper from Hal and opened it, eyeing the others over the top edge. The men were now perched on their berths, Fin and his band standing in the doorway. All were looking anxiously at him, awaiting his judgement.

'I didna believe the lad at first,' Robbie stammered. 'I swear, Jamie.'

'When Robbie proved hard to convince,' Hal went on, 'the errand lad ran to fetch the baker. The breadman took Robbie doon a back lane to the printing hoose to speak to the owner, Mister John Robertson. This Robertson read the paper to Robbie, the same ane ye're reading now.' Hal swallowed. 'Robertson's from the Braes o' Atholl. He spent twenty years in exile in France fer his loyalty to the Stuart cause. Now that he's hame and times are safer, he uses his newspaper to keep Edinburgh acquainted wi' the king's colonising wars. He reports on campaigns and the king's underhand recruiting in the Highlands. He's a friend, Jamie. He told Robbie his information came from the castle, from a senior soldier of the Northern Fencibles, a man who didna wish to gie his name but kent what the authorities planned to do and wished to prevent it.'

Robbie nodded. ''Tis what he said, Jamie.'

'The lad canna read, but Robertson says dragoons are billeted in byres and barns around the city, mair mustering daily, preparing to storm the castle and force us abroad the ships.' Hal scowled. 'We're sold, Jamie, unless we fight it.'

Jamie lowered his gaze to the broadsheet and scanned the page. Frowning, he read the piece again, slower this time, his stomach churning. 'Twas even worse than he feared. He looked up. 'It seems we're betrayed.'

Hal nodded. 'I've spread word to the men on guard. They're nae fer having it. Every man stands wi' us.'

'Every man? Then why the need to overpower our guards?'

'Nay, lad, we didna. I only meant to speak wi' them. Explain our plight and bring them roond to our thinking and hae ye released. Only the three were well-bladdered. They reeked that foully o' drink, I feared fer my lamp. And my brows,' he added, smoothing his fingers over his bushy eyebrows. 'Had they breathed near my flame, I might've lost these beauties. Anyhow, there was nae wakening them.'

Jamie frowned, remembering what Fin had said: he heard a man he believed was McBeath drinking with the guards outside their cell.

'What'll we do?' Hal pressed. 'I thought ye'd ken. Only there's nae going back now.'

Jamie thrust the newspaper back at Hal. Bitterness tightened his throat. The Black Watch's treatment had revealed what the authorities were capable of. Damned if he'd let these men be treated the same way. Nay, by God, they would fight.

He let his breath out, his chest tightening. He had promised to return to Morven, swore it on bended knee. Only thoughts of her had kept him sane these last months. Lord, that she still thought kindly of him. If he led a mutiny, what would it cost him? The good name he had once enjoyed with His Grace? Certainly, though, he'd doubtless lost that already. His land?

It had never been his. His life? He shuddered. Perhaps, but what choice had he? He could hardly return to Morven from India, and 'twas highland blood pulsed in his veins, same as in these men. Aye, by God, they would fight!

He rose to his feet. 'We must assume every officer is against us unless they prove otherwise. Place guards around the governor's house and the officer's quarters on Palace Yard. No one leaves. We raise the drawbridge and close the portcullis gate, mount guards and pickets on every wall and battery.' He drew a quivering breath. 'No one enters or leaves the castle without my authority. Those wi'out fear,' he glanced around the room, 'come with me. We break into the magazine and seize the arms and munitions. I'll wager more arms lie within those walls than anywhere in the country.'

'Hundreds o' barrels o' powder,' Hal confirmed. 'Cannonballs, muskets, cartridge boxes, bayonets and swords.'

Jamie nodded. 'But make no mistake; what we do tonight is mutiny, the regiment in revolt against its officers and the Crown. Even to plot mutiny is a capital crime punishable by death.' He looked at the white faces around him. The men swallowed and blinked back; young Archie puffed his cheeks out. Grim-faced, they nodded.

Hal muttered, 'What other choice have we?'

Jamie glanced at Fin. He nodded back grimly.

'Any man unwilling to risk his life may join the officers. I swear, no ill will come to him. All I ask is he wait until daybreak and the beating o' Reveille afore alerting the officers and joining them. That'll give us what's left of this night to do what must be done.' Jamie stared around the room, challenging the men, waiting for gazes to waver and slide to the floor. No man changed expression. He nodded grimly, looking at Hal. Hal's face had never looked whiter or more stubbornly resolute. 'Most men are still asleep. I'll speak wi' them at roll call and explain our position. They must be allowed to choose. They may board the ships if they wish. No man will stop them. Equally, no man should be forced to join us. But until then, we've work to do.'

'What aboot the officers?' This was from Fin. He was grinning wickedly. 'They'll nae be expecting this.' He laughed. 'They'll be outraged. Captain Cumming will spit feathers. Ye ken how he likes to carry on, the strutting peacock. He'll go rampaging ower the castle. Or at least,' he chuckled, 'the Palace Yard.'

Jamie shook his head. 'Captain Cumming doesna care to humble himself by quartering at the castle wi' his men. He prefers to lodge in town, far from the soldiers he commands. Better fer us, though.' Fin was right. When Captain Cumming learned of their actions, he'd be incandescent.

'Weel,' laughed Fin, 'he'll still spit feathers, only we'll nae hae to witness it or suffer his temper or the sight o' his raging face. Thon's a blessing.'

Jamie nodded. Captain Cumming's wrath was something he was happy to forgo. 'One more thing. I believe the drummers and fifers should beat commands as usual; Reveille and Tap-too, and Alarm to warn of any danger. We should beat Troop every morning to assemble the men and share the duties, relieving those on watch so every man plays his part. Our days should continue as afore, with no man sliding into sloth or indolence. If we behave like the trained soldiers we are, taking turns at guard duty and chores, we'll show the officers there was never any reason to kick or beat us. We're civil men; we're better than that.'

'Weel said,' Hal muttered, and the others cheered.

Jamie grimaced in relief; he had no wish to act the taskmaster. 'We must keep the officers prisoner. 'Tis certain they'll try to stop us. And I think we all ken Sergeant McBeath will never be with us. We must keep the devil under lock and key with the other non-commissioned officers who oppose us.' He smiled at the thought of turning the tables on McBeath. 'But in confining our officers, I believe we should show them as much courtesy as they showed discourtesy to us.'

The men spluttered their objection.

Jamie listened to their protests before explaining. 'It appears we enjoy the respect and good opinion of Edinburgh's townsfolk. Ye saw it at yesterday's parade. The crowds cheered us and jeered His Grace. The levelling societies are likely behind that, but the townsfolk mostly support us. The newspapers speak o' little else. I say we harness that good opinion and dinna squander it with bad behaviour. The townspeople's support lends our action authority, for 'tis plain the War Office mean to misuse us.' He sighed. 'We mustna waste that support but harness it and pray 'tis enough to make His Grace and the War Office see sense.'

As he spoke, Jamie began to see it all in his mind. The guns of the Half Moon Battery were already trained down the Royal Mile to Holyroodhouse, where Lord Adam and Lord Barrington would be sleeping. His Grace was likely lodged nearby in the best accommodation money could buy. Captain Cumming too. Come morning, they would know the

Northern Fencibles had taken the castle—a loaded gun pointed at their heads. Power was all these entitled leaders understood. In wrenching it from them, they might negotiate their freedom. But with the threat of a dragoon charge hanging over them, what choice had they? Only they must hurt no one. Senseless bloodshed would turn Edinburgh against them.

Fin winked at him. 'Ye ken, Jamie, there's ower a hundred French and Spanish prisoners rotting in the castle casements. We could release them if they agree to stand wi' us. Lord Adam willna like that. 'Tis something to threaten him wi'.'

Hal frowned. 'They'll need to be fed. All the men will.'

Jamie nodded. The welfare of the men now rested upon his shoulders. 'Let me worry about that. But by morning's break, we must hold the castle.'

CHAPTER TWENTY-NINE

Druimbeag, October 1781

THE INFANT SNUFFLED, TURNING her head from side to side as she rooted, her instinct to nurse strong for such a tiny soul. Morven kissed her daughter's silky dark head, delighting in her newborn smell, her delicate lips, the translucent lashes on her cheek. The infant uncurled her dainty fingers, and a surge of love ravaged her heart. If only Jamie were here to see how precious she was, how lovely, but she mustn't let herself go to that soul-crushing place. 'Twas weeks since she'd heard from Jamie.

Dinna take her, she prayed. *Oh, please, keep my wee soul safe. Let Jamie come back to us.* She loosened her arisaid where the child was swaddled and lifted the infant to her shoulder. The little face puckered and reddened, heralding a querulous cry. When it came, Morven's breasts tingled; she glanced across at Rowena.

'She's hungry. Away and feed her. I can finish this.' Rowena took the bowl of grain from her and shooed her away. Turning back to the dusty quern stone straddling the ground between them, Rowena turned the quern's wooden handle and poured a trail of grain into a hole in the upper stone. The top stone rattled and grated as it turned against the lower, flour squeezing out from between them. Rowena caught it in a piece of linen.

Morven got to her feet, careful of the precious floor, and glanced across the infield stubble. The birch trees on the druim had turned a fiery gold; some were already bare. A rider mounted the ridge. She stiffened. Lord, let it nae be the factor. She hadna a farthing to give him.

But the rider was slightly built and no more accustomed to handling a spirited garron than he'd been the last time she'd seen him ride one. Unlike the factor, this horseman was young and lean. He wore the blue breeches and tailed blue coat the Scalan master had chosen for his students' uniforms. She raised her hand to Nathaniel, and he waved back, his coat flapping as he made toward her.

'Another visitor,' said Rowena.

Many had come over the past few days—poor hill folk with generous hearts, come bearing gifts and to wet the baby's head in celebration. Many brought things of iron: horseshoes, nails, old hinges, to protect the infant from the *daoine sìth*. The faeryfolk could steal an unguarded infant, leaving a changeling in its place, a faery shadow of the real infant that would grow into a crabbit, misshapen brat, ever crying as it ate the family out of house and home yet failed to thrive. Others brought peat, whisky, and gifts of food. With Jamie gone, few were unaware of her plight with the factor and the risk of her losing Druimbeag.

'Best tak' him inside,' Rowena advised, 'wet the bairn's head in private.'

Morven nodded, glad of Rowena's kindness, although she doubted Nathaniel had come to drink whisky.

As she walked out to meet him, it struck her how fond of Nathaniel she'd become. Once ordained, he would leave for Badenoch to fulfil his father's wishes and follow his chosen path. Or, at least, the path chosen for him. She might never see him again. Worse, since the bishop was already here, he might leave soon. The thought was hard to bear. Yet if Nathaniel wished it, she must be glad for him. She lifted her chin to the breeze and slipped on a brave face.

A few soft words settled Nathaniel's garron. She led the animal to the water trough, careful not to set the hens a-fluttering and squawking. As they passed Rowena at the quern stone, Rowena nodded at Nathaniel, and he made the sign of the cross to bless her. He'd soon be blessing his own congregation. The thought lay heavy in Morven's chest.

She held his garron still while he climbed down.

'How do you do that?' He removed his bonnet and bowed to her. 'I swear all beasts do your bidding.'

She laughed. She'd been around garrons all her life.

Seeing her damp bodice, he stammered, 'Forgive me. I've come at an improper time, I—'

'Nay, dinna go. I'm glad to see ye. I niver right thanked ye fer all ye did fer me when my littlin came. Come in so I can properly introduce ye.'

He waited while she tethered his garron, then followed her inside, staring around the smoky interior. He was too polite to comment on the hum-bleness of her home but looked gravely at her. She supposed there could be little joy in his life, what with all the praying and book-learning he must do, but he seemed troubled.

'Please.' She indicated the chairs at the fire.

He perched on the edge of his, absently playing with the flap covering one of his coat pockets. She sensed it held the source of his strange anxiety.

'Ye'll tak' some ale or whisky?'

'No, no, I've not come to take from you.' He appeared to remember why he'd come and removed the satchel slung across his body, bringing out two items wrapped in linen. 'I bear gifts. A black pudding from Janet to rebuild your strength and a sweet treat. A piece of honeycomb from the Scalan hives.' He rose and placed the items on the table.

'Please thank Janet fer me. 'Twas good o' her.' Her infant began to grizzle in earnest. She loosened her bodice and brought the child to her breast, careful not to compromise her modesty or embarrass Nathaniel.

'Yes, of course.' He averted his gaze, looking for somewhere to direct his attention other than at her. Deciding on his lap, he stared at his clasped hands.

''Tis all right,' she said. 'I'm decent, and nursing is naught to be ashamed o'. 'Tis why nature gave me breasts.'

He nodded, his cheeks flaming, and risked a glance in her direction, careful not to let his gaze stray below her chin. 'What have you decided to call her?' he croaked.

'Ilene. It means wee bird. Though I should likely wait until Jamie gets hame ...' she trailed off. 'Only I dinna ken when that'll be.'

'Ilene.' He explored the word on his tongue. 'A lovely name. You'll have her baptised soon? 'Tis always wise.' He frowned and shifted in his seat, reluctant to explain why that might be.

'I expect so. Might you baptise her?' Had the bishop judged Nathaniel pious enough to take holy orders? In a way, she hoped not, but that was selfish. He would make a fine priest. She wondered what Bishop Hay had made of her giving birth at the college, how the master had explained it.

'Father Ranald, I imagine.' He frowned and lifted the flap of his coat pocket. 'Yesterday, one of my kinsmen brought me a letter.' He fished a wad of paper out. ''Tis from my father.'

'Heavens, efter all this time? What does he say?'

Nathaniel's face tightened. 'He writes that my brother Samuel has died.'

'Oh, Nathaniel. I'm sorry. What happened?'

'He does not give the cause, only that …' he looked fearfully at her. 'That I must return to Badenoch at once. I am now his heir and must take up that role. I must forget about becoming a priest.'

She stared at him. 'But he doesna understand what he asks. He gave ye to the priests as a bairn, never troubling to set eyes on ye again. Now that ye're about to take yer vows, he's cruelly changed his mind!' She choked back anger. Poor Nathaniel. His da cared little for him. 'What'll ye do?'

He swallowed and shook his head. His eyes reddened. Unfolding the letter, he peered at it, blinking furiously. Long moments passed before he could speak. She thought of the lyrical voice he used in prayer, soft with its Gaelic inflexion.

'He writes,' he choked, gripping the letter, *To encourage you to accept this change in vocation, I have laid aside funds for you. Your life will be more comfortable now. But you must return home at once and learn how to manage the land.'*

Refusing to look at her, he refolded the letter with trembling fingers and stuffed it back in his pocket. His tears dripped on the floor. 'Never did I consider the priesthood a vocation,' he choked. 'I knew it was my duty, but I judged it a privilege to serve our Heavenly Father … to … to shepherd the faithful through life. What do I know about farming? I've spent my life preparing for the cloth. I don't even know how to be a man, never mind a farmer or a landowner.'

Morven frowned. Nathaniel was one of the finest men she knew. 'Ye're already a good man,' she countered. 'Look how ye were wi' Struan and the master, how ye helped me when my littlin came. No one had to teach ye to be decent or kind. 'Tis who ye are.'

He sobbed, more tears coming.

She had seen Nathaniel weep before and knew she must allow him time to recover. Lord, let him nae fall to the floor and wail like he did when Andrew died. Father Ranald had said Nathaniel must derive his solace from God. Had no one comforted him since his mam all those years ago? Poor Nathaniel; he'd learned he must look to the spiritual. Showing him tenderness now might make things worse. Fearing that, she made no move toward him but lifted Ilene to her shoulder, her heart breaking. The wee soul hiccuped and lay limply. 'I would trust ye wi' my life,' she said. 'Wi' the life o' my daughter.'

'You're kind,' Nathaniel sobbed. 'Though I fear misguided. I should be mourning my brother, but look at me. My tears are for myself. I wallow in self-pity, so wretched am I.'

'Nay, ye've had a shock.'

'A shock? My whole life has been upended. I believed I'd spend my life with God, that I would follow a higher path, although ...' he swallowed.

'Although?'

He shook his head. 'Lately, I've come to appreciate how much I'll lose on taking my vows.'

'A family o' yer own, ye mean?'

He nodded. 'I believe all I've ever wanted is to love and be loved.' He pulled a kerchief from his pocket and pressed it to his mouth as if he had said something shameful.

'Is that nae what we all want?'

He smiled crookedly. 'It's what I've missed most, I think, what I've been searching for since that night on the riverbank. What I thought I'd found at Scalan, although I see now Scalan was just a place for me to hide.'

She frowned, not understanding. 'Ye've lost yer calling?'

'I'm not sure I was ever called, but lately, I foolishly imagined I might stay here, even near you in Stratha'an. Once ordained, I hoped I might remain close to those I've come to care about.'

'I dinna see why nae. Ye're a grown man. Why should ye do yer da's bidding? He gave ye away. He canna expect yer loyalty.'

He swallowed, looking pleadingly at her. 'Please, tell me what I should do.'

She reached over and took his hand. He flinched but let her uncurl his cold fingers. He was weeping again.

''Tisna my place to do that. Only you can decide how ye wish to live yer life. I think ye should do whatever makes yer heart most glad.'

He stared at her. 'But I no longer know what that is.'

'Look into yer heart. I think ye'll find ye do.'

His brows drew together in a tortured fashion. 'I know only that I wish that for you ... to make your heart glad. If I could give you a better life, if I could alter your situation and bring your husband home, if prayer might do that, I'd gladly spend the rest of my days on my knees.'

'Och, Nathaniel.'

'Such is my affection for you.'

'Hush.' She rubbed Ilene's back. 'Ye dinna ken what ye're saying. I'm spoken fer.'

'Forgive me,' he sobbed. 'I shouldn't have said that. It's just that after reading your husband's letters, feeling his devotion, and ... and witnessing yours for him, I've seen that mortal love can be as fulfilling as God's love. Maybe more.' He swallowed, aware of the enormity of what he'd said. 'I think it's what I long for.'

'Ye're confused. 'Tis hardly surprising.'

He nodded, trying to recover his composure and looked at her sleeping child. His throat spasmed. 'Since meeting you, I've witnessed how powerful mortal love can be, especially when compared with the more distant, divine kind.'

Seeing the extent of his doubts, she looked sadly at him. Had *she* done that? If so, it had never been her intention. A barrier had always existed between them, an unseen boundary of propriety, necessary, she supposed, if he was to become a priest. It was crumbling away.

She got down on her knees before him.

He looked fearfully at her but let her put her arm around him. He shivered and closed his eyes. Still cradling Ilene, she lowered his head to her other shoulder and stroked his hair, murmuring the words of comfort no one had said to him since his mam all those years ago. He sobbed, afraid to touch her, but after a moment, brought his arms up and clumsily held her. How long they stayed like that, Nathaniel sobbing, she hardly knew—until the child caught between them gave a disgruntled mewl, bringing them back to reality.

'Bless you,' he whispered.

CHAPTER THIRTY

Edinburgh Castle

'Let him pass,' Jamie said. 'He may keep his sword as a mark of respect fer his rank, but he must give up his flintlock.'

The guards lowered the drawbridge and waited for Adjutant Abercrombie to cross the wooden bridge before a private thrust the muzzle of his musket in the young officer's face and held out his hand for his pistol. Abercrombie handed it over without hesitation, then followed Jamie through the gatehouse to the inner portcullis. As he passed under its spikes, soldiers eyed him warily.

'I trust I needna search you?' Jamie said mid-stride.

'You may have my sword,' Abercrombie replied. 'That is my only weapon. I come as negotiator, nae adversary.'

'Keep it, but try to draw it from its sheath, and a hundred or more blades will fall upon ye. I promise mine will be first.'

Abercrombie swallowed as he hurried to keep up. He clutched a bundle of paper and quills and peered up through his round spectacles at the ramparts of the Half Moon Battery from where taut faces peered down at him. They made their way up Hawk's Hill, passing the governor's house under heavy guard, and turned to pass through Foog's Gate to the summit and heart of the castle. Once through, they veered toward Saint Margaret's chapel.

'We're going to church?' Abercrombie said in surprise.

'I've long held that whatever is said in the presence of the Lord will more likely be the truth.'

'You're doubtless right, Corporal,' Abercrombie conceded, 'but I haven't come to lie to you. I am to hear your grievances and relay them to His Grace and Lord Adam in the hope of ...' he swallowed, glancing at the many openings in the rock walls from where musket muzzles pointed at him. 'Of bringing this shameful situation to its remedy before the king need learn of it. Surely you see bringing disgrace upon the regiment and its officers will do no one any good?'

Jamie snorted; he couldn't give a tinker's curse about the officers. Only the men concerned him. And whether the adjutant intended to tell him the truth remained to be seen. At least Abercrombie appeared a diligent sort with a civil tongue in his head, unlike Captain Cumming. The captain's shameful performance of the day before still galled.

To his relief, they took the castle without bloodshed and without awakening a single officer. In the light from a half-moon, he and a chosen band of men slipped into the officer's quarters and silently removed every musket and pistol. They did the same at the governor's house, relieving the ageing governor, General John Campbell, Earl of Loudoun, a former colonel in the Hanoverian army at Culloden, of his ceremonial pistols. As a gesture of courtesy, he let the officers keep their swords. Being Highlanders, he and his men understood the importance of a man's honour. He would have no one call them brutes. And whilst an angry lieutenant might attempt a shot from an open window with his musket or pistol, he could do little harm from there with a sword.

Captain Cumming arrived at the castle gates early the next morning in ignorance of their night-time activities and unaware that the castle governor and the regiment's officers were detained in their quarters under guard. Jamie was still explaining to the assembled men what he knew of the position they had been forced into, asking them to choose if they supported the mutiny or wished to join the officers when the captain made himself known at the gatehouse, his enraged bellows clearly heard by every assembled man.

Finding a yawning gap where the drawbridge used to lie and the gatehouse shut against him, Captain Cumming flew into a bewildered rage, demanding the guards admit him. Did they not know who he was? God's blood, he was the most distinguished captain in the duke's regiment. When they refused, he threatened to shoot any man who denied him entry. A private was swiftly sent to fetch Jamie.

Cumming took one look at him and exploded with anger. 'You, by Christ! I might've known. Innes, is it? You've proven yourself a rogue and an agitator from the start. What are you, drunk? Get this gate open. Keep me waiting one more moment, and I'll have you on a summary charge. Move, blast you!' He cracked his cane against the drawbridge wall. 'Wretched sod. This is an outrage!'

Jamie drew a curt breath and addressed the captain across the empty moat with as much civility as he could muster.

'Sir, the Duke of Gordon's regiment has risen in revolt,' he stated boldly. 'Every company to a man.' He hoped that were true, for he had yet to allow the men time to decide where their loyalties lay, although he had a fair notion it was not with the Crown. 'We hold the castle but in taking it, have spilt no blood. Our officers are in excellent health, although we have naturally had to detain them.'

Captain Cumming stared at him. 'Good God! You've gone stark raving mad. Mutiny's a capital offence. I'll have you shot. You and every damn fool rebel.' He drew his broadsword. 'Lower the drawbridge this instant, you coward. We'll have this out man to man!'

Jamie waited until the captain had finished his tirade, then spoke calmly, ignoring the challenge. 'Sir, no man here will board the king's ships, even at the point of a dragoon's sabre. We're not ignorant of what goes on. Not every man here is incapable of reading a newspaper.'

'Insufferable whelp! God blast you. I'll not stand for your impudence.'

Jamie tightened his jaw, biting back the response poised on his tongue, namely that Cumming was an entitled bully who liked nothing better than to see good men flogged. He said none of that. 'You may return to His Grace,' he said stiffly, 'and inform him of our actions, he and Lord Adam and the Secretary at War. I foolishly imagined we had already made our position clear, but perhaps they will be more willing to listen now that we hold the castle with its heavy guns and vast arsenal.'

The captain's face grew sweaty and darkened with rage. 'Damn you for a bugger!' He shook his broadsword and hurled a blast of foul oaths across the empty moat.

'Thus far, we have hurt no one,' Jamie returned through clenched teeth. 'Nor will we, although I can give no such assurance if we are attacked and forced to defend ourselves. We ask for a written pledge from His Grace and the Secretary at War that our terms of enlistment will not be breached. As you know, the men were recruited to defend Scotland. Our enlistment papers made it clear we were not to leave her shores or cross her border unless England was invaded. I think we both know England has not been invaded.'

Cumming gaped at him. 'Do we, by God? What foolishness. England is in peril from her enemies. None but cowards would refuse her aid.' He jabbed his sword at Jamie. 'I have you marked, Innes. You're a traitorous dog who's betrayed his country. Had you the backbone to come out here, I would run you through.' He plunged his sword into its scabbard as if stabbing it through Jamie's body. 'But since you're too spineless to face me, I'll see you court-martialled.'

Jamie had expected no less from the captain.

'The Edinburgh papers claim we've been sold to the Indies,' he threw back at him. 'So, I ask who has committed the greater betrayal? I say 'tis the duke, the king, and his war office, whose sail-ships anchor off Leith waiting to carry us away. Not a man of us will board them. We'll hold the castle until the threat of transportation is withdrawn. We'll see the ships gone and assurances given that the terms we put our names to will be honoured. The men are prepared to die before they let themselves be sold.' He swallowed, hoping that would not be necessary.

'Sold? What foolish wind you blow. I've never heard anything so absurd nor witnessed such miserable ingratitude in a soldier. The men have been treated with the utmost kindness, my company especially, as you should know, and that no matter how poor a soldier or wretched a creature he might be.'

'That has not been my or my fellow men's experience.'

'God's blood!' Cumming cracked his cane against the drawbridge wall. 'I've fagged myself about like a post horse to make it so.' He stared at Jamie, his breath whistling. 'You will bring the men back to their duty. That is an order, Corporal.'

Jamie stared stonily back.

'Blast your cowardly heart! Then I promise every mutineer will suffer the full consequence of the king's wrath.'

Jamie fought to keep his expression impassive. The captain had fagged himself about like at post horse? Cumming hadn't even seen fit to march with his men. In the last months, Captain Cumming had spent more time at his estate in Moray than with his men.

'I'm giving you notice of our actions and intentions, sir,' he returned. 'I ask you take our demands to His Grace and the authorities. We wish no trouble, but we'll not be sold or mistreated.'

'You wish no trouble?' Cumming gaped at him. 'Then I fear you will be sorely disappointed. Trouble, you will most certainly find. You're a disgrace to your regiment, a landless cowherd beholden to His Grace for every blade of grass your beasts chew.'

Jamie's heart threatened to pound out of his chest. He exhaled through his nose. *Dinna let the arrogant blatherskite gall ye into something ye'll regret. Stay focussed.* He swallowed, letting the captain's taunts blow about him like fallen leaves.

'Am I to understand those deluded wretches have chosen *you* as their leader?' Cumming jabbed his cane at the towering castle walls. 'Then, God help them!'

'I speak for the men, aye, Highlanders with little but the Gaelic.'

'Do you? Then you lead them to the firing squad.'

'That is the last place I intend to lead them.'

'What of your sergeant? McBeath, isn't it? The best drill sergeant in the regiment. The poor man's done his best to set a standard for you, whipping you highland sluggards into shape, instilling some discipline in you hill-dwelling rogues. This is how you repay him? I've seen him in town, doubtless on some errand for his ungrateful men. I presume you have him under guard. He can hardly support this.'

At mention of McBeath, the last of Jamie's restraint began to desert him. His fingers tightened around his primed and charged musket barrel, the urge to discharge it at this arrogant buffoon threatening to better him. With the last of his control, he loosened his grip and stepped back, indicating their exchange was over.

What more could he say to such a man? They stood as far apart as centuries of privilege and breeding could place them. He released a long breath through his nose, thinking of his father. His pounding heart began to slow. His da was hopefully looking down on him with pride. He must hold onto that thought.

'Then on your head be it. Devil take you!' Cumming turned on his heel and stalked away over the castle mound, the ostrich plume in his hat quivering with rage.

Jamie held the door open for the adjutant and ushered him into the hushed dimness of the chapel nave. 'Sir, in the interest of fairness, I ask that ye wait here whilst I bring a soldier from every company.' He indicated the chapel pews. 'We must speak as one, with no man forcing his will.'

He returned with Fin and eight others, a crowd in the tiny chapel. All were grim-faced. Abercrombie swallowed as he flicked his gaze from one drawn countenance to another. They had all heard the young adjutant speak fluent Gaelic, so he must have some connection with the Highlands. Might that bring a degree of sympathy for their plight? Jamie prayed so.

'I am to take back a list of your grievances,' Abercrombie said, 'and convince you to give up this folly forthwith.'

'Then ye can tell the feathered peacocks we'll nae be sold as slaves to the Indies,' Fin blurted.

Jamie grimaced. Fin had perhaps not been the best man to bring. He spoke bluntly and lacked the tact and finer graces needed for diplomacy, although Fin likely spoke as most men would want. At least every fencible soldier had chosen to join the mutiny. They would stand together as one and hold their treacherous commanders to their promises.

'The regiment has not been sold, Corporal,' Abercrombie replied. 'I can assure you of that.'

'Then why do the Edinburgh papers say it has?' Fin thrust his chin out. 'And why are the king's ships anchored off Leith, waiting to carry us awa'?'

'The source of those rumours is still unclear, but I promise they are unfounded. The levelling societies are believed to be the culprits. These people like nothing better than to embarrass the authorities, but the transports are only to carry you to the south of England. No further.'

'Against oor terms,' Donald Forbes of MacKay's company growled.

'I agree that would breach the terms of your enlistment, but His Grace and Lord Barrington now regret adding that clause.'

''Tis ower late fer such regrets,' Donald growled. ''Twas upon that promise the duke and his duchess managed to levy so many.'

Abercrombie nodded, looking uncomfortable.

Jamie leant forward, pinning the adjutant with his stare. 'As ye ken, sir, we publicly refused to volunteer fer England, believing it a trick. Much o' Edinburgh witnessed our refusal. If we hadna taken the castle, would the authorities have driven us aboard the ships at the point of a dragoon's sabre?'

Abercrombie swallowed. 'That I cannot say.'

'Cannot or will not.'

'My understanding is you were to be encouraged to do your duty and honour the call made upon you, but no force was to be brought.'

'Ye expect us to believe that?'

'I cannot tell you what to believe.'

Fin scowled at Abercrombie. 'Ye speak in riddles, man. Tell the truth. Already, there's ower much suspicion atween the men and thon buggers in charge. Nae man here trusts the Crown and its treachery.'

Abercrombie blinked at him. 'I'm beginning to understand the extent of your mistrust, Corporal. All of you.' He glanced around. Wary eyes stared back at him from beneath taut brows, men in scarlet and plaid, all clutching their bonnets.

'Then if we're nae to be forced aboard the transports,' Corporal Willie Graham of Lord Haddo's said, 'why are dragoons surrounding the city as we speak?'

Abercrombie moistened his lips. ''Tis true a cavalry corp was summoned at the first whiff of resistance, but thus far, only one troop has fully mustered here.'

'Summoned to put doon any resistance wi' armed force?'

Abercrombie struggled to meet Corporal Graham's gaze. He swallowed and nodded.

'Then, sir,' Jamie pressed, 'since the dragoons' presence has been widely reported in the Edinburgh papers, ye can perhaps understand why we felt obliged to take matters into our own hands? Once alow deck, we'll be prisoners o' the king. He can send us wherever he pleases. To the Indies, America, Lord knows where.'

Abercrombie considered. 'I can see how it might look that way, especially with the rumours circulating.'

Jamie exhaled. His head was beginning to ache. 'Ye're saying there's nae truth to the newspaper reports?'

'That is my belief.'

Jamie frowned; they must have more to go on than one man's belief. 'But are the papers nae correct in saying dragoons are indeed gathering, awaiting orders to overpower us and force us aboard the ships, doubtless now at an accelerated pace.'

'That I cannot say.'

A chorus of frustrated curses erupted around the room.

'Then, what *can* ye say?' Jamie snapped. 'Ye expect us to put our trust in men who've lied to us from the start, the king and his military commanders, men who withheld our pay so we'd barely coin to buy food and naught to send home to our families. The duke, who forced us to enlist, then failed to pay us our promised bounty. Men who made us sign our names on worthless scraps o' paper stating we'd nae leave our country and then urged us to board ships for Lord knows where. Are ye saying we must place our lives in the hands o' these men?'

Abercrombie swallowed. ''Tis my understanding any arrears due were to be paid before you embarked. That it had been agreed with His Grace.'

Fin hooted. 'Anither airy promise to vanish in the mist.'

Abercrombie adjusted his spectacles. 'You must not imagine I lack sympathy for yer plight. I am of highland blood and understand Highlanders' troubles, the ravages wrought upon our land and its people. I've no wish to see you come to harm. I'm here to negotiate the terms of your surrender and find a way out of this without bloodshed, but I see no value in clinging to unfounded suspicions. They will not lead ye safely out of here.'

Corporal Graham rose to his feet, his face heavily lined. 'Fine talk, sir, but how are we to believe a word o' it? The Edinburgh papers tell a different story, as do her people. They urge us nae to let ourselves be betrayed. What have they to gain in lying to us?'

'I cannot answer to the townspeople's motives, Corporal, although I have also read the stories. Someone with evil intent may have put those rumours about.'

'To what end?'

'Presumably to cause trouble, although I cannot imagine who would benefit from that.'

Fin snorted. 'Who would do such a thing?' He sat back in his pew, then blinked and turned to Jamie. 'Christ, are ye thinking whit I'm thinking?'

Jamie closed his eyes for a moment, his head now pounding. He nodded slowly. 'The devil's been whispering in my ear since Fort George. Playing with my head.'

'Who?' Willie Graham demanded, retaking his seat.

'Sergeant McBeath of Cumming's company.'

'Thon divil. Why would he?' This was from John Michie of Fraser's. 'What would he gain?'

Jamie rubbed his aching brow. 'Revenge, I suppose. We have history. He perhaps hoped if he enraged me enough, I might poke my head above the parapet and get myself shot.'

Fin's explosion of blasphemy shocked in the solemnity of the chapel. 'Is that nae what ye've done, Jamie? Mebbe got us all shot?'

The blood drained from Jamie's face. Was Fin right? Had he played into the devil's hands? 'I ...' he stammered, scrambling for clarity. 'If I've led ye into peril through thon devil's false claims, by God, I'll kill the blaggard!'

'Nay, Jamie,' Willie soothed, 'dinna blame yerself. There're still the troop transports anchored in the firth—a blatant betrayal by those in command.'

He nodded at Willie, but his aching head had been joined by a sickness in his stomach. Had he led the men into a trap of McBeath's making? He turned back to Abercrombie. 'Ye say ye wish to help us, sir. Then, might ye get word to a Mister John Robertson, the owner of the *Caledonian Mercury*?'

'If you think it will help.'

'Please urge Mister Robertson to come to the castle and ask fer Corporal James Innes. I wish to learn the identity of his informer. He spoke to one of my men. He told him a senior soldier of the regiment had warned him His Grace intended to sell us to the East India Company. This man claimed he wished to prevent that. If that was Sergeant McBeath, any information he gave will have been fer his own ends. He's been stoking my anger since Fort George, whipping up a blaze of injustice in my breast.'

'Then I'm sure His Grace will wish to hear of it.'

'I'd be grateful if ye'd keep this between us fer now, sir. I believe Mister Robertson means well and has already suffered for his loyalties. I dinna wish to bring more trouble to his door.'

Abercrombie frowned. 'Very well.'

Jamie tried to push this new worrying possibility to the back of his mind, yet something still bothered him. 'Might I ask one more thing, sir? Was England ever at risk of attack?'

Again, the young officer's expression slid into lines of discomfort. He looked at the white faces around him, anxiously awaiting his reply. Light filtering through the leaded windows played upon their faces, giving them a ghostly appearance. He pressed his lips together. 'There was some threat of it, I believe, but never a serious one.'

A hiss of indrawn breath echoed off the chapel walls.

'Then why the need to ship us to the south of England?'

'Perhaps,' Abercrombie offered, 'so you might demonstrate your loyalty to the king.' He sighed. 'But if that was the reason, it has failed utterly. First, you disgrace yourselves with your insolent rejection of the Crown's appeal and now even more thoroughly with this scandalous mutiny.'

Fin snorted. 'Wonder whit the puffed-up peacocks are saying aboot us taking the castle?' He looked expectantly at Abercrombie, who shrank back in his seat. 'To be a fly on the candlesticks atween His Grace and his uncle at dinner these last nights, that'd be a fine thing. Even wi' ten troops o' cavalry, they've little hope o' taking the castle. They'd need to lay siege to flush us oot. How long might that take?'

''Twould be ower bloody,' growled Donald Forbes.

'The Edinburgh papers would mak' hay ower our clash wi' the Crown whilst the townsfolk bring us food and supplies and wish us well. Did ye ken, sir, on our march here, folk lined the streets and cheered us all the way to Castle Rock?'

Abercrombie frowned at Fin. 'Don't fool yourself, the townspeople would support such bloodshed. That is what I am here to prevent.'

'Then, the king doesna yet know of our actions?' Jamie asked.

''Tis hoped I can bring you back to your duty before such a dispatch is needed. 'Twould go better for you and would avoid bringing disgrace upon the regiment. But you must abandon this folly at once.'

'And board the ships in breach o' our terms?'

Abercrombie nodded, avoiding Jamie's gaze.

'Niver,' came the men's shared response.

'Highland backbones are stronger than that,' said Donald Forbes. 'And we hold all the cards.'

Abercrombie sighed and began laying out paper and ink. 'Then I will take back written record of your grievances and what ye hope to achieve. But once the king learns of your actions,' he shook his head. 'As the law stands, all your lives will be forfeit. Once the mutiny becomes common knowledge in London, swiftly abandoning this folly and pleading for the king's pardon will be the only way to save those who only followed the ringleaders like sheep.'

Jamie's chest tightened.

'I will, of course, inform the authorities that you wish to avoid bloodshed.' Abercrombie dipped his quill into a small pot of ink. 'But with every day that passes, you heap more humiliation upon the Crown. Your actions have been reported in every Edinburgh newspaper, some of it a mite fanciful. This humiliation will not be forgiven.'

Fin grunted dismissively, prompting Abercrombie to heave another sigh. 'Have it your way. Might I at least suggest a gesture of goodwill to gentle the king's wrath?'

'Such as?'

'Releasing your officers unharmed might show your willingness to treat with the Crown.'

CHAPTER THIRTY-ONE

'Mister Robertson, good of you to come.' Jamie shook the print-maker's hand and led the way up Hawk's Hill, taking pains to explain the desperate position the fencibles found themselves in as they walked. 'So,' he concluded on reaching the barrack building, 'do ye think ye would recognise yer informer again?'

'I've little doubt I would.' Robertson looked up at the imposing grey building. 'The sergeant who came to me was powerfully built, handsome as a young man, I'd say, though his looks have faded. He's more grizzled now than chiselled, his face cut from craggy rock nae smooth marble. He had a peculiar mannerism.' He raised a hand to his left eye. 'A spasm of the eyelid, perhaps only apparent when agitated. Or lying.'

'Ye think he lied to ye?'

Robertson grimaced. 'I printed what he told me in good faith. As a senior soldier of the regiment, I assumed he would wish to protect his men, that revealing the Crown's deceit would bode ill for him; hence, he'd nae do so without good reason. From his speech, he wasna a highland man, though undoubtedly a Scot. Maybe a Moss-trooper.'

Jamie frowned. He had heard of these border bandits but had no idea if McBeath was one of them. Hadn't his father been a Kirk minister?

They entered the building and made their way to the orderly room where Jamie had kept McBeath under guard since the first night of the mutiny. 'I must warn ye, sir, the man can be foul-mouthed.'

'I'll swear to that,' one of the guards muttered.

Robertson half smiled. 'I doubt he can say anything I've not heard before.'

Jamie nodded and unlocked the door, giving it a push. It swung open, revealing McBeath sitting back with his feet on a desk. He was unwashed and unshaven, his uniform dishevelled, although he was quick to don a galling smirk.

'Well, well,' he drawled, getting to his feet. 'If it's no' the chief mutineer. And ye've brought the newspaper man.' He flicked his gaze to John Robertson. 'Might I be of further service?' He swept him a mocking bow. 'Another news exclusive, perhaps?' He laughed.

'That's him,' Robertson confirmed. 'That's the man who told me the regiment was sold. He spun a persuasive tale and convinced me, I'm sorry to say. You believe he lied?'

'That's what I need to find out.'

'Lied?' McBeath pulled a face. 'I wouldnae say I lied, more …' he waggled his head, then sniggered. 'More inflated and overstated. But then, I needed my pound of flesh.'

'Pound of flesh?' Robertson stared at him.

McBeath ignored the printmaker and glowered at Jamie. 'Five months I rotted in gaol on account o' you. Since my release into the army, I've wasted more months taking orders from strutting scoundrels and bloated gentry, hardly how I wish to spend my days. I've whisky to drink, women to bed. One in particular,' he added with a smirk. 'My fortune to remake since you took all that from me.' His eyelid twitched. 'Though, I'll admit my time wasnae entirely wasted. I spent it sowing seeds.'

'Sowing seeds?' Robertson echoed.

A slow smirk spread across McBeath's face. 'Aye, every other day, I'd scatter a few and wait for them to root. I knew they would, given the rich soil I was sowing them in.' He winked at Jamie. 'I aimed them at a heidstrong fool choked with pride and born of a race o' lawless rogues quick to rise in rebellion.' He chuckled at his own cunning.

'If you mean a Highlandman,' Robertson said, 'I am also a proud member of that race.'

'Are ye now.' McBeath laughed. 'I never would've guessed. I tended my seedlings well, and they soon grew into strong, rebellious shoots. Then all it took was a regular spreading o' fresh dung.' He snorted with laughter.

'Ye mean lies,' Jamie growled.

'I may have spread a few doubts and suspicions, but as any good farmer knows, a thick layer o' muck yields the best harvest. You could say I became a farmer, tending my crop. I knew if I waited long enough, I'd bring in the harvest I'd long been dreaming of.'

Mystified, Robertson turned to Jamie. 'Does he mean he misled you into taking your present action?'

'Aye,' he growled.

'Then he must also have lied to me.'

Grinning, McBeath looked out the window at the castle battlements guarded by mutineers. 'Look what those seeds have brought me—a full-blown mutiny in hardly any time. That's how revenge works. Ye must be patient, twisting and colouring until things appear how ye want. 'Tis how you steer your quarry where you want him.' He laughed. 'Kneeling with his head on the block.'

'Scheming blaggard,' Jamie growled. 'Ye risked all the men's lives fer yer petty revenge.'

'Nay, 'twas you risked their lives.'

'I acted to save them,' he stammered.

'Aye, that's the best part. That's why my plan worked so well. It hinged on yer hatred of injustice, something I knew about to my cost since it brought us to our swordplay last year. You were clay in my hands, what with your noble principles and loyalty to the muck-the-byres of the regiment, although the War Office did much of the work for me, betraying the regiment at every turn. All I did was overplay what any fool could see was a blatant betrayal by those in command.'

Jamie choked with rage. 'Are we sold to the Indies?' he rasped. 'Or did ye make that up?'

'I doubt ye'll ever know. After your treachery, I'll wager the castle mound is the closest you'll get to the south of England. That's where they'll make you kneel to face the firing party.'

'God blast ye! Did ye lie?'

'Maybe I did. Then again—'

'*Did ye lie?*'

McBeath smirked delightedly. 'Of course. I'd have spun any tale if I thought it would get ye hung.'

Jamie was upon McBeath before the smirk could die on the devil's lips. He launched himself from the doorway, his weight and fury bringing the man down in a clatter of overturned chairs. He swung his fist, smashing it into the grizzled face. His next swing went wide, angry blood thrumming through his veins. It caught the tip of the weasel's jaw, loosening a few teeth by the crunching sound.

McBeath grunted beneath him, spitting blood, struggling to worm himself free. The hated face was closer than was tolerable, the man's foul breath rising in Jamie's nostrils. Exhaling, he thought of Morven and the child he might never see and tightened his fingers around the devil's throat, squeezing with every ounce of his hatred.

'Corporal Innes! *James!*' Robertson pulled at his arm. 'Dear God, this isna the way.'

Robertson's cries were but the buzzing of a fly in his ear. Jamie straightened his elbows, the better to tighten his grip, his knee in the weasel's groin, and pressed down for all he was worth.

McBeath's eyes bulged. His face reddened; his cheeks ballooned out. The veins at his temples stood out like twisted cords. Slowly, his face turned purple.

'*James!* Fer the love o' God. Ye mustna. 'Tis madness. They'll hang ye. Think o' yer family.'

He jerked his head as if swatting away a pesky fly.

'I have a powerful voice through the *Mercury*. It reaches far, turning the hearts and minds of many. I can help you. Between us, we will bring this man to justice.'

Jamie blinked and drew a steadying breath. The thrumming at his temples eased a little. Slowly, the hot tide of hatred receded, and he slackened his grip on the devil's throat.

Choking, McBeath dragged in a desperate gulp of air. His teeth were stained with blood. 'Ye're a madman,' he wheezed.

Jamie took his hands from the devil's throat and sat up, his knee still pressed in McBeath's groin. He used it to take his weight as he pushed himself to his feet, his chest heaving. McBeath shrieked and curled in a ball.

'Ye're right,' he panted. 'He's nae worth hanging fer.' He stepped back before he changed his mind, then booted the weasel in the buttocks. 'Fer Hal,' he growled.

'Thank God.' Robertson sagged in relief. 'I thought ye were—'

'Aye, fer a moment there, I thought so, too.'

'We should fetch the surgeon.' Robertson grimaced down at McBeath. 'Let's pray the man's nae seriously harmed, that no excuse might be made to prevent him facing the full force of the law.' He stared at Jamie. 'Is there somewhere private we might talk?'

Panting, Jamie leant forward, his hands on his knees. 'If ye wish. We've the run o' the whole castle.'

'Somewhere far from that man.' Robertson shuddered and moved to the door.

Leaving McBeath where he lay, still moaning, Jamie righted chairs and ushered Robertson from the room. He locked the door and asked a guard to fetch the surgeon, then led the way to his barrack room. His quarters were empty, the room neat and orderly, berths made, the floor swept, and the hearth cleaned of ashes. The men had kept army standards without the need for inspection and punishment. That pleased him, although the orderly state of his quarters contrasted sharply with the chaos in his mind. He sank onto his berth and looked at the printmaker in despair.

Robertson sat on the bed opposite, clutching his satchel. 'Can I ask how this ill feeling arose between you and that man? Am I to understand ye fought a duel?'

'Aye, last year.'

'I only ask as I believe your story would make a compelling feature for the *Mercury*. I'd go as far as say 'twould capture the hearts of my readers, the townsfolk of Edinburgh and the Lothians. That could portend well for you and the soldiers holding the castle.'

Jamie frowned quizzically at him.

'Since the Northern Fencibles began arriving here, the townspeople have shown an uncommon interest in the regiment. They view Highlanders as fierce, exotic warriors and were pleased to learn such men had been sent to protect them. I've taken full advantage of that, promoting the virtues of highland soldiers, stirring up the levelling societies. These people are quick to denounce the government and authority.'

'Thank you.'

'You may not think it to look at me, but I was an active Jacobite in my youth. I paid dearly for it, although nae as dearly as some, but I understand the Crown's intentions, their wish to turn as many disaffected Highlanders into loyal redcoats as possible. Fewer rebels to cause trouble in the north, and with so many highland men beholden to the Crown for their living, less chance of another uprising. Of course, once they have you in the army, they can send you to fight in the king's wars with France and the American colonies, even to conquer the natives of foreign lands.'

''Tis what we fear.'

'Rightly so, James. I've been following the fortune of the Northern

Fencibles since before you got here and the fortune of other highland regiments far longer, chronicling their mistreatment in my newspaper.'

'I can only thank ye fer that, sir.'

Robertson waved away his thanks. 'My readers much admire Highlanders' mannerly conduct. They've been cheering on your refusal to volunteer for England, a move that would leave Edinburgh defenceless. In short, they've developed an uncommon interest in yer fate.'

'Then I hope they understand we had little choice but take up arms if we're ever to see our families again.'

'They do, James, but telling your story would flesh out the man behind the mutiny, an act of defiance the townsfolk almost universally support. With all the facts, I could better explain your reasons, highlight your daring and passion for justice and reveal how that man slyly played you. I can present you as a victim, which, of course, you are. A brave one, if I may say so. My readers will enjoy that, although the authorities will not. With my pen and printing press, I can stir the hearts of the people, giving them someone to focus their passion upon. Feelings in the capital ride high, but I can fire that passion further, rallying it to the mutineers' advantage. With your help, we can make it a great surge.'

Jamie blinked, a flicker of optimism beginning to kindle inside him. Hal was right; Robertson was an ally. 'We hope His Grace and the War Office will see sense,' he said, 'and honour our terms. A forlorn hope, perhaps, but 'tis what we pray fer. They sent Adjutant Abercrombie to record our grievances. He's a Gaelic speaker. Through him, we've asked for a written pledge that we'll be allowed to serve out our term in Scotland. 'Tis what was promised when we enlisted. We intend to hold the castle until we receive that pledge, 'til the ships are gone, but the more we can shame the War Office into honouring their promises, the better.'

Robertson nodded. 'You must understand, the Crown will not wish to give in to mutineers. In doing so, they lose face and authority. As soon as they have a regiment of dragoons fully mustered here, they will surround the castle to prevent fresh supplies reaching you. Yet if the authorities expect you to give up the castle without bloodshed, they must yield to some degree.'

'We've enough food to last months,' Jamie replied. 'The castle stores are piled wi' sacks o' flour and grain, salted beef, many foods highland men have never seen afore, and there's ale and whisky, though I've urged restraint. We need our wits about us.'

'Then, at least you'll not starve.'

''Tis our kinfolk's bellies that are empty.'

Robertson nodded thoughtfully. 'The authorities will wish this humiliation swiftly ended and the ringleaders punished.' He frowned and leant forward. 'They will have you firmly in their sights, but if we can shift their scrutiny to another, to a man lacking principles and integrity.'

'McBeath?'

'Exactly. By his own confession, that man incited a mutiny for his own selfish revenge. Or rather, he plotted to have you incite one. How did he put it? He sowed the seeds of rebellion, leaving you to bring it to fruition, knowing you would since you wished to protect your fellow men. If you'll allow me, I would like to tell that story.'

Jamie looked sceptically at him. 'Ye think it'll help?'

'Undoubtedly. Behind every revolt lies a human story—real people with real lives ravaged by injustice. Honest men with faces that reveal their despair. I've seen many such faces here.'

'I dinna doubt it.'

Robertson glanced at the satchel in his lap, neatly tied with ribbon and holding the implements of his trade. 'Your story is powerful, and your face, if I may say so, uncommonly handsome.' He allowed himself a ghost of a smile. 'That always helps. Perhaps I might bring an artist to capture you,' he mused. 'Do you have a family, James, who await your return?'

Robertson's question prompted a tightening in Jamie's chest. 'A young wife. Morven is my life, Mister Robertson. Wi'out her ...' he swallowed, grief clogging his throat. He hadn't even written to confess what he'd done, hadn't known how or where to begin. 'Wi'out her,' he choked, 'I wouldna wish to live. Yet, like a scoundrel, I left her carrying my child.' He clutched his head. 'The infant is perhaps born. I pray the Lord will watch ower them until I can.'

Robertson sighed. 'I'll wager you had little choice but to leave them.'

Bitterness rasped Jamie's voice. ''Twas the only way to keep a roof over their heads. The duke demanded military service to safeguard the leases on all my kinfolk's holdings.' He swallowed. 'Last year, I fought a duel to protect the last o' my kin. I could hardly let them be dispossessed.'

Robertson's jaw hardened. 'The duke threatened to evict all your kin?'

''Tis how he obtained my enlistment.'

The printmaker seemed lost for words. He blinked several times, his nostrils flaring. 'I fear you were not the only man treated so. I've heard many such tales, although yours is particularly egregious. If I may, I would like to use your first-hand account.'

Jamie frowned at him. 'Ye wish to write about my family?'

'If you'll allow me.'

'Ye're sure 'twill help?'

'I aim to stir sympathy, James, especially among Edinburgh's educated society, to bring news of your treatment into fashionable drawing rooms and let men of law and politics argue the rights and wrongs of your actions. Remember, thus far, you've hurt no one if we discount that wretch back there.'

'I've long stressed the need to act wi' restraint, to make our stand wi'out needless violence.'

Robertson nodded at him. 'The adjutant told me you were a reasonable man. He also said you can read and write both English and Gaelic. You're far from a highland brute. In truth, I believe most ranks of society will relate to you, at least on some level. That makes you dangerous. With the aid of my newspaper, you could help the world see the truth.' He leant forward, staring intently at Jamie. 'Once the authorities realise the influence you wield, I've little doubt they will wish to treat fairly with you.'

'Ye think so?'

Robertson nodded, his eyes flashing. 'I do, James. You have the power to shame and humiliate the Crown and its War Office, to reveal their deceptions and win the people's hearts.'

Jamie sat back, bewildered. *Did he?* 'Ye understand, I dinna wish to cause trouble, Mister Robertson? We've asked only that the War Office honour our terms.'

Robertson inhaled with a smile. 'That is because you are a tolerant man, James. You ask for naught but to have the promises made to you honoured. Am I right in thinking the men's pay has been withheld?'

'And our bounty.'

'More ammunition to fire at them. Trust me, crowds like to see justice done. By the time I'm finished, the townspeople's sympathies will lie firmly with the mutineers. They will wish to see you treated fairly and Sergeant McBeath punished. There can be no question of the authorities letting that man off. Should they try, they'll have civil unrest on their hands. Nay, they will need to punish him and be seen to do so.'

'But will they honour our terms and let us serve out the American war in Scotland like they promised?'

Robertson sighed. 'You must understand, I cannot force the Crown's hand, but I can make it difficult for them to send a defensible regiment overseas. The world will be watching. Or at least Scotland's capital and beyond. The War Office seem bent on exploiting men innocently recruited in the glens to defend their own country. Once my readers understand that, indeed, learn the whole disturbing story, I doubt they'll allow it. Through you, James, we can enlighten them.'

Jamie stared at the printmaker. Never had he imagined one man could wield such power; the pen was indeed mighty. His heart gave an eager leap, a torrent of emotions rippling through his innards. 'Then, Mister Robertson,' he said, 'if I am to tell ye my story, I would have ye call me Jamie.'

Robertson smiled and began drawing paper and ink from his satchel. 'I'd be honoured, but only if you'll call me John.'

Jamie laughed, a weight lifting from his shoulders. 'Where should I begin, John?'

CHAPTER THIRTY-TWO

Druimbeag, Samhain 1781

'Morven, you're hard at work, but should ye nae be resting?' Father Ranald stood in the barn doorway with what looked like a wad of rolled-up paper tucked under his arm. 'Alec. Sarah.' He nodded to her brother and Sarah. 'Good to see you helping.'

Alec lowered his flail, brushing dust and chaff from his flushed face. 'I'll always do what I can to help my sister, Father, even if I hadna promised Jamie. I ken she'd do the same fer me.' At his side, Sarah glowered, her face as begrimed as Alec's. She had still to forgive the father for delaying their wedding.

'Grand, lad, grand.' Father Ranald looked back at Morven. 'Am I the last to meet the child born at Scalan?'

'I dinna think so.' Jamie had yet to meet his child, but Morven bit that back and came forward to show off her daughter. 'I thought I'd call her Ilene.'

'Ilene. A bonny name.' Father Ranald peered at the tiny face, all that was visible of the infant in her swaddling. 'Och,' he breathed, 'nae just a bonny name. What a precious lamb. I see a resemblance to her father, something in her eyes.'

Morven smiled, glad others also saw a likeness to Jamie, and she hadn't imagined it. Ilene was her physical link to him. 'Will ye come in fer some ale, Father?' She glanced at Alec and Sarah. 'I'm thinking we could do wi' wetting our throats.'

They had spent the morning threshing her barley, separating the grain from the straw, Alec and Sarah doing the most strenuous work. Armed with rope flails, they'd toiled for hours, beating the sheaves as they lay on the barn floor while she pulled away the straw and gathered the precious grain. She hoped to distil her barley into whisky, but she could hardly do that in time to pay her rent. 'Twas due in ten days. When she lay down to sleep, bone weary with the wee soul swaddled beside her, the factor's men came striding through her dreams, tramping over the infield waving an eviction notice. How would McGillivray react when she offered him excuses instead of coin?

Peering through the dusty air, Father Ranald considered the sheaves still awaiting threshing. His face appeared more lined than usual. 'I've no wish to hamper your work, but 'twould be best, I think.'

So, they put aside their flails, brushed themselves down, and followed the father to the cot-house. Morven coaxed some warmth from the fire, and they sat around it clutching quaichs of watery ale. The father shifted the roll of paper from his underarm to his lap, covering it with his hands. He sipped at his quaich, put it down, and frowned across at her.

'The factor hasna been here, lass?'

'I've nae seen him, no.' Her heart fluttered.

'I suspect he'll be here soon. When might ye want yer bairn baptised? Sooner is always better, although I understand ye may wish to wait until Jamie returns.' Father Ranald's frown deepened. 'I would counsel against that. You must think on yer child's soul. Should aught tragic occur,' he looked gravely at her. 'Forgive me, but we both know these tragedies happen more than we'd like, yet to receive God's grace, the child must first be cleansed of the sin she was born with. Only then may she receive the Lord's salvation.'

Morven was aware of the Church's teaching that a child who died unbaptised would linger forever in a state of limbo, not in hell but deemed too sinful to enter heaven, yet she struggled with the concept. What sin had wee Ilene committed? Any sin inherited from Adam's long-ago slip in the Garden of Eden hardly seemed to belong to her. What would Nathaniel say? But he had also urged her to have Ilene swiftly baptised.

'Might Nathaniel baptise her?' she ventured. 'Has the bishop made him a priest?'

The father cleared a hoarseness from his throat. 'That was one of the reasons for Bishop Hay's visit, but there is some difficulty with Nathaniel's father.'

'Aye, he told me.'

The father exhaled irritably. 'The man expects Nathaniel to give up all hope of the cloth, even after his many years of diligent study. The poor lad's quite overcome with the strain of it all. We can only pray for him, but any decision must be his.' He swallowed and glanced at the papers in his lap. 'But now, with these dire tidings, Nathaniel frets all the more.'

Morven craned her neck for a look at the papers the father was concealing, struggling to understand their significance.

'He makes himself ill. I understand he is anxious not to disappoint his father; Lord knows he's spent most of his life trying to please that man. Yet he seems set on remaining in Glenlivet, especially now, and dreads telling him.'

Morven's heart thumped. 'What dire tidings, Father?'

'I'd gladly have him as my curate,' the father maundered on, 'to take over when the time comes if that is his wish. Lord knows I could do with the help.'

'What dire tidings d'ye mean?' she persisted.

He stared at her, and it struck Morven how stark his face looked. 'You might come to Scalan to see him, my dear. If anyone can heal his tortured mind, I'm certain 'tis you. Nathaniel always seems happiest in your company.' The father shifted in his chair. 'And I hope he may help you, that ... that he might strengthen your heart and, with prayer, may,' he swallowed, 'help console you.'

'Console her?' Alec set his ale down, his thirst forgotten. He had kept quiet during the father's ramblings but could do so no longer. 'Is there news o' Jamie, Father?'

Father Ranald turned to Alec with some reluctance. 'During the bishop's travels, His Excellency strives to maintain correspondence with Rome and the seats of power at home and abroad, even at Scalan. A rider brought a package this forenoon, directives from Rome and a letter from a fellow priest in the capital, along with a copy of an Edinburgh newspaper, although I fear the paper is days old. Only the news it contained ...' he swallowed, staring into his lap.

Sarah scowled at him. 'Whit news?'

He appeared loathe to answer, finally raising his gaze to Morven's anxious face. Her heart shrank at his expression. 'Have ye heard from Jamie, lass?'

'He wrote to me from Aberdeen, said the fencibles had been ordered to Edinburgh. Nathaniel read his letter to me.'

'But naught since?'

She shook her head, her chest tightening. 'What did the bishop's letter say?'

The father puffed his cheeks out. 'That the duke's regiment has mutinied. The Northern Fencibles have taken Edinburgh Castle with all its armaments. They're holding their officers prisoner. The city's in ferment, the townsfolk cheering the fencibles on, especially their daring young leader.' He moved his hands from his lap, revealing the rolled-up sheets of a newspaper. Morven could see naught but dense lines of printing. He unrolled the paper and held it up.

Alec's hissed breath made her jump, and she stared in horror. The front page was half-filled with a sketch of a handsome young man in military tartan. He sat astride a great cannon, his gaze trained over a city landscape looking out to sea where ships were visible in the distance. The drawing was a perfect likeness of Jamie.

'*Mother Earth*,' she breathed.

Alec leapt to his feet. 'Holy God, what've they forced him to? 'Tis my doing. It should be me. I should be there in Jamie's place.'

'Alec!' Sarah grasped his arm and tried to force him back into his seat. 'What are ye saying? Dinna be shaming me.'

'Nay, Sarah.' He shook off her hand. 'I'll nae be quiet. I should've spoken afore. Morven's my sister; I would have her ken the truth. It should be me in the firing line, never Jamie. He'd do naught like this unless sorely provoked.' He stared at the priest. 'Ye ken as well as I, Father, they'll want his life fer this.'

Morven stared at Alec in horror.

Ilene's face puckered and reddened. She began to wail.

'I'm certain you've made the right decision, Corporal. This can only aid my negotiations on your behalf. With your officers freed unharmed, the War Office will be more willing to discuss the terms of your surrender. That is presumably what we all want.'

Jamie's jaw tightened. 'Twould depend on those terms, but he nodded at Abercrombie, praying the man was right. Following the adjutant's suggestion, he had addressed the men at morning assembly, repeating Abercrombie's counsel that they free all their officers and staff. He urged the men to speak their minds and voice their opinions freely. Most were against it, believing that holding their officers strengthened their hand in negotiations. Perhaps they could exchange these commissioned men for their freedom, although no man had been able to explain how that might be achieved. Arguments flowed back and forth until, with all talk exhausted, Jamie called a ballot. Almost to a man, the fencibles chose to release all their officers. He was relieved. If naught else, it meant fewer men to worry about.

'Ye understand it wasna my sole decision,' he muttered. 'We do things fairly here. I've little quarrel wi' these men,' he nodded at the approaching column, 'beyond their sense o' entitlement and lack o' respect fer highland folk. My quarrel lies wi' His Grace, Lord Adam and those commanders who broke their promise and now presume to do what they please with us.'

Abercrombie turned to him with a look of open regard. 'Since reading your story in the *Caledonian Mercury,* I believe I understand you better, Corporal. Your life has been far from easy.'

Jamie grunted. 'I doubt my life's been harder than other men's. Mine was just the story Mister Robertson chose to tell. His readers now understand how my enlistment was obtained, the threats made and promises broken, and more importantly, that I was far from the only man treated that way.'

Abercrombie frowned. 'But what on earth possessed you to let him do that? I imagine you were known to the authorities before the mutiny, at least to a degree, but now they will certainly name you the ringleader.'

Jamie shrugged. ''Tis what I am. Besides, Captain Cumming had me marked from the start and better me than some other poor glensman.'

Abercrombie raised his brows. 'That is extraordinarily generous of you.'

They were standing at the back of the line of fencible soldiers, Jamie a head taller than the adjutant. As the column of officers and staff drew level with them, they fell silent, watching the men Jamie had relieved of command file past.

Jamie sighed. 'We decided to show our officers the courtesy they long denied us.'

'So, I see.' Abercrombie nodded in approval. ''Tis well done. Those in authority will note it.'

Jamie doubted that.

The Northern Fencibles had formed into two lines, flanking the officers' route from the governor's house, where they had lately been kept, through the portcullis gate to the gatehouse and drawbridge and ultimately their freedom. The men stood respectfully to attention, facing to the front as the castle governor and the regiment's senior officers marched past, stiff figures in crimson coats and gold braiding, most wearing smouldering expressions. Taking up the rear some distance from the main body, Sergeant McBeath hobbled to keep up, his face bruised and swollen.

As he limped by, he turned his head, scouring the ranks to find Jamie. They made eye contact. The weasel's eyes were hooded, little visible but a dark gleam. 'Twas enough to convey the force of his hatred. Jamie stared icily back.

''Twas prudent of you to release that man.' Abercrombie followed McBeath's limping progress with a disapproving frown.

'I feared some despairing soldier might slit his throat in the night,' Jamie replied. 'Perhaps me.'

Abercrombie blinked at him.

Sergeant McBeath's actions were now common knowledge at the castle. Robertson had named him in his newspaper, revealing that he had lied to his men and the *Mercury*, deliberately inciting the men's anger and resentment. He'd goaded one man in particular: Corporal James Innes of Strathavon, the man leading the mutineers. McBeath had never been popular, but such was the men's festering hatred of him now, Jamie judged it unwise to hold him at the castle, this for the weasel's own safety. 'Twas anyhow better the devil suffered British justice; any home-grown kind could jeopardise the position they'd taken. Thus far, they had hurt no one. They must keep it that way, maintaining the moral high ground, but with the truth out, he could no longer guarantee that. Even the officers had disowned McBeath, holding him partly responsible for their humiliation. At least they would waste no more food on the devil.

Once the officers had passed through the portcullis gate, Jamie climbed the steps of the Lang Stairs to the Half Moon Battery with Abercrombie and joined John Robertson on the ramparts. From there, they could watch the officers leave the castle by the drawbridge. Robertson grinned at him.

'It appears some in town have gotten wind of the officers' release. Members of the reforming societies by the looks of it, joined by a spirited crowd from the tenements and wynds of the Grassmarket. Hardly the most welcoming reception party.'

Jamie peered down to the castle mound where a crowd had gathered.

Robertson chuckled. 'These folk have taken the regiment to their hearts. I knew they would once they understood the contempt the authorities have shown you. I expect they've come to taunt these commissioned men whom they view as arrogant gentry.'

Jamie stared in alarm. John was right. The officers crossing the drawbridge were met by jeers from a crowd of ill-wishers. They instinctively bunched around the ageing castle governor, some drawing their swords. A detachment of dragoons was waiting to escort them to Holyroodhouse for debriefing. The dragoons charged forward, pressing their horses between the crowd and the officers to prevent a rushed attack. Jamie glanced along the ramparts. The soldiers who had lined the officer's route to the drawbridge were now crowding along the battery wall. Hal and Fin appeared at his shoulder and peered down to the crowds below. Sight of the colourful Highlanders on the battlements prompted much cheering from the townsfolk below. The men raised their bonnets and waved back.

Loosely ringed by dragoons, the officers made a tense and undignified procession as they marched stiff-backed over the castle mound, followed by a jeering mob. A few stragglers in the crowd remained. To Jamie's horror, they began darting back and forth, gathering up dung left by the dragoons' horses. Laden with armfuls of muck, they ran after the procession, lobbing clods of dung through gaps in the ring of cavalry. The commissioned men hunched over, arms over their heads as a volley of filth rained on their backs and heads.

Appalled, Jamie turned to Abercrombie, who gasped in horror. These folk could sling balls of horse dung with astonishing accuracy.

Robertson only chuckled. 'I swear the crowds back the fencibles more each day. They devour everything I write about you.'

'These folk can read?' Jamie looked at him in surprise.

'Many can. Menfolk, mostly. Women are still wretchedly disadvantaged. The Kirk run the parish schools here, teaching lowland bairns to read. They plan to establish a similar network of schools across the Highlands, especially in the remote glens, teaching English language and culture, something they slyly promote as cultural advancement. In this way, they hope to deter highland attachment to popery and rebellious notions, replacing Gaelic culture with Sassenach ways and language. If highland youngsters can be made to embrace English at an early age, they doubtless imagine the

Gaelic culture will die with its old folk.'

'Scheming devils,' Hal growled.

John had used the Gaelic term for the Highlands, *à Ghàidhealtachd*, land of the Gaels. At mention of his home, Jamie's chest tightened. He dragged his gaze from the shameful scene on the castle mound, where dragoons were now charging into the crowds to disperse them, and looked anxiously at Abercrombie.

'Sir, I hope the authorities willna imagine we sanctioned the demeaning of our officers or somehow encouraged it. We've treated all our officers with respect, ever mindful o' their rank.' He frowned. Despite restricting their commissioned officers to their quarters for almost three weeks, they had treated these men with the utmost courtesy.

Abercrombie nodded. 'I'll inform His Grace and the Secretary at War that this outrage was not your doing. You've treated your officers properly.'

'Thank ye, sir.' Any suggestion that they had mistreated their officers could jeopardise Abercrombie's negotiations. Jamie glanced along the battery wall to where the regimental chaplain stood slightly apart from the men. Reverend Gordon had refused to leave with the officers, and for that, Jamie admired him. An educated man of the Kirk, the reverend felt his duty lay with the men, even though most of those he must minister to were Catholics whose future seemed anything but certain. The reverend acknowledged Jamie with a courteous nod. They were lucky to have him. In the days ahead, they would perhaps have need of his guidance.

Chuckling, Robertson drew back from the parapet. 'They've all gotten away safely, though nae entirely unscathed.'

'Thank the Lord,' Abercrombie muttered.

'What now?' Robertson quirked a brow at the adjutant.

Abercrombie frowned at him. 'You surely don't expect me to discuss my negotiations with you. You're not even a military man. You own a newspaper, for God's sake; you'll only broadcast whatever I tell you to all and sundry, undermining my efforts at diplomacy.'

'These men have a right to know how the Crown intend to treat them.'

'They'll learn that soon enough,' Abercrombie replied, 'once they have peacefully surrendered.' He adjusted his spectacles. 'Negotiations are at a critical stage, but I hope to engineer a pardon for most of these men. That's why releasing the officers was so important.'

'*Most* o' these men?' John glared at him. 'And Corporal Innes? What o' him? The lad's put his neck on the line fer his fellow men.'

'Yes, Mister Robertson, and thanks to you, every man and his dog knows it.'

Robertson bristled. 'I merely called attention to the Fencibles' plight. Telling Corporal Innes' story powerfully illustrated the gravity of their situation.'

Abercrombie sighed. 'Congratulations. Did you expect those in command to be pleased?' He met the printmaker's glare with a measured front. 'These men have heaped shame and disgrace upon themselves and their regiment, most of all upon His Grace and the Crown's senior commanders who now understandably wish to see those responsible punished. Trust me, the authorities will not let this pass. There will need to be a reckoning.'

Jamie swallowed. He had always known there would be a price to pay, doubtless a heavy one. 'Twas only right he should be the one to pay it. He thought of Morven and the child he might never see, and his guts clenched.

'You'll do your best fer him?' John pressed.

Abercrombie massaged his brows. 'As I say, my negotiations are at a delicate stage, but I am in the business of saving lives, Mister Robertson, not sacrificing them.'

Robertson nodded, appearing marginally placated. 'Then best be remembering the strength o' feeling I've whipped up here. Make Corporal Innes a scapegoat, and I promise there'll be hell to pay.'

Abercrombie's brows shot up. 'You're threatening me?'

Robertson glanced at Jamie, who grimaced and shook his head. 'Only reminding ye how high passions run.'

'Trust me; I am fully aware of those passions.'

At Jamie's look, John grudgingly let it drop. He meant well and doubtless knew Abercrombie was doing his best. Since their first meeting, John had been fastidious in bringing a copy of the latest edition of his newspaper to the gatehouse as soon as it left his press. The mutiny and its many causes still dominated the paper's columns, even pushing news of the American War and how badly it went for the British to the back pages. At morning muster, Jamie took pains to relay every word printed about the mutiny to the men.

The *Mercury* had conceded that the transports lying at anchor in the firth were waiting to carry the men to England, not India, and the regiment had not been sold. That was a lie fabricated by Sergeant McBeath to fuel the men's resentment. The men feared they would never see their families again, and John argued the rebellion was therefore understandable. But shrewdly, he also printed the full wording of their attestation papers, showing that the duke and the War Office had broken their promises.

Jamie was grateful but feared he had let the printmaker go too far. John Robertson was a persuasive man. Against his better judgment, he'd let John publish a personal piece describing the ill blood between himself and McBeath. The feature gave a colourful account of their duel and the events that led to it. To Jamie's embarrassment, John even brought an artist to the castle to sketch him.

That edition of the *Mercury* sold out within hours, with Robertson forced to authorise another print run to keep up with demand. The people of Edinburgh were hungry for news of the Northern Fencibles' bloodless clash with the British military. They particularly craved information about Corporal James Innes, the mutineers' handsome young leader. According to John, he was now a household name in the capital.

Such notoriety made Jamie uneasy. Elevating him must only rile the authorities further. But John believed the more acclaim Jamie could garner, the harder the Crown would find it to punish him and his fellow High-landers. Opinions mattered, particularly when they were held so firmly and by almost every class of society.

The *Edinburgh Evening Courant,* Robertson's more prestigious rival, had also published commentary on the mutiny, the information leaked to them by Robertson. Although in competition for readers and not always of a mind politically, both broadsheets supported the Highlanders, although the *Mercury,* with its Jacobite leaning, was their most ardent backer. The papers were hailing Jamie as both a hero and a victim, something the authorities must hate. Jamie imagined the duke now regretted recruiting him.

With Edinburgh's lower and merchant classes both now invested in their cause, families were bringing gifts of food and supplies to the gatehouse. The castle was well stocked for a siege, both in food and munitions, and they had adequate water from the castle well, provided the authorities could find no way of poisoning it. A stealth attack was Jamie's greatest fear. Past attackers had scaled the sheer face of Castle Rock to gain entry, and he constantly stressed the need to be vigilant. But until they received the written assurances they had asked for, there could be no question of surrendering the castle.

He sighed and turned to stare out over the firth. The transports were still there, dark hulks on the horizon. 'Lord Barrington shows no sign o' relenting?' he pressed.

Abercrombie appeared wary of saying too much. 'You must understand; the authorities cannot be seen to give in to mutineers.' Meeting Jamie's gaze, his own softened. 'Yet with the Fencibles showing such blatant disloyalty, I cannot see how there can be any thought of sending the regiment to England. That scheme must surely lie in tatters.'

'They nae longer intend to ship us away against our will?'

'I didn't say that.'

'Nae to England,' John finished.

Abercrombie sighed. 'Today's actions will have pleased His Grace and Lord Barrington. You must be content with that for now. I still have work to do.'

CHAPTER THIRTY-THREE

Two days later, after the drums had beaten Reveille, Jamie crossed the parade ground to the Argyll Battery with Hal to relieve the men on guard duty.

'Corporal.' A young private stood to attention as he approached. 'What does it mean?' He looked north over the scaffolding and building work of the New Town, out over the firth, still hazy in the morning mist. Following his gaze, Jamie blinked and stared. There was no sign of the troop transports that had lain there at anchor for almost three weeks.

'They're gone,' Hal breathed.

Jamie squinted in the half-dark, his steaming breath making it harder to see.

'Does it mean we've won?' The private could barely keep the excitement from his voice.

'Doubt it,' Hal muttered, but when he turned to Jamie, his weather-worn face creased in jubilation.

'I pray so.' Had Abercrombie managed to win them their freedom? Lord, let it be so. Yet it couldna be that simple. Where were the written assurances they'd asked for?

It was nearing midday when Jamie was called to the gatehouse. Adjutant Abercrombie had arrived and wished to see him. Jamie led the young officer to the chapel, his stomach churning, and bade Abercrombie wait while he fetched the other men. His tongue itched with questions, but one look at the adjutant kept him silent.

The men came crowding in, clutching their bonnets. They had all seen that the troop transports were gone, but did it mean what they hoped? Abercrombie's expression was difficult to read.

The adjutant waited for the men to be seated, then cleared his throat.

'His Grace has authorised me to put proposals to you for the peaceful surrender of the castle.'

They looked at each other.

'Despite your demand for written assurances, His Grace will pen no such thing—deeds that could be leaked to the press to humiliate His Majesty and His War Office. You must accept His Grace's word, although he is willing to come to the castle and put his terms to you in person if you wish. He, of course, assumes that will not be necessary.' The adjutant removed his spectacles, and the official stance he had maintained since his arrival seemed to lift away with them. He looked at the anxious faces around him. 'You have my word these are the most lenient terms I could secure.'

Jamie nodded, his heart thumping. 'Thank ye, sir. What does His Grace propose?'

Abercrombie busied himself removing a sheaf of papers from his satchel and peered myopically at the men. 'That you will vacate the castle by sunset without incident and peacefully surrender its possession to the Perthshire Highlanders. Thereafter, you will be quartered in tents around the capital before marching by company to coastal defences around Scotland, where the discipline of the regiment may in some manner be restored. You will defend these ports from the ravages of French and American privateers and will put down any local unrest. Away from the capital, 'tis assumed you will no longer be prey to the influence of the reforming societies and other poisonous intermeddlers and will keep rigorously to your duties, entertaining no more rebellious notions.'

'Ye mean,' Hal pressed, 'we havena to go to England?'

'After the scandal of your disobedience, there can be no question of that.'

'Thank the Lord!' Hal whooped and turned to Jamie, flashing him a triumphant grin. A murmur rippled around the nave, and the tension palpably lifted.

Abercrombie went on, 'You will surrender your ammunition. All powder, cartridges, and flints in your possession must be handed over and your bayonets unfixed and piled by the gatehouse as you pass through. You may keep your muskets and swords but will collect the regimental sporrans you so childishly discarded in a fit of temper and belt them properly in place.'

'Fair enough, I suppose,' Fin muttered.

'Are you saying we're to be pardoned?' Jamie asked incredulously. Abercrombie's taut and unsmiling countenance was beginning to unnerve him. 'We're nae to be disciplined? No man will be seized and thrown in the Black Hole?' Hadn't Abercrombie said there would need to be a reckoning? This seemed too good to be true.

Abercrombie swallowed, avoiding his gaze. 'You must understand Lord Adam demanded the mutiny be crushed under a dragoon's boot. To avoid that and secure favourable terms for your surrender, I have been obliged to give certain assurances on your behalf. Assurances, I hope you will understand were necessary.'

'Those being?'

The adjutant moistened his lips. 'I have assured His Grace that you regret your rebellious behaviour and will submit to the Perthshire Highlanders without trouble. If permitted to remain in Scotland, you will act with dutiful obedience. Your misconduct was brought on by groundless suspicion, obstinacy, and folly, and you now repent it wholeheartedly. In giving these assurances, I allowed the authorities some scope for leniency, letting any climbdown by His Grace appear gracious and causing him and the War Office the least degree of humiliation. In return, they have agreed to pardon all the mutineers, but—'

A shared gasp echoed off the stone walls. Men turned to each other, grinning, clasping forearms and exclaiming in Gaelic, pounding each other on the back.

Still, Abercrombie had not smiled. 'All but those deemed the ringleaders.' His face tightened. 'Those men being Corporal James Innes of Captain Cumming's company and Corporal Finlay MacKay of MacIntosh's. Forgive me, James.' He looked wretchedly at him. 'The Perthshires are to take you prisoner. You'll be tried by court martial in the next few days, charged with mutiny and you, Corporal MacKay, with incitement to mutiny. Captain Cumming spoke forcefully against you, James. Forgive me, I could do little to counter his arguments or change Lord Adam's mind.'

Jamie swallowed as bile rose in his throat. He knew the penalty for mutiny; they all did. Any court martial would be a formality.

'Niver!' Hal shouted. He leapt to his feet. 'We'll nae agree. We'll fight; God blast them. They'll nae take Jamie!'

'Nor will they have Finlay MacKay.' Donald Forbes rose to his feet with a growl. Wooden pews scraped against the stone floor as the others rose around him.

Jamie remained seated, his heart bounding, a sudden sweatiness in his flesh. He'd always known leading a mutiny could cost him his life, but what choice had they left him? He was a proud Highlander; he had other highland men in his care. He swallowed, thinking of Morven. Would he ever see her again? Pain crushed his heart, and he struggled to breathe. Yet he'd made his choice weeks ago. He shook his head.

'I'll have no blood spilt in my name; no lives wasted. I'm grateful fer yer efforts, sir, we all are. If we can trust His Grace's word and the word o' these lords, then, thanks to you, they've given us what we asked for. If I must be the price,' he swallowed, a muscle tightening in his jaw, 'so be it.' He looked at Fin.

Fin's eyes were wide; his face looked ghastly. For once, he had little to say. He looked at the glensmen standing guard around him, at their fiercely loyal faces. An answering swell of pride and grief surged across his features, and his eyes watered. He raised his chin. 'Aye,' he rasped, 'I'll have no man spill his blood in my name.'

The river was higher than Morven feared. Stained amber with peat, its waters swirled around hidden rocks, weak sunlight glinted in its depths. Fording the Avon here was safe enough on the back of a surefooted garron; she'd done it hundreds of times. But afoot with an infant swaddled at her breast was another matter. Her pony was long gone. She'd weeks ago exchanged it for winter fodder for the beasts.

Faltering at the water's edge, her stomach churned. Fresh snowfall in the hills and mountains had swelled the river. 'Twas a blessing the strath had not been buried. Nowhere for miles was it possible to cross without the risk of being swept away, other than with the boatman Robbie Grant, but she had naught to give Robbie, and Father Ranald had urged her to go to Nathaniel. She longed for his counsel.

The thud of hooves and murmur of voices came to her through the trees. She drew back into the riverbank's frozen underbrush. They spoke in English and came quickly into sight: two men on horseback. The factor rode in front, his bloated figure clad in woollen breeches and knee-length coat. He wore no wig, but a tricorn covered his baldness. Doctor Dalrymple followed behind on his great draught-horse. Like McGillivray, he wore well-cut woollen clothing, although his head was bare. Three brace of grouse hung from his saddle along with a small fowling piece. Loping behind came four gun dogs, their noses to the ground. They quickly flushed her out.

'Mistress Innes.' The factor frowned down at her. 'Why do you skulk in the bushes?'

'I wasna skulking,' she replied indignantly.

Dalrymple snorted. 'This is the henwife I told you about, William. The brazen piece has beguiled the priests hiding at Scalan. She imagines herself qualified to administer potions brewed from poisonous weeds and is clearly a witch. Doubtless, she was in there plucking more weeds.'

'Yes, yes, I know of her.'

'She claims to understand more about medicine than a trained physician. Perhaps she imagines her husband's infamy grants her potion-peddling nonsense legitimacy.' Dalrymple snorted. 'Then again, among the ignorant tenantry of this glen, perhaps it does. I assume you know who her husband is? You read the same papers I do.'

'I make it my business to know about His Grace's tenants,' the factor replied. 'I granted James Innes the tenure of Druimbeag last Martinmas, and this is how he's repaid me. He has disgraced himself and his regiment. The duke writes to tell me the scoundrel awaits trial in the vaults of Edinburgh Castle, charged with mutiny. A capital offence.' He made a disgusted sound in his throat. 'His court martial's set for tomorrow. Pity. I should've liked to bear witness. I sorely misjudged the rogue.'

Morven stared at him in horror. 'It canna be,' she choked. She backed away, staggering into the trees. 'Lord,' she whimpered, 'protect him, I beg ye.' Her legs buckled, and she sank to her knees in the withered bracken. 'Ye promised, Jamie. Ye swore ye'd come back to me.'

Ilene began to wail, prompting the dogs to bound into the trees to investigate. They crowded around, wagging their tails, trying to lick her face. Only then did McGillivray appear to appreciate what Morven carried in her shawl. He made no attempt to call the dogs to heel but climbed down, frowning, his hands on his hips. There was a sudden commotion in the river. He spun around with a start.

Nathaniel came surging through the swollen river mounted on the master's horse. 'You mustn't harm her,' he cried. 'You don't understand how precious she is.' He urged Rufus up the banking, scattering the dogs. They barked in excitement, weaving through his horse's legs. Rufus reared, almost throwing him, but by some miracle, Nathaniel kept his seat. His face was white, his eyes wild. He managed to calm Rufus and turned on the factor and his companion.

'You don't understand. The Lord has blessed Morven with the gift of healing. She's an angel who heals the sick and the hopeless. Her skills are without equal, as is the goodness of her heart. You must leave her be.'

Morven gaped at him. What was Nathaniel doing here? And from where had his new-found boldness come? She rose to her feet, clutching at a tree to steady herself. Nathaniel's earnest face brought a surge of gratitude. She could have wept, but she'd not give Dalrymple the satisfaction.

'No one is hurting her.' Dalrymple rolled his eyes as if explaining to a child. 'I expect William was about to evict her. The shameless piece is no angel but a witch, and her husband is a notorious traitor. Hardly praiseworthy tenants. Not that it's any business of yours. I suggest you return to your saints and Hail Marys.'

'Evict her?' Nathaniel gasped. 'But he can't. She's done naught wrong.'

'I think you'll find the factor can do what he likes. His Grace has given him the authority.'

'Then he mustn't, I ... I won't let him.' Nathaniel dismounted and faced the two men.

Dalrymple laughed. 'How, pray, do you intend to stop him?'

'I have faith,' Nathaniel stammered, 'faith that the Almighty will right the wrongs done to Morven and her husband.'

McGillivray huffed impatiently. 'Who in God's name is this deranged youth?'

'He's one of the priestlings from Scalan,' Dalrymple replied. 'I forget his name. How His Grace can allow that abomination on his land is beyond my countenance.' He glowered at Nathaniel. 'So, you've ventured out to rescue this brazen witch. How Christian.'

McGillivray remounted his horse and fixed the physician with a cold stare. 'I'll thank you to remember that *I* decide who is fit to be His Grace's tenant, not you.'

'Forgive me, William, but this woman's husband is an acknowledged traitor. You surely don't intend to let the cunning piece remain here?'

'Jamie's no traitor,' Morven choked. 'He was pressed. Ye ken it as well as I.'

Nathaniel nodded vigorously. 'Mistress Innes speaks the truth. The Edinburgh crowds are hailing her husband a hero. The capital's newspapers are full of his story. They say he was forced to join the duke's regiment or see his family evicted, that the men of his regiment have seen never a penny of their pay. A damning accusation they level at His Grace. Having read the man's story, I found his account powerful and convincing and can understand why the drama has enthralled Edinburgh for weeks. I'm sure you know what the papers are saying.'

'Outrageous drivel,' Dalrymple snapped.

'You think so? Readers of the Edinburgh papers don't agree. They've taken Corporal Innes to their hearts and want him pardoned. Crowds gather outside the castle walls to demand his release. I imagine his supporters would be eager to hear news of their hero's wife and child, an infant he has yet to see and never will if the authorities have their way. Should they learn his family are being threatened with eviction, I expect they'll be justly enraged.' He grimaced. 'Who knows what that could lead to.'

Dalrymple's brows shot up. 'What are you suggesting?'

'Only that I imagine the news would cause great furore if it were to be splashed over the front page of the *Caledonian Mercury* or the *Edinburgh Evening Courant*, papers I assume the duke and duchess read.' He looked from one man to the other. 'I expect letters to the owners of these newspapers would be enough to enlighten the townspeople.'

Both men blanched in disbelief.

'You wouldn't dare!' Dalrymple spluttered.

Nathaniel held the physician's challenge, his eyes glinting. 'You doubt it?'

Morven stared at him. From the unflinching look on his face, Nathaniel *would* dare.

'Such an act would constitute an outrage,' growled McGillivray.

Nathaniel turned to him. 'Telling the truth, you mean?'

'Well, I ...' McGillivray blustered. 'What I mean is, let's not be too hasty. If Mistress Innes can pay the tack duty she owes, I see no need to have her removed. Particularly now there is an infant to consider. Although I suspect she cannot.'

Morven's stomach clenched. Here was the crux: she hadna a farthing to her name, yet she mustna lose Druimbeag. With Jamie accused, her promise to him meant more now than ever.

'I'll get it,' she stammered. 'I swear, sir.'

'How?'

She looked hopelessly at Nathaniel.

''Tis what I've come about.' He held out his hand to her. 'The bishop wishes to speak with you. If you will, I am to take you to Scalan.'

''Tis where I was going,' she said, grasping his hand. He helped her and Ilene up onto Rufus' broad back. Mounting himself, he took up the reins, and Rufus lurched forward. They plunged back into the river.

CHAPTER THIRTY-FOUR

Edinburgh Castle

For five days, Jamie languished in a dark cell beneath the vaulted castle casements, waiting for the Crown to gather evidence and testimony against him. Shackled in irons and isolated from Fin, every inch of him bitterly cold, he had naught to fill the bleak hours with but the guilt-ridden thoughts festering in his head.

He had achieved his aim. The Northern Fencibles would stay in Scotland, and in winning that victory, they had fired no shots and spilt no blood, although he doubted that would count for anything at his court martial. If His Grace and the Secretary at War could be trusted, the men would serve in Scotland until the end of the American war, when the regiment would be disbanded. Then they'd return to their hills, their duty done, albeit with ill grace.

Only, what had it cost him? He would not return with the men, breaking his promise to the woman he loved. In truth, he had already betrayed her. In his heart, he knew he would never see Morven again. He groaned and rolled on his side. His flesh was deathly cold, a chill in his bones. He closed his eyes, hoping to conjure her image, and a yearning sound wrung from his lips. He would never again feel the extraordinary directness of her gaze other than in his dreams, never feel the inner melting her smile kindled.

He opened his eyes and stared into the darkness, a surge of grief choking him. He dragged himself upright, his chains rasping over the stone floor, and sat with his back against the wall. His head swam, a wave of nausea washing over him. The cold was pitiless. He shook as if from an ague. Hunger and cold had weakened him in body and spirit, the watery pap the guards occasionally remembered to bring him unfit for swine, while the endless darkness served only to deaden his soul.

Since giving himself up to the Perthshires, he had been allowed few visitors beyond the regimental chaplain, who came daily bearing a candle and was a welcome face in the darkness. When he could, Reverend Gordon smuggled a morsel of bread to him, hiding it beneath his robes. The minister's compassionate prayers helped ease the guilt eating at his heart. Reverend Alastair MacGregor, minister of the Gaelic Chapel-of-Ease on Castle Wynd, had also visited and had volunteered to act as interpreter for Fin at their court martial. Jamie could do little but thank him. The trial would be an ordeal enough for Fin without the added torment of understanding little his accusers said.

During his visits, Reverend MacGregor described fighting through the crowds outside the castle to reach those he wished to help. 'I swear, they shout louder fer yer release every day.'

Jamie peered at him through the gloom. 'These folk call fer my release?'

'You and thon poor MacKay man.'

'But why? How do our woes trouble these folk?'

The minister took a moment to answer. 'They sympathise wi' yer plight. They see ye as one o' them, a brave man doing his best fer his men, something they do every day fer their families, only to a lesser degree, of course. To them, ye stand fer every common man doontrodden to further the ambitions o' powerful men.'

Jamie blinked at the minister but could think of naught to say in response.

Abercrombie had also been to see him. From his face, it was plain the young officer struggled with a heavy heart. Any pretence at maintaining the official distance between them demanded by his rank had gone. He warned Jamie he could expect no leniency; the authorities wished to make an example of him. Any compassion they might have felt had been expended upon those more innocent men they had agreed to pardon. Jamie should use the time left to him to put his affairs in order. To that end, the adjutant brought a candle, paper, and ink.

Abercrombie pushed a battered table across the stone floor toward him, but Jamie's shackles would not allow him to sit at it. Grateful nonetheless, he hugged his knees on the frigid floor while, in the flickering candlelight, the adjutant, who knew how these things should be worded, penned his will. Jamie owned naught in the world but his father's old plaid and the pay and bounty coin still owed to him, coin which he feared might never now be paid. He left it to his wife Morven, who, in bringing together the pieces of his broken life, had made him whole again. He hoped she might one day find it in her to forgive him. He had little to show for his life, but Abercrombie promised to ensure his last wishes were respected.

On his second visit, the adjutant again brought paper and ink.

'Lest you wish to write a letter to your wife,' he explained, 'making clear what's befallen you.' He frowned down at his hands. 'Something she might keep to remember you by and read to your child once the infant is old enough to understand. That way, he will learn something of his father. Your bravery,' he choked. 'Or she will if your child is a girl.'

'My wife canna read, but aye, I must find the strength to explain why I'll nae be returning to her and beg her forgiveness. Our priest will read my words, though what I am to say ....'

Abercrombie sat on the cold floor and handed Jamie paper, ink, and a long quill, then turned and offered him his back. 'I'd be glad to assist with the wording if I can be of use, though I understand this must be a personal message.' He looked over his shoulder. 'And I'd be honoured if ye would call me James. In this grim place,' he wrinkled his nose at the gut-wrenching stench, 'and at this even bleaker time, I believe we are merely two men, equal before God. There should be no rank or division between us.'

Jamie had to clench his jaw to keep the emotion from his voice. 'I'm indebted. We share the same name, though I think far from the same life.'

'Aye, sadly. Given the chance, I'd have liked to know you better, Jamie.'

So, while Abercrombie leant forward, holding the guttering candle high, careful not to drip wax on the thick paper Jamie pressed to his back, Jamie wrote his last letter to Morven. Every word was torture. His hands trembled almost as much as his heart. Grief so tightened his throat he could barely breathe. When it was done, Abercrombie took the sheet from him and folded and sealed it. He promised he would have it sent north with the swiftest despatch rider. He would be dead before Father Ranald could read his words, but Jamie prayed Morven might understand why he'd taken such desperate action, although he had no right to expect her forgiveness.

After the torment of the letter, it was almost a relief to be led the next day to his court martial.

The authorities assembled for the trial in the great chamber of the officers'

quarters on Palace Yard, where Jamie had kept the regiment's officers prisoner. He and Fin were now the prisoners, and the irony was not lost upon him. Guards unshackled his ankles so he could trudge up the stone steps into the light. As they led him into the chamber, his wrists bound, sunlight streaming through the many panes of the high windows pricked his eyes, and they smarted and streamed. A fire blazed in the ornate fireplace, most of its warmth blocked by the sixteen members of the military board who sat closest to it. Even standing far from the blaze, swaying with weakness, he felt warmer than in days and was able to nod to Fin when he was also led stumbling into the chamber.

Abercrombie had told him the accused were not represented by counsel at a court martial and there would be no right of appeal. Still, several young Edinburgh lawyers had come forward to offer their services. The Judge Advocate had refused them all. Glancing around the chamber, Jamie found Abercrombie in the gallery behind him. The sight of his white, bespectacled face calmed his nerves a little. Reverend MacGregor came to stand close enough to Fin that he might whisper a translation of the proceedings in his ear, and Jamie nodded respectfully to him.

A hush fell, and the staff and board members who would act as their judge and jury rose with a shuffling of feet. The judge advocate, Lieutenant Colonel Ralph Dunbar of the eleventh dragoons, entered the chamber. A large man, the lieutenant colonel made an imposing sight in his expansive scarlet coat, all bright buff facings, gleaming silver buttons and lace. His face, beneath his silver-edged tricorn, was impassive and hard to read, his thick wig lending him a frowning appearance. Abercrombie had explained that Dunbar would preside over the court and guide the officers of the board, deciding what evidence they heard and how they should apply the law. Regardless, any final decision and sentence must be confirmed by the king, or at least Lord Barrington as the king's representative.

The adjutant's face had pinched then; he'd been unable to meet Jamie's gaze. 'Yet I fear,' he confided, 'given the enormity of your crime, the verdict and sentence must be inevitable.'

'I understand I have no cause fer hope,' Jamie answered. 'But I pray they might spare Fin's life.' His voice thickened. 'And I pray God stiffens my courage so I make no unseemly show o' myself at the trial or ... or at what must come after.'

Abercrombie made a small, distressed sound. 'As you know, the events leading to your court martial have been widely reported in the press. The peoples' sympathy lies with you and Corporal MacKay whilst they criticise the duke and the authorities.'

'I'm sorry if that makes things difficult fer ye.'

Abercrombie shook his head. 'My point is the papers make the argument that ending the life of a man seen as a hero by many in a brutal, public display can only hurt future recruiting in the Highlands. By executing you and the near legend you've become, the authorities may choke off its source of highland warriors, something the Crown and its War Office have come to depend upon.'

Jamie nodded slowly. 'Then I may yet make a difference, even make my dead father proud. My da was a good man, but his struggles against injustice beat him down. Eviction. 'Tis a shameful treatment too many in the Highlands endure, what they threaten us wi' to make us enlist.'

'I know. I'm sorry for it.'

'But if my death can expose the ill-treatment of Highlanders, then it may yet bring some good my life did not.'

'Please,' Abercrombie choked, 'don't belittle yourself. You've brought hope to many, not least to your fellow soldiers.'

Jamie sighed. 'Then I pray that when my final moments come, I dinna disgrace myself or those I presumed to speak fer.'

Abercrombie had been unable to answer, and Jamie felt sorry for distressing him.

He shifted his focus back to the chamber where the drawn-out procedure of formally swearing in the board members and administering oaths was going on. His legs began to tremble, and he longed for a seat.

The trial finally commenced with the president of the board calling forward the first witness for the Crown. Jamie groaned when Captain Cumming mounted the witness box. Stern-faced, the captain puffed his chest out, stretching himself to his full height. He swore his oath through clenched teeth. Both his evidence and the tone of its delivery were damning. He testified that the mutiny had been premeditated and meticulously fore-planned by Corporals Innes and MacKay, particularly Innes. The pair had planned the whole thing whilst incarcerated together in the castle's Black Hole. That punishment was for rebellious behaviour at a formal dress parade for their colonel, His Grace the Duke of Gordon. However, their conduct had been equally outrageous at an earlier parade performed before Lord William and Lord Barrington. On both occasions, Innes had broken ranks and urged his fellow fencibles to refuse to board the king's ships. His language had been seditious, his claims outrageous. He'd whipped up the men's minor grievances to preposterous heights.

'The man is unquestionably a rogue and an agitator,' Cumming growled. 'A traitorous dog unworthy of the king's uniform.' He thrust his chin out. 'From the start, I found his character to be thoroughly blasted. Innes dared address his colonel and laird directly, insolently levelling false accusations at him, claiming the duke had broken his promise to the men. I can still hear the upstart's strident voice directing the rebels in their mischief. Later, whilst his officers slept, the scoundrel had the audacity to take command of Edinburgh's ancient citadel. A lowly cowherd! I ask you, gentlemen,' he glared at the officers of the board. 'The man's a rebellious Highlander. Like the rest of his race, he doubtless passes much of his time soused in whisky. From what I've seen, most Highlanders are drunken sots.'

The judge advocate allowed the captain to rant on until Jamie's head swam, and he felt sick with despair. He closed his eyes, letting his thoughts flee north to the sanctuary of Strathavon. He saw himself in his home glen, turning Druimbeag's dark soil, Morven by his side with their child in her arms.

Others were called after Cumming; all officers he had taken prisoner. Some clearly held a degree of sympathy for him, yet without exception, all identified him as the mutiny's ringleader. Most agreed the Northern Fencibles were rascally fellows, led further astray by their rebellious leader. Jamie glanced over at Fin. Reverend MacGregor was whispering furiously in his ear. *How much more o' this must we endure?*

But it went on for the rest of that day and the next. Many officers testified that although the mutineers had used no violence and had always been courteous and mannerly, that was only because their actions had gone unchallenged. Other than assaulting Sergeant McBeath, and Innes had carried out that attack, they had hurt no one. But that was more by chance than design. What if the castle had been attacked? Carnage would have ensued, the mutineers turning the castle's heavy guns on the city and its people. Most voiced the opinion that since the majority of mutineers had been pardoned, the full force of military justice should fall upon the two men charged with inciting and leading the rebellion.

Abercrombie took the witness box at the end of the second day. He testified that at the shambolic parades mentioned by other officers, Corporal Innes repeatedly pleaded with his fellow soldiers to sheath their weapons. Rather than whipping up the men's anger, Innes had urged restraint, telling them their wrongs could be settled peaceably. Although outspoken, he had assured His Grace the men wanted no trouble, but they would not stand by and let him break their terms of enlistment.

'I believe Corporal Innes is a principled man,' he finished. 'A man moved to act by the injustice he saw meted out to his fellow glensmen, men that, in my negotiations with him, I saw that he cared about. He and Corporal MacKay feared the regiment had been sold to the East India Company. I also read with dismay such speculation in the Edinburgh newspapers, as I'm sure we all did. It has now been established that Sergeant McBeath started those rumours, a man with a deep-seated grudge against Corporal Innes. For his actions, Sergeant McBeath has been stripped of his rank and returned to his unit as a private soldier.' The corners of the adjutant's mouth twitched. 'I'm certain the men of his unit will deal with him as they see fit.'

Jamie's eyes widened, and he stifled a smile. Hal and the others would relish the chance.

Abercrombie paused to gather his thoughts. 'Although there is no question in my mind that these men must be punished, I urge the board to show mercy. Both are good soldiers and repent their actions. In my opinion, neither man deserves to die.'

Abercrombie returned to the gallery to a rumble of discontent from the board, many members glowering at him. His gaze flicked briefly over Jamie's face. He nodded imperceptibly.

The board then retired to deliberate on their verdict while Jamie and Fin were led back to their cells.

The guards brought Jamie back to the chamber early next morning and made him stand beside Fin. His ankles were bleeding where the leg irons had chafed, while the chains around his wrists so weighed him down that in his weakened state, he could barely stand. He glanced at Fin, wondering if he looked as wretched as his comrade. Fin's head was bowed. His face, beneath the dark shadow of his beard, looked sickly and grey, his eyes sunk in their sockets. Once brash, Fin now trembled.

The board members filed in, preceded by their president, all wearing ornate headdresses. They waited until the judge advocate had entered and seated himself, then sat and removed their hats. Their president, a Captain Fraser, remained on his feet and cleared his throat.

'Your Honour, the board has reached its verdict.'

'What verdict have you come to?'

'We find the charges of mutiny and incitement to mutiny under the Articles of War brought against the accused, Corporal James Innes and Corporal Finlay MacKay, proven. These men are therefore guilty of all charges.'

The expected outcome elicited nary a murmur in the chamber, although upon Reverend MacGregor whispering it to Fin, Fin visibly sagged. The court orderly saluted the board members and the judge advocate, and they all rose and replaced their hats. They filed out to consider what sentence they would pass.

Jamie supposed there could be little to consider, but the process must be made to look fair. Left to stand beside Fin, he could at last feel the heat from the fire, and they both shivered with the pleasure of it. He must look wretched and smell worse, but that hardly mattered. Inside, he felt dead already.

They were not left to wait for long. The board members and Lieutenant Colonel Dunbar returned within the half-hour and retook their seats. It remained only for Dunbar to pass sentence. He did so with terse brevity.

'Corporal MacKay,' he stated, 'having committed the lesser crime, will be shown mercy. He will receive five hundred lashes on the bare skin of his back, the punishment laid on upon two successive days. Corporal Innes, his crime being graver, will be shot to death, his sentence carried out in three days by a firing party from his own company.'

CHAPTER THIRTY-FIVE

Scalan

Nathaniel paused at the study door and whispered, 'You should correctly address the bishop as Your Excellency, Morven, although Bishop Hay is a humble man. He may prefer you call him Father.'

She nodded, and Nathaniel opened the door and ushered her inside. The bishop was seated at the fire between Father John and Father Ranald. In his late middle years, he wore a long purple cassock and matching skullcap. A silver crucifix hung on a long chain about his neck. He was thin with hunched shoulders and a brutally long nose, although his hooded eyes appeared kindly.

'Mistress Innes.' He extended his right hand to her. 'I've heard much about you. Please, come forward so I may have a better look at you.'

She knelt as Nathaniel had instructed and kissed the gold ring on his outstretched hand. It was quite the most splendid object she had ever seen, with many small sparkling stones arranged around a larger purple one. As she rose to her feet, still bowing, Ilene grizzled in protest.

'Ah, yes, you have a child.' The bishop frowned. 'The infant born at Scalan in breach of almost every one of Bishop Gordon's rules.'

'Forgive me,' she stammered. 'It wasna my intention to break the rules, Yer Excellency, but bairns come when they come, and she took me by surprise.' She swallowed and glanced at Father John, who struggled not to smile. 'I've called her Ilene.'

'Please, may I see?'

She pulled her shawl back so the bishop could peer at her daughter in her swaddling. Father John also leant across.

'Why,' the bishop chuckled, 'she's quite charming. But please, you must call me Father.' He flicked his hand at Nathaniel. 'Fetch the lass a chair, Nathaniel.'

While Nathaniel brought another rush seat, the bishop continued to talk to her as if she were an old acquaintance. 'I read your husband's story in the Edinburgh newspapers—a rash man, although I understand something of the treatment he and his fellow soldiers endured. As a youth, I was imprisoned in Edinburgh Castle. I passed another miserable year at the king's pleasure in London for my part in the Jacobite Rising; hence, I know what it is to displease the British Crown.' He frowned. 'But I understand your husband's situation is far more desperate.'

Morven struggled to answer. She had no notion what the Edinburgh papers were calling Jamie's story. She knew only what Father Ranald had told her—the authorities claimed Jamie had led the duke's regiment to mutiny. If true, she knew he wouldn't have done so without cause.

'I'm shamed to say it,' she replied, 'but like you, I once doubted Jamie. I can be quick to judge and foolishly thought ill o' him when I shouldna have.' She looked the bishop in the eye. 'I'll nae do that again. My husband's an honourable man. Faced wi' injustice, he will try to owercome it. Knowing that, nae matter what the authorities say he's done, or those who write o' his rashness, I ken better and will stay true.'

The bishop raised his brows at her. She supposed no one had spoken so bluntly to him since he was a bairn.

'You misunderstand,' he said. 'I admire your husband's principles. His courage. He committed an act the king and government consider outrageous but did so to help his fellow men. He must have known he was risking his life. I believe that makes him a champion, not a traitor.' Frowning, he turned to Father Ranald and the master. Their faces were now registering some discomfort. 'Does the lass not understand what the papers have reported? Namely, that His Grace broke his promise to his own regiment. Further, as a result of his actions, Corporal Innes has gained support from almost every sector of Edinburgh society, almost to the point of threatening the Crown's authority. Would I be correct in assuming she cannot read?'

'Aye, Your Excellency,' Father Ranald replied. 'Like most in these glens, Morven had no opportunity to learn. I regret I didna think to read the news reports to her.'

'Then you must, Ranald, so she understands. Or Nathaniel.'

'I long to, Your Excellency,' Nathaniel said.

'Then do. The sooner, the better.' The bishop turned back to Morven.

'I appreciate things look hopeless for your husband, but you must put your faith in the Lord. Every soul at Scalan includes your husband in their prayers, hoping for his deliverance. But as to your own plight, there I may be of assistance. Nathaniel tells me tack duty is owed on your husband's holding. At Martinmas, I assume.'

She nodded, a thickness in her throat. 'I havena the coin to pay it, though I doubt His Grace will want Jamie as a tenant now.'

The bishop frowned. 'That you cannot pay is hardly surprising. You've been on your own for months while the authorities, in their deceit, have not paid your husband what is honourably due him. Now you have an infant to care for, yet despite your troubles, you have given your time to the care of others. I'm told we have you to thank for Father John's life.' He turned to the master, who still looked pale. 'What would we do without dear John?' He patted the master's hand. 'And you saved young Struan and have kept all our scholars well.'

'The lass is a skilled healer,' Father Ranald said, 'unlike that charlatan, Dalrymple. I took the liberty of dismissing the rogue. Young Andrew died through his neglect.'

'You did right.' The bishop nodded tightly. 'A terrible tragedy. Yet we have not paid Morven for her trouble. I appreciate John felt he could not employ her, a young woman, without my approval. I now give it and wish to pay her.' He drew a leather pouch from his robes. It jingled softly. Morven's eyes widened. She stared incredulously at him.

'I'll have a contract drawn up between us, but perhaps a verbal one will suffice for now. Provided you are amenable, I hereby engage you to act as physician to the Scalan community, your duty to keep the scholars and staff as well as you can.' He leant forward, his eyes kindly. 'Does that sound agreeable?'

Bewildered, she looked at Nathaniel, who nodded vigorously.

'Aye, Father,' she stammered.

'Splendid.' He handed her the pouch. 'You must understand this money does not come solely from mission funds. In the last few days, a small but significant sum has been left for you with Father Ranald at the chapel at Findron and a similar sum with Father John here at our own chapel. Hard-earned coin, I might add, from the families of those men your husband's sacrifice has freed.'

She turned to Nathaniel in confusion.

'The authorities have pardoned all the mutineers,' he said. 'All but your husband and another man. The verdict of their court martial is not yet known, but ...' he swallowed, his face tightening. 'But it seems there can be little grounds for hope. Those pardoned have finally been paid, and their kinfolk have not forgotten you.'

'Hastily paid,' Father Ranald muttered. 'No doubt to counter the accusations in the press levelled at His Grace.'

Morven stared at Nathaniel. 'Ye mean—?'

'I mean, you can now pay your tack duty and hold onto Druimbeag.'

She gasped, tears coming. She swiped at them with trembling fingers. *But what was Druimbeag to her wi'out Jamie?*

'Take the lass to the kitchen, Nathaniel,' the bishop instructed, 'and see that Janet gives her a dram to soothe her nerves. And read her every news piece we have about her husband.'

The trail of old men and womenfolk waiting outside the stone steading McGillivray used as his estate office wound around the yard and its outbuildings, reaching the sloping lawns of Inchfindy Hall. They were waiting to pay their tack duty and have the factor assure the lease on their holding for another quarter. Clutching Bishop Hay's pouch, Morven glanced at her da and nervously joined them.

'Dinna fret,' he muttered. 'Ye've as much right to be here as anyone.'

She nodded, a lump aching in her throat. But it should be Jamie. He should be the one standing with the cottars and smugglers of Strathavon, men and women he was proud to know now called him friend.

Donald Gordon of Craigduthel turned to greet them, then moved aside to let them through. 'On ye go, lass,' he said. ''Tis an honour to stand wi' ye. And you, Delnabreck.'

'*Tapadh leat*,' she murmured. Thank you.

Those waiting in front turned to see what Craigduthel was about. Their faces fell when they saw her. Whispering in hushed tones, one by one, they moved aside to let her through. Hal's wife Eilidh murmured, 'God bless ye, lass. May the Lord watch ower ye and Jamie's littlin.' She gripped her shoulder and gently pushed her forward.

More hands propelled her forward, folk parting like the Red Sea before

Moses and the Israelites to let her through. Annie Shaw brushed her hand as she passed, then others did the same, even grizzled old bodachs. One herdsman used his crook to shepherd folk back so she and her da might pass. As she stumbled forward, folk murmured how sorry they were, many reaching out to touch her child, knowing she was Jamie's. One or two whispered a blessing. Without exception, every face tightened with sorrow, gazes cast down and heavy with sadness.

When she reached the steading's open door, McGillivray glanced up from his ledger, then raised his head and stared. His manservant hovered at his shoulder. He also quirked his brows.

'Mistress Innes, I hardly expected to see you.' Frowning, he indicated she should approach the great desk he sat behind. 'Though you have saved me a disagreeable journey.'

He had said he would not need to evict her if she could pay the full tack duty owed. Swallowing, she held out the bishop's pouch and let it drop on the desk with a soft thud.

McGillivray sat back, quill poised in hand. 'What's this?'

'The rental coin I told ye I would get.'

He stared at it as if transfixed, then laid his quill down. Untying the purse strings, he tipped the contents on the table. 'How in the devil?' He gaped as silver and copper coins spilt across the table's smooth surface. Instinctively, he began to count them, piling coins in neat columns. Turning back to his ledger, he flicked the pages until he found what he was looking for. 'Druimbeag,' he murmured. He smoothed his finger across the page, then snorted, 'You have overpaid!' He slid two copper farthings back at her. 'What is your given name, then? I'll alter the record to show it.'

'I dinna understand.' She turned to her da.

'Why would ye do that?' her da growled. 'The rental o' Druimbeag is correctly held in my son-in-law's name. James Innes.'

McGillivray fixed him with a weary look. 'Because as you doubtless know, Mister MacRae, Corporal James Innes has been found guilty of mutiny. He will be executed tomorrow at Edinburgh Castle. Hence, I must amend my record.'

Morven staggered back against her da, her hand flying to her mouth.

McGillivray scowled at her. 'Come now, don't pretend ignorance. You must have known your husband's defiance could only end this way.'

She made a choked sound, and her da stepped forward to speak for her.

'She feared,' Malcolm stammered. 'We all did when we heard Jamie hadna been pardoned wi' the rest. But she didna ken the ... the court's decision 'til now.' He slipped his arm around her as she sagged against him. 'I've long held that where word's scant, there's aye room fer hope. But when ye're educated and wealthy and bide in a great hall, I'm supposing news travels on swifter wings.' He shook his head. 'Thon's nae how it works fer common folk.'

The factor frowned at his manservant, waiting for him to interpret her da's words, spoken in his thick rural accent. In his anger, Malcolm MacRae had spoken blunter than was wise. Understanding, McGillivray raised his brows at her da's impudence. He shifted his attention back to Morven. The hardness in his eyes softened a little. Perhaps she even saw a trace of pity.

'In that case, I pray you'll forgive me.' He opened a drawer and drew out a sealed letter. 'A rider left this for you, a mounted infantryman. It seems he was not able to find Druimbeag.' He held the letter out. 'Or perhaps was disinclined to try.'

Morven's hand shook as she took it. She recognised Jamie's sloping longhand, the letters splintered and broken, made with a trembling hand. Turning away, she pressed it to her heart.

Her da tossed his payment on the table. 'Betraying bastards,' he growled. 'Every promise broken, but what else can we expect? 'Tis the same army and commanders oor fathers fought on Culloden Moor.' He tightened his hold on Morven and cradled her to him. 'Och, lass,' he mourned. 'Ye must ken how sorry I am.' He tried to steer her away. 'We'll find Father Ranald; he'll read this to ye.'

'Wait a moment.' McGillivray rose to his feet, his chair scraping on the hard floor. He frowned at Morven's stricken face. 'I daresay I could spare a moment to read whatever that is.'

Morven shook her head. She needed Nathaniel; he would understand and be kind.

''Twill be writ in Gaelic,' her da said scornfully.

McGillivray's face closed. 'Have it your way.' He flicked his hand to dismiss them.

Morven barely saw. Grief rose like a tidal wave and dragged her under.

CHAPTER THIRTY-SIX

Her da guided Fergan with a sure hand, yet it felt as if the garron already knew the way. His hooves drummed with Morven's heart, pounding over McGillivray's lush pastures, then they were on heathland, floundering, hooves sucked into wet peat, then on again into scattered woodland, the scent of pine and loam sharp in her nostrils. They skirted Gallowhill, swaying down the braeside, her da's home-crafted saddle made to hold an anker of whisky on either flank, creaking with the strain. Cold air chilled her face. She clung to her da's back, pitching forward when he did, bending under the trees that fringed the Livet. At the ford, the sound of rushing water filled her ears. Fergan plunged into the river, and they surged across in a froth of icy spray. She held wee Ilene close. The infant's face looked so small and delicate; Morven's heart wrenched. The wee soul would never know her father. Hers would be a lifetime of loss.

Gaining the far bank, Fergan crashed through the undergrowth, then the land blurred past again, a haze of russet and gold. Morven pressed her cheek to her da's back and closed her eyes. He smelled of whisky and peat smoke, scents familiar to her all her life. A yearning for home and the commonplace welled. Beneath the wool of his homespun plaid, she could feel his muscles working while she felt fragile and weak. Never was she more thankful for his powerful presence.

On they thudded, Fergan grunting and blowing hard. When Morven opened her eyes, they were in the Braes of Glenlivet, surrounded by the dark hills Nathaniel had once called his armour. She clutched Jamie's letter. *On the morrow, they would kill him.* What would they do to him, shoot him to pieces? But she mustna think of that, of how they would make him suffer. They may as well shoot her, for without Jamie, she would sicken and die.

Yet on her heart thudded, each beat counting down Jamie's last moments on earth with her powerless to help him. Would she feel him leaving? Know when he was gone? But he was far away, on the other side of the mountains separating the Highlands from the civilised south. She would be left to imagine, oh God, the pounding of his heart, the dryness of his mouth and raggedness of his breathing as he waited, likely blindfolded, for British justice to fall.

Finally, they were on the lonely stretch to Scalan. One more curve in the road and the seminary revealed itself, encircled by its shield of dark hills. Her da had long known of Scalan but had never been there and never spoke of the place. The penal laws that decreed the college illegal were still in force, and he would not endanger his faith or those who risked everything to protect it. He slowed Fergan to a walk as they entered the courtyard and pulled his bonnet from his head. Morven could see Nathaniel's herb garden all planted out. The sight brought the sharp sting of tears. Her da tethered Fergan by the water trough and left the lathered pony to drink while he helped her to the door. He rapped on it with his fist. She shivered beside him. The wind was always rawer here, naught in the bleak landscape giving any hint of the warmth and graciousness of spirit she had found here.

A servant cracked the door open and peered warily out, doubtless conscious that Bishop Hay was sheltering within. He recognised her, his face tightening in sympathy. 'Ye'll be wanting Nathaniel?'

When she nodded, he ushered them inside and left them standing in the hallway. He returned with the master. Father John knew; she could see it in his face.

'My poor child,' he said. 'What can we do?'

She clenched her jaw. Since girlhood, sympathy, no matter how well-intended, had brought tears, and she had a lifetime yet for tears. She held out Jamie's letter.

Father John stared at it. 'I can only imagine how precious this must be. Perhaps you would rather Nathaniel read it to you? He has decided to disobey his father, although he has yet to tell him. The bishop means to ordain Nathaniel as soon as possible, lest his father should think to come here and cause trouble.'

The news should have quickened her heart, but it thumped dully, all the joy sucked from her soul.

'Thank ye,' her da replied. 'Morven particularly spoke o' the Gunn lad.'

'I understand. They have become friends. Please go up to my chamber, child. I'll send him to you.' The master turned to her da. 'You must be ...?'

'Malcolm MacRae o' Delnabreck.' He bowed, clutching his bonnet. 'Here to aid my daughter.'

'You have my thanks, Mister MacRae. Our housekeeper will look after you.' He looked at Morven. 'Perhaps Janet might also mind your child?'

She shook her head. She'd not be parted from her.

So, while her da went with Father John, Morven climbed the staircase to the master's chamber and waited by his desk. Nathaniel entered a few moments later. His face looked pale and wretched; the suffering of others always distressed him.

'Please.' He pulled the master's chair out and stood back, wringing his hands.

She lowered herself onto the seat, careful not to awaken Ilene, and looked up at him. His breathing was quick and panicked, the boyish lines of his face tight with concern.

'I hardly know what to say,' he stammered. 'We heard the terrible news this forenoon. A rider came with correspondence for the bishop. His Excellency called us together to tell us of ... of your husband's sentence. I've spent the hours since on my knees, praying he'll be granted a reprieve. Edinburgh's been in turmoil since the verdict. An angry mob protests outside the castle, growing by the hour both in size and volume, demanding the authorities pardon him.' He was babbling and seemed to know it. He drew another breath.

'Please.' She smiled crookedly and held out Jamie's letter. 'Will ye read it to me?'

He stared, appearing to immediately appreciate what it was. 'I'm glad you at least have this.' He lurched to the master's desk and rifled amongst his things. Finding a silver opener, he broke the wax seal and unfolded the letter with trembling fingers. Peering at it, he retreated to the master's bed and sank into the stuffing. He looked anxiously at her, trying to ascertain if she was in a fit state to hear whatever it contained. Appearing unconvinced, he nevertheless cleared his throat and read:

'My love, please forgive me fer nae finding the courage to write to you sooner. I fear that at heart I'm a coward, and now, at this late stage, this is the hardest letter I have ever written. There are no words to say how sorry I am. What I must tell ye will come as a terrible shock. I pen this from the vaults

of Edinburgh Castle, my court martial set for the morrow. I'm charged with leading a mutiny, and since I'm guilty o' that, I'm told I can expect no mercy. I can give no excuse for my actions other than to say that what I did, I did in the hope of protecting my fellow men. Never did I wish to hurt anyone. The authorities intended to ship us to England or to foreign service in the king's colonies. Only by rebelling could we frustrate their plans. I thank God the men have been pardoned their part. Only I and another stand accused. On the morrow, a military board will sit in judgment o' us. I pray they'll show Fin mercy. He was only ever guilty of high passion and perhaps some brashness. For myself, I understand I must suffer the full force of British justice.'

Nathaniel faltered and glanced fearfully at her. She kept her head bowed, gripping the edge of the master's desk. When she appeared incapable of saying anything, he read on:

'I havena the strength to tell ye the whole sorry tale, but Hal has promised he'll tell ye everything when he returns. 'Tis enough to say the army's treatment of my fellow soldiers incensed me. They're fine men, men I've come to love like kinsmen, though I hope ye'll nae imagine I chose them ower you. You are my life. Yet you know how much I despise injustice. I await judgment of my actions, knowing my punishment will certainly be final and will force me to break my solemn promise to you. That I'll nae keep my promise undoes me. Only a wretch would forsake the woman he loves and the child he put in her belly. I pray ye might find it in ye to forgive me, though I've no right to ask such a thing. I scarce know how to say how sorry I am. It sounds so pitiful. Never did I wish for this. I hoped to spend my life with you, building a home and a family. Now I fear how you'll manage. I pray yer kinfolk will take ye in, and McGillivray will allow it. Yer da's a good man, but that you and yer family should suffer on my account grieves me sorely.'

Nathaniel made a choked sound.

'Please,' she whispered. He nodded and rasped on:

'I'll likely be dead afore this reaches ye, yet I wish ye to know that from the first moment I saw ye, all fierce in my defence, I loved you. Never was a man more blessed than me, for I was loved by you. Our time thegither was cruelly brief, but my love for you is endless. That I didna meet our child is my bitterest regret and seems the hardest thing. I pray the infant thrives, that ye'll tell the lamb I didna leave my family willingly.

'Yet in all this, I clutch at one grace. My death in this public manner may focus the eyes and sympathy of the nation on the treatment of highland folk.

If so, I may yet achieve something. I ramble, my love—forgive me. Cold and hunger have addled my mind, but I canna help but wonder if this is why I was spared. I cling to that thought in the bitter darkness and find it brings me ease.

'My fingers ache, and I fear I've taken advantage of my friend James Abercrombie long enough. Despite what I've done, I pray ye might remember me fondly. I will always love you. Your devoted husband, James.'

There was silence but for the soft rustle of paper as Nathaniel laid the letter down. He was weeping, and she daren't look at him. The tightness in her throat grew unbearable. Her face twisted, tears breaking in a choking rush. *'Jamie,'* she wailed. *'Dinna leave me. Please.'* Sobbing, she slumped forward on the desk.

'Morven, I ... oh, Lord, what can I do?' Nathaniel rose and stood before her, his home-cobbled shoes coming within her blurry field of vision. 'I'm here for you. Always. Whenever you need me. Let me pray with you ....' His voice trailed away as he realised how feeble that sounded in the face of her despair. Ilene began to cry. He winkled her gently from Morven's arms. 'Hush, dear soul.' He rubbed her back, holding her awkwardly to his chest. She settled with a snuffling sound, laying her head on his shoulder.

After a time, Morven's grief exhausted itself. She dried her face with her arisaid. 'I'm sorry,' she whispered. 'I must be strong, yet I feel so helpless. Jamie risked his life to free men from this and neighbouring glens. What can I do? There's little time, and he is my life.'

'I hardly know,' Nathaniel croaked. 'Naught, I fear. But you mustn't worry about how you'll manage. I'll take care of you. You and Ilene. It's what I want and ... it would be an honour.'

She looked wretchedly at him. 'What d'ye mean? How can ye?'

He frowned as he thought, cradling her child—Jamie's child. She sensed his hesitancy as he searched for the right words. He would not want to shock or offend her. He returned to Father John's bed and sat down, blinking and breathing hard. It struck her that whatever he was wrestling with had been on his mind for some time and would have stayed there were it not for the desperate nature of her situation. He must summon all his courage to voice it.

'I mean, I wish to care for you as ... as a man,' he stammered.

She looked blankly at him. 'But ye're to be a priest. The master said ye've decided to disobey yer da. I'm glad.'

'Yes, but I don't have to. Rather than take the cloth, I could ... marry you. Then, as my father's heir, I could provide for you and Ilene.'

She stared at him.

'You needn't say anything,' he rushed on. 'I realise how this must sound. In your grief, this is the last thing you wish to hear. But I hope you will consider it. I would ask nothing of you but your companionship, which I value. I don't expect love, Morven. I know you don't love me.' He swallowed, his eyes brimming. 'But I confess I have feelings for you for which I have no name.'

She blinked at him. 'Ye'd do that? Give up the priesthood, throw away everything ye've spent all these years studying fer?'

'I would do it for you,' he said softly. 'I've spent the morning thinking about it. I could learn to farm. You've taught me that I need a family like any man.' He gazed into Ilene's sleeping face. 'We could be a family. Not all men are made the same. Some choose the priesthood, but I did not. 'Twas chosen for me.'

'But I thought 'twas what ye wanted.'

He crossed the room, still holding Ilene, and knelt before her. He was trembling, his eyes shining with sincerity. He gingerly took her hand. 'I thought that too, but now I see my calling lies elsewhere.'

She frowned. 'Ye dinna ken what ye're asking.'

'I ask only that you might think about it. Will you do that?'

Her heart shrank, more tears coming. 'I canna, I'm sorry. I hope ye can understand.'

'You love Jamie too much to ever replace him with me? But I wouldn't ask you to. I wish for naught but your friendship. You need not lie with me or do anything to betray his memory. Don't you think Jamie would want you to be safe and cherished? You and his child. I would do that. Always. I promise.'

'Ye're kind, Nathaniel.' She looked into his earnest face, and her chest tightened with grief. 'But it wouldna be right. Or fair to you. Just last year, I stood in chapel afore God and the folk o' Stratha'an and gave Jamie my pledge. I couldna repeat those words to another. Even you. Dinna ask me to, please.'

He nodded sadly. A muscle in his throat convulsed, and his face twisted with grief. Lifting Ilene, he gently gave her back. 'You once told me you were a faithless creature. Do you remember? Yet the woman before me is the truest, most loyal soul. You refuse to save yourself. Don't you see how that proves your faithfulness? And through all this, you have striven to hold onto Jamie's land, although the tragedy is he will never know it. I pray you'll not regret your decision.'

Morven looked into Ilene's face, into her eyes, so like Jamie's. 'I have my daughter,' she whispered, 'and my memories to see me through the lonely years.' She touched Nathaniel's hand. 'Yer offer means a great deal to me. I hope ye might understand why I canna accept it.'

He swallowed and squeezed his eyes shut.

'What will ye do?'

A moment passed before he was able to answer. 'What I've spent my life preparing for. I'll take holy orders if the church will still have me and pray I make an adequate priest.'

CHAPTER THIRTY-SEVEN

Edinburgh Castle

JAMIE HAD NO NOTION what hour it was. He passed his last night on earth staring into the foul-smelling darkness of his cell and the blackness behind his eyelids. For days, he'd felt naught but an inner deadness; now, with his life almost at an end, his heart filled with love and gratitude. Rather than dwelling on what lay ahead, the dread of it, he flowed over with longing for Morven and the life they briefly shared. What he would give for another moment with her, a chance to hold their child. It took all he had not to weep.

He remembered her at her father's bothy working her da's illicit still, and his heart clenched. 'Twas where he'd first kissed her, as enthralled by her beauty and candour as he'd been intoxicated with heady whisky fumes. He pictured her at Druimbeag, sowing the grain he had hoped to harvest and distil into whisky, charming wisps of chestnut hair trailing from her kertch. He saw her treading blankets in the shallows of the Avon, laughing, her legs bare and skirts hitched at her waist. He thought of their last morning together, her face flushed from their lovemaking. He evoked her herb-rich scent, the silken feel of her skin, the breathless little sounds she made.

The rasp of an iron bolt drawing back jolted him from his memories, and he sat up as candlelight flooded in. Reverend Gordon stood haloed in the doorway.

'Forgive me, James. I fear 'tis time.'

The chaplain had come to pray with him and would accompany him on his last walk over the drawbridge to the castle mound, where he would face a firing party of his own glensmen. The reverend had promised he would only leave him at the last moment.

They knelt together on the cold floor, guards standing over them as the chaplain prayed for his soul. Reverend Gordon was not a Catholic and could not give him the Last Rites, but Jamie still drew comfort from the minister's compassionate words. His prayers were full of understanding and evoked a humbling sense of gratitude, something Jamie could not fully communicate. At length, the minister whispered a final 'Amen,' and the guards released Jamie from his shackles and hauled him to his feet.

His mouth was dry, the weakened muscles of his legs cramping painfully. They bound his hands behind his back and led him stumbling up into the chamber of the officer's quarters, where he had days ago been court-martialled, through the building and out into the damp November air. Fin was waiting at the corner of Palace Yard with Reverend MacGregor from the Gaelic chapel. He was bareheaded, his face deathly white, his hands also tied behind him. Before he suffered the first two hundred and fifty lashes of his sentence, that day's allocation, Fin must witness his fellow mutineer's execution.

Muffled drums began a slow ruffle followed by a long roll and tap, echoing the dull beating of Jamie's heart. A company of Perthshire Highlanders moved forward to surround them, and at a signal, he and Fin were slow-marched through the arch of Foog's Gate and down Hawk's Hill. Jamie glanced across at Fin. Fin stared back, his eyes wide, his face twisted in an agonised expression. He made a futile little gesture with his head, conveying his despair.

They passed under the spikes of the Portcullis Gate, Jamie's legs trembling. He clenched his teeth, willing them to steady. He belonged to a proud race of warriors. He mustn't let his courage desert him—'twould shame his regiment and the loyal men who made up its ranks. Finally, they crossed the drawbridge to the open expanse of the castle mound to be greeted by a deafening wall of sound. His heart lurched. At first sight of men on the drawbridge, what must look like two pitiful, bareheaded wretches, an angry roar erupted from the crowds pressing up Castle Hill. The mass surged forward, up from the wynds and back closes off the Grassmarket, the bustle and commerce of Lawnmarket. He gaped. Even three ranks of sabre-wielding dragoons struggled to hold them back. They appeared a disparate mix of shopkeepers and merchants, pedlars and beggars, even respectable gentlemen and their families come to enjoy the spectacle—a grisly morning's entertainment.

He staggered on, deafened by the din, the slow roll and tap of the drums beating in his throat. Ahead, six companies of Gordon Fencibles were drawn up in a hollow square, all friends and comrades, recently pardoned men who had passed the last days quartered in tents around the capital. A triangular scaffold of halberds had been erected within the square as a flogging post. A group of burly drummers waited there, wearing the Perthshire's tartan. He glanced at Fin, praying these men would exercise some restraint.

He returned his gaze to the front, his heart faltering when he saw what waited for him: a lidless coffin and standing by it, a double row of his own glensmen, their muskets held at the ready. Pity tightened his chest. He knew every man of them; every face was as familiar as his own. All were openly weeping.

The Perthshires left Fin to wait by the flogging post, Reverend MacGregor promising to return to him. Both churchmen then walked on beside Jamie, flanking him as the Perthshires led him to the open box. They made him kneel beside it, his stiff muscles cramping as he fell to his knees. His vision blurred, and he feared he would swoon. Lord, let him nae dishonour himself. He clenched his teeth, praying his head would not visibly tremble.

The noise from the crowd intensified, growing ugly and more agitated. He tried to shut it out, to ease the dread in his belly by summoning Morven's beloved face. Let her smile be the last thing he saw before a volley of musket balls blasted his soul to judgment.

Reverend MacGregor knelt beside him, praying softly in Gaelic, a major from the Perthshire Highlanders standing at his shoulder. Gordon men came forward to blindfold him and asked his forgiveness. He gave it as he went into the darkness.

'Minister, if you'll allow me, I have newly issued orders I must read out.' A rustling sound suggested the major had produced a scroll of paper.

Jamie was aware of the minister getting to his feet. The drums ceased. The major's clipped voice seemed to come from a great distance. '... court has found the accused guilty of mutiny ... Articles of War ... military board sentenced Corporal Innes be shot to death.'

His knees began to tremble, and with his hands tied behind his back, he feared he might topple over. He stared at the thin strip of weedy ground visible beneath the lower edge of his blindfold, praying he would not. The crowds fell to a great wailing and keening, and it began to dawn on him that the pressing hordes had not come to enjoy a gruesome spectacle but to show him and Fin their support. The realisation brought a gladdening in his heart and the sharp sting of tears. The keening rose in volume, threatening to drown out the major.

'His Majesty,' the major struggled on, 'in his great compassion, has graciously agreed to offer the condemned men mercy provided Corporals Innes and MacKay accept certain conditions. Those terms being ...'

Reverend MacGregor dropped to his knees, frantically translating the major's words so Jamie would be in no doubt of their meaning.

'... that the men will endure public degradation and dismissal from His Majesty's forces and will return to their miserable hills and never again attempt to enlist in His Majesty's army or speak out against the British Crown.'

'Lad,' the minister gasped. 'They dinna wish to mak' ye a martyr or others who might rise in yer defence. They mean to cashier ye.'

Jamie turned blindly in his direction.

'They intend to shame ye, lad, nae shoot ye.'

'Does the condemned man accept His Majesty's terms?'

Swaying on his knees, Jamie shook his head in bewilderment.

The major exhaled in exasperation. The crowds pushing up Castle Hill were beginning to force the dragoons back. 'His Majesty requires an answer. A swift one.'

'Ye must say aye, lad,' the reverend urged.

Jamie's head ached as he struggled to understand. The Gordon Fencibles had already been pardoned, all but he and Fin, so sacrificing himself now would help no one. He twisted his head but could see naught. Was this another mealy-mouthed trick by the War Office, mocking the stand he'd taken? Weakened in body and mind, he hardly knew. They would simply let him go home?

'*Corporal Innes,*' the minister implored. '*D'ye understand, lad?* Ye must agree, or they will shoot ye.'

He nodded, moistening his lips with his parched tongue. 'Aye,' he rasped. 'I'll go hame, then. Gladly, I will.'

'*Buidheachas do'n Tighearn,*' the minister gasped. Thank the Lord.

They removed his blindfold, and he blinked and looked across at Fin. Fin was gripping the flogging post, his legs sagging beneath him. The major lowered the scroll and signalled to the Perthshires. The drums struck up again, now beating a lively march, their muffling felt removed. Two soldiers collected the coffin, about turned, and marched back to the castle with it.

Dazed, Jamie struggled to his feet, the minister rushing to help him. The Perthshires unbound his hands and lifted his arms above his head in a victorious gesture to the crowds. The townsfolk roared their approval, surging forward, straining against the barricade of horses. Wrestling with their skittish mounts, the dragoons fought to hold them back, their horses prancing sideways. Jamie was left to stumble into the weeping embrace of his fellow glensmen, men who had moments ago been awaiting the order to shoot him.

'Thank God.' Hal crushed him to his chest. 'I thought I'd lost ye.'

'I thought it, too.'

Trembling, young Archie wept with joy. 'I couldna have shot ye,' he sobbed. 'I swear, Jamie.'

Jamie drew the lad to his chest. 'I like to think ye could have. I'd nae have ye flogged again fer my sake. Ye've suffered enough.'

Archie's cracked laugh dissolved into a sob. Hal put his arm around him.

Abercrombie pushed his way through a crush of Gordon men. His face was white, his spectacles knocked askew. 'James.' He gripped Jamie's hand. 'I cannot tell ye how relieved I am. I misjudged your printmaker friend. You have John Robertson to thank for your life. Since your arrest, he has written exhaustively about this injustice in his newspaper, aiming his criticism at the authorities, warning what their actions would likely achieve. Thankfully, the Secretary at War has listened and recognised his folly. Ending your life, a Highlander widely viewed as a hero in a gross public display, would only injure future recruiting in the Highlands. Fear of losing their mountain reserve of men has won you your freedom.' He stared around. 'That and the scale of unrest your sentence has stirred. Lord Barrington feared the spilling of more blood and the trouble that would bring.'

'I wish no blood spilt,' Jamie rasped.

'It seems trouble has been averted for now.' Abercrombie looked anxiously at him. 'I pray you'll forgive me. I learned of this sickening charade a day ago but was refused entry to speak with you. This travesty is the work of Lord Adam. He wished to punish you for your impudence and shine a compassionate light on the Crown by granting you mercy. His cruelty nauseates me, though 'tis not the first time the War Office has sanctioned such a thing. It has become almost commonplace to grant a last-moment reprieve when it suits, along with the despicable practice of making men draw lots to decide who lives and who dies. I witnessed that once.' He shook his head. 'The men's hands shook so violently, the poor souls could barely grasp the straws.'

'Aye,' Jamie growled. 'I've seen military justice first-hand. The injustice o' it.'

Fin fought his way toward them. 'Is it true?' His eyes were wild. 'We're to go free?'

'I can scarce believe it, but the adjutant tells me 'tis true.' Jamie put his arm around Fin.

'You are to be publicly humiliated,' Abercrombie confirmed. 'But will live.' He allowed himself a flicker of a smile. 'And may go home to tell the tale.'

The dragoons were now struggling to hold back the jubilant crowds, scuffles breaking out on all sides. Gordon men swiftly dismantled the flogging post and formed themselves into a three-sided square. Two Perthshires grasped Jamie under the arms and dragged him inside. There, he and Fin faced a stern front of senior officers, men who days before had given evidence against them.

Captain Cumming quivered with rage. He had expected them punished; the flesh flayed from Fin's back, and the traitor James Innes, a landless cowherd he'd called him, blasted to Kingdom Come. Notwithstanding their terrifying ordeal, they would go home to their hills. Cumming appeared so incensed by that he was incapable of civil speech.

'Wretched sods!' he roared. He snatched his hat off and struck Jamie across the face with it. 'You're not fit to wear the king's uniform.'

Jamie flinched but stood his ground, a gasp echoing through the crowd.

The captain's chest heaved; his face was purple. He tore at the worsted epaulette on Jamie's right shoulder, the insignia marking him a corporal. He ripped it free and threw it in Jamie's face. Jamie stood motionless, his gaze lowered to protect his eyes from the rabid spittle flying from the captain's lips. If he need only endure Cumming's wrath to return to his wife, he would suffer it gladly. Never had he asked to wear the king's uniform.

Cumming next turned his wrath on the facings and yellow lapels embellishing the front of Jamie's red coat. He tore at them, ripping them free and dashed them to the ground. The buttons followed. He yanked at them, Jamie bracing himself to prevent being wrenched forward. They refused to give. Cursing, Cumming doubled his efforts, his face twisted with rage. Still, they refused to budge. Incensed, he drew his *sgian dhu* from his hose and slashed at the front of Jamie's coat.

'Insufferable wretch. Damn, your cowardly heart. You seduced the minds of the men. God rot you! You embody the wicked spirit of the lower classes.'

Jamie stood tall, stoically enduring the onslaught, the captain's hate-filled words rolling off him like rain off a sheep's back. He let his eyes close, and as he stood there in disgrace, his heart flew, and he couldn't help smiling. He would keep his promise. He would return to Morven and their child and as quickly as his legs could carry him. His smile broadened, joy coursing through his innards. A laugh bubbled up. Try as he might, he could not stifle it.

'Intolerable wretch. You think it amusing? You disgust me!'

But all Jamie could think about was how much he longed to be with his wife, of the glorious, heather-clad hills he would journey through to find her, how his heart would soar amongst their peaks. He imagined the moment he'd hold her, her smallness, the tumble of chestnut hair he would loosen from under her kertch. He even dared imagine the child he had thought never to see. He pictured the infant's face, the curve of the child's head as he cupped it in his hands.

'Blast you to buggery!'

When the captain finally appeared done, Jamie's uniform hung in tatters, the sleeves torn away, his waistcoat and stock slashed to ribbons. Breathing hard, Cumming thrust his hand out. A private handed him a sword, a weapon Jamie could see had been filed almost in two. Raising it high, he broke it over Jamie's head and hurled the pieces away. The crowd gasped in horror, and a rumble of anger grew. Seen from a distance, the act must have appeared an impressive feat, but Jamie knew better. He'd barely felt it and let out a gust of laughter. There was a collective gasp, and then the crowd began to laugh, a rumbling release of tension.

Cumming gaped in horror. Running with sweat, his face liver-red, he roared, 'Get out of my sight! If ever I see you again, I swear I will run you through.'

Jamie stepped back with his head held high to a chorus of whistles and cheers from the crowd. Incensed, Cumming spun on his heel and struck Fin across the face with the flat of his hand. Fin staggered but righted himself, standing impassively to receive the humiliation he knew he must suffer if he wished to go home.

CHAPTER THIRTY-EIGHT

JAMIE GLANCED ACROSS AT Fin, drooping in the saddle beside him. He looked done in, so weary he could barely stay upright. 'We'll bed ourselves down here, will we?' He brought his garron to a halt. 'Stirling must be well behind us and seems as good a place as any.'

Fin groaned as he slid from the saddle. They tethered their garrons in the trees and left them to graze, then lay down by a burn at the side of the road, wrapping their cloaks about them. The trees were bare, a tapestry of stars sparkling above, frost glistening on the withered bracken. They had no strength to make a fire but hardly cared; they'd grown used to the cold. Fin was asleep within minutes, and Jamie soon would be. Yet as he pulled his cloak up about his ears, his mind was restless, his heart swollen with gratitude for those who'd intervened on his behalf that he might return to his wife. James Abercrombie, John Robertson, the many concerned readers of his newspaper; if not for them, he would lie in a traitor's grave. How could he repay such a debt?

After being publicly disgraced, he and Fin were drummed out of the regiment, and their fellow fencibles ordered back to their tents. The joyous Highlanders marched away singing outlawed Jacobite songs, ballads their officers, without Gaelic, likely assumed were the simple country songs of an uncivilised race. The crowd parted to let them through, many raising their voices alongside them.

He and Fin found themselves hoisted upon shoulders and carried down Castle Hill to the Grass Market, where an air of festival prevailed, news of their release having spread. Market stalls had been closed for the day, animals tethered while the townsfolk climbed the hill to the castle to voice their fury at the authorities' treatment of the Highlanders sent to protect them. Now, they returned in triumph, carrying their trophies high. He and

Fin were passed from shoulder to shoulder, folk clutching their hands and tearing yet more strips from their ravaged uniforms to keep as mementoes. The procession halted outside the White Hart Inn, where their supporters set them down, urging a continuation of the revelry inside. Liberal swigs of whisky and ale would soon restore them to heart and health. A breathless John Robertson caught up with them at the door.

'Corporal Innes,' he gasped, 'I canna help noticing ye're nae in uniform.'

Jamie grimaced at the tattered rags clinging to his bones. 'I apologise if my appearance gives offence.'

'Nay,' Robertson laughed. 'Ye're a sight for sore eyes, but if ye'll allow me, I have more suitable clothing for yer journey north.' He gestured for them to follow him and set off up the thoroughfare before turning down a back lane.

It was with some regret they left their new friends to celebrate without them and followed John. Within minutes, they were in his printing house, surrounded by stacks of paper. High windows allowed the light to flood in. The interior was rich with the aroma of walnut oil, turpentine, iron, and soot. Jamie breathed in the wonder of it. 'Twas the scent of freedom. John had used the printed word to argue their plight and sway opinions. In truth, he had wrought a miracle.

'John.' He gripped the printmaker's hand. 'I hardly ken how to thank ye.'

'No need.'

'But there is. But for you, I'd be a corpse in a wooden box.' He squeezed John's ink-stained hand. 'How can I ever repay you?'

'Aye,' Finn rasped, 'if it werena fer you, I'd be face-doon in the infirmary wi' my back laid open awaiting another flogging on the morrow. I'd have lost the best man I ken.' His voice faltered. 'I've naught to gie ye but my thanks, but I do that in all earnest.'

'As do I.'

Robertson brushed away their thanks. 'I'm only glad I could do something to help. But I imagine ye'll want to get home to yer families.'

Jamie smiled. 'Ye'll perhaps forgive us fer nae wishing to tarry owerlong in the capital lest His Majesty should change his mind.'

John laughed. 'I'll nae be offended by your swift departure, but ye canna be travelling like that.' He nodded at the tattered remains of their uniforms. 'I've more prudent clothing for ye and twa sturdy garrons to carry ye through the glens.'

Jamie looked searchingly at him. 'But how did ye ken they'd let us go?'

'I only hoped, Jamie, but I knew how high passions rode in the capital. After all, I helped arouse them. And I know something of the minds of those in authority, how much weight they place upon how things appear. Executing you would've been disastrous, but releasing you both unharmed brought the mob back from the brink of revolt. 'Tis how they'll view it, although, in my opinion, discontent isna so easily put down.'

John opened a wooden chest and drew out two bundles of clothing: frock coats in shades of drab, linen shirts, knee breeches and stockings in the English style, and two warm woollen cloaks. Wearing the Englishman's dress meant they would more likely go unremarked by the occupying troops. John left them to wash and dress and returned with flasks of ale and a large mutton pie from the baker's shop they had passed as they hastened after him. Fresh from the oven, it smelled savoury and delicious. They fell upon it, scorched fingers and tongues be damned. Never had food tasted better.

Despite the clothing not being Jamie's usual style, once washed and dressed, he felt more like himself. He could have slept for a week but was anxious to be on his way home. John led them through the print house to the stables behind and saddled two garrons. 'I have wealthy friends on the continent,' he explained. 'They help fund my activities here.'

'In Rome?' Jamie asked.

'At the Palazzo del Re,' John confirmed, 'court of the exiled Stuart kings. I believe my benefactors would approve of today's work.'

John had little spare coin to give them, but they were unarmed and weak as babes, so 'twas likely as well. He gave them water and bags of oatmeal and urged them to trust no one on the road. When they were ready to leave, he clasped them close and wished them Godspeed.

Jamie gripped his hand. 'If I can be of service in the future, John, I hope ye'll nae hesitate to ask.'

John assured him of that. They led their garrons to the opening of the close, pulling their bonnets low as they emerged. No one cast them a second glance.

Letting go of his memories, Jamie looked at Fin's shadowy figure in the darkness. Curled on his side, Fin was snoring softly. He let his own eyelids close.

When he awoke, the morning was cold and grey, the sun already well-risen but lurking behind thick cloud. They drank the last of their water, refilled their flasks and rode on. As they travelled north, the landscape became hilly and more forested. They both welcomed the change. Jamie's heart lifted, and beside him, Fin began to whistle. They kept back from the road, guiding their ponies through dense woods, the forest floor cushioned with leaf litter.

In the aftermath of Culloden, the government had built a network of roads through the Highlands, linking their new forts and garrisons. Both soldiers and locals now used these roads, but having no wish to be stopped or questioned, they shunned openly travelling them. The king had granted them mercy and commanded they go home to their hills, but his decision would not be known or even welcomed by some they might meet on the road. They wished no trouble, and with their highland garrons used to fording rivers and negotiating steep braesides, travelling rough country was no great hardship.

They lay down for the night to the north of Perth near the ancient town of Scone, once seat and enthronement place of the old Scottish kings. Jamie had learned of Scone from his priest teacher, Father Tobias, who spoke with awe of the abbey where kings were made. They fell asleep to the sound of roe deer foraging in the leaf litter with the weight of history pressing all around them.

They rose at dawn, a thick mist hanging in the air, and rode north through rolling hills and rich farmland, reaching the foothills of the Cairngorms before the light began to fade. There were few trees now, the ground rising around them. As they climbed, the mist turned to drizzle, then sleet, a growing wind driving it in their faces. They hunched themselves, ruddy hands clawed to the reins, cloaks hooded over their heads as they followed the Shee Water into Glenshee. Toiling toward the Spittal of Glenshee, where they hoped to shelter for the night, Jamie thought of the many travellers before them who had taken refuge at the spittal from reivers and wolves. The call of home grew strong in his breast, and he shivered with anticipation.

They saw no one until they reached the crumbling Chapel of Ease just south of the stone shelter. Families were leaving the ancient place of worship, and it dawned on Jamie it must be the Sabbath day. Hooding their plaids against the sleet, these folk cast them wary looks. He and Fin were strangers and by their dress, must look every miserable, sodden inch of it, yet the priest cautiously approached them to offer shelter within the walls of his chapel. When they thanked him in Gaelic, he smiled in relief and bid them welcome. They spent a dry night on the knave floor, watched over by a statue of the blessed virgin, their cloaks hanging over the backs of pews to dry, their garrons sheltering in a stone hut at the rear.

The next day was fairer, and Jamie awoke with an eager thrill in his belly. If all went well, they would reach Fin's home that evening, and he would make Druimbeag the day after. He worried about what he might find when he got there. In the long months of his absence, he had sent nary a farthing home. His promised bounty had never materialised, and he'd not see it now. In what strait had that left Morven? Did she even still live at Druimbeag? McGillivray would not tolerate missed payments; had he evicted her? Jamie's belly gripped. He'd taken the king's shilling to prevent that, but to Morven, his betrayal must seem complete. She might even imagine the fault hers, for she had promised to keep Druimbeag safe, but without silver, such promises were empty. And what of their child? Did it live? He couldn't help remembering Druimbeag as he'd first found it—a crumbling ruin, the land run to seed. No place to bring up a child. Yet despite its place in his heart, Druimbeag was naught but land and a pile of stones. 'Twas Morven that mattered. Lord, that she hadna suffered because of him. Yet she must have. He had promised to return to her and would keep his promise; only he returned in disgrace. Would she even want him? The authorities had judged him a traitor; His Grace must surely agree. What of the folk of Stratha'an? Would they also turn against him? He groaned. Morven deserved better.

Fin's holding lay west of Corgarff Castle, an isolated tower house now an army garrison. Fin had assured him only a handful of foot soldiers would be stationed there, men invalided out of active service and now keeping watch for whisky smugglers, but Braemar Castle was more heavily garrisoned. They must pass it to reach Corgarff. Wary of soldiers, they kept off the road, leading their garrons through fragrant woods of larch and fir, rejoining the road out of sight of Braemar's turrets. 'I've had my fill o' castles,' Fin muttered.

Safely past Braemar, they slogged through open moorland, their garrons rasping and blowing hard. The land rose and opened out, falling away in great treeless slopes and folds, the hills wearing their winter colours, summits cloaked in snow. As they turned west toward Fin's home, Corgarff lay below them in the near distance, its stark walls pale against the dark hills. In the cold air, their breath billowed like clouds, and they felt as if they stood at the top of the world.

When they reached Corryhoul, Fin's holding, the sky had deepened, and the mountains were aglow with fiery colours. The stone cot-house looked abandoned and forlorn, the stubbly strips of land around it mostly bare.

'At least my hairvest's in,' Fin muttered as he got down. 'I feared 'twould be rotting on the ground.'

Two young lads were carrying water and set their pails down to stare. Fin whistled and snatched his bonnet off, waving it above his head. They shrieked and ran toward him. At their cries, a woman came to the door with a babe at her breast. She also shrieked, her cry flushing three girls and a dog from the byre. In moments, they were surrounded by smiling faces, woollen-clad bodies, and the soft lilt of Gaelic. The dog ran in circles, barking in excitement.

Fin's wife half-heartedly punched him. 'Where's the king's siller ye promised me, Finlay MacKay? I might've kent I'd nae see a farthing o' it.'

'Bridget. I can explain.'

She threw her arms around him. 'Never heed. Nae doot ye've drunk it. Are ye nae going to greet yer new bairn?' She pulled back her shawl, revealing a wizened infant with great dark eyes. 'I thought we'd cry him Murdo efter yer granda.'

Fin peered at the shrunken face and stroked the child's cheek. His face tightened and reddened, and he clenched his jaw. 'Aye,' he rasped, 'a guid name.'

'Who's this?' Bridget nodded at Jamie.

'A friend. Jamie Innes o' Stratha'an.' Fin tugged him forward. 'He'll be biding the night wi' us.'

'A friend, eh? He's dressed the same as you.' She laughed. 'Like a pair o' *Sassenachs*. But ye're welcome, Jamie.' She turned back to Fin and ran an appreciative eye over his garron. 'Ye'd better be coming in. Ye can tell me why ye're nae wearing the duke's uniform.'

Jamie left the explanations to Fin and sat back from the fire in the half-dark, letting Fin's family surround him with the warmth of their welcome. Bairns clambered all over him, tucking themselves under Fin's arms. He hardly seemed to mind. Jamie wondered if his own infant would look as starved as little Murdo and prayed not. But as warmth from the peat fire began to seep into his bones, he let go of the thought and shivered with pleasure. 'Twas the warmest he'd been in weeks. The flames began to lull him, and with a bowl of broth filling his belly, his eyes soon closed.

Come morning, he awoke stiff from the chair but eager to be on his way home. He gave what remained of his oats to Fin's wife, his yearning for home stronger than his desire for food. When it came time to go, he and Fin grew awkward.

'Ye'll mind and bring yer family to visit?' Fin twisted his bonnet in his hand. 'I hear yer wife's a beauty. I'm keen to meet her.'

'I will, aye.' Lord, that she was still waiting for him.

'Best be mindful o' thieves,' Fin said with a wry laugh.

Besides the pony, Jamie had naught worth stealing.

Fin explained that a drover's track crossed the duke's grouse moors to meet the river Avon at Inchrory. From there, another track followed the course of the Avon to the ford at Druimbeag. 'If ye're content wi' naught but hare and deer fer company,' he said, 'riding through the hills will be yer quickest way hame.'

Jamie grinned. 'Hare and deer suit me fine.'

They clasped forearms and embraced fiercely. Neither man had words for the bond that had grown between them. They parted, Jamie squeezing Fin's shoulder, and he mounted and urged his garron away.

Glad to abandon the military road, Jamie urged his garron west, picking his way through an old forest of scot's pine, emerging into open hills. He was alone now, but for the stout-hearted garron he had named Otter for his love of plunging into rivers. Jamie hardly minded. He was almost home, on His Grace's land, the bare heather slopes studded with grouse butts. Fragments of rounded stone walls topped with turf were scattered over the hills, built to give the duke and his shooting companions somewhere to hide with their guns. When the flushed birds flew over, they could more easily pick them off. He thought of the waste, and his empty belly growled in protest. These entitled men must return with more food than they could eat in a year.

He reached the abandoned military camp at Inchrory before the sun had gained its full height and was rewarded with his first sight of the Avon, a sight he'd thought never again to see. He got down so Otter might drink and sank to his knees, cupping his hands in the surging water. He drank and washed his face, thinking of how John the Baptist had long ago cleansed the sin from those who repented in the waters of the river Jordan. If only he could do the same. He would wash away the betrayal inflicted on he and his fellow glensmen.

Revived, he urged Otter on, following the Avon north through a wild landscape of scree-strewn slopes topped with rocky crags. Closer to home, the hillsides softened into grassy shielings groved with birch, rich pastures flanking the river. At last, his heart thumping, Jamie came to the ford near Druimbeag. Otter needed little encouragement to surge across. They crested the ridge, something he had done in his dreams more times than he cared to count. The cot-house lay ahead, just as he remembered it, only with no welcoming trail of smoke escaping from the roof.

His stomach gripped, and he hastened their pace. When they reached the infield, he led Otter across on foot. The rigs were naught but stubble. He thanked the Lord his harvest was in, yet an insidious suspicion now wormed in his belly. Had Morven sold the grain to pay the factor? That would mean her starving over the winter. Lord, let her nae have done that to keep her promise. He had foolishly talked about how much Druimbeag meant to him when she was all that mattered.

Inside, the cot-house was unchanged, but there was no sign of Morven. The fire was out, and the ashes cold, unthinkable to the superstitious folk of Strathavon. Yet when he crossed to the table, he saw some of her things—piles of dried roots, her pestle and mortar. Herbs hung from the roof timbers. Spread over the bed were the linen and blankets her parents had given them as a wedding gift. He stroked the soft wool and lay down, pressing his face into the weave. Morven's sweet, herb-rich scent rose in his nostrils. He groaned, his heart wrenching.

As he rose to go, something on the far side of the bed caught his eye. His heart fluttered. A cradle, old and battered yet beautiful, passed down through generations of glen bairns. Lined with moss and linen, a little blanket was folded over one side. He whimpered and reached to touch it, knowing it must have held his child. Returning to the firestone, he knelt and stirred the ashes. Beneath, a faint smoulder still lived. He blew on it and fed it with tinder, coaxing the fire back to life. Letting it go out brought ill luck.

He found his cattle in the byre, three cows with sturdy calves, healthy beasts with a shine on their coats. Morven hadn't sold them; she hadn't needed to. Relief calmed his thumping heart. But how had she managed? And where was she?

He had left Otter tethered to a gorse bush and returned to find the bush ravaged to the wood, Otter's jaws still busy. 'Forgive me, my friend. Our search isna yet done.' Rowena might know where Morven was. Failing that, her da or perhaps Alec.

Jamie saw no one until he reached Balintoul. After the quiet of the last few days, the village square seemed to seethe with people and beasts. He dismounted and approached a group of familiar faces, his stomach churning. They were cottars and hill farmers, most also whisky smugglers. How would they treat him? Half starved, bearded, and dressed like an Englishman, would they even recognise him? He abandoned his wife and child and led the Gordon Fencibles into danger, rebelling against the king's authority. They might view what he'd done that way. Yet here in the glens, would they even know about the mutiny? How would they? Lord, he would need to confess.

The closest man glanced at him. 'Twas Archie's father, Angus Munro of Ardriachan. He grimaced at Jamie's breeches and stockings with undisguised scorn, then focused on his face. 'Jamie.' He reared back. 'Jamie Innes! But it canna be.'

'Can it nae?'

'By Christ, it is!'

Frowning, old Craigduthel peered into Jamie's face, then tentatively fingered his sleeve. 'I dinna ken how,' he gasped, 'but 'tis truly young Druimbeag.' Grinning, he threw an arm around Jamie's shoulders. 'We supposed ye dead. Shot at Edinburgh Castle. Father Ranald read a newspaper to us in chapel. It said a military court found ye guilty o' mutiny and sentenced ye to death. We all got doon on oor knees and prayed fer yer soul. I've niver seen folk so grief-strick.' He swallowed. 'Nae since Cumberland's men hung my lads ower thirty years ago. The womenfolk keened that hard I could scarce hear the father speak. I might even hae blubbered a bit mysel'.'

'Then I hope ye'll forgive me, Craigduthel. It wasna my intention to distress ye.'

Craigduthel grinned. 'I will that.'

Men were shaking his hands now, exclaiming at his resurrection from the dead, clasping him to their chests in wonder.

''Tis the grandest news,' Peter Cameron declared. 'Father Ranald said the authorities betrayed the Gordon Fencibles as expected, but ye raised the men and stood against the blaggards. His Grace was fer shipping ye to England or some faraway land, but ye seized Edinburgh Castle to stop it. Ye risked yer life so the men might stay in their ane country like Her Grace promised.'

'Ye know o' that?'

'Aye, the whole glen must ken o' it by now.'

Jamie blinked in astonishment. Never had he imagined word of the mutiny would reach the glen so fast, especially the truth of it. He shook his head. Was there naught John Robertson couldna do? But if news of his sentence had reached Stratha'an, Morven must think him dead.

'I dinna ken how ye escaped,' Angus said, 'but I'm mighty glad o' it. If it werena fer you, they'd have shipped my Archie awa devil knows where.' Grinning, he linked arms with Jamie and spun him around, whooping and kicking up his heels. Jamie staggered giddily, his head spinning. 'I'm fer wetting yer thrapple to celebrate.' Angus tried to steer Jamie toward the Balintoul Inn. 'Who's fer joining us?'

'I will!' Craigduthel cried, and the others seemed as eager.

'Where's Delnabreck?' the miller cried. 'He'll be cock-a-hoop. Since word came o' the lad's court martial, there's been nae talking to him. Delnabreck!' he shouted.

Jamie searched the square for Morven's father, but it was Alec he saw walking up the street toward him. Alec slowed his steps as he struggled to make sense of the scene before him. His face drained of colour. Sarah caught Alec up and also stared, then she was sprinting toward him, her face alight, elbowing her way through.

'Jamie!' She hurled herself at him, almost knocking him over. 'I kent ye werena dead. Ye're my cousin, bold and fearless. Ye bettered the Black Gauger wi' naught but an ancient broadsword. I kent ye'd escape somehow.' She looked at his strange clothing. 'Are ye in hiding from the redcoats?'

'No,' he croaked. 'I was ... pardoned of sorts. 'Tis a long tale, but afore I tell it, I must find Morven.'

Alec hung back. He was thinner, and his face had a hunted look, yet his likeness to his sister was so uncanny Jamie's heart clenched. 'Praise the Lord,' Alec choked. His face tightened. 'Ye must hate me. I dinna blame ye; I should've suffered fer my foolishness, never you. What ye must've endured.' He swallowed, his face twisting. 'Forgiveness is too much to ask, yet I do humbly ask it.'

'Och, Alec.' Jamie strode toward him and clasped him to his chest. 'There's naught to forgive, and I could never hate ye.'

'But efter my drunken—'

'I mean it. I canna think what drunken foolishness ye mean.'

Alec's eyes filled. 'I dinna deserve yer kindness, or ... or even to be yer kinsman.'

'Nay, Alec, I'm the fortunate one. The day Morven became my wife, I gained so much more. I was blessed wi' her family as kin, good folk who value me nae matter what I've done.'

'Always,' Alec sobbed, embracing him. 'Ye're one o' our own.'

'You honour me. But Alec, where is she?'

Alec released him. 'Gone to Scalan. Her and her bairn—your bairn.'

'Scalan?'

'The hidden college in the Braes o' Glenlivet—a student is being or-dained. If ye'll let me, I'll tak' ye there.'

CHAPTER THIRTY-NINE

Scalan

Morven glanced around the little chapel. She should feel joyous; a new priest was being made, yet her heart thumped dully and her stomach churned. Light from the lone window spilt across the altar where Bishop Hay stood, picking out the gold in his flowing robes, the richly embroidered band on his mitre. Flanked by Father John and Father Ranald in their plain cassocks, he shone like the beacon of faith he was. She glanced behind her. With the singing over, the boys sat with their heads bowed, their hair combed flat and faces freshly scrubbed. Farther back, the college servants stood in their best clothing, their eyes shining with pride. Janet beamed at her. Nathaniel had been here since he was eight, and Janet had watched him grow into the pious young man they knew. She was the closest soul to a mother Nathaniel had known since he came here.

Morven tried to smile back, but grief had so broken her, her features felt set in stone. She glanced at Ilene. Newly nursed, the infant was sleeping soundly. She prayed she would not awaken and disturb the solemnity of the ceremony. They had been honoured with a seat at the front where Nathaniel's family should be sitting, but his mother and brother were dead, and his father had refused to attend. After a lifetime of obedience, Nathaniel had finally found the courage to disobey his da. He wrote to inform him that after years of diligent study, he wished to be a priest, not a farmer. Incensed, Mister Gunn sent his reply with the swiftest rider. Henceforth, Nathaniel was the Catholic Mission's problem, not his. He never wanted to see his ungrateful son again.

Nathaniel was hurt but not surprised. 'You grew up blessed with a loving family,' he told her. 'I envy you. I've always felt unwanted and unworthy, yet I'll soon be anointed to do God's work, administering the sacraments, proclaiming the word of God. I imagine it may be lonely work. We have no family connection, no kinship of any kind, yet we are both alone in the world now in our different ways.' He frowned at his hands, aware that his words must sound brutal. 'Forgive me; it was not my intention to distress you, but you would do me the greatest honour if you would allow me to consider you and Ilene my family. Not in blood, of course, I don't make such a presumption, but in the ways that matter.' He sighed. 'I understand why you could not wed me. I was foolish to imagine you might. But I want you to know I'm still here for you, even after I take the cloth. I hope you will let me care for your spiritual needs if not your physical well-being.'

Morven already knew something of the spiritual world; through that realm healing was wrought, but she could understand Nathaniel's need for kinship. 'I'd be honoured,' she answered.

Nathaniel's eyes filled with tears, and he bit his lip. She sensed there was more. 'Thank you. As my kinswoman, you would honour me further if you would attend my ordination.'

She faltered. Her grief lay between them, solid and impregnable as a castle wall. Nathaniel must feel it. It changed everything, made everything harder.

He smiled hopefully. 'If you could find the strength, Morven, seeing your face among the sterner, churchly ones would lighten my heart.'

'Of course,' she whispered. 'I'd nae miss it fer the world.' These last days, despair had been her constant companion, yet no matter how hopeless she felt, for the sake of others, she must summon the strength to carry on.

'I can scarcely imagine your heartache, but your presence on the day would mean everything.'

His smile was such a grateful, poignant thing she'd been forced to turn away lest her wretchedness should taint him. She must be strong, not only for Nathaniel but for her daughter. She shifted in her chair now, trying to feel joyous whilst inside, she had never felt so empty.

Nathaniel lay prostrate on the floor before her, wearing a long white robe, his arms outstretched in supplication whilst the bishop chanted over him in Latin. Morven knew few Latin words, but Nathaniel had explained the bishop would evoke the Holy Spirit to come down upon him and set him apart for the ministry. Once ordained, Nathaniel would be gone from her almost as surely as Jamie. So much loss. Yet that was selfish. In declaring her his kinswoman, Nathaniel hoped to maintain their friendship. Had she done the right thing in turning him down? But she couldn't make him happy. There was no room in her heart for any man but Jamie. No amount of wishing or exchanging vows could change that. Letting him sacrifice himself would've been unfair. Nathaniel deserved more than she could give him.

At length, the bishop raised Nathaniel to his knees and placed his hands on his bowed head in what was called the laying on of hands. He turned to Father John and Father Ranald. They came forward in turn and did the same. In a solemn voice, the bishop recited the prayer of ordination and blessed Nathaniel's new vestments. He passed them to Father John, who pulled the chasuble over Nathaniel's head, fixing the folds so they draped properly. Lastly, he slipped the silken stole around Nathaniel's neck.

Nathaniel glanced up and caught her eye. He looked beautiful, almost unearthly. He lowered his head and in a trembling voice, made his vows: he would be celibate his whole life; he would always obey the bishop. The bishop then anointed Nathaniel's upturned hands with sacred oil. Over the years, those hands had turned the pages of hundreds of books, had taken notes and made beautiful sketches; they had even helped her gather healing herbs. Now, they were holy instruments. Nathaniel would use his hands to bless the sick, the dying, newborn infants, women in childbirth, perhaps even men going into battle.

Smiling, the bishop raised Nathaniel to his feet and kissed him on the cheek, then sank to his knees for Nathaniel's blessing. Nathaniel made the sign of the cross and cupped the bishop's hands in his own. 'Blessed art thee,' he murmured.

Applause rippled around the chapel. A new priest was made: Father Nathaniel Gunn. He would guide the folk of Glenlivet and beyond in the true faith. Morven shivered. How did she feel about that? She was in too much turmoil to tell.

Rising, the bishop stepped back and urged the students forward to be blessed by their new priest. Amidst a commotion of scraping chairs and shuffling feet, Morven slipped out. A strange feeling had come upon her, a need to be amongst trees, to gaze at the wide sky. She stumbled down the stairs and out into the courtyard, her heart thumping. She paused to catch her breath. Ilene had woken. Cradling her close, she crossed the courtyard and slipped through the gate.

To the side of the college, a piece of land had been laid out as a kailyard for growing food. Bishop Hay had directed an avenue of trees be planted to encircle the place. 'Twas known as the Bishop's Walk. The holy man liked to walk there; it helped him feel closer to God. Nathaniel confessed he also liked to walk there whenever he felt overwhelmed.

The trees were mostly rowans and gave some shelter from raw winds, yet amongst their bare boughs, the breeze still brought tears to Morven's eyes. Her tears had been lurking anyway, all through Nathaniel's ordination. Here, they could fall unnoticed, and they streamed and dripped. Over the years, fierce gales had battered these trees, yet they stood resolutely, bent and twisted, crusted with lichen.

The strange tingling came upon her again. Morven loosened Ilene's swaddling and whispered to her, letting the infant grip her finger. The wee soul was so innocent and trusting. She had no concept of grief. What *was* grief? Surely 'twas just love with nowhere to go, love that kept gathering since the man 'twas meant for wasna there to give it to. Jamie was gone yet love for him still lumped in her throat and reddened her eyes. It ached in her chest, leaving an empty hollow where her heart used to be.

'Ye must be brave,' she whispered to the infant. 'I love ye so I can scarce bear it.' She stroked her cheek. 'I promise I'll give ye all the love Jamie would've given ye. Ye willna want fer love, my lamb.' Though she would doubtless want for other things.

Ilene gazed raptly at her, trying to coo back. Every day, she appeared brighter, trying to copy expressions and sounds. Jamie would never see it. The pity of that tore at her, and Morven fell to her knees. '*Why?*' She raked the leaden sky for answers, but it only frowned back, the same sky, the same God, that must have looked down on Jamie in his final moments and did nothing. Sobbing, she stared at the empty landscape, then back at the college. Nathaniel was walking towards her in the robes of his new office, wearing the strangest expression.

'Morven, forgive me, but ... your brother is here. And ... he has brought someone with him.'

'Alec? Here? Is something wrong?'

'No, far from it.' He stared at her, his lips trembling, then turned and beckoned.

She struggled to her feet. Two men were walking toward her. She recognised Alec. He was smiling, and behind him walked a tall man in a cloak, the hood mantled over his head. The strange feeling tingled around her heart again, and the hair rose on her nape. Lord, 'twas Jamie's ghost still wrapped in its shroud.

Alec stopped, but the ghost walked on. Coming closer, he drew back his hood. He was bearded, his dark hair clubbed at his nape, his lips full and sensual, familiar, for they had kissed every inch of her body. The breath left her, and she staggered back.

'My love.'

She shook her head. He wasna real. She'd barely slept; her mind was playing tricks on her.

He nodded uncertainly and opened his arms to her. When she did naught but stare, he walked forward, his gaze fixed on her face.

Her breath came in gasps. 'Jamie. Oh, Jamie. Tell me ye're real. Tell me ye've truly come back to me.'

'Did I nae say I'd come back?'

Sobbing, she pushed Ilene into Nathaniel's arms and ran to him. He welcomed her into his embrace, and she wound her arms around him, pressing herself into the bones of him. His arms tightened around her. He smelled of peat moss, of pony and hard toil ... of Jamie. Lord, he was real. Joy coursed through her body, her heart singing. He was so thin, she could feel his ribs and the sobs racking his body. She stroked his back, then loosened her hold and stared up into his face. Her throat spasmed. 'I thought ye were ... that ....'

'My letter. Forgive me, I believed I would meet my maker and never see ye again. I wished to explain and seek forgiveness for breaking my promise.' His face twisted. 'But at the last, I was shown mercy.'

Morven thought of all those at Scalan who had offered prayers for him, the Strathavon cottars and smugglers who had remembered him in theirs, his fellow glensmen, freed through his sacrifice. All had likely prayed for him.

He fell to his knees. 'But my love, do ye still want me? I come in disgrace.'

'I want ye 'til my heart's sore wi' the wanting.'

'And I you.' He gripped her tightly, pressing his cheek to her belly. 'My love, my love.'

Sobbing, she ran her fingers through his hair and buried her face in his dark locks, choking on her sobs. He rose and searched her face, drying her tears with his thumbs, then tentatively kissed her.

She returned his kiss, her heart fluttering. A little yearning sound slipped from her lips. He groaned, plundering her mouth, and she felt his hunger for her.

'Forgive me.' He broke away, remembering where they were and those waiting. 'Then, knowing what I've done, will ye have me back?'

'Ye need to ask?'

'Nay, but forgive me, maybe to hear the words.'

She nodded. 'My love, ye are the shore I've beached my heart upon. Wi'out ye, I'm lost, hopeless and despairing.'

He choked in relief and took her hand, pressing it to his lips. Ilene began to fuss. He spun around, looking for his child.

Nathaniel held her out.

'Yer daughter,' Morven whispered. 'See how lovely she is.'

He gazed at the infant in wonder. 'A lass. I thought never to see her. She's beautiful, like her mother.'

Nathaniel placed her gently in his arms.

He gazed into his daughter's rapt face, cupping the curve of her head. When she tried to coo to him, his throat convulsed, and he kissed her forehead. 'I feared I'd lost ye both.'

'Ye thought me so faithless?'

'Nay, but I abandoned ye, and I'm judged a traitor.'

'Nae by me. Nae by anyone in this glen.'

'Bless ye,' he sobbed. 'I'm told I have a home to return to, because of you.' He looked at Nathaniel. 'And the priests o' Scalan, especially Father Nathaniel.'

Morven smiled, not yet accustomed to Nathaniel's new title. 'Nathaniel is my dearest friend. I hope he will be yours. I consider him my kinsman. Did I nae promise I'd keep Druimbeag safe?'

'I should never have doubted ye.' Jamie held Ilene to his shoulder and slipped his fingers through hers, kissing the back of her hand. 'I've learned home is more than a scrape o' land. 'Tis where you are.'

She pressed his hand to her cheek. 'Then, ye're hame, my love.'

'I thank the Lord fer it. I never mean to leave.'

Smiling through her tears, Morven held her other hand out to Nathaniel. He stumbled forward and gripped it. He was weeping.

Jamie inclined his head to him, a small gesture of friendship. 'I congratulate you on yer ordination, Nathaniel, and ...' he swallowed. 'I can only give ye my heartfelt thanks.'

Unsure what to say, Nathaniel smiled back, his dimples appearing.

'Blessed art thee,' he whispered.

'Lord, that I am.'

Grinning, Alec threw his arm around Nathaniel's shoulders. 'Welcome, kinsman,' he said.

'Bless you,' Nathaniel sobbed. 'To be part of a family again, especially this one, I cannot explain what joy that brings me.'

'Och, we're glad to hae ye.'

Morven squeezed Nathaniel's hand, and he turned to her, tears shimmering on his long eyelashes. She thought of that long-ago boy crouching fearfully beside her in the undergrowth. He gave her hand an answering squeeze and with Jamie's arm around her waist, she walked back to the college surrounded by family.

Author's Note

THANK YOU FOR READING *Where The Heart Beats Strongest*. If you enjoyed it, I would be grateful if you would leave a review on the book's Amazon page. Reviews are important to me and only need to be a few words, but let readers know that my work is worth reading. If you do, thank you so much!

This is the third novel in the Strathavon Saga and follows Morven and Jamie into the first year of their marriage. During this time, the American colonies were fighting for their independence from the British Crown. The Revolutionary War did not end until 1783. The war tested Britain's military capabilities to the full, with her losses vast, both financial and in terms of men, although the Crown considered this a price worth paying. Britain was now also dealing with an increasing number of enemies. Following America's victory at Saratoga, France allied with the new American government and formally declared war on Britain in 1778. Spain followed, with Britain already at war with the Netherlands.

America was now receiving both financial and military aid from France, with the French navy and American privateers harrying the long shoreline of the British Isles, including raiding Scottish ports. With Britain's regular forces overstretched and overseas, an urgent call was put out to raise fencible regiments to defend Britain and her ports, fencible being a term used to describe defensible companies raised solely to defend the homeland.

Culloden was the last pitched battle fought on British soil and took place on the 16th of April 1746 on Drumossie Moor near Inverness. It was a massacre, a crushing defeat for the Jacobite army led by Prince Charles Edward Stuart and marked the end of the Jacobite risings. The wounded were bayoneted where they fell or rounded up and blasted with volleys of musketry at close range. Few escaped. The atrocities that followed have been largely glossed over, but the bloodletting spilt out to neighbouring villages and townships and across the Highlands, with reports of whole communities burned. Scalan was razed to the ground on the 16th of May. Prisoners, along with many innocent bystanders, were crammed into the holds of ships and transported south for trial. Imprisoned for months, many died of typhus; more still were hanged. Around one hundred and twenty were convicted of high treason and hung, drawn, and quartered. The Highlands came under martial law, with the occupying army free to inflict what it liked upon a population viewed as ignorant, superstitious, and without virtue.

Yet a little over thirty years later, the British Crown had come to see the Highlands as a source of expendable fighting men for their many conflicts. After Culloden, Highlanders were ruthlessly hunted down and slaughtered. Now, the War Office actively sought them out to defend the same Crown that sanctioned the killing, rape, and harassment of their families in a crusade to 'civilise' the rebellious Highlands and its Gaelic culture. The mountains of the north were now recognised as home to a hardy and intrepid race of men who would fight valiantly for their laird or clan chief when called upon. This resource should be called out for the king, dressed in faux highland garb and plundered as cannon fodder to defend the authority that still oppressed it.

Eight new highland regiments were formed at this time. One of these was the Northern or Gordon Fencibles, raised by Alexander, 4th Duke of Gordon, known as the Cock o' the North. Of the eight regiments raised, five mutinied, and for all the reasons I describe. The Gordon Fencibles did not mutiny at this time, although they came close. This mutiny is my fiction. However, the distrust and resentment I describe was real. A later fencible regiment raised by the duke in 1793 did mutiny. If you would like to read more about the highland regiments raised in the 18th century and how they were treated, I can recommend the wonderfully readable *Mutiny* by John Prebble.

The duke and other lords sent recruiting parties into the glens to round up men, using the warrant the king had granted them as an excuse to exploit traditional clan loyalties and obligations. When it became clear those loyalties were no longer held so firmly, any man unwilling to enlist was coerced to take the king's shilling using the threat to evict his family. Recruiting parties were determined to get their man, with families forced to hide their young lads until the levy had passed through their area. Resentment simmered. The traditional highland way of life had been outlawed and repressed for decades; now, the Crown was stealing its youth. In the Highlands, the British Army had gained a reputation for selling highland recruits to the East India Company as they neared the end of their term of service or upon a whim. This is the historical reality in which my fictional tale unfolds.

Nathaniel Gunn is my creation, but Scalan, the hidden seminary where he and other young boys secretly trained to enter the priesthood, is a real place and still stands in the remote landscape of the Braes of Glenlivet. Following the spread of Protestantism, the Catholic faith was outlawed by Scotland's Reformation Parliament in 1560, with the Pope's authority abolished and Mass banned. It was forbidden to train as a Catholic priest. In the years that followed, the existing Catholic clergy slowly died out, leaving fewer and fewer priests to care for the dwindling Catholic population. This population was principally concentrated within the Highlands in a narrow band stretching from the north-east coast to the Western Isles. People in this area still lived in a feudal clan society bound by age-old ties of kinship and common faith, and it was here, on the Duke of Gordon's land, that Scalan was founded in 1716.

At first, the seminary was no more than a shieling hut, but over the years, subsequent bishops and college masters extended the building. As Scalan grew in size, so did its importance. For much of the 18th century, Scalan was the only place in Scotland where boys could train to enter the priesthood, and these young men became known as 'heather priests'. Despite frequent attacks, around one hundred priests were trained at Scalan, and Catholicism survived in Scotland largely thanks to their courage and devotion.

Father John Patterson was the master at Scalan from 1770 until his death there in 1783. John died of consumption in his mid-thirties, having been master for thirteen years. Bishop Hay, who was present at his death, declared that no master had been more dedicated, prudent, humble, caring, or devout in his leadership—or more fruitful. Under John's guidance, two dozen boys went on to serve as ordained priests.

The penal laws were finally repealed in 1793, allowing Catholics to worship freely for the first time in over two hundred and sixty years. Scalan had been chosen for its remoteness and the degree of protection its location enjoyed on the Duke of Gordon's land. However, with the penal laws lifted, remoteness became more of a hindrance than a necessity, and Scalan closed in 1799. The boys were moved out of the hills to a grand new house near Aberdeen with four floors and extensive grounds. It must have felt like a palace compared with cramped and chilly Scalan.

With the Church relinquishing its lease on Scalan, the duke's factor divided and re-leased the land. The college and its outbuildings became tenants' homes with mill buildings added to serve the community. Eventually, the site was abandoned and fell into disrepair—a sorry end to such an important place.

Thankfully, today, Scalan has been restored and is open to visitors as a museum under the care of the Scalan Association, a charity dedicated to preserving the heritage of the Catholic Church in Scotland. Fittingly, the humble college is now a place of pilgrimage. The building stands as a monument to the survival of the Catholic faith in Scotland through long years of religious persecution.

You can learn more about Strathavon and see some images of the area at: https//www.angelamacraeshanks.com

Or on Facebook at:
https://www.facebook.com/angelamacraeshanksauthor

You can contact me at: angela@angelamacraeshanks.com

Please see over for a glossary of Scots words and expressions used throughout this novel.

The Scot's Tongue

THE SCOT'S LANGUAGE IS wonderfully expressive, and I have used it freely to add both authenticity and a sense of time and place. I hope the meaning can be generally inferred, but for the more challenging words, I provide a glossary below.

arisaid – a long draped garment worn as part of female Highland dress
bairn – a child, male or female
bannock – a round, flat, thickish cake of oatmeal or barley baked on a girdle
Beltane – Gaelic May Day festival marking the start of Summer
bide – to dwell or reside
birl – to revolve rapidly, whirl round, especially in dance
bether/blatherskite – a silly, foolish person; a babbler
blither blather – nonsensical rumours
bodach – an old man
bodhran – hand-held traditional Celtic drum
boll – a dry measure of oats or barley
bothy – a primitive dwelling or shelter
breeks – breeches, trousers
byre – a cattle house
ceilidh – a social gathering, usually with music and dancing
clabber – soured milk with a thick, yoghurt-like consistency
close – a narrow passage or alley
cottar – a tenant occupying a cottage and the land attached to it
crabbit – bad tempered or out of humour
crag – a rocky hill or mountain
creel – a deep wicker basket carried on the back by means of a strap

dirk – a short dagger worn in the belt
dram – a small drink of liquor, especially whisky
droukit – soaked, drenched
druim – the ridge of a hill
dyke – a low wall made of stones
factor – an agent who has charge of administration of an estate
fash – fret, worry
garron – a small sturdy highland horse or pony
gauger – an exciseman
gloaming – evening twilight
guddle – to grope for fish with the hands in water
kailyard – a kitchen garden
ken/kent – to know or be aware of
kertch – a traditional head covering of linen worn by married women
kirk – a church, generally Presbyterian or non-Episcopalian
Kirk – when capitalised, refers specifically to the Presbyterian Church of Scotland
kist – a chest, box, or trunk
lowp – to bound or walk with long springing steps as if through heather
lugs – ears
midden – a dunghill, ash-pit or refuse heap
mind – to remember or call to mind
mooth – mouth
muckle – large in size
plaid – a length of thick woollen cloth up to six metres long gathered into pleats and belted at
the waist with the upper half draped over the left shoulder or over the head for protection
quaich – a shallow two-handed drinking bowl or cup, usually wooden
quern – a hand mill for grinding grain where two matched circular stones rotate one over the
other
quine – a young woman
reiver – an armed cattle raider
rig/runrig – narrow strips of arable land, part of the system of agriculture of the Highlands
Samhain – a Gaelic fire festival celebrated on the 1st November marking

the end of the
    harvest and beginning of winter
    sark – a shift or shirt worn near the skin
    Sassenach – English or English-speaking person
    shieling – upland pasture where cattle were driven for the summer
    spaewife – a woman who foretells the future
    spittal – a shelter, especially in mountainous country for travellers
    stook – a shock of cut sheaves of grain set up to dry in a harvest-field
    tacksman – a tenant farmer who leases land to sublet
    tatties – potatoes
    thegither - together
    thrapple – the throat
    thrawn – contrary, obstinate, or stubborn
    wynd – a narrow often winding street or lane leading off a main thoroughfare

www.ingramcontent.com/pod-product-compliance
Lightning Source LLC
Chambersburg PA
CBHW021033310726
48969CB00006B/1640